Let Me Fall

LILY FOSTER

Also by Lily Foster

THE LET ME SERIES

Let Me Be the One

Let Me Love You

Let Me Go

Let Me Heal Your Heart

Let Me Fall

When I Let You Go

THE BLACKBIRD SERIES

When the Night is Over

Your Hand in Mine

Ghost on the Shore

All Your Life

Let Me Fall

Cover by Cover Me Darling

First paperback edition January 2017

IBSN 9780990594185 (paperback)

Shorefront Books

Let Me Fall

Prologue

I wasn't a fool.

I knew what was being said about me, if the wary side glances and stifled giggles were anything to go on. But I could hear them now, and Lord, it made the words cut so much deeper.

"Aubrey, I feel so bad for you."

"Talk about losing the housing lottery," another one chimed in.

My roommate let out a weary sigh for sympathy and then practically whimpered, "I'm afraid to go to sleep at night. It's so eerie. She's like a character right out of *The Walking Dead*."

I could picture Aubrey in that moment: wide-eyed, drawing everyone in around the campfire, gearing up to spook them with the most gruesome part of the ghost story. I could hear her damn gum snapping from the other side of the door too, and could easily conjure up a visual of her chewing in her very own irritating way, slow and lazy like a dumb effing billy goat.

"I don't think she's washed her hair more than two times since we've been here."

"Gross!" both of her minions shrieked in unison before they all broke out into a cruel fit of laughter.

"I don't want to be mean," she insisted. *Oh come on, Aubrey, sure you do.* "But Carolyn is just so...odd. This isn't what I signed up for."

I pulled a few long, stringy brown strands in front of my face and examined them, running them between my fingers. I'd been away at school for nearly five weeks now. Washed my hair twice? No, I could definitely recall three, possibly four washings.

I crossed the room and stood before the full-length mirror, looking at this girl for the first time in God knows how long. I took in the gaunt cheeks, the pale skin, the cracked, chapped lips and the shapeless clothes that hung off my too-thin frame.

I shook my head, taking in the pathetic sight before me. *This is what you wanted, dummy. Are you satisfied now? You had to get as far away from there as possible, remember?*

To get away—it was more like a burning need to escape. It drove me to follow through on my plan, even though I knew I wasn't on the most stable ground, mental health-wise. But now, standing in my room alone, listening to all of them talk about me as if I was some sort of freak? I missed home desperately.

I missed my mother and father. Missed the way they took care of me, surrounded me in a cocoon of safety, love and care. I missed my little brother, although at some point during the past six months he'd gone from idolizing his older sister to observing me from a distance, ashamed and fearful of what I've become.

I looked around this room. My side was barren, prison-cell chic, while Aubrey's side looked as if some bubble gum, sunshine, sparkle and happiness-inspired apparatus had crop-dusted over her belongings. Aside from the black satin comforter, which I can only assume was meant to communicate to her male suitors that she had a dark and naughty side, most everything was pink—hot, nauseating pink. She dressed well, but her interior decorating instincts were for shit.

The wall above her bed was covered with photos, each one picked to highlight how beautiful, popular and perfect she was. Since I didn't spend much time outside of the room after classes, I often found myself studying the pictures. Handsome boys with athletic builds draped their arms around Aubrey, gazing at her, wanting her. A group of girlfriends in bikinis at the beach, hamming it up for the camera. In another they were dressed in cheerleading uniforms. There was a prom picture, too. A boy who looked like he was straight out of central casting for homecoming king type was dressed in a fitted tux, his eyes fixed on the ample cleavage spilling out of Aubrey's hot pink bodice. *Believe it or not, Aubrey, you and I probably would have been besties in high school.* Just the thought, the reminder of my former self—God, it burned like bile rising up the back of my throat.

Really, Aubrey was as much of an anomaly around here as I was. This was a seriously competitive school—one of the hardest to get into on the East Coast—so there weren't many head cheerleader Barbie types like her around. Most of the students here were sophisticated, albeit bookish types. You had your hipsters, your artsy kids, intelligent jocks and loners also. I guess I fit into that last segment of the campus population. But I'll be honest, even among that group I was more seriously messed up than anyone else I observed. And I would know, as I spent countless hours standing watch, day after day after day, peering down over the quaint courtyard from my second-story window.

We couldn't have been more mismatched as roommates, even if someone in student housing was intentionally pairing freshmen up to ensure certain misery. I was now awkward, quiet and easily rattled. Aubrey, in contrast, was socially outgoing and bubbly—a natural and skilled networker. While I had yet to succeed in pairing "hello" with eye contact since arriving here, Aubrey had already secured herself an entire circle of BFFs and she'd had no less than three romantic encounters.

After the first night of freshman orientation when I politely declined to attend some mixer, Aubrey and the others didn't include me in their plans. So I was already in bed with the lights out by the time she'd come back to the room, giggling and buzzing. I therefore had the pleasure of listening to Aubrey and her hook-ups bump, grind and moan. It was excruciating. I wasn't a prude or anything, but lying there in the dark pretending to be asleep as they went at it made it even more obvious to me that I was, in fact, an absolute weirdo.

One night I overheard a semi-thoughtful boy whisper to Aubrey, "Yeah? You wanna do it with your roommate right over there?"

Tipsy Aubrey giggled, shucking off her jeans. "Who cares? It's like I don't even have a roommate."

Exactly.

I didn't exist.

I remember the screaming. It went on and on. Coarse, primitive and rage-filled. A welcome silence followed by the relentless pounding of fists against a door. Sparkling bits and pieces. Shards of glass refracting light in the most beautiful way. I remember red, so much red. Red splattered and smeared across every square inch of that damn photo collage.

Sirens, the police restraining me?

I have no memory of that.

They filled me in on everything later, after they'd taken me far, far away.

Chapter One

JEREMY

Everyone was talking shit, even before I showed up for the first day of try-outs. No one just walked onto varsity as a junior. Everyone else had to pay their dues, grinding it out on JV, proving themselves. They earned their positions.

Whatever. I *was* walking on and they all knew it.

I was seventeen, a full year older than most of the other juniors, thanks to being held back in the second grade. I was already well over six feet tall and I was not lanky or scrawny by any means. I'd been shaving since eighth grade and was now easily mistaken for being in my early twenties.

The decision to come to Westerly High was not mine. Apparently, my specialized private school tuition cost the state upwards of sixty-thousand a year. During my last annual review, the school district administrators (much like a prison parole board) deemed I was fit to reenter society. Academically and socially, I was considered rehabilitated.

I was furious—scared really. I didn't want to go back to a place where I knew every day would be a struggle. My teachers assured me that I was ready but I was doubtful.

The one and only incentive I had for returning was football.

First morning of practice and the August sun is beating down on me as soon as I leave the air conditioned cocoon of my '97 Chevy. My truck is old and rusty, but there's enough freon in its AC to freeze a side of beef. I stalled for a full five minutes before cranking open the cab's worn, rusted door. I figured a pep talk of the *No fear, Yield to no one, Strike hard*-variety was in order.

"If he's as good as they say he is, then sorry, but fair's fair."

Tall and slim, with a haircut right out of some prepster store catalogue, I pegged him as the quarterback. A beefy, angry looking kid—pegged him as a linebacker—challenged him, "Loyalty counts for nothing, right Spence?"

"We're here to win games," Spence answered leisurely, lacing up his cleats, "not to give out prizes for fucking loyalty."

They caught site of me standing there, promptly clammed up and went back to the business of suiting up. I was trying not to feel awkward, but I was standing there with all my gear and had no idea where to settle in. For all my bravado, arriving somewhere you're clearly not wanted sucks, even on the best of days.

I looked to Spence, figuring he was a potential ally, but when he locked eyes with me and then looked away without so much as a head nod, I figured I was on my own.

That's all right. I don't need any of these pansy ass bitches for friends.

I read last year's roster online one night when I was looking for some information on the coaching staff. All but a few of the players had douchebag first names like Spencer, Emory, Parker, Chase or Landon. Typical for this town full of wealthy, stuck-up pricks. I always had a take-no-prisoners mindset on the field, but now I'd be out for blood.

I turned towards a deserted section of the locker room, figuring I could find an unoccupied locker to stash my gear.

"Hey," I heard someone call from behind me.

This one was close to my height, leaner build, friendly face—not that I was looking for friends at this point.

I tried my best to affect an *I don't give a shit* attitude. "What's up?"

"Do you have a lock?" When I shook my head, he handed me one. "Take this, it's an extra. I wouldn't leave my shit unattended. You're not the most popular guy at the moment."

"I can see that."

"I'm Will Clarke," he said, extending his hand. "You're Jeremy, right? I definitely remember you from Driscoll Elementary."

"Yeah," I said, shaking his hand, "Jeremy Rivers."

"You left in what, fifth or sixth grade? Did you move away or something?"

I heard some asshole cough into his hand and mumble, "Juvie."

That earned him a few cheap laughs. So that's where all these fucktards thought I'd gone? Made sense, I guess. I did leave Driscoll on a pretty low note.

"See you out there," Will said with a sympathetic look as he backed away.

The air was muggy and thick. The sun blazed without any breeze to take the edge off. I was always in top condition and I'd been running sprints and doing stair drills at a punishing pace all summer long, but today was rough. Not nearly as tough for me as it was for some of the others, who were red-faced, pulling for breath and trailing behind. Several of these good ol' boys had obviously spent the summer hanging out poolside, sucking down booze from daddy's liquor cabinet.

As we filed back into the locker room, I could feel a few of the guys actively hating on me. The negative vibe was hanging in the air. One kid I'd consistently burned during sprints and receiving drills purposely pushed into me, nearly knocking me off balance as he made his way past me down the narrow locker room aisle. *Nope, this shit is not starting today.* I reached out and grabbed the collar of his jersey, jerking him back. "I wouldn't do that again," I said evenly, leveling him with a menacing look.

In truth, I was scared shitless, fairly certain that forty guys were about to jump me and start beating the shit outta me at that very moment. But I knew better than to show fear.

"Do *what* again?" he challenged.

I turned my attention back to the locker, doing my best to appear bored. "You heard what I said. I don't think I need to repeat it."

I had to walk a fine line in this school district. One misstep and I'd be out. I didn't want trouble, wasn't looking to start anything, but I wasn't backing down either. Anyone who messed with me had better be ready to back it up.

Spencer Davies' interest was piqued now. "Aw, throwing a tantrum, Baker? You just got smoked, plain and simple. Deal with it."

"Fuck you, Spence," Baker shot back.

"You're the one getting fucked. Just fucked yourself right outta your starting position."

As Baker slammed his locker loudly and went for the showers, another moron chimed in. "It must be nice, just strolling in and passing over seniors...Guys who've left their blood and sweat on that field, earning their way onto this team."

"Holy shit, Chase, you sound like a fucking drama queen," Will said, exasperated.

When someone added, "It's Chase's time of the month," a few of the guys laughed, easing the mood in the locker room.

Those first two weeks, every damn day was the same: I'd outperform my competition at practice, shrug off the hatred and ignore the snide remarks. No one actually ever stepped up to me. My reputation was earned long ago. When you punch a teacher out, people tend to remember. So they taunted from afar, never fearless enough to challenge me directly. My therapist would have been proud if she witnessed how I was putting my anger management techniques into practice *every* minute of *every* fucking day I was around these guys.

They weren't all bad. Will Clarke, Drew Oliver and Mike Hanson weren't exactly my new best buddies that fall, but they didn't support the few guys who were campaigning to make my time at Westerly High unpleasant. They respected my ability, and despite my bad reputation, gave me the benefit of a fresh start.

Just the same, I gravitated towards the rougher element. My friends were the pot smokers, the class cutters, behavior problems, and occasionally, the petty thieves. Keep in mind this is one of the more affluent suburbs in the country, so behavior problems were fairly mild in comparison to say...anywhere else in the world. For the most part, these kids were do-gooders. You had your exceptions to the rule—the over-privileged, unsupervised kids looking to get back at mommy and daddy by developing an alcohol or meth problem—but overall it was pretty tame.

I just felt more comfortable on the periphery, on the fringes. Always had. In this town, I was an outsider from day one and I knew it.

"How did it go today?"

"It went, Dad."

It took some effort to calm the scowl, but I managed a genuine smile as I slid the salmon from the sauté pan onto our plates.

"Another gourmet meal. What have we got here?" my father asked, taking his seat at the table.

"Panko crusted salmon over quinoa with balsamic glazed brussel sprouts."

"Thank God I was blessed with a six-foot-three teenage boy who enjoys watching the cooking channel."

"Like I have a choice," I cracked, rolling my eyes. "Your repertoire is limited to grilled cheese sandwiches."

"Yup. Your mother, though...You take after her. That woman could cook. I'd drive home from work every night looking forward to dinner because she made it an event." His eyes were closed and he was smiling, fully back in the memory. "She was making dinner for me, a handyman, but she had the table set like she was serving the King of Siam. I loved walking through that door. Hmm, the smell of bread baking, onions frying. There's nothing better than the smell of home-cooking. And your mom truly enjoyed it, just like you."

I nodded and then we ate in comfortable silence. As we cleared the table together and loaded the dishwasher, I told my dad about the days' drills, what I thought I did well and where I thought I could improve.

"What are your teammates like?"

"Not my teammates yet, Dad." I let out a breath. "I don't suppose I'd be too enamored with me if I was in their shoes. I'm bigger than most of them and I'm faster. They see me as a threat." Then I let it all out. "And I'd rather eat glass than be in that school anyway, you know? All those stuck-up assholes...And the work," I added, shaking my head. "You know it's gonna be too hard for me."

My father was quiet for a moment. He understood my fear. He'd lived with it, still struggled with it himself. "I don't imagine any of this will be easy on you, but I do think it's all going to work out just fine, Jeremy. I feel it in my heart."

My father was good like that, supportive, and he always made me feel like he was right in there, taking the blows and fighting alongside me.

Us against the world.

It was just me and my dad in the small brick house that sat at the edge of this massive property. The house was larger than the one we left, even though these were technically servants' quarters. Those first few years after she died, sometimes it was too quiet.

My grandparents lived in a modest house closer to town, right off Main Street. It was better having them around. My mother's parents did their best to help out. They had my mom late in life though, their only child, so they were pretty old by the time I came along. My Grandpa could throw the ball around the yard with me and he let me tinker while he hobbied in the garage, but I didn't have any sort of structure really. There were many nights back then when my dad didn't bother with the whole bath, brush teeth and bedtime story routine that my mother had established. And put it this way, after she was gone, no one was sitting at the dining room table in the evenings helping little Jeremy with his homework—homework that I simply could not do.

I can still picture my mother sitting with me, tirelessly flipping through flashcards. Each letter of the alphabet, she'd train me to name them and then to pair a sound with each one. It took repetition, day in and day out, for me to master this basic skill. My mother always smiled patiently and paired the painful task with cookies, hot chocolate, kisses and hugs.

She got sick when I was in first grade, so the tutoring sessions went by the wayside. When I entered second grade in this new school district, I think the phone calls and meetings with Dad started right away. The appeals to have me tested when they realized I couldn't read at all. Maybe I needed glasses, maybe I was intellectually impaired. I overheard it at the time but didn't know what they were talking about, other than the fact that I couldn't read. Of that, I was already painfully aware.

In this school, not only were the other kids in my second grade class reading, they were reading full on chapter books with many, many pages and no pictures. *How could anyone enjoy a book without pictures?* But these kids were the offspring of doctors, high-profile trial attorneys, astrophysicists for fuck's sake. Their DNA gave them reading superpowers, while I was lacking in every academic skill area. Even math, which came easily to me, was now giving me trouble because I couldn't make heads or tails of the word problems.

My father was in no state to even think about getting me help at the time. Getting through a day's work, remembering to shower, to shave, remembering to eat—those were now priorities. He was grief-stricken. I repeated second grade and struggled my way through third, fourth and fifth, growing more frustrated and angrier year by year.

The last day of August, our last practice before Coach was announcing the starting line-up—that's when I saw her. She was part of the reason I'd been "asked" to leave school all those years ago.

We had to walk through the gym on our way to the locker rooms. Every other day it was empty because football practice started a few weeks before school began. Today though, the girls' volleyball team was having tryouts. *When did volleyball uniforms get so hot?* I took in the shorts that barely covered their ass cheeks and the tight, formfitting tank tops. Some of the guys started hooting and hollering as they took in the scene, the girls preening, laughing or looking annoyed in response.

Back in the locker room, Chase, one guy I had come to truly dislike, called out, "I know who I'll be whacking off to tonight... Samantha Cavanaugh. That girl has the sweetest tits I've ever seen."

"You mean, the sweetest tits you've *never* seen, don't you?" Will asked.

"Only a matter of time, young Will," Chase shot back, stupid smug grin on his face. I pretty much always had the urge to slap that kid.

"I'd take Carolyn Harris over her any day of the week. She's a lot nicer, and those legs...I can envision those long, beautiful legs wrapped tight around me," Mike said, making a crude gesture with his hips.

"Shut the fuck up. Carolyn is mine."

"Take it easy," Mike said.

Drew's face changed from menacing to light in the span of a second. "I'm just fucking with you, but she is going to be mine. I've been waiting to ask her out for a year."

I raised an eyebrow looking to Will. The mention of her name got my full attention. Will explained, "Carolyn's parents won't let her date until her sixteenth birthday, or at least that's what she tells Drew to make him back off."

"October twenty-ninth, baby," Drew said absently, tossing a football into the air repeatedly.

Spence pushed Drew's shoulder so that he missed the ball. "That's a little ass backwards. Are her parents Amish or something?"

"No, they're cool, just a little protective. I'm good with it. And when Carolyn does go out with me, at least I'll know she hasn't already sucked off every other guy in our grade...unlike Chase's babe."

The locker room erupted in laughter with a whole lot of "burn" and "oh, shit" taunts thrown in. Chase looked like he was about to charge at Drew for a second before he started to laugh along with everyone else.

"Yeah, I wouldn't call Taylor pure as the driven snow, I guess. I wouldn't call her my babe, either."

There was no more talk of Carolyn, but I couldn't get her out of my mind. Will slapped my back, startling me out of my stupor when the coaches came into the locker room to announce the starting line-up for our first game that following Friday.

"You daydreaming, Rivers? Thought you'd be more excited about being our starting cornerback."

I smiled, nodding, recovering myself. I looked over to see Landon Westfield scowling in my direction. He was a senior who would now be sitting on the sidelines unless I got injured. I did feel bad, kind of. Being him sucked right about now. But this was football, not girl scouts, and I appreciated that the coaches respected talent and work ethic.

As I lay in bed that night, I thought about her, about the way it was between us back then. Mostly, I thought about that one week, and the day that changed my life.

With my learning delays and the surly attitude I used to mask my embarrassment, I tended to frustrate my teachers. But even though I wasn't the most respectful kid in class, I knew my place. I never made an enemy out of any teacher. Sixth grade, though, brought Mr. Witt. A few of the kids nicknamed him Mr. Zit due to his post-pubescent case of acne. He wore glasses, he was my height exactly, and he was mean. He had me pegged as an outsider, poor and stupid, inside of a week.

I didn't think I dressed shabby or anything, but these kids dressed differently. They seemed to have new sneakers every few weeks, while I got new ones only when I let my dad know that my big toe had a blister from being crammed in too tight. Other boys dressed in khaki pants, some wearing button down shirts and loafers when there was no dress code. What kind of twelve-year-old boy willingly does that? Anyway, I guess I looked, dressed and acted...different.

The first day Mr. Witt called on me to read aloud, I swear I caught him smirking. He knew. Fucking bastard knew and he was trying to make me look like a fool in front of the entire class. After stumbling over a few words, I shook my head, hoping he'd pass over me and give another kid a turn. He raised his voice and ordered me to read again. I said, "No," meeting his gaze without raising my voice. He told me to stand in the corner next to his desk, where everyone had no choice but to stare at me. I tried to think of anything else—the new snowboard I was hoping to get for Christmas, Beatles' lyrics, the Patriots' chances of making it to the Super Bowl that year—anything to take my mind off where I was at that very moment and why.

I stood there for the duration of the class. He was our Social Studies teacher too, so I had to stand for the next period also. When the bell rang for Gym, I went to move and he yelled, "You will stay right there!" As the other kids filed out, he lowered his voice and said, "You will stay there until you learn to listen."

The other kids came back from Gym, one or two chuckling over my predicament when they saw I was still standing there, but most looking uncomfortable or sympathetic. Carolyn Harris, sitting right up front, looked as if she was fighting back tears. I had to look away or else I knew I'd start crying too, and I was not crying in front of Zit. I wouldn't give him the satisfaction.

The entire day I stood there. I was told to eat lunch standing while the other kids went to the cafeteria, and he held me back when the other kids went to Music. He tried to speak to me a few times, but I just stood there stock still, defiant in my silence. He swapped one failed strategy for another, changing from tough guy to good cop, to "doing this for your own good" bull-shitter. I gave him nothing.

At dismissal, gathering his things and walking out of the room, he announced, "Perhaps Mr. Rivers will demonstrate respect tomorrow, like the rest of you." He tried to sound casual, but his voice was shaky from what I guessed was either nerves or fury.

A few boys smirked as I angrily grabbed my things from my desk, but most steered clear. One douchebag named Trent teased, "I c-c-can't ruh-ruh read."

I kept my head down for a second, grinding my teeth to keep from swinging. When I peered up at him, I must have looked set to kill because he literally ran around a desk and scooted out of the classroom at lightning speed.

I felt a hand on my shoulder and spun around to see Carolyn, her eyes full of pity.

"I'm sorry, Jeremy. He's a jerk."

No.

Stop.

No more.

"Shut the fuck up," I snapped, pushing her back.

She tripped over the leg of my desk and landed on her ass, stunned. I took off running at full speed. I ran out of the class, out of the school, and through the backstreets of this town that did not feel welcoming or familiar to me. I didn't stop running until I was at the lake, lungs burning, the early December air freezing the tears on my cheeks.

I was mad at Zit, I was mad that I still couldn't read better than a damn first grader, and I was mad at Carolyn. Why did she look at me that way? Why couldn't she just leave me alone? I hated myself when I pictured the look on her face. Quivering bottom lip, tears in her eyes, hurt and betrayed. Me—I did that to her.

Carolyn had never been anything but nice to me and to everyone else in class. She smiled whenever she caught me looking her way—a sweet, shy smile. And Carolyn was always kind to the class misfits. The fat kid who always had boogers in his nose, the one girl who'd sprouted giant knockers by fifth grade, the quirky autistic kid—she made attempts to include everyone. *Is that how she sees me? Another misfit, the one who can't read?* Didn't matter. Fact was, she'd been nothing but good to me and I'd just forcefully knocked her on her ass, cursed at her and left her crying.

Carolyn was smart—I'd say the smartest girl in our grade. I would smile inwardly listening to her answer questions, amazed by how much she knew. And when she read out loud to the class, it was like her voice put me under a spell. Carolyn read with emotion, changing her tone to match the mood and intention of the characters. She read so well that sometimes our teachers would let her read several pages in a row, rather than stopping her after one page and choosing the next narrator. I think they enjoyed listening to her voice as much as I did.

Carolyn was also beautiful. Not prettier than the other girls necessarily, but something radiated from her and drew everyone in. Happiness? Kindness? Whatever it was, I wanted some of that goodness to rub off on me. Carolyn was everything a lonely, hot-tempered, foul-mouthed, hopeless boy could ever dream of.

We weren't friends back then. It was more like I was a distant admirer. She'd never know it though, as I made a point of scowling or turning away whenever she caught me staring at her.

As I sat in class daydreaming, I would imagine myself talking to Carolyn, making her laugh, amusing her with my smooth, clever lines. Back in reality-ville though, I lacked the confidence to interact with her in any way. And I couldn't trust in her kindness. Even though she was nice, I figured she also thought of me as stupid and incapable, someone to feel sorry for.

The anger slowly bled out of me that cold afternoon as I made my way back towards my grandparents' house.

By now, my grandmother was not in her right mind. She remembered me and could sometimes hold a lucid conversation, but she was not a caretaker anymore. And my grandfather's hands were full caring for Grandma. I'd go there after school, attempt homework for no more than fifteen minutes, and then watch television with them most days until Dad picked me up.

That afternoon, I sat and had a soda with my grandfather and then asked him for five bucks. I needed to perform some act of penance.

I always saw Carolyn breaking pieces off from a triangle-shaped chocolate bar and handing them out to her girlfriends. As I walked into the grocery store, which in this town was like a gourmet food emporium, I saw the bars displayed up by the register. *Figures...she likes candy bars that cost three freaking dollars apiece.* I plunked my money down and went home to write a note that I taped to the weird triangular box.

I got into class before everyone else the next morning and shoved the candy into Carolyn's desk before taking my seat. It felt like everyone gave a quick look my way as they filed in. That is, everyone except Mr. Zit. He didn't acknowledge my presence.

When he was handing out permission slips for next month's class trip, instead of just giving a stack to one kid or giving the first person in each row papers to hand back, he called each child up one by one in alphabetical order. He greeted each with a smile and some phony friendly comment as he handed them the paper. It was a trip to the Bruce Art Museum located a few towns over, and I was excited about it. I knew they had a few Rodin pieces and I was looking forward to seeing them up close. The closer Zit got to R, the itchier I got.

My grandfather loved tinkering with clay, metal, wood—he even carved soap. He would make the weirdest, coolest looking sculptures out in the garage. He gave me my first sculpting knives, sketch pads, pencils and charcoals when I was seven. He used to call me his Rodin, in reference to the fact that I was self-taught and my "art" could be a bit on the wacky side. When my grandmother would look at my work, wide-eyed and bewildered, my grandfather would say, "Don't listen to the masses, Jeremy. Rodin was an outsider—son of a clerk, self-taught, rejected from that snooty art school in *Pah-ree*. He went on to create some of the most famous works of art in the world. Don't you ever listen, just create."

When Zit called Trent Ralston's name, I knew in my gut he

would not be calling me next. Yep, next name called was Amy Simms. *Stay calm*, I told myself, but I knew my face was turning an angry shade of red. My knee was knocking with nervous energy against the underside of my desk.

Zit was downright gleeful after he finished handing out the permission slips. He clapped his hands twice and then told everyone to take out their book. We were reading *To Kill a Mockingbird*. I hated that book. I hated certain characters in the book, namely Atticus and Calpurnia, who happened to be two of the truest, most genuine people, but I hated them because I stumbled so badly over their names. I came to like Boo of all people. His name? Piece of cake.

I had a pit in my stomach. *Here we go again.*

"Chapter four everyone," he chirped. "Mr. Rivers," he said without looking my way, "I'm being generous and giving you an opportunity to redeem yourself. Please start us off."

I took one look at that opening sentence: *The remainder of my school days were no more auspicious than the first*. There was no way. I couldn't even make heads or tails of the second word. A long minute passed.

"Jeremy? We're waiting," said the smug little shit. "Is there a problem?" I stared down at the page and angrily swiped at one hot tear before it could escape. "I didn't want to have to do this, I really didn't," he said in a saintly tone, meant to convey to the others that he was truly sorry about what my incorrigible behavior was forcing him to do. "Jeremy, come stand up front."

I sat frozen, my body too big for the desk I was crammed into. In truth, being tall to begin with and a year older than the other kids, the desk was small, but this was different. I felt large, overheated, agitated and trapped.

"Jeremy? The *entire* class is waiting."

I rose up and slowly made my way to the front. I heard someone behind me sniggering, probably Trent. Some kids looked up as I walked past, but most kept their eyes fixed straight ahead. Carolyn sat right up front, head down, shoulders slumped. She was clutching the boxed chocolate in her hands with a white knuckle grip.

I took my place next to his desk and turned to face the class, staring at the back wall. My blood was hot liquid rage, pump, pump, pumping through my veins. My fists were clenched and my jaw ticked angrily. Underneath all that anger, though, was shame. I was so fucking ashamed. Ashamed that I was stupid, ashamed that everyone knew I was stupid, ashamed that people—that Carolyn—felt bad for me on account of the fact I was stupid.

I was this man-child, bigger than the rest of them but less capable than every single person sitting in that room.

Zit came and stood right in front of me, nose to nose. His hot, sour breath hit me when he hissed, "You will do this *every* day. Do. You. Understand?"

Lights out.

I knocked him to the ground with one punch. And I'm sure that punch was painful, as it packed every ounce of fury that had built up inside of me over the past two days.

I stood there for a moment, shocked, cradling my sore fist. I remember seeing his glasses, bent and broken on the floor. I'm pretty sure I also saw a tooth.

My class erupted as I ran out of the room, racing down the hallway as fast as my legs could take me. I ran straight into a lady as she rounded a corner, nearly knocking her over. By then I was crying big, scared-shitless kinds of tears.

"Jeremy? Are you all right, honey?"

She worked in the main office. I remembered she was someone who had spoken with my dad and she'd given me a letter to bring home to him once. She was short and skinny, but she held me firmly by my shoulders and spoke in a sure and commanding voice. "It's going to be okay. Whatever happened, it's going to be okay."

For some reason, her words soothed me. She led me to her office.

After calling someone to go check on my class, she sat me down, and in between tears, coaxed me into telling her everything.

Mrs. Connolly. From that day forward she became my advocate, my biggest cheerleader. She was petite and looked sweet, but the lady was fierce. When the principal tried to lay into me after hearing Zit's side of the story, she stood up and faced off with him. "With all due respect, we will examine *all* sides of this story before Jeremy is assumed to be the one who bears all of the blame here."

I never returned to Mr. Witt's class, and following an immediate evaluation, both psychiatric and educational, I was deemed to be severely dyslexic and dysgraphic—a fancy way of saying that I was not only reading disabled, but my writing also sucked. On the plus side, I was gifted in both mathematics and nonverbal reasoning skills, whatever they were. And contrary to what Zit was stating as fact, I was not psychotic or emotionally disturbed.

I'm sure if I hadn't punched Zit and if I'd had the reputation of being a calm, good boy, the school would have kept me and arranged for remedial services there. Since I had, in fact, assaulted a teacher, the school approved funding to send me to a private school that specialized in educating kids with learning disabilities.

They wanted me gone.

I remember Mrs. Connolly reassuring me, telling me that I would love this new school. I wasn't convinced. I also remember her telling me how smart I was. When I smirked, she took me forcefully by the shoulders again and said, "Some people are not smart, you're right. Some people, though, are smart in different ways. You can do math at a tenth grade level, did you know that? *I do* because I tested you. You can arrange puzzles better than ninety-seven percent of kids your age. Did you know that? *I do* because I tested you. The mathematicians and the puzzle solvers of the world are the inventors, the artists, the builders...the creators. Thomas Edison, Albert Einstein, Ansel Adams...All great men who failed abominably in school. Trust me when I tell you, Jeremy, everything is going to be okay."

I cried walking out of her office with my dad that day, but they were tears of relief. And within two weeks of going to that new school, I had hope.

* * *

CAROLYN

"Are you all right, Carolyn?" Erica cocked her head to the side, taking me in. "You look kinda sick."

"Uh, yeah," I said, recovering.

Drew had just sidled up to me as the guys were making their way through the gym towards the locker room. He tugged on my braid when he whispered, "It's August twenty-ninth. The countdown is on." He proceeded to raise one and then two fingers up in the air, smiling sweetly at me.

"I don't know if Drew is going to last two more months. Stop teasing him," Samantha scolded. She was smiling, but sometimes, like now, I felt an undercurrent of animosity simmering just below the surface with her.

Kerri's auburn curls bounced as she trotted over. "Drew is such a hottie. And it seems like he's hopelessly devoted to you, bitch. I'm jealous."

"Yeah, Drew's nice," Samantha shrugged noncommittally, drawing her words out slowly, "but the question is, will he wait for Little Miss Innocent here to finally say yes to a date? Really, most guys aren't into being tortured."

I said nothing. Drew had been playing this game with me since last year, teasing me—although taunting is more what it felt like. When he first asked me to the movies, I panicked. I don't know where the lie sprang from, but before I knew it, I was bound by it: no dating until my sixteenth birthday. Since then, he'd been counting down the months, which would soon be weeks.

Drew was gorgeous, well-mannered, at the top of our class and a great athlete. He was effortlessly popular and girls flirted with him given any opportunity. Drew and his closest friends, Will Clarke and Mike Hanson, were three of the most sought after boys in our class.

I couldn't figure out what Drew saw in me, Little Miss Innocent. And that moniker? It sickened me. Samantha and the rest of those girls—my supposed closest friends? They didn't know me at all.

Kerri looked positively dreamy-eyed. "No, I think Drew would happily wait for Carolyn."

"Boys like Drew do *not* wait." Apparently Samantha was now the authority on everything. "Do you think any of those boys have turned down Taylor, Lara Reynolds or that goth slut, Vanessa?"

Erica's eyes widened. She looked around to make sure no one was listening as she waved us in closer, whispering, "Ohmigod, do you know what I overheard Taylor saying last night?" Erica sounded like she had some grade-A dirt to dish. "She was telling Lara about some new guy. Just moved here, I guess. She told Lara she met him at a party down by the lake and," she looked around a second time to make sure no one else was eavesdropping, "Taylor said his cock was so colossal she couldn't take him all the way in. His dick," she was cackling now, "choked her!"

We talked trash about Taylor and girls like her—girls deemed slutty, easy—but in truth we were fascinated by them. Taylor was sixteen, nearly seventeen, but she seemed light years older and more sexually aware than the rest of us. There was a rumor floating around that she'd lost her virginity to her much older stepbrother when she was thirteen, and she didn't give anyone reason to doubt it. She didn't seem to care that everyone gossiped about her. Taylor was gorgeous, rich, she was into guys, she dressed in a way that was sexy and provocative—she owned it.

I wondered what it would be like to be Taylor sometimes. She was confident around the boys, in control. She pranced around in a teeny bikini at pool parties, sat in boys' laps, purred in their ears—she was no virgin, that much was obvious.

The way I assumed she was with boys both excited and repulsed me. The mere thought of metaphorically taking a walk in her shoes thrilled me as much as it made me feel shame.

It would never happen. Carolyn Harris was virtuous, smart, accomplished, serious—a good girl.

At least that's what everyone thought.

Chapter Two

JEREMY

"Mr. Rivers, how did you *feel* reading this chapter? What emotions did D.H. Lawrence evoke in you?"

I loved Ms. Margolis. She was my English teacher and a part-time struggling actress. She lived and breathed the plays and novels she taught, and she inspired us to do the same. With me, she didn't bat an eye that my earbuds were plugged into my audio e-reader as the rest of the class read their paperbacks, and she counted my spoken answers as equal to the written responses the other students gave. She also treated me like my opinions were intelligent and insightful.

"I guess in this chapter it was humiliation. I could feel the mother's prideful anger at being ignored by the waitress in the pub and the humiliation Paul felt on her behalf."

"Yes, yes, yes, Mr. Rivers! The pain of feeling less than, of being judged, discounted..." She went on, dramatically waving her arms and moving about the room, calling on other students, most of whom felt like I did about her. People like her made my transition back to Westerly High bearable. English Lit my favorite class? Who would have guessed it? The rest of my classes were a mixed bag. Science: mheh, Math: easy, Global History: painful. I was managing.

"Want to cut after this class?"

"Can't, Vanessa. I have practice. Seems stupid to cut and then just come back here later, right?"

We walked to the lunchroom together and then joined the rest of what had become my group at our table. Vanessa was beautiful, with porcelain white skin, jet black dyed hair, and a really nice body. She was also into Ms. Margolis, Tori Williams, Samantha Cavanaugh and every other good-looking female at school. She let me in on that nugget after I tried to kiss her, slightly drunk one afternoon when she and I had skipped class and went wandering down by the lake. After that she became a close friend, and I was honored to be the only one she trusted with her secret.

Vanessa was the only girl in this group and she liked it that way. She wasn't comfortable within the girl cliques. She had no girl friends. Because she dressed the way she did and patently ignored them, the other girls assumed Vanessa was a slut who preferred to be passed around among the rough crowd of guys she spent her time with. She liked to let them think that. As a joke, she'd bat her eyelashes at me or wiggle herself into my lap when one of the "it" girls was paying attention. As a result, the entire school assumed I was banging Vanessa. You would think this would keep other girls at bay, but certain girls liked the challenge.

"Mike, Jeremy, Blake," Taylor purred as she came up behind me and placed her hands on my shoulders. Mike and Blake were teammates of mine. Taylor addressed the three of us, ignoring Vinny Roman and Frank Carr, two of my less popular friends—ones who inhabited my same income tax bracket.

Taylor made me uncomfortable. She licked her lips when she paused in conversation, trailed her nails down my chest for no good reason, or might rub my shoulders in a way that was overly familiar. The week before classes started up, Frank dragged me to a party down by the lake. I was introduced to Taylor that night. She wasted no time, groping me about ten minutes after she told me her name. I hardly knew the girl, but fuck, she scared me.

"I'm having a party after the game Friday night. You better be there," she teased.

Vanessa pretended to gag on a carrot, simulating a blow job. Taylor ignored her and leaned down to whisper in my ear, "Please *come*, Jeremy." Yes, she put full emphasis on the word come. "You keep blowing me off. You're hurting my feelings."

"We'll be there," Blake assured her. "Make sure the Jacuzzi is a comfortable eighty degrees."

"You got it. Bye guys," she chirped, raking her nails lightly along the back of my neck before walking away.

Vanessa looked to Blake. "Why do I get the feeling Taylor is going to be the only girl at this party?"

"Nah, I've been to her house before, it's not like that. She's a schemer, though. It'll be the one guy she has her eye on and then she tries to figure out who else to pair up."

Vanessa looked disgusted. "So it's totally for the purpose of hooking up?"

"Absolutely," Blake answered. "Her parties are actually border-line weird. The music is low, the lighting is soft. It's very *Eyes Wide Shut*, you know?"

"She's after you, Rivers," Frank teased.

"You can have her."

"She doesn't want me. Believe me, if she was rubbing *my* shoulders and scratching *my* back like that, I'd be at her house getting that blow job you know she's itching to give you."

"Yeah," Blake teased, "she likes initiating the new guys."

"You've got that bad boy thing going on," Vanessa said, glaring at me. "You're brooding, kind of guarded. You're her pet project this fall."

Vinny looked to Vanessa, cocking his head. "That doesn't piss you off?"

Vanessa got up and grabbed her tray. "Jeremy's a big boy. He can do whatever or whoever he wants. I don't own him."

After she left, Vinny looked to me. "What was that? And what's up with you two anyway?"

"Nothing," I said, shaking my head. "We're friends, that's all."

"Then tap Taylor this weekend. Take my word for it, she won't leave you alone until you do," Mike Hanson chimed in.

Frank and I walked to our next class together, Studio Art, with him teasing me about Taylor the entire way.

The absolute best thing about being in an affluent school district was the enrichment programs. My basic art class was taught by a working artist who was—hello—a graduate of the School of the Art Institute of Chicago. Insanity. And Chuck Watters also taught an after-school figure drawing class. Chuck—he insisted all his "fellow artists" were on a first-name basis with him—only allowed a few serious high school students into this class. I thought my chest would burst with pride when he invited me to join the group that met once a week after school hours in the studio. It was a mix of local college students and a few of us juniors and seniors.

Frank was jealous. Not because he wanted the instruction, but because figure drawing meant nude models.

Frank and I became good friends after reconnecting this September. I knew him from Driscoll, but we'd lost touch after I left. Like me, he wasn't an honors student, and the fact that we both came from single-parent homes, weren't filthy rich, and both liked tinkering with crap bonded us.

Frank's dad was a cop who worked a side job doing carpentry. Frank used his dad's equipment to fiddle around, making chairs and other furniture. He blew me away with his talent, but he downplayed everything. "Get off my dick, Rivers, it's just a table," he'd snap in his smart-ass way, even though I knew he was proud of his own work.

On Sunday mornings I'd help him haul his pieces to craft festivals around the area. He was making a decent buck, too. People who trolled those markets were usually upscale. They'd smile, all giddy as they handed over their cash, knowing they were getting a steal.

It was cold that Friday night, one of our last games of the regular season. Still, I was set on going to the bonfire down by the lake. I'd rather freeze my ass off than be snared in Taylor's web. Maybe because I looked older people assumed that I was experienced, but nothing could be further from the truth.

My encounters were limited to heated make-out sessions with a good friend from my old school, Andie. She was pretty, funny, a talented artist and a fellow dyslexic. We were each other's first kiss in ninth grade. I was thrilled to have a girl to kiss and some soft, bare skin to touch. We never rounded more than second base. I didn't push Andie and she never offered more than that, so Taylor's advances seemed like jumping from the sandbox into the strip club.

Vince, Mike, Frank and I piled out of Will's shiny new truck. I was beginning to really like Will and some of the others, but man, all of these boys were spoiled. A truck like that with a big cab and flatbed was wasted on Will. The boy was never hauling payload, that's for sure.

We made our way towards the party with people stopping me, Mike and Will to slap our backs and yell their congratulations on another win. I'll admit, to be recognized and told you're good at something felt great, but it was still a somewhat alien experience for me.

There had to be two hundred kids clustered in small groups around the lake, mostly juniors and seniors. Spencer Davies, my new BFF who was coming around because my interceptions at cornerback made his job easy, waved me over. Just then, Samantha Cavanaugh all but plastered her tits up against Will, whispering in his ear. I was happy to leave them to it. As I made my way over towards Spence and his boys, I looked in the direction Samantha had walked over from. Carolyn and a few of her friends were there, nursing their beers. Drew was there too, leaning into Carolyn. She looked up at him, smiling that same shy smile I could never forget.

Drew had made good on his promise, asking Carolyn out the night after her parents treated ten of her girlfriends to a Broadway play and a fancy dinner in Manhattan—stretch limo transportation included, naturally.

Vanessa heard about Carolyn's mellow, understated Sweet Sixteen celebration and laughed bitterly as she tallied up what the small gathering had probably cost, which was way more than a month's salary for someone like my father. It burned Vanessa more than it burned me—the have and the have-not nature of this town. I was resigned to it, whereas Vanessa was resentful.

As I stood there bullshitting with Spence and a few of his buddies, who slinks up next to me and wraps her arm around my waist but Taylor.

"Hey there, Taylor," Spence greeted her, eyeing her from toes to tits. He never once made eye contact with her.

"What's up, Spencer? Long time, no see," she answered, drawing her words out in a way that pretty much oozed sex.

"Well," he faked a hurt expression, "I don't seem to be on your guest list anymore. You found someone new? I thought we were going steady," he teased.

"Well you were my first, Spence, so you'll always be special to me," she teased right back.

This kind of advanced flirting was foreign to me. I stood there mute. Taylor turned her body towards me then, so close I could almost feel her crotch pressed up against the side of my thigh. "I do have a new friend, though. You *are* coming tonight, right, Jeremy?"

"Uh, I don't know what I'm doing yet."

She put her hand inside my jacket and dragged her nails across my chest when she said, "I'm heading back there now with Lara and Kim. Don't disappoint me."

She slowly drew her hand out and licked her lips before walking away. She was too much—a caricature of how you pictured the fast, easy girl at every high school.

Spence raised his eyebrows. "Please tell me you're not contemplating turning that down."

I shrugged. "Don't think I'm that interested in going where so many have gone before, you know?"

Spence nodded, thinking it over as he drained his beer. "Yeah, I don't think I'd stick my dick in that either, but a blowjob? Best one I've ever had."

Drew joined us and zeroed in on me, smiling. "Heard you're heading to Taylor's tonight."

"Who'd you hear that from?"

"Right from Taylor's very own talented mouth." He must have sensed my unease. As Drew patted my back, he said, "I can relate. I was shitting a brick the first time she invited me over. I was a babe in the woods."

Spence smirked. "And now you're a man of the world, Drew? Popped Carolyn's cherry already?"

"Shut the fuck up, Spence." He wasn't angry, though.

Spence smiled. "No, Carolyn's a girl you take your time with. She's," he rolled his eyes, "special."

Drew shrugged. "She is."

The conversation moved onto other topics, onto other girls then, but my thoughts were stuck on Carolyn. She hadn't acknowledged me once since I'd been at Westerly. To be fair, we didn't share any classes because she was in all honors and advanced placement. The one time I did pass her in the hallway and our eyes met, I didn't get the feeling that she even recognized me. Just as well, I guess. I didn't need her remembering the learning disabled, hot tempered delinquent I'd been.

She may not have noticed me, but I, on the other hand, was pretty much actively stalking her. I'd watch her pore over books in the library, I'd sneak glances at her table in the cafeteria, I'd lurk in the gymnasium doorway when her volleyball team was playing.

Carolyn had changed. She was tall, slim but curvy, with long brown hair that hung half-way down her back. I won't lie, I'm a guy and my eyes lingered on the way her body filled out her skimpy volleyball uniform, but it was more than that. When I'd spy her laughing with her friends or smiling at someone, it felt like my heart was breaking just a little bit. It was that same feeling I had back in sixth grade—of wanting something so badly and knowing I'd never have it.

Drew bumped my shoulder. "I'm off," he said, nodding his head in the direction of Carolyn and her friends. "I'll be thinking of you tonight when I go home with a set of blue balls."

Well, I did not go home with blue balls. Drew's comment snapped me back to reality. Made me realize how futile crushing on Carolyn was. Instead, I made my way home late that night after getting an education in life.

Taylor was not what I expected. She was surprisingly sweet. You couldn't fool girls like her. She knew inside of ten minutes that she was dealing with a virgin, and that made her even hotter for me. How can I describe it besides saying that she took care of me?

Taylor took it slow that first night. It was like she was the guy, asking for my unspoken consent when she looked up at me before unbuttoning the fly on my jeans. I tried to take control but she would gently turn the tables on me, easing me onto my back, kissing me and whispering encouraging words in my ear as she urged me on, instructing me as I did things to her.

That night was the start of a month-long romance. It was a

romance on my part, anyway. I was in awe of Taylor, whipped by the first girl who gave it up to me.

In English Lit we were still working our way through D.H. Lawrence. Now we were on *Lady Chatterley's Lover*. I pictured Taylor's face when I read about Connie, while I was Oliver—the hired hand with the rich, privileged girl. One line stood out when I thought about us because I knew, even in my lust-induced infatuation, that I was not her only one. To paraphrase my new pal, Lawrence: *The bitch-goddess was trailed by thousands of gasping dogs with lolling tongues.*

Taylor and I didn't act like girlfriend and boyfriend in public. That wasn't my choice, but I quickly understood that Taylor didn't operate like that. I would have held her hand, taken her out, defended her when other guys leered at her or made crude comments —all of it. But Taylor didn't seem to need or want that. She liked the world on her terms. If she wanted you, she'd plop into your lap when you were hanging out with your friends and make it obvious. Otherwise she'd wave, blow a kiss and keep on going when she saw me passing in the halls at school.

After a month of feeling like I was, in fact, a gasping dog, it got old. Like every guy who'd gone before me, I resigned myself to the fact that she was probably already with someone else. I saw it for what it was, got my kicks a few more times, and braced myself for the pain I felt when I saw her pushing up against some new guy.

I acted like I didn't give a shit, that she was just a lay and nothing more, but it hurt.

CAROLYN

Samantha had her arms wrapped tight around Will's middle as they walked towards us. He looked amused while she looked smitten. "Let's all go back to my house. My parents are away."

A few people, Drew included, accepted the invite, but Will shook his head. "Can't. Anna has friends over. I need to head back and check on them."

She rested her head against his chest and squeezed tighter. "You are *such* a good big brother."

"Uh, thanks," he said, easing himself away from her. "But you all go. I'll catch up with you tomorrow."

He looked down at Samantha and gave her a half-hearted smile before turning to walk towards the field where all the cars were parked. I noticed, and so did Samantha, that he quickened his step to catch up with Tori Williams. I saw him place a hand on her shoulder and he smiled, beamed really, when she turned to talk to him.

"Tori is the fakest bitch on the planet."

"Excuse me?" Erica challenged her, shocked. "Tori is *not*, in any way, shape or form, a bitch. She's one of the nicest girls in our class, Samantha. What's the matter with you?"

"I don't know," Drew said, nodding his head in their direction. "Tori acts like her and Will are just friends, but I think she gets off on leading him around by his di—uh, manhood."

I laughed inwardly. It's true that I don't care much for foul language, but I thought it was funny that Drew considered me so innocent that he needed to watch his words around me.

"So," he went on, "your house, Samantha?"

"Sorry, I'm not feeling it anymore," Samantha said absently. She looked lost in thought for a minute before her expression changed. She smirked, asking no one in particular, "Did you see Taylor all but do the deed with Jeremy in full public view?"

Drew pretended to look at his watch. "I predict that Jeremy is getting the Taylor Special right at this very moment."

Erica shook her head. "Why do guys go for her?"

Drew threw his head back and laughed. "Uh, I don't know, Erica, why do you think?"

"But do boys really want that, Drew?" she asked, truly wanting to know his thoughts.

He glanced my way before answering, "That's not really what guys want, no." *What a liar.* "But for someone like Jeremy, she's perfect. She's a step up...Or a step sideways from that one Vanessa, right? And Jeremy doesn't seem like the warm and fuzzy boyfriend type."

"No," Samantha said, eyes like a predator, "he seems like he's dark, moody and—"

"Hot!" Erica interrupted. She looked to me, Samantha and Kerri, who'd just joined us. "You have to admit, that boy is gorgeous."

Jeremy was gorgeous and so...big. He was bigger than all of the kids when we were back at Driscoll, but now he seemed like a grown man amid a sea of boys. You could tell he needed to shave every day and his body was well defined. Those days when my timing was just right, when I was fortunate enough to catch him straddling his motorcycle after school and revving the engine before pulling away, I thought he looked more like a teacher than a student.

I was stunned when I saw him that first week of school. All of my friends had been talking about the new boy. The new boy was sex-on-a-stick kinda hot and he was dangerous—a juvenile delinquent who'd just gotten sprung from a detention center. The one whose junk was, according to Taylor, colossal.

Erica poked me in the ribs when we passed him in the hallway. "That's *him*!"

"What's his name?" I asked, even though I already knew without a doubt that it was Jeremy.

"Jeremy Rivers," she said, sighing dreamily. "He's hot but too much of a bad boy for me. I draw the line at criminal activity. But," she said, grabbing my arm and turning me to look at her, "I would love to have just one session with him. I bet that boy can kiss!"

Seeing him that day brought me down. I couldn't concentrate. I was back to that week in sixth grade. Back to that teacher, whose name I couldn't even recall, torturing Jeremy. I remember how strong the urge was to throw my arms around Jeremy and hug him, to let him know he had a friend in me, to let him know that I cared about him. Angry at myself for remaining silent, for not standing up in the middle of that class and screaming, "Stop it!" to that sad excuse for a teacher.

I cried every day for a week after they kicked Jeremy out of school. In my lame little form of rebellion, I'd say I had a sore throat every time I was called on to read. I was so angry, and I was worried. It was a month before the not-knowing drove me crazy enough to go see the school psychologist. I broke down in her room, telling her about the emotional abuse Jeremy endured before snapping and hitting the teacher. When I angrily asked why Jeremy had been punished and not the teacher, she assured me that Jeremy wasn't punished and that he was at a good school where he could get the help that he needed. It was Thursday when I spoke with the psychologist. By Monday morning we had a new teacher. I never saw that sadistic jerk again.

Was it true what they said about him? Was Jeremy a criminal? Did something happen, did something change him? He always had a rough edge—I vividly recall being the recipient of one of his angry rants. But I always believed there was a tender soul, a sad little boy beneath that tough façade. I guess he now looked and dressed the part of delinquent, but I still didn't buy it. I knew how the rumor mill could be at Westerly. You couldn't believe half of what you heard.

The party was breaking up at the lake. It was too damn cold to be standing around outside. Drew looked to me. "Want to hang out at my house?"

"You're not looking for an invite to Taylor's?" I teased.

He made a disgusted face and shook his head. "Why would I want ground beef when I have filet mignon?"

I couldn't help but laugh. "I don't know if I like being compared to meat."

He pinched my ass as he moved in closer. "You are my sweet, tender, juicy girl. Now come to my house, *please*. We only have an hour before you have to be home."

"All right," I said, although the thought of being alone with him made me nervous. Drew was intense. I mean he was funny, life-of-the-party and all that, but there was a side of him that was serious and single-minded. I felt like the day I said yes to going out on a date with him, I committed to being his girlfriend, to being exclusive. I still wasn't sure how I felt about that.

There was a part of me thanking the heavens above because Drew was Mr. It at Westerly. He was the gorgeous football star, the top student, the popular guy every girl wanted. The fact that Drew was into me burned Samantha, and I guess that pleased me too. It was almost like I could see her shaking her head, wondering how Drew could possibly want me when she was available. I was happy, but at the same time I couldn't totally tune out the nagging little voice in my head that was setting off warning bells.

Drew showed up unannounced at my house the day after my birthday with a giant bouquet of red roses. He asked my father's permission before asking me out on a date. I remember my dad quirking an eyebrow as he gave Drew the go-ahead, totally baffled by how formal Drew was behaving. I was so glad Drew didn't mention the age sixteen dating rule-thing in front of my parents, as they had no knowledge of the lie I'd concocted.

He was a perfect gentleman on our first date, and after that night he started calling me every day, meeting me at my locker every morning, sitting at my lunch table and making plans for us on the weekends. I was a willing participant who just sort of went along with it all.

"Come here," he said, patting the space next to him on the couch in his basement. When I went to sit he pulled me onto his lap. "You know what today is?"

"Um, Friday?"

"Yes, my brainy girl, it's Friday. It's also one month since we started dating."

"Oh."

"Do you like being my girlfriend, Carolyn?"

I turned my body to face him, straddling my legs over his. He sounded unsure and it made me nervous, wondering if *he* was happy going out with me. I did like Drew. He made me feel special. And though it shamed me, I liked how dating Drew had upped my social standing. It's not that I was on the social outs before, but over the past month I noticed how his friends, all juniors and seniors, now made a point of calling out to me in the hallways just to say hello. It was a level of status I didn't have before.

"Of course I like being your girlfriend." After a pause I asked, "Are you happy with me?"

He nuzzled into my neck as he pulled me closer. "So happy."

Drew was kissing my neck then, moving up to my jaw and then softly taking my lips. We'd kissed a lot over the past month, but never with our bodies in this position. Drew moved slowly with me. His hands had never touched any part of my body besides my hands, face or waist before tonight. But now I could feel him pressed against me, and as he kissed me his hands roamed up my sides and rested alongside my breasts. I tensed a little. Not because I didn't like the feeling, the tingling in my belly that moved lower and the way my breasts stood at attention. No, it was because the last time a night started out like this, things hadn't ended so well for me.

He sensed my apprehension and pulled back. "Hey, pretty girl. No pressure, ok?" he reassured me. "Your body feels amazing, I'm not gonna lie, but there's no rush. I don't ever want you to feel rushed, all right?"

I nodded my head and forced a smile before leaning back in to kiss him.

My body might have been there with Drew, my lips kissed his, but I was far away. Memories of that summer dogged me. They pushed through even as I shut my eyes tight in an attempt to hold the ugly images at bay. Memories of *him*. The way he looked at me. The things he said. The way he made me believe that I was funny, smart and beautiful. The way he made me feel cheap, used and so, so stupid the next morning.

Once. That's the number of times I gave myself permission to cry over it. Don't cry over it, don't talk about it, don't dwell on it—forget. But I never could manage to put it behind me. The sound of his voice, the feel of the cold ground beneath me, the ache in my chest—I'd never be able to forget.

Chapter Three

JEREMY

The verdict was in. Academically speaking, my year was so-so. Passed English with a mediocre C, passed Art with flying colors, aced Math, passed Science by the skin of my teeth and failed Global History. With words like Mesopotamia assaulting me constantly and no audio version of the textbook to rely on, I was screwed. I tried, I really did, but it was a struggle to manage all my classes. With the exception of Art, they were all really hard for me. I did the best I could.

The rule read: two failures and you were automatically cut from the team. With my History grade and the D in Chemistry, my coach informed me I was on academic probation. They were going to "figure something out" for me in the fall.

I trusted Coach and hoped for the best because I was determined to play football my senior year. It's not like I was looking to go further with it; I wasn't interested in a college scholarship or anything. It's just that football, like art, made me feel good. It made me feel accomplished, maybe even a little important in this world that I sometimes felt so out of place in.

41

As school was ending, everyone yammered on about their plans for the next two months. Vinny, Frank and Vanessa would be around, working their asses off all summer like me. The rest of them? It was surreal listening to them talk about meeting up in Nantucket, Marblehead, or having one another as guests in the Hamptons. Some kids would even be abroad, their parents insisting they should have a European experience.

My summer experience, *if* I was lucky, would include sneaking a dip in the pool on the estates where I'd be working. I was pumped for the opportunity I had this summer, working for a licensed electrician who was a friend of my father's, Denny Roberts. I needed to rack up a minimum of two hundred hours under the supervision of a licensed professional so that I could enroll in an apprenticeship program next year.

I had a plan for my future, one that did not include college. I no longer hated school, but I didn't embrace academics to the point where I was willing to torture myself for an additional four years. I wanted to build, to fix, to make things.

Electricians, especially if you ran your own company, made good money. Yes, I wanted money. I didn't want what I saw in this neighborhood—the sprawling mansions, the garages filled with luxury cars that were rarely driven—but I wanted to be comfortable, to be able to take care of the people in my life. So I would work this summer, snag a union apprenticeship right after graduation, and hopefully, within two years I'd be on my way to becoming a licensed electrician who could run his own show.

Working this summer was also a necessity because I needed to start paying my own way. My father did all right, but money was tight lately. My grandmother's health had deteriorated, her dementia more severe now. The second time she left home wandering aimlessly, we weren't able to find her for several hours. She'd managed to venture a full town over wearing only a light house dress and socks. After that episode, the decision was made to move her into a nursing home. My father and grandfather had to chip in out of pocket to keep her in a better home, rather than the state-funded facility she was entitled to. My father didn't complain, but I got the impression that it was really expensive. I wanted to do my part.

My grandfather was heartbroken that his "bride" was gone. He hated being in their house without her ,so Dad would drop him off at the nursing home first thing every morning. My grandfather spent every day there, sitting by her side, feeding her and talking to her. She no longer recognized him, but he didn't care. He just needed to be near her.

Watching the two of them together didn't make me sad. As he sat reminiscing, flipping through pictures that Grandma couldn't even focus her gaze on anymore, I felt content. That kind of love, the kind you couldn't walk away or move on from—complete and total devotion to another person—it was incredible.

* * *

CAROLYN

My parents didn't push back when I announced that I wanted to stay close to home again this past summer. I was relieved. Last year I tried to act cool when I shrugged my shoulders and offhandedly told them I just wasn't into being a counselor at that academic enrichment camp anymore. To say they were surprised is an understatement.

I used to love that place. I started going there when I was ten, and every year I'd look forward to it: six bliss-filled weeks of being immersed in science with like-minded nerdy kids.

Among my hometown friends I always felt like a fish out of water, a poseur. I trudged through outings to the mall and pretended to absolutely *love* applying make-up and trying out new hairstyles. But in reality, I was happiest with my nose buried in a book or tinkering with my mother's cast-off chemicals and Bunsen burners in the garage.

Summer camp was the place where I felt a sense of belonging. When I laughed *there*, it was with real joy, among true friends. But after my stint as a junior counselor, I was done. Resigned and determined, I would never step foot on those campgrounds again.

So this summer I commuted with my dad. I spent four weeks working alongside a supervising neurologist and a few undergraduate students at Yale, assisting as they conducted research on brain development as it relates to dyslexia. As a high school student, I shouldn't have been there. I knew I was given the opportunity only because of my mother's connections. But I was all for nepotism now, because this place gave something very special back to me—something that awful experience at camp had taken away. In that lab I felt like I was finally back, geeking out with people from my tribe, and I'd found my life's work.

I was excited to get home every day, anxious to try out my newly acquired teaching strategies on Thomas.

My brother was eleven now. Born on my fifth birthday, he was the best present ever. I treated him as if he was *my* baby from the day he came home from the hospital. I fed him, read him bedtime stories, played with him and loved him unconditionally from the very first day I laid eyes on him.

When Thomas had trouble learning his ABCs in preschool, I worked with him every day, as did my mother and father. I was in the fourth grade then, and sadly, thanks to Jeremy Rivers, I had a fast-forward idea of what Thomas's future might look like.

Thomas now attended a school for children with dyslexia and other learning disabilities year-round, as did his friend, Zach. In the summer they had half-day sessions, so I didn't feel too bad about torturing the two of them every day for a little while so they could help with my research. I'd always bribe them with a trip for ice cream or cheese fries afterwards. On one particular day, though, they wanted to go to the lake.

"Really? Why the lake when we have a pool right out back?"

Thomas bounced on his toes, a dead giveaway that he was nervous. "Our pool is lame."

"Chrissy and Marissa Nader said the lake is cool," Zach chimed in.

Hmm...little brother's got a crush. "The Nader twins said it's cool, huh?"

Thomas blushed and then barked, "Are you gonna take us there or what?"

I was still smiling to myself as I flipped my towel out onto the grass and watched the boys wade in. The lake was peaceful, and being there during the daylight hours felt different. I'd only been there at night for bonfires or after-game parties when you couldn't see much of anything. During the day it was beautiful. Tall reed grass created a border on one side, and made a gentle whooshing sound when the warm breeze kicked up. I sat across from it, watching the birds nose their beaks into the sand. In the middle of the lake there was a floating dock. The boys swam out there and proceeded to do cannonballs over and over—jump, climb back up, repeat.

Spending the entire month of July in the lab had left me pasty white. I slathered on some sunblock with minimal SPF and took off my tank top and shorts. I was keeping half an eye on the boys while people watching, taking in the few others who sat along the shore. This was the place the townies used for a swimming hole, so there wasn't one familiar face. My friends would be hanging out in their resort-like backyards, each with a spacious heated pool, most tricked out with underwater lighting, state of the art sound systems and Jacuzzis.

A young mother at the waterline playing with her two toddlers caught my attention. She looked content and happy as her boys busied themselves shoveling the muddy sand into small buckets. I imagined them heading home later on that afternoon, the mother turning on the sprinkler so the boys could clean off while she cooked dinner. Her husband? I conjured up an image of a man who worked with his hands, dressed in work boots, jeans and a flannel shirt. It's July, but I was in the middle of my daydream so I just went with it.

She is genuinely happy to see him when he gets home, watching through the kitchen window as he picks the boys up one by one, tickling them into fits and getting himself wet in the spray of the sprinkler in the process. When he comes inside with one toddler under each arm, they smile at each other in a way that tells you they're not only in love, they are connected in that soul-deep kind of way. I fast forward through their family dinner to the two of them sitting on their front porch swing. They pass a bottle of beer between them, taking sips and talking about nothing and everything. She has one leg resting over his lap and he rubs her knee as she threads her fingers through his hair. All fades to black when he looks over to her in that intimate way and gestures inside the house. "Come with me," he's saying, looking for the homecoming he can only get with her in his arms.

I'm drawn back to reality when I notice two girls around Thomas's age making their way out to the float. The Nader twins?

Watching them, I remember how I was at that age. I remember the mad crush I had on Jeremy, so certain at the time that it was true love. I'd write his name and my married name, Mrs. Carolyn Rivers, in the journal I kept stashed under my bed. I even named our children: Rory, my favorite character from *Gilmore Girls*, and Jared—at the time I had an obsession with watching *My So Called Life* re-runs. Back then I would smile in triumph every time I caught Jeremy looking my way. I knew he only scowled out of embarrassment when he got caught. Oh, the heartache I'd felt in the weeks and months after he left school.

I found myself stewing then, wondering why he kept ignoring me, acting as if he didn't know me this entire year. It's not like we never saw one another. With me dating Drew and Jeremy being a teammate of Drew's, we did wind up at the same parties. One night this past winter we were both among a small group huddled in Mike Hanson's garage. Sitting on a couch watching Drew and Jeremy play each other in a game of pool was weird. He laughed and conversed comfortably with my boyfriend, but he didn't once look my way, smile or give any indication that he knew who I was or cared to get to know me. I sat there feeling awkward and uncomfortable in my own skin.

"You're burning."

His deep voice snapped me back to the present. I whipped my head around and came face to face with a set of strong, sculpted legs. I looked up and was momentarily blinded by the sun before my vision adjusted and I was staring right into Jeremy's eyes. His hair was longer, falling past the nape of his neck but not long enough to skim his shoulders. He had the kind of hair that effortlessly hung in shaggy, sexy layers. My eyes drifted over his torso, and God, he looked so much more like a man than Drew did. Jeremy's shoulders were broad, and his chest was smooth and muscular. His waist descended into a V, a faint line of wispy curls trailing from his belly button to a place down, down below.

When he cleared his throat a moment later, I became aware that I was biting my bottom lip and pretty much gawking at him. I tried to think of something to say but came up empty.

"Your back...It's burning, Carolyn."

"Um, you know my name?"

He chuckled. "Yeah."

Embarrassed, I stood and put my tank top on. I wanted to say something witty. I wanted to have the conversation, the flirty banter I'd been practicing since that first day I saw him in the gym last fall. Instead I stood there tongue-tied, shy and awkward.

He broke the uncomfortable silence. "Have you heard from Drew?"

Who?

"Oh, yeah," I said, recovering. "Sounds like he's having a lot of fun in Germany."

Jeremy's expression was easy and kind. "Yeah, he tries to make it sound like it's all work, no play, but I know he's full of it. When is he due back?"

"Third week in August. Just in time for football, I guess."

"I can't wait for football," Jeremy said, smiling as he looked out at the kids jumping off the dock and splashing each other in the water. Then he looked back to me and said, "All right...I'll see you around, Carolyn."

I watched as he turned and walked back towards the lot. He must have just finished a workout. The sun glistened off the beads of sweat that clung to his back. I wanted to lick him, lick those few beads of sweat that were slowly making their way from the nape of his neck down his back, all the way to that curve right above his...*You're insane, Carolyn.* I shook my head and grabbed my towel off the grass.

So he *did* know who I was after all. The thought pleased me. I knew I was an awkward mess and hadn't made a stellar impression during our encounter, but I was happy regardless.

I was happy that he remembered.

All this year, I wondered how he could forget me. Jeremy had been my hero ever since fifth grade, when he pushed Trent Ralston to the ground after he'd snapped my training bra strap and said something vulgar that made all the other boys laugh. I would never forget that day *or* the day Jeremy turned his hot temper on me. I couldn't be mad at him, even though I cried enough tears of hurt and embarrassment that night to fill an ocean. I could feel his shame and could only imagine how he suffered. The sweet apology Jeremy left hidden in my desk the next day nearly broke my heart.

I could never forget him, even if decades and a million miles separated us.

* * *

JEREMY

I slid in, my wet, sweaty back sticking against the hot leather seat of my pick-up. Damn, I was missing my post-workout dip in the cool lake. I had to bolt, though. After finally working up the nerve to talk to Carolyn, I was rattled.

I stood back, just watching her for a few minutes. She had creamy white skin that stood in stark contrast to the black one-piece reining in her curves. I never knew a one-piece could look so hot. The pretty girl I once knew had grown into a beautiful woman.

I watched Carolyn's face and found myself smiling as her lips curved up at the corners. She looked like she was lost in good thoughts. But a minute later her brow creased and her lips turned down in a grimace, as if the memory of something harsh or hurtful had surfaced. Just then, she reached both hands up as she undid the band that was holding her hair in a loose knot. She was sitting Indian style, and when she reached up her back arched, drawing my attention to her breasts. My eyes fixed on the sweet curve peeking out from the side of her suit. As her hair fell in loose waves down her back, I don't remember making a conscious decision to approach her. It was more like my feet just started moving, driven on by a will of their own.

"You're burning."

Real smooth, Jeremy.

She just stared at me. Even if she didn't remember me from Driscoll, she had to recognize me from school now. We passed each other in the hallways, we hung out at the same parties, I was even friends with her boyfriend. She couldn't be that oblivious, could she? Once I brought up Drew she seemed more relaxed.

Yeah, I reminded myself, Carolyn has a boyfriend.

Every time I saw Drew with his arm draped over her shoulder or snug around her waist, I had to turn away. They looked like they fit together: the brainy beauty and the guy in our senior class who was going to be voted Most Likely to Succeed. She fit with him, not with me.

I was surprised to see her at the lake. Hardly anyone from our school came here. Most were off vacationing who knows where, and if they *were* unlucky enough to be home, they didn't have to venture more than ten yards out their back door to reach a cool, blue oasis.

Some of the houses I worked on this summer blew me away. I expected them to be luxurious but I was just in awe sometimes, wondering how much money these people actually had to be able to afford it all. The house I was working on now had a pool that looked like pictures I'd seen of Italian grottos, complete with a secluded cave-like nook and cascading water feature. It looked incredible, and I *would* have taken a dive in that pool at the end of my day if it wasn't for the sex-starved cougar who'd hired me.

Mrs. Peterman had actually hired Denny, but after the job was deemed to be within my skill set I was pretty much left on my own. This week I was installing outdoor lighting. Mrs. Peterman, or Beth, as she insisted I call her, was probably no more than thirty-five. Denny let it slip one day that Mr. Peterman was pushing sixty. I guess Beth was what they call a trophy wife. I didn't like her. She made me nervous and she was *always* around.

As I worked on the deck, she'd saunter out in heels and a cover-up that barely skimmed her ass cheeks. Then she'd slowly peel the top over her head to reveal herself in a teeny bikini before planting herself on a lounge chair by the pool. I could feel her eyes on me the entire time I worked. I wasn't obvious about it, but she had my attention too—the woman had an insane body. I'd sneak looks in Beth's direction only when I knew her back was turned. I'd watch when she rose and made her way to the pool, and again as she'd slowly move her hips side to side as she climbed the stairs back out, her dark hair dripping wet down her back.

Today, before I managed to escape unnoticed and head out to the lake, Beth had nearly propositioned me. It was so hot, had to be over ninety, but I didn't dare take my shirt off while I worked. Figured she'd think I was extending an invitation. So I couldn't wait to get out of there and dive into that cool water. As I was packing up my tools she came over, as she did every day, and asked me questions about my life, about school, football, whatever. I was polite but didn't feel the confidence or the desire to answer her in the same flirty way she spoke to me.

When I was just about ready to leave, she asked me if I'd come inside and help her get something from a shelf that she couldn't reach. I swallowed, nervous, and followed her inside. I knew damn well she didn't need the glass bowl she was gesturing to in the upper cabinet, but I went along with it anyway. I wasn't used to saying no. Beth was older, assertive, and she was, in a way, my employer.

She pointed up to the bowl and stood close behind me as I reached up to grab it. She placed her hand on my lower back, on my damp t-shirt, and I froze in place.

"Jeremy, you poor thing, you're so sweaty from working in that hot sun. Let me make you a cold drink," she insisted as she trailed her hand lower still, resting it on my belt.

"I'm good, Mrs. Peterman, really."

"I know you're good, Jeremy," she teased. She turned away then and took a pitcher of lemonade out of the fridge. "Sit and cool off," she commanded.

Beth was wearing a bathing suit, I knew that, but the little kimono wrap she was wearing gave the illusion that there was nothing underneath. When she hopped up onto the kitchen island next to where I was sitting on a stool, the slit opened, revealing her thighs all the way up to the apex. I swallowed as my eyes fixed on the sight.

"Do you have a girlfriend, Jeremy?"

My knee was tapping against the base of the counter as I stammered, "Uh, no-no one right now."

"Really?" she asked, her voice now a cutesy, girlish squeal. "Wow, I find it hard to believe that every girl in this town isn't after you. I practically have to fan myself every time I see you swing that hammer of yours."

I choked on the lemonade. *What was she playing at*, I asked myself, even though I knew full well what she wanted.

"Thanks for the drink, Beth. I really have to go."

"Are you sure?" she asked, playfully pouting.

"Yeah, I do," I said as I got up and put the glass in the sink.

I thought sadness clouded her eyes for a moment but then she switched gears and flashed me a mega-watt smile. "All right, see you tomorrow then."

You'd think my dick would be hard as a rock after witnessing that display but it wasn't. I had a lusty, busty babe practically laying herself on a platter for me to feast upon, but she did nothing for me. Carolyn, on the other hand? Just an innocent glimpse of her bare skin and the sound of her sweet, unsure voice had worked my body into a painful state. As soon as I got home from the lake yesterday, I jerked off in the shower thinking about her. We were in the water together in my fantasy, her arms draped around my neck as I held her up, her slick body pressed against mine. After I got my release, I sagged against the tiles.

Carolyn would never be mine.

Chapter Four

CAROLYN

Three days in a row.

Jeremy was here yesterday but he didn't come over to talk to me. He stayed on the other side of the lake. I watched him from the corner of my eye. I watched as he stripped out of his t-shirt, toed off his running sneakers, peeled off his socks and then took a running dive into the water. When he came up for a breath, he shook his hair out like a shaggy dog, blissfully happy to be cool and refreshed again. So beautiful. He was like watching a living, breathing work of art.

I came back again, day three, even though Tommy and Zach requested a trip to the local batting cages instead of the lake. I coerced the boys only after succumbing to them amid some serious negotiations. Not only would the batting cages be first on the agenda tomorrow, but there would be no tutoring before or after.

After my first run-in with Jeremy, I'd taken care to shave anywhere on my body that might be remotely visible, slathered on self-tanner, and took the time to straighten my wayward wavy hair into sleek, glossy submission.

I'd always liked Jeremy, and maybe we weren't exactly friends at Driscoll, but we did go back a long way. As I primped and picked my bathing suit out with care each day, I told myself that it would be nice to get to know him again, to have him as a friend.

I knew I was lying to myself.

Today I sat on my towel in a blue seersucker string bikini. The fabric gave the suit a sense of innocence, but the cut of the top and bottom were anything but chaste. I pretended to read a book but was scanning the shore for him at regular intervals, my searching eyes hidden behind sunglasses.

Hottie on the horizon.

I swallowed and sat at attention observing his daily routine. He slowed to a stop and rested his hands on his knees, bent at the waist, regaining his breath after running in this hot, humid weather. After a minute he dropped and banged out one hundred perfect push-ups. The muscles in his back, shoulders and arms flexed with the movement. As his body dipped down, I imagined myself lying beneath Jeremy, caged in by his strong arms, his body pressing into mine. I swallowed again and shook off the thought. I felt a little ashamed of how I was stalking him, totally perving on him. I stood and put my feet in the water, figuring I needed to cool off some. I kept watching, smiling as he took off running, taking those first steps trudging through the water before launching himself into a dive.

"Are you going into the lake with all the creepy, slimy lake things?" Tommy teased as he and Zach made their way back to the shore.

"No, I am not," I said, laughing and shaking my head.

"Can we go get ice cream now, Carolyn?" Zach asked.

"Um, sure," I said, slightly disappointed. "Just take a few minutes to let the sun dry you. Riding a bike in a wet bathing suit is no fun, trust me."

Dammit. I didn't want to run off just yet, but after several minutes the boys started getting restless. I stalled for as long as I could, dressed in slow motion and then picked up my towel and shook off the sand, frustrated.

The boys were cramming their sandy feet into their sneakers when Jeremy approached. "Hey, Carolyn."

"Oh, hi," I answered, trying to act surprised at the sight of him. Jeremy was dripping wet, his shorts clinging to his body. Yes, my eyes darted right *there* before I quickly looked away. *God, I hope he didn't just notice that.*

Disaster averted. Jeremy was looking down, taking a towel out of his drawstring bag when a football tumbled out and fell onto the ground.

Tommy tapped his arm. "Hey mister, can we borrow your football?"

"Mister?" I laughed. "His name's Jeremy."

Tommy persisted, oblivious to me. "Mister Jeremy, can we use it?"

Jeremy looked at me and started laughing when he saw the smile I couldn't contain. "Yeah, sure. Go long, you two."

Zach and Tommy took off, looking back to Jeremy every other second. He held the football perched above his right shoulder as he waved them further out with his left hand. "Get ready," he called to them as he launched a perfect spiral through the air for what seemed like a mile. He pumped his fist when Tommy caught the ball and smiled as he turned back to face me.

My cheeks heated when I sensed him taking me in from head to toe. Jeremy cleared his throat and said, "You get tan pretty fast, huh?"

"No." I smiled, looking down and shaking my head. "This is what they call fake and bake." He looked confused so I clarified, "Self-tanner? I figured my ghostly white skin might be scaring the rest of the lake-goers."

Tommy ran the ball back then and asked Jeremy for another throw. "You don't need to run it in, buddy, just throw it back to me, ok?"

"I can't throw it so far."

"No worries, I'll run in for it. It's good practice for me."

The three of them spent the next ten minutes tossing the ball, Jeremy getting a workout by running after their lame throws. He was patient and encouraging with them.

"Thanks."

"For what?" he asked, looking over his shoulder at me as he launched another perfect spiral.

"For this," I said, motioning to the boys. "I torture them for nearly two hours every day after they get home from school. This is a nice break."

He cocked his head to the side. "Tutoring," I replied in response to his expression.

"They have school in the summer?"

"Um, yeah. My brother goes half-days in the summer. It's good for him…You know, so that he doesn't regress."

He smiled warmly. "Spoken like a teacher, Carolyn."

I shrugged my shoulders and smiled. I closed my mouth quickly then, remembering I'd scarfed down tuna on a mini poppy bagel right before heading over here. Tuna breath plus the potential for poppy seeds stuck in my teeth. *Way to go, Carolyn.*

Oblivious to my inner psychotic dialogue, Jeremy asked, "What school does he go to?"

The boys came running at us full-speed, Thomas knocking into me as I answered, "Tommy and Zach go to Briarwood Country Day School."

"You two go to Briarwood?" Jeremy asked, surprised.

Tommy nodded his head happily but Zach cast his eyes down before muttering, "Yeah."

"Do you know Mrs. Mitchell?"

They both look at him, puzzled. Thomas answered, "Yeah, she's my favorite teacher."

Jeremy smiled, nodding. "She was mine too. Do you know Mr.

Ramirez? I was his worst student. He nearly lost his mind trying to teach me guitar. I was hopeless."

Zach brightened up then. "He lets us call him Diego. I'm his best guitar student," he added proudly.

"Next time you see him, tell him Jeremy Rivers says hi. Oh," he added, laughing, "and tell him I'm the lead guitarist in some hot, new alternative rock band. He'll pass out!"

"But you're not, right?" Tommy asked, speculating. "You said you stink at guitar."

I closed my eyes for a moment and smiled. My sweet, quirky, he-who-speaks-without-a-filter little brother. When I opened my eyes, Jeremy was staring right at me, smiling. He kept his eyes fixed on me when he spoke to Thomas. "Right, dude. I just wanna mess with him."

Thomas joined in laughing then, as if to say, *Ok, now I get it.*

Zach asked timidly, "You don't go to Briarwood anymore?"

"No." Jeremy gestured his head in my direction. "I go to Westerly with Carolyn."

"So," Zach pressed, "you went back to regular school?" He looked hopeful.

"Yeah, last year. I miss Briarwood, though. The teachers were great there. Best teachers I've ever had. Before I went there, I hated school."

"I like it there too," Zach nodded, agreeing with his new hero.

"Briarwood's awesome," Tommy chimed in, fist bumping Jeremy. "Hey Jeremy, teach us to throw a spiral like you."

"Tomorrow," he said as he looked to me with a tentative expression. He corrected himself, "Or the next time I run into you."

"Come on, Jeremy," they pleaded.

Jeremy smiled wide. "I really can't...Gotta go see my Grandma and Grandpa. But I promise, I will teach you next time."

And then Jeremy was pulling on his shirt—what a shame—and stuffing the football and his towel back into his bag. He twirled his key ring around his index finger a few times and then looked up at me and said, "See you around, Carolyn," before looking over to the boys. "It was good to meet you two. Make sure you say that to Ramirez, ok?"

They both nodded, giggling, and fist bumped him again before he turned and headed for the lot.

The next day it rained buckets...and Drew Skyped from Europe.

We talked for half an hour, me faking enthusiasm as Drew rattled off the minutia of his daily comings and goings. He looked the same as he always did—gorgeous. Drew already had the look of a well put-together businessman at the age of seventeen. He looked believable in his crisp dress shirts, expertly trimmed hair and in his cool, blue, determined eyes.

Drew was over in Germany getting more exposure to his father's business. His dad was like some ex-Navy Seal or something who now owned and operated a consulting firm that advised the government on high priority security issues. Drew didn't share details with me, but I got the gist that what his dad's company did was something along the lines of fulfilling government contracts by running special-ized covert operations. Very cloak and dagger.

Drew had it all planned out. Acceptance to Annapolis, five years rising through the officer's ranks in the service before moving onto the civilian side to join his father's very profitable company. Lately, even though we'd only been dating eight or nine months, he'd talk about his plans as if my inclusion in them was a given.

"I think Alexandria would be a great home base for us when I get deployed, don't you, Carolyn?"

I'd laugh him off, gently trying to get the message across that his assumptions were off base. "Drew, hello? I'm sixteen."

"And I'm seventeen," he'd tease back. "I'm seventeen and I know what I want when I see it, Carolyn Harris."

"I don't even know where I'm applying to college yet, Drew."

"I thought you were set on Georgetown? That would be great... Less than an hour apart."

"I'm not one hundred percent sure," I said, standing my ground as we chatted with the distance of an ocean between us. "I really like being at Yale this summer. And I might want to stay closer to Tommy."

"Yale? Staying in Connecticut? That's hardly a new experience, Carolyn. And we'd be nearly six hours apart."

Did he have some stored bank of knowledge, a detailed catalogue of the driving distances between all locations? Everything preconfigured? Yes, he did.

"We'll talk when you get home, Drew. I don't want to make any big life decisions just yet."

"Two more weeks, baby. I miss you so much. I keep thinking about the night before I left...in my pool house." I swallowed, blushed and turned my face away from the screen for a moment. He chuckled. "Did I embarrass you, sweetheart."

I shook my head and forced a smile. That night we did more than we ever had before. His parents took us out to dinner at some upscale steak house and Drew snuck me a shot of something warm that burned my belly in an oddly soothing way before we got into the car. I think he needed something to ease his nerves too. Mrs. Oliver was nice, I guess, but Drew's dad was formal, demanding. He was kinda harsh. Drew called him sir, and that alone made it awkward to be around his family. Even his mother seemed a little stiff and wary in her husband's presence.

My parents were more laid back and were openly affectionate with one another. When I spent time at Drew's, I felt bad for him.

That night, Senior Chief Petty Officer Oliver was in his usual form. After Drew was pressed to give a status update on his Annapolis application process, I was grilled about my plans. I noticed that he scoffed when I told him I planned to major in neuropsychology. Drew chimed in to smooth it over, clarifying that I was *not* looking to be a therapist but someone who's more like a doctor or a research scientist, studying neurology and the role it plays in learning disabilities. I felt like saying, *Don't defend me to this jerk.* And what *if* I wanted to be a psychologist? Was there something the matter with providing people with mental health services?

We went out to the pool house after we got back. Drew collapsed in a chair, seemingly wiped out by the effort it took to deal with his father. He pulled a flask out from underneath the chair, took a swig and then passed it to me. I took a little sip in an effort to show solidarity with him. I really did feel for Drew. His father was stoic, cold and demanding. It would be hard to live up to his expectations. Drew was typically self-assured, cocky even, but he was the complete opposite in the presence of his father.

I sat in his lap and draped my arms around his neck as I kissed him. I wanted to make him forget.

"God, Carolyn," Drew moaned into my mouth. "Do you know how hot you are?" He pulled back a few inches and looked into my eyes. "You don't even know and that makes you even hotter. You're this sweet and innocent beauty that's oblivious to the fact that every guy in our grade wants you." He began kissing my neck then and said in between kisses, "But *I've* got you. You're mine, Carolyn."

I winced slightly at the mention of my innocence but didn't lapse into self-recrimination like I usually did. Tonight Drew's sadness made me feel different.

I repositioned myself so that I was straddling him and I unbuttoned the front of my dress. He slid the straps down my shoulders and cupped my breasts through the lace of my bra. Then he kissed me. His mouth felt hard against mine. It wasn't the kind of kiss that unleashed butterflies in your stomach or set off fireworks in your mind, but it was passionate. I could feel him pressing against me as he rocked his hips up into mine.

"Does that feel good, Carolyn?"

It did feel good and I nodded as I breathed in deep. Drew had touched me there before and I'd stroked him, letting him come in my hand many times. But I never came. At least I wasn't sure if I had or not. Samantha had relayed, in detail, that her few experiences were earth-shattering events where her vision blurred, the stars aligned and her satisfied coochie sang a happy tune. I, on the other hand, had learned to whimper and moan so that at a certain point Drew was satisfied he'd done his job well and he would stop.

After he slid his fingers beneath the lace of my panties and worked me up into what he thought was a frenzy, I went to undo his belt and his zipper. He leaned back, looking at me reverently as I slid my hand into his briefs. I kissed his jaw and then down his neck as I worked him. "Fuck, that feels good." As I moved and kissed along his collarbone, I felt his hand gently push on my head, urging me lower. I guess I must have hesitated for a moment because he spoke again, urging me on sweetly, "Please, Carolyn. Please do this for me."

So I did.

I hated it the first time I was coerced to do it and didn't like it any more this time. Drew wasn't *him*. Drew cared for me deeply, I knew that. But it brought me back to that night, alone with *him* in the woods. *His* hands fisted roughly in my hair, pushing me down onto him, not caring that I was just a kid or that I was gagging. I tried not to think about it. I tried to block it out.

At one point Drew's hold became a little frenzied and he began jerking his hips up into me. I felt the tears coming as I went to move myself away from him. He didn't notice. At that same moment he pulled out and rubbed himself roughly as his release spurted onto his stomach.

He opened his eyes after a moment and kissed the top of my head. "Carolyn, that felt incredible. Thank you, sweetheart. I love you. You know that, right?"

I nodded and kissed Drew's chest. I couldn't look up at him—he'd see I was on the verge of sobbing. I collected myself as Drew cleaned up. He came back in and laid on a lounger, bringing me down to rest beside him, tucking me in close as he whispered sweet words to me and told me how desperately he'd miss me this summer.

I couldn't get to sleep thinking back to that night. I did miss Drew but not in the way other girls seemed to truly miss their boyfriends—the boys they *loved*. The first night Drew said those words to me, I repeated them back immediately. It was only four months after we'd started dating. I didn't know if I loved him or not. Did I care about him? Did I want only good things for him? Did I enjoy being on his arm, basking in the admiration of others now that I was officially Drew Oliver's girlfriend? Yes was the answer to each question.

But did I love him?

The sense of wanting, the hopeful feeling I had when I wondered if I would see Jeremy at the lake the next day—Drew never stirred up those kinds of feelings.

Thoughts of Jeremy kept me up late that night. I fantasized over what our next encounter would be like and then no sooner would guilt wash over me. It was terrible to think about Jeremy in that way when I had Drew.

I was Drew's girl.

The self-imposed guilt trip was pointless, as any ridiculous notions I had about me and Jeremy were squelched the next time I saw him at the lake. Yep, just like a bucket of ice water being dumped over a few weak, smoldering embers.

* * *

JEREMY

By day three I was pleading with no one in particular for this godforsaken rain to stop. The only upside was that I was working on an indoor project with Denny in the meantime, giving me a much needed break from Beth Peterman.

When I finally woke to bright sun and a coating of sweat on my skin, I was pumped. Today was really hot and Dad and I were probably the only people in this town without central air conditioning. I didn't care, though. The sun and the heat upped the odds that Carolyn would be at the lake. Hopefully she'd be wearing that tiny blue-checkered bikini she was wearing the other day. Oh my lord, Carolyn looked good in that.

I was thinking about Carolyn all day, hardly noticing that—surprise, surprise—Mr. Peterman was home for once. The day couldn't get any better. With her husband home, Beth had no choice but to ignore me.

I knew even thinking about Carolyn was stupid, but I couldn't help it. I wanted to be around her. More than that, I wanted her. And when she was around, things were more exciting and fun. I knew she got rattled when I was nearby and I liked that I made her feel unsettled. Everything about her seemed orderly, methodical and disciplined. I liked that with each passing day, Carolyn's bikinis seemed to show more skin, her hair was down and more tousled, and that reserved, prim veneer seemed to show a few cracks. I think I even heard her snort when she laughed at something her brother said the other day.

She didn't disappoint today. I was relieved to see her when I pulled up. She was standing on the shore in a pink bikini, her brown hair falling in loose waves around her face. She took in a shaky breath and smiled when I walked up behind her and said, "You made it."

"Hey," she greeted, still breathy as she watched me strip off my sweaty shirt and drop it next to her towel. "How are you?"

"I'm good. Happy it finally stopped pouring. I've been cooped up working indoors the past few days."

"Where are you working this summer?"

"I'm doing apprentice hours for a local electrician. He's training me."

"That sounds interesting."

I chuckled. "I don't know if you'd find it interesting, but I like it. I like working with my hands."

She put her hands on her hips in a defiant pose but she was smiling. Those hips were sweet. "Don't assume anything about me, Jeremy Rivers. You haven't been around me in a *very* long time." After a moment, her expression became more serious when she asked, "Is it hard? I mean, learning all of that. I would think electrical work is very complicated...and dangerous."

"I still have a lot to learn but I've been helping my father since I was a kid with repair work and carpentry. I've done some basic electrical work at the estate we live on, too. And Mr. Roberts is great. He's a good boss."

Carolyn nodded. She looked out at the boys and their friends playing on the dock and then practically whispered, "It is *so* hot today."

I was tempted to tease her, asking her how she could be hot with so little clothes on, but I wouldn't. She was too nice to make fun of. And I'd be a fool to say anything that might encourage her to keep her beautiful body covered.

I started walking backwards, slowly making my way into the lake. "Well, I'm heading in. You coming?" She looked longingly at the water but raised her eyes to me and shook her head. "Suit yourself, Carolyn."

After spending a few minutes hurling Thomas and Zack off the dock as they laughed like pair of hyenas, I made my way back out to her. She looked like a goddess standing there—long, graceful limbs topped by deadly curves. As I came closer, I noticed she was twirling a lock of hair around her finger. I stilled for a minute, remembering her as a girl, that same nervous habit she had back then. It was stupid, but I felt my heart swell a little as I took in the sight.

When I got to within a foot of her, I shook my hair out, wetting her, making her squeal and laugh. I liked the sound of her laugh.

"So missy, Thomas told me your secret."

"He's a little rat. What secret?" she demanded.

I cocked my head and asked in disbelief, "You are *afraid* of the lake?"

She giggled nervously. "I can't stand how the bottom feels. It's slimy!"

"You're so spoiled, Harris. Only your clean, shiny pool will do?"

"No," she protested, swatting my chest. I had to resist the urge to grab her hand and hold it in place because damn, her hand felt too good on my skin. "I like the feeling of sand between my toes when I'm at the beach, Jeremy. I go in the ocean. It's just the lake. I always imagine a snake or a viper wrapping itself around my ankle as I sink into that mushy yuck."

"First off, a viper *is* a snake, and there are no snakes in that water. And you don't have to touch your feet on the mushy yuck at the bottom if you can swim."

She screamed bloody murder when I tossed her over my shoulder and ran her into the lake. Everyone nearby turned at the sound of her shrieks and laughter. I lowered her when we were chest deep. I wanted to put some distance between our bodies because mine was beginning to react to the feel of her, but she freaked when I put her down, wrapping her arms around my neck tight so that I was holding her up. Goddamn, her chest was pressed up against mine and I could feel her nipples hardening against me. This couldn't happen.

"I've got you, Carolyn," I assured her as I created a slight distance between us, holding her up by her hips. "Wow, you really are afraid, huh?"

"I know it's ridiculous," she said, shaking her head in embarrassment.

"No, it's not. I shouldn't have teased you."

She looked up at me, still holding onto my shoulders and treading water. "The water does feel great, though. I felt like I was going to spontaneously combust back on the shore."

"Can you touch one foot to the bottom?"

She considered it for a moment. "Yes," she said, nodding and laughing.

She tentatively touched one foot down and then the other. Carolyn was on her tip-toes, her face a grimace.

"I guess that's enough desensitization for one day," I said as I lifted her up and slung her behind my back cross-wise as I waded back to shore.

"I feel like a sack of flour."

What you feel like is a walking, talking wet dream. Shaking off the thought, I said, "Here you go, back on semi-dry land, safe and sound."

When she looked up at me, her smile made today the best day I'd had in a really, really long time.

* * *

CAROLYN

"Well, isn't this cozy," a snarky voice called from behind me. Jeremy froze and then instinctively backed away a few steps.

"Hey, Vanessa," he said. He sounded uncomfortable, guilty even. Maybe that was just me projecting though, because all of a sudden I was feeling exposed, the guilt of acting this way and wanting another boy washing over me.

I turned to see her, arms crossed, looking completely out of place in her calf-high combat boots, her snug black shorts and her tight tank that exposed her belly. She was beautiful in her own way, with jet black hair, fair white skin and pouty lips painted a candy apple shade of red. She narrowed her eyes and scrutinized me, and let's just say that if looks could kill, I'd have been six feet under.

Jeremy asked, "Carolyn, do you know—"

"Vanessa. Yeah. Hi, Vanessa," I offered. She gave me a tight smile and no greeting in return.

Then Vanessa patently ignored me, smiling sweetly up at Jeremy. "Come on, big boy. You promised you'd help me with that *thing* after we stop in and see your Grandma, remember?"

"Yeah, sorry."

He looked back to me without smiling and said his regular parting words, "See you around, Carolyn."

Vanessa linked her arm through his and pressed into his side as they made their way up the hill together. She said something that he replied to and then they both laughed. Vanessa looked back over her shoulder at me, smirking.

I got the distinct impression that the joke was on me.

As I lay in bed not sleeping that night, I decided that what I'd been playing at with Jeremy was unwise and it was over. Drew would be home in a few days and my life would get back to normal.

Watching Jeremy with Vanessa, I could understand what he saw in her. She was exciting, ballsy, daring—a risk-taker. Me and my nerdy research projects would probably bore the crap out of Jeremy inside of a week.

They fit together.

Chapter Five

JEREMY

The rest of the summer dragged.

I fell back into my old routine. Work, dodge Mrs. Peterman's advances, punishing workout, cool shower, visit with my grandparents, and then either sketch or fall into bed with my e-reader set on an audio book.

I avoided the lake. I did go back there once, the day after our last awkward parting. I wanted to smooth things over, apologize in some way for Vanessa's rude behavior and my weird reaction. I wanted it—whatever *it* was—to continue. But Carolyn wasn't there and I took that as a sign.

The next time I saw her was a few days before classes started back up. It was just like last year. Chase was a few paces ahead of me, howling like a wolf. He was the first to catch sight of the girls' volleyball team in the middle of tryouts. The coach tried to hush him but as the rest of us made our way into the gym, the catcalls and whistles only got louder. Their coach eventually threw her hands up, exasperated.

I watched Drew make his way over to Carolyn, lean down and whisper something in her ear. She smiled up at him. He reached a hand down to help her up and then pulled her close once she was on her feet. He whispered in her ear again and then ran his hand over her ass before she swatted him away and laughed, blushing.

Fuck, it hurt. And I knew I had no right to feel that way.

I didn't shower after practice. Just needed to get out of there. I threw my gear into the truck and took off, driving aimlessly. Not really without a destination, I suppose, as I found myself pulling into the Petermans' driveway under the pretense of picking up the last of my tools. I *had* left a cable cutter in their garage, but Denny could have gotten it when he came to settle the account with them.

I rang the bell and Beth answered. She was alone, as usual. She looked me over from head to toe, taking in the sweaty clothes that clung to my skin. She told me she was just about to take a dip in the pool.

Did I want to join her?

This time I didn't say no.

* * *

CAROLYN

It was as if those two weeks had never happened, like I'd imagined it all. Jeremy passed me in the hallways at school as if he didn't even know me.

The first time it happened I was mid-smile, about to say hello when he strode past. I turned around to follow him only to lock eyes with Vanessa, who was standing by his locker waiting for him. The look she shot me was pure evil.

Unlike last year, it seemed like I crossed paths with him constantly now. That first day, after ignoring me, I practically crashed into him as I absentmindedly made my way out of AP Calculus. He didn't stop to help me pick up my notebook or calculator, leaving me to scrounge on the floor as hundreds of bodies hurriedly pushed through the hallways. The icing on the cake? As I made my way into the cafeteria I heard Drew call my name and saw Erica waving me over to our table. Who's sitting at the other end of the table with Will and Mike? Gets even better. Samantha's sitting next right to him, super close, her hand resting on his shoulder. He says something, apparently something hilarious, because she throws her head back and laughs before fixing him with a look that I could only describe as hungry.

No, not her.

Will called over, "Hey Harris, how was your summer?"

I gave the standard reply, "Great!"

Mike greeted me with, "What's up, Carolyn."

Even Frank Carr nodded his head in acknowledgement, and I hardly even *knew* him. Jeremy, meanwhile, didn't so much as glance in my general direction.

Drew pulled me onto his lap and kissed my neck, murmuring, "You look lovely today."

"Why thank you," I replied, mimicking his formal manners. I needed to laugh, to be seen and heard having fun—needed to mask the agony, the hurt that was threatening to take over.

Samantha called from the other end, "Carolyn, they think I'm lying. Did you or did you not spend your entire summer in a lab coat cooped up indoors?"

I took a deep breath. A lot of things had changed about me since that awful summer. Before *him* I was confident and sure of myself— not boastful, just happy with the girl I was. Now I made a habit of second guessing myself, questioning my decisions, wondering constantly if I measured up. Samantha seized on my weakness, and I noticed that now, with increasing regularity, she gave me compliments that were anything but complimentary and she sometimes made jokes at my expense. The kind of jokes people justify with follow-up statements that are supposed to make you feel better about being dissed, like: *I'm just messing with you*. In Samantha's case, she followed up with the same sorry line every time: *I'm kidding...You know I love you, right?*

Erica came to my defense quickly. "Back off. Carolyn will be at an Ivy League school next year and you'll be where, Samantha, Bumfuck Community College?"

Erica was kicking the hornet's nest and Samantha could be one nasty bitch of a hornet when she wanted to be. Before Samantha could think of some way to embarrass Erica in front of these boys, I piped up. "I didn't spend the entire summer at Yale. I was at the lake...a lot."

He still didn't look up. In fact, he angled his body away from everyone else and started up a side conversation with Frank. I knew he heard me, though.

Coward.

Will started talking about how he used to love the lake when he was younger and I was telling him about Zach and Tommy doing cannonballs non-stop off the dock when Samantha mock shivered and said, "I wouldn't swim in that dirt pit if you paid me a million dollars."

Will glanced at Jeremy and then asked her, "Why not?"

"It's filthy! I mean, c'mon, the sand is like dirt. And the people..." she trailed off, scrunching up her nose.

I saw Jeremy stiffen, but Samantha was so lacking in empathy that his scowl didn't even register with her.

I raised my voice. "Well, I loved it there, even though some of the people *did* turn out to be rude."

Gotcha!

Jeremy's head whipped around and his eyes met mine for a split angry second before he righted himself, stood, took his tray and mumbled some parting words to the group.

Something about him brought out my inner ballsy chick. She'd been in hiding for nearly two years now—so long that I hardly even recognized her. I wanted to bait Jeremy. His blatant snubs had hurt me, and hurt that's left to fester eventually turns to anger. And yes, now I was pissed off. Jeremy had to know I was speaking directly to him, and my message was: *Go ahead, jackass, pretend you don't know me.*

All of the boys left then, heading outside to toss a ball until the bell rang. That left just me, Samantha, Erica and Kerri.

"Are you into Jeremy?" Erica questioned Samantha.

Samantha narrowed her eyes at Erica, trying to decide if she should let Erica's insubordination from before go. She decided to be a benevolent queen bee and make nice. "Well, that's what I want Will to think, duh." When no one commented, she added, "Let him see me with Jeremy. I want Will to know exactly what he's missing."

Kerri pushed to her feet as she gathered her things. "You're wasting your time on Will. He's into Tori, one hundred percent. She lives next door to my freshman buddy, Lauren Paine, and she said Will pops by there all the time."

Samantha glared in Kerri's direction as she left for the library. Kerri and I had at least that much in common—she was a student.

"What the hell does he see in Tori?"

Erica tapped her chin. "Hmm, I don't know, maybe that she's smart, pretty and nice?"

She emphasized that last word. Erica was feisty and she liked to give it right back to Samantha, even though when push came to shove, we all deferred to her. But I needed some of that attitude. Over the past year I'd become Samantha's pathetic underling.

Samantha rolled her eyes. "Please, she's like under house arrest— she never even goes out. And I heard she *has* to work at the hardware store because her parents don't have a pot to piss in. Sounds like lots of fun, you're right."

"Her parent," I corrected. Samantha could be such a bitch. "I feel terrible for Tori. She's responsible for taking care of her little brothers…It's like she's like their mother now." I kept at it, wanting to stand up to Samantha, but looking down at the table as I did it because I didn't feel confident enough to take her on. "And for the record, they're not destitute. People in this town are under the impression that if you don't get a BMW for your seventeenth birthday then you're as good as on welfare."

"I didn't know her mother was dead. Now I feel bad."

This was the Samantha of days past—my *friend*. It was nice to be in her presence every now and again.

Our mothers were close friends, so Samantha and I were introduced while we were still in diapers. I did love Samantha like a sister at one time. We shared so many secrets, so many adventures, but something happened in seventh grade. It was like Samantha's interests shifted to include nothing but clothes, boys and gossip. She was bewildered and annoyed when I still wanted to bake, get messy with my science experiments or play with Thomas. If it didn't include a mani-pedi, a trip to the mall or making snarky comments at someone else's expense, then it wasn't worth her time.

My walk down memory lane was short-lived, as Samantha's mood shifted from sympathetic to carefree inside of a minute. "Anyway, Will *is* interested. He just needs a little nudge." She giggled before adding, "And if I wind up getting nudged by Jeremy in the meantime, that wouldn't suck, right? He's hot."

Erica stuck her thumb into her mouth and dragged it out with a loud pop. "By nudged you mean fucked?"

I shushed Erica. "You are so crude."

"I'm crude says the prude…What about her?" Erica nodded in Samantha's direction, smiling. "She's mean!"

Erica was teasing, sort of. No one came out and really told Samantha the cold hard truth, even Erica.

"I *do* like Jeremy, though, so I'm *not* being mean." She waved us in closer before she whispered, giggling, "I kind of want to see if what Taylor said about him is true, you know?"

Erica nodded knowingly. "I've checked him out in those football pants. The rumors are true."

I was weary from this conversation. "He's a person, not a freakin' piece of meat."

Samantha licked her lips and winked at me, laying it on thick. "I think I need to uncover the facts for myself."

She was trying to make me laugh, but what she did turned my stomach. I was pissed at Jeremy for ignoring me, even though I knew I really had no right to be. But I could *never* be hurt or angry enough to wish Samantha on him.

She would hurt him.

He walked by me without so much as a nod of recognition for the next two weeks. I saw him at least three times a day, if not more. It started to sting less. But while Jeremy patently ignored me, Vanessa made it her mission to lock eyes with me whenever the opportunity arose. I even stopped going to the local ice cream parlor with Tommy because she worked there, opting for some crappy frozen yogurt place instead. Who in their right mind hired someone whose idea of a greeting was to practically growl at people? I mean, aren't ice cream parlors supposed to be happy places? I heard she also had a job answering the phone at a tattoo parlor one town over. At least I didn't have to worry about running into her there.

What was their deal? She seemed like she had some kind of hold over Jeremy, but he also seemed like he did what—or whom—he pleased. Anytime I saw Vanessa or saw the two of them together, it reminded me of that last day at the lake and it burned. I felt foolish and embarrassed all over again.

You have a great boyfriend, Carolyn, I reminded myself. *You will be far away from Westerly next year, far away from bitchy losers like Vanessa and far away from boys like Jeremy Rivers.*

Chapter Six

CAROLYN

I'd just exited the college counselor's office, high off his prediction that my latest SAT scores would be good enough for Yale, when I heard my name called. When I turned, I saw a petite lady with glasses and a warm smile. She looked familiar but I couldn't place her.

"Oh my, it's so wonderful to see all of you kids again. You've all changed so much since Driscoll."

"Mrs. Connolly?"

"The one and only," she replied, smiling. "Do you have a minute?" she asked, already ushering me into her office.

"Sure."

"First, how have you been? I was talking to your guidance counselor and he said you're aiming for Yale?"

"Yes, I mean that's my reach school. I'm also looking into UPenn and Georgetown...Columbia also."

"Impressive. He told me you had an interesting experience at Yale this summer." She didn't wait for my reply before explaining that she'd known my parents for years, as she was involved in Thomas's initial evaluation—the one that landed him in Briarwood. "I think it's wonderful that you've taken an interest in that field."

"I'd like to see where it takes me, Mrs. Connolly. I know how hard people like Thomas have it. I want to make a real difference for kids like him."

"So would you be interested in doing some tutoring work? Helping some of your peers here at Westerly?"

"I've done it in the past, but I gave it up last year. My schedule has been heavy with AP courses."

She nodded in understanding but pressed on. "It's a paid position." She paused, smiling. "It's nominal, just a few hours a week at minimum wage, so I don't want to get your hopes up. But it would *also* come with a glowing letter of recommendation, and from a Yale alum, no less." In response to my raised eyebrows, she pointed to herself. "Class of eight-four."

Acceptance at Yale was not a sure thing for me, so this? *This* was like dangling a carrot in front of a starved horse.

"How many days a week?"

"Two days a week, ninety minute session each day. You would start this coming Tuesday. It's helping mainly with test preparation and homework."

"How many students?"

"Um, just one."

"Who is it?"

She began looking through some files on her desk when she answered absently, "All of the details haven't been worked out yet. There will be a few other tutors so we'll see who matches up best based on strengths and weaknesses. Are you in, Carolyn?"

I could almost feel Yale's acceptance letter in my hot little hands. "Yes, I'm in."

* * *

JEREMY

"She won't want to work with me."

Jeez, she would *not* let this go. I appreciated Mrs. Connolly's tenacity when it benefitted me, but she could be a pain in the ass otherwise.

I was so happy when I ran into her the first week of school—glad even for the budget cuts that split her position between the elementary school and the high school. Mrs. Connolly met with me and Coach in early September to devise a plan, taking me under her wing yet again. Yeah, I was happy then, but now? Not so much.

"We don't have many options here, Jeremy. You have—" I think she was about to say something like: *bombed the last few tests you've taken*, but she caught herself. "You are struggling, even with your educational accommodations. And frankly, insisting on having Paul Wiseman as your tutor, a math whiz, when *your* strength is math? That's just plain foolish. Carolyn Harris is akin to having a reading specialist working with you. She's been working with her brother for years, has solid research experience under her belt...C'mon Jeremy, she can tutor you better than I can!" Then she pulled out her trump card. "Do you want to finish the football season? I hate to say it but you are on the verge of being deemed academically ineligible. That's the cold hard fact."

I'd been in a sour mood for the past three weeks. I wasn't failing everything, just History and Physics. I didn't even know how I was failing Physics. I actually understood the material but when it came time to take the tests, I was just tanking. Two failures and I was off the team. They didn't do exceptions here, and in truth, I didn't want any. I didn't want to be given any special treatment. Didn't want to be the slow, learning disabled kid who couldn't pass.

I was desperate so I agreed.

I stopped by Connolly's office a few minutes early on my way to meet up with Carolyn in the library. Poking my head in, I asked, "So she's ok with this?"

"Why wouldn't she be?" Mrs. Connolly snapped without even looking up from her computer screen, dismissing me.

My fucking palms were sweating as I sat there waiting for her. I was rubbing them against my jeans practically every five seconds. There was just one other kid seated in the study room across the hall. My eyes were glued to the corridor, waiting on her. I saw her come in then, chatting easily with Paul Wiseman, two brainiac peas in a pod.

Carolyn looked down at a paper to see which room she was assigned to. In about a nanosecond she'd be wishing her paper read anything but Room C. She paused with her hand on the doorknob, meeting my nervous gaze through the glass. She drew in a deep, steadying breath before entering the room and then she strode in with her game face on.

"Jeremy."

"Um, are you ok with this? Tutoring me?"

Her look was defiant. "Why wouldn't I be?" She sounded exactly like Connolly—Connolly's evil spawn. I must have been smirking at the thought because now she looked offended. "Is something funny?"

"No," I assured her, shaking my head. "Look, I appreciate you working with me, really."

"I'm getting paid, Jeremy." Her tone was sour. "Believe me, it's not out of the goodness of my heart."

Fucking ouch.

She was in professional mode. We split the next ninety minutes prepping for my physics test and then outlining the chapter for next week's history exam.

She didn't work like Paul did. She took my old tests, broke down how my science teacher asked questions, and then predicted how this chapter's test questions might look. For history, she jotted down my text book's publisher and edition number before she left and told me she'd have a better way for me to read the text by Thursday.

I sat there for a few minutes after she left, reeling. I was in awe of the girl. I felt like I'd been under the tutelage of an expert for the past hour and a half. It was like she understood how my mind worked and could break things down for me so that I wasn't so damned confused. I always knew Carolyn was smart, but I don't think I understood how truly gifted she was. That, in turn, made me hopeful. I believed she could help me dig myself out of this hole.

The time spent with her also left me feeling lonely.

Seeing her back in Drew's arms a few weeks ago started me off on a series of meaningless, shallow hook-ups. Spending time with someone I cared about—someone that I genuinely liked as a person —made every other interaction seem that much more superficial and shitty.

I was now in the habit of swinging by Beth's once a week. She would have preferred three times a week, minimum, but I felt so dirty after leaving there that I couldn't bring myself to answer her texts most of the time. I did start to see her in a different light, though. She was lonely too, married to some old guy who was trying to relive his youth. A guy who really didn't know her, left her for weeks at a time in a town where she knew no one, and where the local society gals looked down on her as the uncultured gold digger that she was.

But wrong was wrong. She was married so I was guilty for my part in it. She was wrong too, obviously. I mean, if my life was an episode of *Law and Order*, what she was doing could—save for a few months—technically be construed as rape. I did *not* see it that way, though. I looked way older than eighteen, so Beth probably didn't know she'd been luring in jail bait. I don't think she did, anyway.

Beth wasn't the only one who left me feeling empty. I started up again with some girl Willow, who'd graduated last year and was now attending college less than an hour away. Some nights she'd just text and show up at my house. I was willing. We started hooking up last year after Taylor and I burned out. I liked Willow but she dumped me right around the time prom dates were being negotiated. I offered to take her, and her response was to look at me with a mixture of pity and humor. Was I serious? She couldn't go with a junior. Dumb ass me, right? When I thought about it, she and I never did anything but get it on in her pool house. We were never a couple in public. Fine. She used me last year and I was using her now.

Using people and being used—it felt like crap.

Thursday at 2:40 sharp I was waiting in Room C, anxious and afraid that she wouldn't show. She walked in at 2:45, right on schedule. Carolyn was all business again—no smiles, no small talk. I couldn't tell what she was thinking.

She didn't waste any time. She set me up with a tablet that had both my Physics and Global History books uploaded on it. Carolyn explained that it was audio enabled, but the text was also converted to a dyslexia-friendly font. "To me it just looks like the letters are bottom heavy and slightly squiggly, you know?" Her eyes lit up then and she smiled. "But to you and to Thomas, it makes the letters look more distinct. It's amazing, Jeremy. You'll make way fewer errors. Isn't that crazy?" Her excitement was infectious. "It's downloaded onto this tablet so any book you read will be written in this font. And," she dug a device that looked like a digital thermometer out of her bag, "this is a pen device that you can drag over text. It reads the words aloud, can give you definitions, and you can also record your own voice on it and then plug it into your computer and it will convert it to text. I had Mrs. Connolly order it for you. Use it when you're having a difficult time decoding specific words. It can read entire passages but you don't need that."

"Wow," I whispered, looking it over.

"This is fairly new. They didn't have this when you were at Briar-wood, right?"

"No." I looked up at her then. "Thanks, Carolyn."

She shrugged her shoulders, brushing me off. "It's nothing. Come on, let's get to work."

And so it went.

I thought I'd feel uncomfortable around her, maybe embarrassed having her teaching me, but I never did. She might not like me, but Carolyn was always respectful and never condescending. She always made me feel at ease when I didn't get something. And with her, I didn't care about stumbling over a word here and there.

Two weeks later when I got my first science test back and scored a seventy-eight, I was ecstatic. I slapped it down on the table grinning when I walked into the room.

She looked at it and then looked up at me, tilting her head. "Are you satisfied with that?"

"Hell yeah! That's passing. It's *more* than passing."

Her smile was soft as she nodded her head and looked down at the paper again. "But you're really smart. You can do much better than this."

I swallowed the lump in my throat and took a seat across from her. "Listen, if I pass then I can play. I'm not looking to get into Harvard, all right?"

She reached across and laid her hand on top of mine. "Hey, I'm sorry, Jeremy."

When she said my name it did something to me. Shook me up, made me dream of things. What would it be like to hear her say my name all the time—if she was mine, if she was my girl?

When I looked back up at Carolyn, she was smiling. "You're right, I *was* being a bit of a buzz kill. And Rome wasn't built in a day, you know?"

My hand felt cold when she slid hers off mine.

✱ ✱ ✱

CAROLYN

"How slow *is* he?" Drew asked as we sat together studying for AP Physics.

"He's actually really bright, just like Thomas is. Like a different type of intelligence where you're just held back by reading."

"Couldn't one argue that if you cannot read, then you're not intelligent?"

Drew wasn't being a jerk, he was asking innocently.

"No. I mean, it's like the brain just isn't wired for reading. If you speak the information to people like Jeremy and then let them speak their answer, you see that the reasoning process is fully intact. School is just extremely frustrating for people like him. He is smart, though, without a doubt."

"How are you two getting along?"

"Fine, I guess." That wasn't a total lie. Things had gotten somewhat easier between us over the past few weeks. "We're not BFFs but he's polite and I think he appreciates the help."

"I find him hard to read, you know?"

I nodded because, yes, I certainly did find him hard to read. There were times when we would have a moment during our sessions —a shared laugh, a smile of appreciation—and then he'd flip the switch and go back to being taciturn and sort of irritated.

"Will and Mike think he's a great guy but I don't know...I think he's got hard edges. And that girl, Vanessa? What could anyone see in her?"

"You don't think she's pretty?"

"If you're into that, I guess. I predict she'll be unmarried with three kids and three different baby daddies by the time she's thirty. I can kind of picture her, tattoos covering her bony arms, smoking a butt on the steps of her double wide in the trailer park."

"You're just mad because you know she could probably kick your ass," I teased, tickling Drew.

He pinned my wrists and flipped me over onto my back, straddling me on the couch. "Oh, now you're gonna get it, Harris."

I did like working with Jeremy. It was a challenge but I was learning so much, getting a window into the way his brain worked, and gaining a deeper understanding of why certain teaching strategies were more effective than others.

While those were perks, there were challenges—lots of them. For example, I found it hard to concentrate at times, especially when Jeremy would take his pencil and tap the eraser against his bottom lip when he was lost in thought...or when Jeremy would run his hands through his hair when he was frustrated...or when Jeremy smiled in triumph as he mastered a difficult concept.

I liked him.

Like, I *liked* him.

The warm, buzzy feeling I had in my chest when I was with Jeremy wasn't very different from the butterflies I'd felt for him back in sixth grade. The only difference was that instead of daydreaming about an innocent kiss, now I'd find myself gazing off into space, wondering how it would feel to have his hands grasping my hips, holding my body close as he kissed me deep, his tongue exploring my mouth.

As I took my seat across from Jeremy today, though, I wasn't lost in naughty thoughts. Today I was wondering why I felt lightheaded and sweaty all of a sudden. And why the room was kind of spinning.

"Carolyn? Are you all—"

I darted up, knocking my chair out from under me. I clamped my hand over my mouth as I struggled with the doorknob and then ran to the girls' bathroom. I just barely made it, sweat pooling on my forehead, before falling to my knees and heaving into the toilet. It felt never ending. How much food was in my stomach? I kept heaving even after there was simply nothing left. Oh yeah, those really *attractive* noises you make when you dry heave? I realized mid-lurch that Jeremy was witnessing the whole show.

I wiped my mouth on my sleeve when I felt him come up behind me. He gathered my hair and ran a wet paper towel across my forehead and down along my neck. I was about to laugh it off and attempt some clever comment, but my stomach was overtaken by aliens again. I think what I ate last month decided to make a comeback.

How humiliating.

And how sweet he was.

After what seemed like a lifetime, I rested my head in my hands and slid my butt onto the bathroom floor. "God, don't look at me, I'm gross."

He chuckled softly. "I've seen worse."

He wet some more paper towels and wrung them out before handing them to me. I wiped my mouth and my hands. Then Jeremy reached down and gently pulled me up.

"Thanks, Jeremy."

"You good? Think you're done?"

"I'd better be."

"Jeez, you look green, Carolyn."

"I feel like death warmed over."

"Do you have a car?"

"No, my mother's picking me up."

"Give me your phone."

"It's back in the room."

When I tried to take a few steps and teetered, he steadied me.

"Whoa. You stay here," he said as he propped me against the wall, "and I'll get your stuff. I'll be right back."

By the time he returned a few minutes later, I'd slid down the wall into a sitting position. I didn't even have the energy to stand. I felt like absolute crap.

"Hey, you doing all right?" he asked as he crouched down next to me. "I called your mom, she's on her way. I'd have driven you myself but I have my bike today."

I croaked weakly, "Yeah, I don't think I'm up for being on the back of a motorcycle right now."

He laughed. "And I don't think I'd be able to drive the thing knowing you could puke on me at any moment."

I tried to laugh but just keeping my eyes open was a major effort at that point. I noticed Jeremy looping both of our backpacks onto his shoulders and before I knew it, he was reaching down to scoop me up in his arms.

"I can walk," I offered, even though I was grateful that I didn't have to.

"Nope, I've got you. And before you go getting all mushy on me, Carolyn, I'll remind you this is purely selfish on my part. I need my tutor to make a full and speedy recovery. Next week I've got two huge tests, got it?"

"Got it, Daniel-san."

"Huh?"

I breathed out, exhausted with the effort of speaking—of thinking, for that matter. "Karate Kid. You're Daniel-san, I'm Mr. Miyagi."

"You're *who*? Holy shit," he whispered. Then he placed his lips against my forehead. What the? Was he kissing me? *That's nice*, I thought, but messed up, considering I probably smelled of puke. "I think you're delusional with fever."

Oh, checking my temperature—no kiss.

I closed my eyes at that point and didn't perk up again until I felt him lower me into the car.

"She's really sick, Mrs. Harris. I don't think I've ever seen someone throw up that much."

"Ok, let's get you home, sweetie," my mom chirped as she clipped my seat belt over my lap. "And thank you...Um, I didn't get your name."

"Jeremy Rivers. Carolyn tutors me."

"Jeremy? The one Thomas talks about? Did you go to Briarwood?"

"Yes, ma'am."

"Well thank you, Jeremy, for taking care of Carolyn. I'm so happy I finally got to meet you."

The next twenty-four hours were a blur. When I woke up on Wednesday afternoon I was covered in a sheen of sweat, thirsty and a little hungry. That was a good sign. Like a mind-reading angel, my mother entered my room with toast and tea on a tray.

"Ah, how did you know?"

"I could tell the fever broke. I knew you'd need a little something in your tummy."

"What time is it?"

"Four o'clock."

"What day is it?"

She smiled. "Wednesday."

"I feel so much better."

"Good, but I think you should stay home to rest tomorrow."

"I really don't want to miss another day, Mom."

"Why? Your grades won't suffer."

I couldn't tell her why. "I just need to go in. If I feel bad tomorrow morning, I won't go, I promise."

She sighed. "All right." As Mom went to prop my pillows up so I could sit up and eat, she said, "What a nice boy that Jeremy Rivers is."

I nibbled on my toast as I gave a noncommittal nod of assent.

"How has it been for him, coming back to Westerly?"

"I would say good overall. He's kind of a big man on campus, football star and all. He's popular with the girls," I added, rolling my eyes.

She sat next to me on the bed, smiling. "I meant academically, Carolyn."

"Oh," I said, recovering. "He has accommodations like extra testing time and technology assistance, but it's a struggle for him."

My mother looked disappointed. She was thinking about Thomas. "I mean, he's passing, Mom. He doesn't complain. But I feel bad sometimes. It's like he doesn't expect to excel. He's happy with just getting by."

"All those years of just anticipating failure...I imagine it's hard to set new expectations for yourself."

"Yeah," I answered absently. I was thinking, wondering if I could help Jeremy to see himself in a different light. I felt terrible about the day I shot down his happy mood when he showed me his mediocre test grade. He was proud of himself but I knew he could do better. I was determined to make him see himself the way I saw him.

Thursday I returned to school and was disappointed when I realized there would be no tutoring that day either. When I saw Kerri at our lockers in the morning she relayed the lunchroom scene from the day before, telling me how Jeremy, looking positively green, practically knocked Samantha off his lap and onto the floor as he rushed to the bathroom. Apparently I was contagious. She laughed as she imitated Samantha's attempt to play the concerned girlfriend, which lasted for all of about two seconds. Samantha took off once she caught a whiff of puke.

I had a substitute teacher last period so I ditched. Not having a license when all of my friends did—it just blew. I walked the distance home and then took my mother's cast-off old beater, a Volvo wagon that I assumed was still in the garage because it would one day be mine. I drove with my permit on the seat beside me. I figured that if I was pulled over, I'd play dumb.

By the time I reached Jeremy's place, I was a nervous wreck. I was relieved to see his truck in the driveway, but parking parallel alongside it took several attempts. Forget how I must have looked backing into that spot on Main Street—I can only imagine.

"Hello."

The man who opened the door was so good-looking he startled me for a split-second. He looked to be about forty, with clear, bright eyes and tan skin that looked like he spent a lot of time outdoors. It was Jeremy, twenty or so years from now.

"Hi, I'm Carolyn. Is Jeremy home? I heard he was sick."

He nodded his head, smiling. "He was sick, all right. That was some virus he had, but now I think he's back among the living. I heard the shower going before and was just fixing him something to eat."

I held up the paper bag in my hand. "I brought him some soup. A peace offering."

"Well, let's see if he's up for visitors."

He closed the door behind him and led me back outside and around to the other side of the house. As we made our way, I took in the scene. It looked like a cottage right out of a storybook, where you'd imagine Goldilocks came across the three bears' place out in the middle of the woods. It was serene and quiet, the only sound being the crunch of fallen leaves underfoot.

He opened the door and called out as I followed him up the stairs, "You decent, Jeremy? You have a visitor."

"Yeah, you can send Vanessa up."

Her name coming from his mouth felt like a jab. Why? *Why* did I come here? I felt small and foolish all over again.

"Is Vanessa on her way?" I asked. "I can leave. I just wanted to drop this off for you."

His hands stilled at the sound of my voice, the towel still covering most of his face as he stopped drying his hair. "Carolyn?" He tossed the towel aside and looked at me.

I felt uncomfortable and embarrassed. However, that didn't stop me from noticing the way he looked sprawled out on his leather couch, flannel pajama pants slung low, no shirt, his skin fresh and damp from a shower. He was a sight.

I swallowed and placed the paper bag on the coffee table in front of him. "I figured this is the least I could do after passing the plague onto you."

He smiled. "Dad, this is Carolyn Harris, the girl I told you about...The one who's tutoring me."

Mr. Rivers smiled at me as he shook my hand. "I'm Michael Rivers. It's nice to meet you, Carolyn. Jeremy has been singing your praises."

Jeremy cleared his throat then, signaling for his dad to stop talking. His dad chuckled and then made his way back downstairs. Jeremy looked back to me. "You do owe me, Harris. I don't think I've ever been that sick before. I probably lost five pounds in one day."

"Well, here's a peace offering...Chicken soup from Le Évier."

"Hmm," he mused as he opened the bag. He breathed in as he lifted the to-go container's lid and closed his eyes. "It smells incredible. I'm starving so I'm guessing I can hold this down."

"I was twenty-four hours to the minute, so I assumed that you'd be on the mend by now. Kerri told me that disaster hit around lunchtime yesterday."

His eyes twinkled as he looked up at me, smiling. "I was sitting there, totally fine one minute, and then thinking, *oh nooo*, the next."

"Been there." I wanted to make casual conversation but I was nervous and coming up empty. So I said the first thing that came to mind. "Kerri told me you practically threw your new babe off your lap when you went running for the bathroom."

"My new babe?"

When I didn't say anything in response, Jeremy began to eat his soup. *Way to go, Carolyn*. Why am I always so freaking awkward? I'd just ruined a nice moment between us, *again*.

"There are some crackers in the bag."

"Thanks."

"So, um, I just wanted to bring you that and to let you know I'm free on Sunday if you want to get together." He must have been starving because he didn't stop spooning soup into his mouth as he cocked his head and gave me a look that made me feel as if I'd grown a second head. "To study," I clarified. "You have tests on Monday and Tuesday, right? I want you to feel prepared."

"You don't mind? You'd do that for me?"

"Of course," I answered. "We missed both sessions this week thanks to me."

"It wasn't your fault."

I was still standing across from him, shifting my weight from one foot to the other. He stopped eating for a moment and one corner of his mouth turned up in a smile. He was looking at my hand. I realized later that I'd been twisting my hair into knots.

"You wanna sit, Carolyn?"

"No, um, I've gotta get going. I took my mom's car and I technically don't have my license."

His eyes widened. "You shitting me?"

"No." I shrugged. "It's no big deal."

"Really? You're a decent driver?"

I laughed as I sank into a chair opposite Jeremy. "No, I'm actually pretty bad. You should have seen me trying to get your soup. I had to back into a spot on Main with a Jaguar on one side of me and a brand new Mercedes convertible on the other. I was shaking by the time I cut the engine."

He laughed with me, shaking his head. "I can picture it. Now this soup tastes even better, knowing you risked your life getting it for me." After a minute he tipped the container over, drinking the last drops. "I think that was the best soup I've ever had."

"Yesterday I thought the same thing about the toast and tea my mom made me. I think you were just starving."

"No, ma chère, that soup was ooh la la good. Très délicieux."

"Your French accent isn't half bad."

"Briarwood." He stood and made his way to a small kitchen where he dumped the container into the trash. "They have a good foreign language program. Better than Westerly...Better for me, anyway. Everything was conversational, as opposed to written, so they really drilled you on proper pronunciation."

"Do you miss it there?"

He grabbed a t-shirt and pulled it over his head before sitting back on the couch. What a pity, covering up that torso.

"Sometimes I miss it, like when I fail a test," he said, winking at me. "But I like Westerly. I love playing football again. I have a great art teacher now, but then...I miss having so many other artistic kids around like I did at Briarwood." He shrugged. "Each place has its plusses and minuses, I guess."

"I heard that you're a great artist."

He shook his head. "I'm so-so at best. But it was crazy at Briarwood. It seemed like every kid there was a prodigy in their own weird way. You stutter and can't read, but you can play the guitar like Mark Knophler. You can't write your name legibly but you can sculpt like Donatello. Not everyone was like that, but a lot of them were."

"Everyone has different types of intelligence. I truly believe that. You should hear Zach play the guitar. And I know building with Legos isn't really a talent, but Thomas can construct entire cities with the most intricate details. He's also a programming whiz. He can do things I could never do."

He nodded. "*That* was the best thing about Briarwood. I never felt stupid there. The teachers made me feel like my art was important, just as important as reading. So I felt accomplished in some way, you know?"

"You're not stupid, Jeremy. Please don't ever say that."

He smiled at me in a way that was affectionate and kind—like we were really friends. I ate all that tenderness up, and it was better than chocolate.

"I don't think that anymore, Carolyn. I really don't."

We sat in comfortable silence for a moment. I looked around, taking in some of the posters on the exposed brick walls. It was eclectic, with colorful modern art prints that I didn't recognize, some alternative rock band posters, one of Miles Davis blowing on his trumpet, and some sketches on canvas mixed in.

"Did you do those?" I asked, pointing to a cluster of small canvases, each with a child in various poses.

"No, my friend Andie did them. She's still at Briarwood."

"They're beautiful."

"Yeah, they are. She's beyond talented…Puts me to shame."

"I bet you're really good, you're just being modest."

He shrugged. "I enjoy it."

I should go, I thought at that moment, *quit while the going's good.* "It's getting dark, I'd better head out."

He grabbed a sweatshirt off the back of the couch and stood, slipping his feet into flip flops. "I'll drive your car and my dad will follow us."

I started to protest, "I'll be fine, I—"

"No way am I gonna be responsible for you wrapping yourself around a tree. It was pretty ballsy taking the car out in the first place." He held his open palm out, gesturing for my keys. "Don't push your luck."

Chapter Seven

CAROLYN

"Carolyn, can we meet at around one on Sunday?" He gestured to Frank. "I promised Frank that I'd help him in the morning."

Samantha's head whipped around and she zeroed in on me. Hell, the entire table turned to look at me as I felt my cheeks flush.

"Um, sure."

"Are we meeting at the library?"

What the hell was Jeremy doing? He'd never so much as spoken to me outside of our study room in the school library and now he was making casual conversation in front of everyone in the cafeteria? I tensed and felt Drew's hand still on my back. I was overreacting. This was no big deal. *Relax, Carolyn.*

"No," I answered casually. "The public library will be too crowded on a Sunday. Come to my house." I turned and looked to Drew. "We're not going out with your parents until five, right?"

He hesitated and then answered, "Yeah."

"All right," I said, looking back at Jeremy. "One o'clock." Then I promptly turned my attention back to Drew.

"Working overtime?"

"We didn't have any sessions this week and he has two major exams coming up."

He scooted in closer and pulled me so that my back was right up to his front. "Maybe I need you to be *my* teacher, Carolyn."

I saw Jeremy look up for a second before turning his attention back to Frank and the rest of the guys.

Drew actually nibbled on my earlobe after whispering in my ear. I couldn't help but squirm in response. I knew what he was doing, he was staking his claim.

"What are we doing after the game tonight, baby."

Baby? The pet name didn't roll off his tongue easily and didn't sit well with me.

I scooted up a smidge, creating some space between our bodies. "Nothing too late. Thomas's game is an hour away tomorrow morning. We're leaving at seven, remember?"

"Aw, Carolyn, I forgot. You mind if I skip it? I have a lot of crap I've gotta catch up on tomorrow. Thomas won't care, right?"

I tried to keep the disappointment out of my voice. "No, he won't care."

Thomas *wouldn't* care and that's what bothered me the most.

Drew never made much of an effort with Thomas. Occasionally Drew acted the part, but he was just being polite; there was no real connection there. Drew obviously thought Thomas was peculiar and that hurt me. Was Thomas quirky? Absolutely. But he wasn't some oddball and that's kind of how Drew looked at him, eyes glazing over as Thomas excitedly presented his newest Lego creation or tried to explain the differences between two obscure but similar species of birds.

Thomas's newfound interest in sports was thanks to Jeremy, really. After throwing the ball with Jeremy that day at the lake, Zach and Thomas got it in their heads that they wanted to play football. Tom badgered my mom until she relented and Zach did the same.

Now the two of them were playing on a team in the neighboring town.

Our town's league was hard core. Most of those kids had been playing since they were four or five. Thomas would never make *that* team. Thomas's league was more...egalitarian. Everyone got playing time despite their level of ability, and effort was highly regarded. Yeah, it was one of *those* leagues: winning isn't everything. I saw Drew shake his head in disgust during the one and only game he attended when he heard the coach say, "Good try," for the umpteenth time. I, on the other hand, thought it was pretty cool that Thomas and Zach wanted to give something new a try. It was brave.

Drew gave me a squeeze and then followed Will, Mike and the rest of the guys outside for the last few minutes of the period.

Erica scooted closer to me. "How is it, tutoring Jeremy?"

"It's going well," I said absently. "He's a hard worker."

"He told me you're...What did he say, exactly...He said you're like a walking, talking super nerd." Samantha laughed but no one joined in with her. When I ignored her, she tried to placate me. "I'm just kidding. He said you're the smartest person he's ever met."

The last sentence was muttered begrudgingly.

Erica looked at her pointedly. "What exactly is going on there, Samantha?"

"A few hot kisses, he's copped a feel...But tonight's the night. I'm inviting people to my house after the game. My parents are away until Sunday." She looked to all of us. "Ask your parents if you can stay over."

"Wouldn't you want him there alone?" Kerri asked.

"No. I mean, I don't even know who it is that I want. If Will is there then that's who I'm going for. But if he really is hung up on Tori, then Jeremy will make a tasty plan B."

"Lucky Jeremy," I said quietly.

"What's that, Carolyn? Don't tell me you're still into him?"

I shot her a look meant to convey a warning: *Don't you dare.*

Samantha was the only one who knew about my crush on Jeremy all those years ago. She was going to marry Warren Wells, I was going to marry Jeremy Rivers. *She* probably hadn't saved the notebook with her married name, Mrs. Samantha Wells, scribbled in it, though. *She* didn't have a note that was once taped to a candy bar, a note that had nearly broken her heart years ago. Pathetic yes, but I still had those tucked away in a box where I kept all my special, private things.

"Are you serious right now, Samantha?" I rolled my eyes in an attempt to convey just how *ridiculous* the very idea of that was. "I just think you're being thoughtless, that's all. Would you like to be someone's back up plan?"

"I don't think getting with me would be, like, suffering for Jeremy. Socially, it will be a giant step up for him."

Thankfully, Kerri changed the subject because Samantha was making me physically sick. I couldn't stomach the thought of Jeremy's hands on her, or worse, the thought of him actually caring about her.

I went home right after the game. I knew that Drew and the rest of my friends were heading to Samantha's. I called his phone after Thomas's game at around ten the next morning. No answer. I tried Erica, Kerri and Samantha. No one was picking up.

"Hey," Drew greeted me, sounding groggy. He finally got around to calling me back at three that afternoon.

"Hey yourself. Rough night?"

Pause. Uncomfortable, long pause.

"Yeah, guess you could say that. I wish you came with me last night."

"Why's that?"

"No reason." His tone was suddenly more upbeat. "I just missed you."

"Sounds like you just woke up."

"I didn't get in until like...five."

"Did *everyone* stay that late at Samantha's?"

"I don't know. I drove home with Will. I think he hooked up with Kerri."

"What?" I blurted out. "Does Samantha know that?"

"Why would Samantha care? She looked pretty busy with Jeremy."

Ugh. "Jeremy was kind of her back up plan. She's probably going to skewer Kerri."

"How was your night?"

"You know I just went home, Drew." He was trying to change the subject but he wasn't getting off that easy. My intuition told me something was not right. "Why were you there so late?"

"It got kind of crazy. I think a lot more people showed up than she anticipated. It was literally wall to wall. I just did too many shots and I, uh...I passed out."

"Alone?"

"What are you asking me, exactly?"

"The same thing you would ask *me* if I told you that *I* was at a party until five in the morning without you, and you didn't hear from *me* until the next afternoon."

"Jesus, Carolyn. All right, you're right...I would ask. And the answer to your question is yes, I was alone." I was silent on my end of the line. "Hey, I'm sorry. I shouldn't have had so much to drink, ok? You want to come over? We'll hang out here and watch a movie. Come have some Chinese food with me. Help me nurse this vicious hangover."

"Sounds tempting, really, but I'll pass."

"Don't, Carolyn."

I blew out a breath. "I'm not mad, Drew. I just feel...I don't know...bitchy. It's just better if we don't hang out. I'll see you tomorrow night."

"We're ok?"

"Yeah."

"All right, baby, I'll call you later."

I felt like snapping back: *Please don't, baby.*

I wanted to bear my claws at him for no reason, really. I was mad at the girls, too. Why wasn't anyone calling me back? And I was mad at Jeremy. And sad for Jeremy. And mad at Samantha.

Ugh.

Kerri came by at around five, looking like hell. I heard my mom let her in downstairs. She burst right into my room after knocking once and flopped herself onto my bed. Her hair was pulled up in a wet ponytail, her face was pale, and she looked exhausted.

"I have something to tell you."

"You hooked up with Will?"

Kerri flung one arm over her face for a moment and then sat up and looked at me wide-eyed. "Drew knows?"

"He wasn't sure." I sounded bitter to my own ears when I added, "Sounds like I missed quite a party."

"I was doing shots...Everyone was. Samantha made these gelatin shots. I think they had grain alcohol in them. I didn't even do that many! I just remember wanting to dance and then feeling really woozy." She started to cry. "I woke up next to Will with no clothes on."

"Oh, Kerri." I held onto her as she wet the front of my shirt with her tears. "What did Will say?"

"I could tell he was as horrified as I was. He doesn't like me that way, Carolyn. He doesn't have any feelings for me. Will asked me if we slept together and I said—" She started bawling again, choking out the words, "I said...I said I didn't know!"

"Shh, it's all right," I said, rocking her. "Do you remember anything?"

"I told Will I remembered kissing him." She shook her head. "When I told him that he looked like he was gonna hurl. He said he didn't even remember talking to me at the party last night."

"Will is a good person. He won't say anything."

"I know he won't and I know he didn't, you know, take advantage of me or anything. He was so freaking nice this morning. He apologized a million times, helped me find my clothes and made sure no one saw us leave the room together. He drove me home before going back for Drew. Oh, Carolyn, I am *so* embarrassed."

"Does Samantha know?"

"I don't know but I'll find out soon enough." She was wringing her hands nervously, looking out my bedroom window. "What if I did sleep with him? My first time and I don't even remember it?" She started crying again.

"It could be worse, Kerri." I spoke from experience. "Really," I said when she looked at me with a raised eyebrow. "It could have been someone like Chase, someone who wouldn't think twice about telling the entire school and branding you a slut. Will Clarke won't let you get hurt. I'm sure of that."

She sniffled and nodded. "You're right."

"Are you sore?"

She thought for a moment. "No. If I'm not sore does that mean I didn't do it?"

"I don't know," I lied. I *was* sore that next day, not terribly, but enough to know that something had most definitely been *there*.

I wished that I could be a better friend to Kerri right now, to confide in her, share my shame to ease hers. Tell her that I *knew* how it could be so much worse. To give tacit consent to something you knew in your heart you didn't want. To remain silent and nod your head like some dumb-struck imbecile when someone was pressing down on you, asking you if you wanted it, when you really wanted to scream.

To lose your voice—that was the worst way of all.

But I couldn't be her friend. There was not one person I trusted with that secret. I decided before coming home that summer that I wouldn't tell a soul—that I'd forget it ever happened.

But I could never forget.

* * *

JEREMY

This girl is a bitch.

I walked in on Samantha as she was laughing, snapping away on her phone, taking pictures of her friend who was passed out naked. Thankfully, I'd turned down every shot she'd tried to force feed me tonight. I was fairly sober compared to the rest of the fools at this party.

After erasing the pictures from Samantha's phone, covering Kerri with a blanket, and then locking Kerri and Will inside the room so that no one could walk in on them, I left.

I'd had enough.

Had enough of Samantha trying to grind on me and slip her hands into my jeans, enough of watching the weekend warriors puke into the bushes, and enough of watching Drew feel up one of Carolyn's closest friends. Yeah, Mr. Perfect had been getting it on with Erica. In his defense, he was so messed up he probably didn't have any recollection of it today.

Fuck that—there was no excuse.

It was times like this when I had the overwhelming sense that I just didn't fit in. I guess one could argue that most people in my age bracket feel misunderstood, but I pretty much always felt like I was on the outside looking in. I didn't want to drink myself into a stupor like these frat boys in training. I didn't think half the shit they thought was hilarious was even worth a chuckle.

Walking up the pathway to Carolyn's house on Sunday, I had a sudden strong urge to hit something when I thought about her going out with that douchebag later on today. I wanted to turn around and go home, angry with her for being so clueless, and tormented because

I *knew* what he was really like but I wasn't going to tell her a goddamned thing.

The door swung open before I had a chance to knock.

"Jeremy! What are you doing here?"

Jeez, this kid was good for my confidence. He looked up to me smiling, like I was the sun and the moon.

"Thomas, my man...Heard you're playing football this year, is that correct?"

"Yep, and I'm a cornerback, just like you!"

"I'm gonna have to check out one of your games."

"Really? There's only two left so you should probably come this Saturday."

"Oh. All right then, I'll be there."

"I'll tell Zach, he'll be stoked." Without taking a breath, he asked, "You wanna see my iguana?"

"Sure, but let me talk to Carolyn first. She's helping me study and she might want to get started right away, ok?"

His eyes dropped to the ground. "Oh."

"I really have to study, Tom. I have to work really hard just to pass my classes, you know?"

"Yeah, I get it." He looked back up to me. "But you'll stay after for a few minutes?"

"Yeah, promise."

Thomas started yelling Carolyn's name only to see her looking down on us from the upstairs landing, amused.

"C'mon up...We'll study in my room."

"Jeremy said he wants to see my iguana after, so let me know as *soon* as you're done, ok?"

"I will, Tom, but we have a lot of work to do, all right? No interruptions."

"Got it."

I met her at the top of the stairs. "He's a great kid."

"He thinks you're a rock star. I think he was actually jealous when he heard my mom telling my father about how you came to my rescue last week when I was puking my guts out."

I looked around her room as she went to get us settled at her long work table. There was an entire wall dedicated to her medals and awards from various science fairs and programs.

"That's my nerd wall. I've got to take that stuff down. Some of it's from, like, eighth grade."

"No, it's cool that you won all this." She snickered, rolling her eyes and shaking her head. "Really, Carolyn, it's impressive."

She had pictures on another wall, a collage of her with friends, some from Westerly, some I didn't recognize. "Who are these kids?"

"That's the group I worked with at Yale this summer, and this group is from a summer camp program I used to attend. They're all science buddies."

"Do you feel like you have more in common with them than you do with your friends here?"

"Besides Kerri, I have nothing in common with any of my friends." She put air quotes around that last word.

"Sometimes I wonder why you hang out with them. You and Samantha? It doesn't add up."

She looked hurt. "I've known Samantha since I was a toddler. We're like sisters," she added quietly. "And what about *you* and Samantha? To me, that doesn't add up, but *you* certainly seem to find her interesting."

"Why would you say that?"

Carolyn let out an exasperated breath as she looked to the ceiling. "*Please*, you let her hang all over you at school."

I played along. "I do?"

"And from what I hear, you two had *so* much fun at her party Friday night."

"Oh, you heard that, did you?" Now I was pissed. "Did you hear that from your boy, Drew?"

She walked past me, brushing me off, grabbing a pen and a notebook from her desk. "It's not important."

"No," I said, grasping her upper arm. "It *is* important because it's not true."

She looked down at her arm and then looked up at me, surprised. I wasn't holding her tight, but damn, I shouldn't have grabbed her like that. I backed up a few steps.

"You weren't with her on Friday?"

"No, I've never been with her. Not for lack of effort on her part, though. What's it to you anyway?"

Carolyn looked tired suddenly. She leaned back against her wall and then sank down to the floor slowly, landing on her ass. "It's *not* my business, you're right. I just...I think she'll hurt you. Sometimes she can be—"

"A mean-spirited bitch?"

She rested her chin on her knees. She wouldn't say it out loud but she was nodding her head.

"I'm not into her, Carolyn."

"Good," she murmured.

I was so tempted to tell her everything that went down Friday night, but she was a big girl—she had to figure it out on her own.

"Are we good?"

"Yeah, Jeremy...Let's start with Physics."

I was sitting in front of my easel in Figure Drawing. It met Tuesday nights at six, so that was my long day. After Carolyn tutored me, I spent around an hour weight training with the team, then I showered quick and made my way upstairs to the third floor studio. I loved it up here. Chuck Watters treated me like an adult, like a fellow artist. He was tough in the way he critiqued my work, but I could take it. He made me better, so much better.

Today we were drawing Laurent, some dude I estimated to be in his mid-seventies. Every week it was someone different: black, white, young, old, strong, feeble. Occasionally I got lucky. The model might be a female grad student from Yale or Fairfield in their twenties or thirties. It *was* all about technique, but still, I'm a guy and gazing at a beautiful woman was a far superior way to pass the time.

Chuck was standing over me, critiquing my hand. "No...It looks too stiff here, you see?"

"The hands always give me trouble."

"It's the single hardest thing to master, Jeremy. You'll get it."

Just then the door opened, which never happened. School was pretty much deserted by that time and the third floor art studios were like no-man's land to begin with. We were in our own little world up here with the door covered to protect the model's privacy.

I was right by the door, so I was the first to see Carolyn peek in with a happy, excited look on her face. She locked eyes with me and then her eyes followed mine as I instinctively looked to Chuck and then to the model. When I looked back, her mouth was hanging open and the paper she'd been holding dropped to the floor. I jumped up and gave an apologetic look to Chuck as I grabbed the paper, ushered her out and closed the door behind us.

"What the hell are you doing up here, Carolyn?"

"I...I...You draw naked people up here every week?"

"Yeah. What do you think figure drawing is?"

"I didn't know. Wow. That's pretty cool. You looked like the youngest person in there."

"You got that from the nanosecond you spent in the room?"

"Yeah," she said, laughing. "I'm pretty observant."

"Ok, freak," I teased. Seeing her laugh or smile always made me feel light-hearted. "What was *so* important that you had to barge in and scare the poor old naked guy half to death?"

"Oh nothing," she said, innocently, "just the *ninety-two* you got on your Physics test." I took the now crumpled paper and stared at it in disbelief. "Jeremy, say something!"

I grabbed Carolyn and spun her around. I couldn't contain it, I could hardly believe it. A ninety-two? Really? When I came to a stop, our faces were an inch apart.

"Thank you, Carolyn."

"It's all you, Jeremy."

I wanted to kiss her, and I was definitely getting the vibe that she wanted me to kiss her too. It was probably no more than five seconds—the two of us face to face, our bodies pressed close together—but it felt like a lot longer. A million thoughts raced through my head but one stuck: *she's not mine.* So I lowered her to the ground and backed away.

"Really, Carolyn, thank you. I never would have gotten that grade without your help."

"You're welcome, Jeremy." Maybe I was imagining it, but her eyes looked a little misty. "I'm sorry I interrupted your class. I ran into Mrs. Parks and she shared your grade with me. I was excited and I got a little carried away."

"No, it's fine, really. I'll see you Thursday?"

"Sure," she said, turning to go. "I'll see you then."

* * *

CAROLYN

The tension at our lunch table was borderline unbearable. Most of the guys were missing in action, so it was just the four of us. Drew hadn't come to the cafeteria once this week, complaining that he was swamped with work and busy polishing up his essays for his back-up school applications.

By Wednesday, Samantha was ready to blow. "It's kind of sad, huh, Kerri? You let Will Clarke screw you, without so much as even a pre-game *conversation,* and he hasn't come within a mile of you since."

Kerri looked to me, desperate.

I put my hand on Samantha's. "Stop it."

"Yeah, don't be a bitch," Erica spat.

"Oh, and don't even get me started on *you*," Samantha hissed back at Erica.

I didn't know what that was about, but it must have been something bad because I never saw Erica back down so quickly.

Kerri squared her shoulders. "Fuck off, Samantha. You're so much better? Every time I turned around I saw you trying to grope Jeremy's dick. You're pathetic."

"Do you think I'm jealous of you?"

"No, I think you're just being a straight-up bitch."

"I'm so *not* jealous, Kerri. If I wanted Will I certainly wouldn't have to strip down naked and throw myself at him."

"I don't think he'd want you even if you stripped down naked and dipped yourself in chocolate, Samantha. In fact, I'm pretty sure he despises you."

"Well, I'm sorry to break it to you, Kerri, but all the guys know. They *all* know you give it up easy. I'm sure you'll have plenty of dates now. Was that your goal?"

I gasped. "Samantha, what the hell?"

I gathered up Kerri's things and followed her as she ran out of the cafeteria and into an empty classroom.

"She saw us. Will told me she walked in on us and took pictures."

"He knew?"

"Jeremy told him. He was there with Samantha." She dug the heels of both hands into her forehead. "Fuck, he saw me naked too."

She was now face-down on a desk, her shoulders shaking with the force of her sobs. I rubbed her back, trying to think of ways to console her but coming up empty. A few minutes later I asked, "Who has the pictures?"

She shook her head without looking up. "Jeremy erased them from Samantha's phone."

"So then Samantha was lying...All the guys *don't* know."

Kerri looked up at me and cocked an eyebrow. "Samantha knows so she'll make sure that everyone we know finds out."

"No she won't. I'll talk to her. Kerri, do you want me to get you out of here? I'll cut class with you."

"No," she said, sniffling. "I have a test next period. I'm not fucking up my GPA because of her."

There was a knock on the door and then Will walked into the room. He looked like crap—like he hadn't slept for days.

"Can I talk to you, Kerri?"

I nodded at Will and left the two of them. Later on Kerri called to tell me that Will comforted her, apologizing again, and promised he'd deal with Samantha on her behalf. Will also wanted Kerri to know that he told Tori everything. He felt he owed it to her. He assured Kerri that Tori wouldn't tell anyone else. Tori was pissed, but also knew how upset Kerri was about the whole thing. Kerri cried when she told me that Will seemed upset and concerned about Tori most of all.

"I wish he did have a thing for me, Carolyn, because I swear, I don't think there's a better person on the planet."

"Yeah, Will is a great guy. Drew loves him like a brother."

"You're lucky, Carolyn, and Tori's lucky. I'd like to have someone like that...A good guy who cares about me. Drew looks at you like you're everything, you know?"

"Yeah, he's great."

I did think Drew was great. Sometimes I wondered how he shouldered everything—football, maintaining a ninety-five-plus average, and especially living up to his father's expectations.

That last time we went out to dinner with his parents, I made the mistake of asking Drew what his back-up school was, just in case he wouldn't be heading to the Naval Academy.

His dad snapped, "*We* don't do back-ups. Drew *will* be in Annapolis at the United States Naval Academy."

I found myself actually praying to God that night, pleading with the powers of the universe to make it so. If Drew didn't get one of those few, coveted spots, I could only imagine the hell his life would be. Maybe it wasn't entirely fair, but I kind of hated his father.

When he took me home, we sat in his car outside my house talking. He had a lot on his mind. He wasn't himself. I wanted to comfort him. And if I was being totally honest, as shameful as it was, being around Jeremy had aroused some need in me. I led him inside and downstairs to the basement. The house was quiet. My parents typically turned in early and I knew Thomas was already in bed.

Drew sat on the couch and I stood in front of him. When I started to slip out of my dress, he rubbed his hands over his face roughly and told me to stop. "Not like this, Carolyn. Not tonight." I pulled the dress back up onto my shoulders. His rejection stung and I was embarrassed. "Come here," he said, gesturing to his lap. "I love you, Carolyn. I want you so badly, I do. I just want everything to be perfect, you know? You're perfect."

Perfect.

That was the closest I ever came to telling him myself. I wanted to confide in Drew, but something held me back. Something always did. It didn't matter, though. What is it they say? Everything comes out in the wash?

Yeah, everything would come out eventually.

My house of cards would fall.

Chapter Eight

JEREMY

The football season ended. My grades allowed me to play through the entire season, as well as playoffs.

So I could have ended the tutoring sessions with Carolyn, but that would mean I wouldn't have three hours a week with her all to myself. I wasn't giving that up. I even asked her to add a Sunday here and there, under the pretense that I had some big exam to study for. I did have tests, and I did stand a better chance of doing well with her help, but I started to need those Sundays for other reasons.

The awkwardness was gone between us. Over the course of the past few months, we became friends—real friends. Talking to her was natural and easy. I felt like I could say just about anything to her because Carolyn had no filter herself. She was pretty much the queen of blurting things out. I could be myself around her and I loved making her laugh.

A few Sundays, like that first time, we studied at her house. I liked being in her room, I'll admit it. I liked sitting with my back resting at the opposite end of the bed from her, sneaking glances as I tried to concentrate on whatever I was struggling to understand.

Her mom would always ask me to stay for Sunday dinner, pleading with me when I hesitated, explaining that my presence would make Thomas's week. I loved that kid. He was different but he didn't seem one bit self-conscious or ashamed.

Sitting around their dinner table felt foreign in a way, but it filled me with something good, like peace, and a feeling of want. It's not like I didn't have a really good relationship with my father, I did, but this was something else. Carolyn's dad was smart, kind and funny, and it was obvious that he was still crazy about Mrs. Harris. You'd see him grab her hand, rubbing his thumb over her palm, or you'd notice the smiles and looks that passed between the two of them. Mr. and Mrs. Harris both had a great way with the kids, too. They gave their opinions but always asked what Carolyn and Thomas thought, treating their ideas as if they held the same weight. It was no wonder that Thomas never believed he was limited or that there was something wrong with him. There was nothing but love and acceptance in this place. I'd find myself looking around the table, thinking that I'd like to have this life someday.

The first Sunday after Christmas break, she met me at my house at noon. We were coming back to mid-trimester exams. Today we were studying for Global History, and after putting in a solid hour, I closed my book and looked up at her. "I owe you lunch."

"Why?"

"You give me Sundays out of the goodness of your heart. It's above and beyond the call of duty. I owe you and I'm starving. Chinese or pizza?" I asked, holding up the phone.

She sat on my couch with her feet bare, dressed in sweats and a snug Westerly Volleyball tee shirt. Her hair was down and her glasses were perched half-way down the bridge of her nose. She looked freaking exquisite. I swallowed as I stood there waiting, thinking to myself that she was the most gorgeous woman on the planet.

"Pizza with mushrooms and peppers, please."

"Very decisive. I like it, Miss Harris."

We blew off studying while we waited for the delivery guy. I asked her about World War Three that was currently raging between Kerri and Samantha. Carolyn reported happily that they seemed to have arrived at a truce and things were returning back to normal, with Samantha even showing a nicer side to everyone. I doubted it. Then Carolyn asked me why Vanessa wasn't around much lately, and while I would never tell her story, I did let Carolyn know that Vanessa was working every free minute she had, trying to sock away money so that she could move out right after graduation.

After coming out of the bathroom, she stood in front of Andie's sketches. "You know, I think about that old guy in your art class a lot."

"I can understand that. He was pretty hot."

She looked back over her shoulder, smiling. "Jerk. I meant that I think about how fearless he is. All of the models who pose for you... They have no fear or shame."

"Why should they be ashamed? The human body is beautiful, don't you think?"

She moved back towards the couch and sat with her back against the arm again, facing me. "You know what I mean, Jeremy. I would be too self-conscious, I'd feel judged. But I admire them, you know? I wish I was free like that...That I didn't care what everyone else thought."

"Well," I said, attempting to lighten the mood, "when you grow a pair of cojones, I'll let Chuck know. My fellow artists would be thrilled to see you walking through the door in your robe."

She raised her eyebrows and smiled. "Not happening." She cocked her head to the side. "I'd love to see some of your sketches, though. Would you show me?"

I was literally saved by the bell. First, I'd have to find a sketchbook that didn't have at least one creepy, stalker-like drawing of Carolyn in it—that would be tough. Hell, I think I had one devoted *entirely* to her. "Sure," I said absently as I went to grab cash out of a drawer, "someday."

After I paid the delivery guy, I flopped back onto the couch beside her and we dug in. A few minutes later, with cheese dripping from her chin, she asked, "Why didn't you speak to me, Jeremy? Why did you act like you didn't know me?"

I leaned over and wiped her chin with a napkin, buying myself some time. "When exactly are you referring to?"

"I know, right?" she teased. "There were so many different times you ignored me. Let's start with junior year. You remembered me, right?"

"I did remember you but I was kind of hoping that you'd forgotten me. Let's face it, before I left school I'd physically assaulted you *and* punched a teacher within the span of forty-eight hours. Not exactly my finest moment."

"Fair enough. How about this past September? Why did you ignore me after we came back to school?"

I took my time chewing. We were wading into muddy waters. "Um, I just...Things were different once we got back to school."

"So different that you couldn't say hello?" When I didn't answer right away, she asked, "Was it because you were looking to hook up with Samantha?"

"What?" I shook my head, disgusted by the thought. "I was never into Samantha. That girl...She's nothing but a cock tease."

I tossed her a can of soda and then popped mine open, wrestling with whether or not I should share more. "Some of these girls are so...forward, you know? Samantha would think nothing of groping my junk at parties or whispering crude crap in my ear. She's no different than a horny guy."

That struck Carolyn as funny. "Samantha wanted to know if the rumors Taylor was spreading about you were true."

"What rumors?"

She shook her head as her cheeks reddened. "Nothing."

I slid the pizza box out of her grasp as she reached for another slice. "Tell me or you starve."

She blew out an exasperated breath. "Don't make me say it, Jeremy. Just put it this way, it's something *every* guy wants a reputation for."

She went to reach for the pizza again but I blocked her hand. "Not good enough, Carolyn."

She fell back against the couch cushions and covered her eyes with her forearm as she mumbled, "Taylor said you were huge, okay? Satisfied now?"

I laughed as I slid the pizza box back towards her. Carolyn scowled at me as she grabbed a slice and then angrily took a bite. A minute later, she pressed on. "You never answered my question. Why did you treat me so badly?"

I turned away from her, staring straight ahead at the wall, focusing my gaze on Miles Davis. "I'm sorry for that. It's just that when we got back to school you were with Drew again, and seeing the two of you together…Talking to you felt wrong, that's all."

"Why?"

"You just fit together, you and Drew. That's what I thought at the time. He's Joe Popular, on his way to high places, and you're…I don't know, the perfect girl."

In response to that, she dropped her slice back into the box and then rocked forward holding her face in her hands.

"What's the matter? What did I say?"

She wouldn't show me her face until I gently pried her fingers from the tight grasp they held. She was practically clawing at her own skin.

"Hey, talk to me."

She looked up at me, her eyes red and glassy with tears. "I'm not perfect. Drew always calls me that. I'm not perfect, I'm not pure, I'm not even…I'm not a virgin."

"So what?"

"So he thinks I am," she whispered.

I let that sink in for a minute. "Wait, you couldn't date until you were sixteen and you've only dated Drew. So you were never with him?"

"How did you know that I couldn't date until I was sixteen?"

"Locker room talk, nothing really."

"That was a lie anyway." She looked away from me and said, "I made that up so Drew would stop pressuring me."

"Why didn't you just tell him you weren't interested?"

She looked back at me, dead on, her expression both sad and bitter. "Because apparently I'm not very good at saying no."

"So who was it, then?" I reached over and placed my hand on her knee. "Only if you want to talk about it."

She put her hand over mine. Carolyn's touch was soft, but it was like she needed to hold onto someone, to anchor herself, to steel herself for what she was about to say.

She took in a ragged breath, shaky but determined. "It was the summer after freshman year. I was fourteen, nearly fifteen. I'd been going to this summer camp for academically gifted kids since I was ten." She stopped to wipe her nose on a paper napkin and then said, "I really loved it there. The entire school year I'd look forward to going back. And that summer," she cracked a crooked smile, "I was big time—a junior counselor." She uncurled her body and rested back down on the couch, nudging her bare toes underneath my thighs. "The junior and senior counselors had different privileges. We could be out later and we weren't really supervised. It felt so good." She smiled for a moment at the memory.

"There was this senior counselor. He was the one everyone else was drawn to. He was good looking and athletic. Most kids there couldn't throw a ball without looking like a complete spaz, so he was like a star athlete. He was really smart—at least he made everyone else think he was—and he was smooth." She shook her head. "When I think about it now, he wasn't cool, he was only cool by *our* standards. King of the nerds, you know?"

She eased her head back, looking up, immersed in the memory. "He didn't pay any attention to me right away and I would never have expected him to. By the end of the first month, though, I'd catch him staring at me. It made me nervous at first, but then I started to look forward to any little crumb of attention he threw my way. I might be walking back to the cabins with my campers when he'd come along, wrap his arm around my shoulder and walk part of the way with me. Or he'd make a point of calling out to me and giving me a head nod as he passed by. Nothing at first, but by the time six weeks had passed, he was making a point of pulling me aside when all of the counselors were out after hours. He might lean me up against a tree and gently press his body into mine, or just whisper in my ear that he thought I was beautiful."

When she stopped to wipe a stray tear from her cheek, I reached underneath me and pulled her feet onto my lap. She looked at me sadly when she asked, "Isn't that stupid, that I was so desperate to be told I was beautiful?" She didn't wait for my answer. "By the beginning of our last week there, he started laying the bullshit on thick and I fell for every cheesy line. But you know what? There was a part of me that knew—I *knew* he wasn't genuine. But that night he led me out into the woods, I didn't listen to that voice. I felt so mature, so grown up the way he kissed me." She laughed ruefully. "In my head I was already imagining how I'd brag about it to Samantha and Erica. Even Kerri had been kissed before. I always felt like an inexperienced baby in their presence."

I could feel my body getting tense, knowing where she was going with this. I cracked my knuckles and then took her feet again in my hands, rubbing them. She didn't comment on it even though we'd never really touched one another like this before.

"So he's kissing me. I pulled back when he started touching me and leading my hand to touch him. He said, 'You want this, Carolyn, just as much as I do' and just like that," she stopped to snap her fingers, "I clammed up and just went along with it." She bit her lip and shook her head. "We didn't have sex that night but we did a lot. I was so ashamed and upset afterwards. He actually held me as I cried before taking me back to my cabin late that night. He comforted me, so how could I think he was a bad guy, right?

"The next day I was shaking like a leaf, I could barely concentrate. I avoided him but he approached me twice that day. Once to tell me how beautiful I was—I guess he knew that was my kryptonite —and once to tell me he couldn't wait to see me later. I decided I wouldn't go down to the bonfire with the other counselors after bed check that night, but he intercepted me right before I was about to walk into my cabin. He was good, I'll give him that. He acted hurt, like I was rejecting him by not coming along, and told me he was sorry that he'd done one particular thing that had upset me the night before."

She stopped when she felt me squeeze her feet hard. I didn't even realize what I'd done. "Is this too hard to listen to, Jeremy? I'm sorry. I don't even know why I'm spilling all this. I've never said any of this out loud before."

"No," I said, shaking my head to reassure her. "It's just the thought of some asshole forcing you...It makes me want to choke that fucker to death."

"I think that's the worst part, Jeremy."

"What is?"

"That he *didn't* force me."

Carolyn cried for a minute, and I let her before reaching over and dragging her next to me so that I could hug her. She sat next to me then, curled up, her head resting on my chest.

"He promised me he'd make it better that night. He told me he wanted to make me his. He was going to miss me so much. He was going away to college and was afraid he'd never see me again.

"I knew I should have stopped it right then, but I didn't. I took his hand when he offered it, and I followed him like some mindless mute, you know? He didn't waste any time that night. He started off kissing me but within two minutes he had my shorts pushed down around my knees. He *asked* me, Jeremy. He *asked* me first but it felt more like a command. 'You want this, right? You want me?' That's what he kept repeating while he was...fucking me."

"Fuck," I practically blew out, shaking my head. I let go of her and pulled at my hair with both hands. I wanted to hurt someone in that moment. "He was going to college! He was probably eighteen, Carolyn. He raped you."

She was comforting me then, rubbing my back. "He was wrong. He was a bastard, I know that." She leaned back against the couch cushions again, thinking, more composed. "What upsets me the most is that I didn't tell him to stop. He was hurting me and I was silent. Why didn't I stop him? Why didn't I *tell* him to stop?"

"Because you were *fourteen* and he was eighteen. And seventeen or eighteen, his age is irrelevant, Carolyn. He was *so* fucking wrong. You can't tell me that you gave consent. I don't care if you said nothing or if you nodded your head and went along. Any *normal* guy would know you were too young, or that you were scared or uncomfortable."

"It was all part of a game."

"What?"

"It was a game for him. The day all the parents came for pick up, I was waiting with my campers and he was standing off to the side with a group of his buddies. They were all slapping his back and laughing with him. His last name is Henley and a few of them were calling him Hat Trick Henley. I heard one of them ask, 'Which lovely young maiden gave you the hat trick?' I looked up to see him gesturing towards me. Apparently I was the third girl he'd deflowered that summer."

"What's his first name?"

"Does it matter?" When I shrugged my shoulders, she said, "If it's all the same, I'd rather never say it or hear it spoken again."

"He's a fucking pig, Carolyn. Someone should have made him pay for what he did."

"I know that, and I'll never forgive him for what he did to me. But whether it makes sense to you or not, I do feel like I bear some of the blame. I'm still working on trying to forgive myself, you know?"

I took her by both shoulders and looked her in the eye. "You bear *no* blame. You *have* to know that."

"Jeremy," she said, smiling weakly, "I'm working on it."

Chapter Nine

CAROLYN

It took a few days for Jeremy and me to get back to our normal. While I was walking around feeling light and unburdened, now he looked as if he was shouldering my pain. But I didn't feel the pain as much anymore. Telling him freed me. To tell someone who didn't judge me or see me differently afterwards brought me peace. I told him all that as he sat across from me in the library on Tuesday afternoon.

"I just want to know one thing, Carolyn. All this time, why didn't you ever tell Drew?"

I said the first thing that came into my head, "Because I don't trust him." And in that moment, it was as if I'd untangled a mangled mass of feelings and everything became clear.

It was the first week of February and I'd come to the decision that I was going to break up with Drew. The day I was planning to talk to him, though, was the same day he received a letter from the Naval Academy telling him he'd been wait-listed. So not only was he not granted early admission, he wasn't accepted outright from the general pool of applicants. This was not a good sign. He showed up at my house at around eleven that night, drunk, and cried in my arms as he described his father's reaction—his father's abject disappointment.

The days that followed were tense. I couldn't comfort Drew. He was angry and sullen. If I suggested anything, any alternate plan, he'd bite back, telling me I didn't understand.

What made things even more uncomfortable was my acceptance into not only Yale, but Georgetown, Columbia and UPenn as well.

"I guess it doesn't matter if you pick Georgetown after all. I won't be in Annapolis anyway so do what you want."

His resentment hung in the air every time we were together.

After about two weeks of the angry young man routine, I was fed up. After being told for the umpteenth time that I didn't understand, I snapped, "You know what, Drew? I *don't* understand. You're acting like you have no options. You've been accepted elsewhere. You've been accepted to *Princeton*! And your father is acting like an absolute ass! He should be proud to have a son like you. Anyone else on the planet would be proud of you, but nothing is good enough for Senior Petty Officer Oliver. You *both* act like it's all or nothing."

He leveled me with a menacing look. "Don't *ever* talk about my father that way. You don't know shit about him or about what he's been through, all right?"

His words and his tone stung. I let out a deep breath and spoke quietly. "I just hate how he makes you feel...Like you're a failure, Drew. You're *not* a failure."

He scoffed. "Everything's easy for you. You hardly even study and you earn straight A's. You pick some major based on a whim. Something that I can guarantee won't earn you any *real* money. But who cares? What does it matter?"

"What the hell are you even talking about?"

"*You* have the luxury of saying it will all work out. No one has any expectations of you besides graduating from a top school, marrying a good guy and raising a family."

"That's insulting. Are you stuck in the nineteen fifties or something? I have high expectations for myself that go far beyond being someone's wife and popping out a few of his babies!" I shook my head in disbelief. "I cannot even believe we're having this conversation."

We didn't speak for two days. When he called on the third day to apologize and to tell me his good news, that he'd been accepted at Annapolis, it was too late. The damage had been done, and really, I'd made my decision long ago.

"I'm so happy for you, Drew, I really am."

"My parents are taking me out tomorrow night to celebrate. My grandparents are coming also. I want you there next to me."

I took a deep breath in an effort to shore myself up, to prepare for his reaction to what I was about to say. "I'm so relieved you got in. I know how much you wanted this. I wish you all the very best, I do. And my decision really has nothing to do with our argument. I'm just...changing. I'm different and I don't think we belong together anymore."

What followed was three days of being bombarded by phone calls, visits and flowers. We rehashed the same conversation over and over. I asked him to tell me what it was that he loved about me. I tried to tell him that he loved this *idea* of me—not the real me. When he brought up the prom, I felt like a horrible person.

"I can't imagine being there with anyone else, Carolyn."

I almost told him we should just go together, but I held back. That was nearly three months away. I couldn't pretend, couldn't wait any longer.

I like to think of myself as a moral person. I'd never intentionally hurt another person and I would never cheat. But really, wasn't what I'd been playing at these past several months as bad as cheating? I cared deeply for Drew but my heart beat for someone else entirely. If there is such a thing as one true love, I believed with a conviction that grew stronger every day that Jeremy was that person for me.

A few days later, I heard Drew got trashed drunk and went home from a party with Lara. Samantha called me first thing Sunday morning to relay the juicy gossip. I'm sure she loved every minute of that conversation, even as she tried her best to act the part of concerned and supportive friend.

* * *

JEREMY

Weeks passed with me and Carolyn continuing this dance around one another.

I could see things had gone sour between Carolyn and Drew. Her confiding in me as we sat in the library one day after school only confirmed what I'd already figured out on my own. Was I happy about the break-up? Yes and no. Yes because it meant that I finally had a chance with her. But no, because I had this feeling deep in my gut that it wouldn't work. *We* couldn't work.

Me and Carolyn? It was too much to hope for.

She made me hope, though. Every time she laughed at something I said, every time she touched my hand, every time I caught her staring at me...I dreamt of it, I hoped.

"Why don't you just nail her already?"

Vanessa just had a nasty outlook on life in general lately.

"Pardon?" I teased, attempting to get her to lighten up.

"You fucking drool over her. She better be worth it. She better deserve you. If you're letting some spoiled princess lead you around by your dick, Jeremy, then that's just sad."

"Carolyn said that you hate her. I guess she was right."

"Hate her? I don't give two shits about her. I just don't want her messing with your head. And you, dumbass, where exactly do you see this going? What happens to you when Madame Curie sets off to college?"

"I'm not with her, Vanessa. Drop it."

It was no use being mad at Vanessa. It would be like kicking a three-legged cat. She wasn't angry at Carolyn, she was just angry in general.

Life was pretty bad at Vanessa's house. Her mother had a new loser of a boyfriend, one who made no secret of leering at Vanessa and giving her his unsolicited advice on how to snag a man. "Shouldn't be a problem with a tight little body like that, young lady." She imitated him, pressing a raisin over one of her front teeth to emulate his toothless, seedy grin. I laughed at her imitation, but really, that shit was *not* funny. When I begged her to just stay with me for a while, she declined. Her mother was a lousy parent, Vanessa acknowledged that, but she still felt protective over her. She didn't trust that this asshole wouldn't beat on her mother—she'd seen enough to suspect he was a nasty drunk. So she stayed. And if Vanessa needed to participate in some verbal lashing out to deal with her fury, then so be it.

I was angry, though, because Vanessa was saying some things out loud that had been gnawing at me a lot lately. Was I good enough for Carolyn? She was going to college and probably graduate school after that. I assumed that one day she would be Carolyn Harris, Ph.D.

It wasn't that I was down on myself—I had a good, solid plan for my future. I just didn't know if Carolyn was the type of girl who could ever *really* be happy with a blue collar guy. I knew that she wanted me, that she cared about me. I felt it, but I just didn't really trust in it.

So even after Carolyn told me they broke up, that they were officially done, I didn't dive right in. No one was using me—never again.

* * *

CAROLYN

It was subtle, but I could feel the animosity rolling off Erica and Samantha.

"What were you thinking breaking up with Drew?" they'd ask, insinuating in their own endearing way that I'd never do any better. "What did he do?" Erica pressed, fishing for details. My explanations didn't satisfy them.

There had been this obvious, yet barely perceptible shift within our group. Erica, who'd always been outspoken and the only one of us who'd dare to put Samantha in her place, now seemed to have taken on the role of Samantha's closest confidant. I felt like a third wheel in their presence. I even felt like I'd lost that close bond with Kerri. I was no longer in on the group texts to meet after school for a trip to the mall. "C'mon, Carolyn, you *hate* the mall," Samantha would shoot back, clearly bored when I'd call her out. I did hate the mall but I hated the feeling of being friendless even more. I wasn't imagining it—the way they'd stop talking mid-conversation as I approached and the lukewarm reception I'd get when I suggested we do something.

I was being frozen out.

Samantha plopped down at the lunch table Friday afternoon. "My father asked me last night which color I like best, red or black. Do you know what that means?"

"He wants you to play checkers with him?" Kerri teased.

Samantha picked a grape from Erica's tray and tossed it playfully at Kerri. Boy, she was in a good mood.

"It *means* that he wants to know what color car I want."

I was baffled. "But I love your car. You want a new one?"

Samantha was gifted a beautiful navy blue Audi coupe for her seventeenth birthday. It wasn't even a year old yet. My parents didn't exactly drive junkers, but they weren't car people and they were very careful and practical about money. I understood the whole argument about fancy cars being a waste, a depreciable asset, blah, blah, blah. But in the middle of February, sliding into Samantha's heated leather passenger seat was *nice*.

She looked my way for less than a nanosecond. "I'm going to be *eighteen*," she said, shaking her head as if she was repeating something obvious to a toddler. Then Samantha directed her attention back to the others. I was being dismissed again. "And," she said, excitedly, "I'm sure he's thinking I'll need a convertible because I just found out I got into Miami!"

"Oh my God!" Erica gasped as she grabbed Samantha's hands in her own.

Wow, they've bonded, I thought bitterly. Wasn't this the girl who gave Samantha a smack down about only being able to get into a community college a few months ago?

I piped up, despite having to fight past the lump in my throat. "Congratulations, Samantha." I *was* happy for her. Getting into Miami was an accomplishment. That was definitely a reach school for her. "I bet you're going to love it there."

"What's not to love?" Kerri asked, smiling at Samantha. "Sun, beach, a tan year-round. Michigan is sounding pretty crappy right about now."

"So come with," Samantha cooed, smiling at Kerri. "We could be roomies!"

"Right, my parents would freak. They met at Michigan, so I will attend Michigan and meet my husband there as well." Smiling, Kerri raised her hand to her forehead in a crisp salute. "And on that note, I've gotta run. I've gotta print out my English paper." As he shoved a thumb drive into her front pocket, she looked to Samantha. "When are you sending out your invites?"

"Yeah," I chimed in, trying to be enthusiastic and supportive. "The big birthday is two weeks from today."

Pitiful and weak. Worming my way back in, desperate for my "best friend" to like me again. I felt like a loser.

"I'm just sending a text invite. And I'm letting it be known that it's *not* to be forwarded or shared. If I don't invite you, do *not* come. The last party I had was ridiculous."

With the mention of that last disastrous party, Kerri's face fell and she left to go to the computer lab.

Erica nodded. "Totally. Some of the people who showed up from school...I just felt like asking them, 'Who *are* you?' This should be more intimate. Just the people we hang out with."

"I agree," Samantha answered. Then she looked pointedly at me. "What are we going to do about you and Drew that night?"

"What do you mean?"

She sighed loudly. "I *mean*, there's not going to be like a hundred people there so you can avoid one another. There's probably going to be no more than thirty or forty. Are you going to make it awkward?"

"Am *I* going to make it awkward? Would you rather I didn't come?" My mouth was probably gaping open as I waited for her to respond.

She inspected her flawless manicure, buying herself some time, although I can't imagine she actually felt bad about cutting me loose. "Of course I want you there, Carolyn, but I don't want Drew to feel bad. Can you blame me? The poor guy is heartbroken."

"The *poor* guy has received blowjobs from no less than two different girls in the past week and a half. I think he's surviving."

Erica's face twisted. "You can't blame him, Carolyn. You *dumped* him. And who can fault him for getting some after spending the last year and a half with you, the last virgin on Earth?"

I looked back and forth between the two of them. "Are either one of you my friend? It doesn't really feel like it from where I'm standing."

"Come on, Carolyn," Samantha said on an exasperated breath. "Of course we're friends and of course you are coming to my party. It wouldn't be March fourteenth without you. I don't think I've had one birthday when you weren't there helping me to blow out my candles. Just don't get all emotional if Drew is with someone else, ok? It's bound to happen."

Samantha shot Erica a look, as if to silence her before she spoke. Then Samantha looked back to me. "Now *please*, let's just talk about something else. I'm *so* bored."

Jeremy came up to me after lunch, looking all chipper. He reached into his backpack and pulled out a paper. "Mrs. Quinn gave the quizzes back at the end of class. Check it out, I got a hundred! I don't even need you anymore."

When I didn't respond, Jeremy rubbed my upper arm. "Earth to Carolyn. Hey, what's wrong?"

Apparently no one needs me.

"Carolyn," he said, louder this time.

I felt like a powder keg ready to blow. "What, Jeremy?"

"Did something happen? Was it Drew?"

And I felt so, so sad at the same time. "I'm fine, really. Just...it's been a weird day, that's all."

He eyed me skeptically as he folded the test paper and tucked it back into his pocket. "I'm not going to that senior athletic awards dinner thing. I really wasn't into it, and I promised Vanessa I'd help her with something tonight. Are you going?"

"No."

"You're not?"

"No," I repeated, my tone clipped.

"Oh-kay," he said, drawing out the word.

"I don't want to see Drew. I don't want to see any of them."

"Are you sure you're all right? I can tell Vanessa I'll help her out tomorrow."

"No, go help *Vanessa*." I dragged her name out and paired it with a face that I'm sure was pretty ugly and fifth grade juvenile for that matter.

"I thought you were over that. What have you got against Vanessa?"

"Oh, nothing," I bit out sarcastically. "She just pretty much snarls at me every time I see her."

"That's just her way. Believe me, she has nothing against you."

"Like I care?" I shot him a glare. "Samantha? Erica? People I thought were my friends? Even Kerri. Kerri and I used to talk on the phone at least three times a day. This past week we talk only if *I* call her. Even she's backing away from me...Just because I'm not part of the perfect little couple anymore." I shook my head. "I'll be gone soon, far away from here."

He took a step back. "Yeah, you'll be gone."

I knew what I was doing. I was taking everything out on him. All of it: the sadness of being rejected by girls I thought were my friends, the loneliness that washed over me every day when I retreated to my isolated corner of the library, and the forlorn feeling I had—the fear really—that Jeremy didn't want me.

Weeks had passed since I'd broken up with Drew, and Jeremy still hadn't made a move. Nothing had changed. He treated me the same but I couldn't help but feel abandoned. He was the only one who knew everything, the only one who really knew me. And I craved his attention, his nearness, his warmth. The fact that he wasn't making any sort of move to claim me, well, it made me fretful and...furious.

"What do you care if I'm gone? You're like the Invisible Man lately. You don't come over on Sundays anymore...You hardly even talk to me. I think telling you everything about that summer was one big ass mistake." I pushed hard at his chest. "Do I disgust you now, Jeremy? Not so interested now that I've tarnished your picture of sweet, innocent Carolyn Harris? Thanks for that, asshole," I spat as I pushed him again.

Jeremy dragged me into an empty classroom across the hall,

towering over me as he backed me against the wall, caging me in with his hands. "Hardly ever talk to you? Are you kidding me? I've been giving you space, sweetheart," he hissed. "You think it's been easy for me? You told me all that shit and then the next *day* I had to watch you walking through the hallways hand in hand with Drew. I had to watch him *kiss* you at lunch! What the hell? I don't know where I fit into all this." He shook his head. "Are you really that self-centered?"

I hung my head and fought back the urge to cry. *Please don't you leave me too*, I silently pleaded. After a minute, I muttered, "I'm so sorry."

He lifted my chin with his finger. "You could *never* disgust me. I'll *never* back away from you. *Listen* to me. I'll *never* not want you. I know you don't like the word, but you *are* perfect to me, Carolyn."

"You...You want to be with me?"

He kissed my lips once. "Always have and always will."

Jeremy came by that night at around ten-thirty, after he finished helping Vanessa do whatever it was she needed to do. After what Jeremy said to me today, I didn't feel the need for a status update on his relationship with Vanessa. I did trust him and Lord knows I needed a friend.

"I'm sorry, is it too late? Will your parents be pissed?"

"Are you kidding? Aside from me, this house shuts down at nine-thirty, no matter what day of the week it is. Unfortunately, that means they all wake up at six, no matter what day it is."

"How are you doing?" he asked as I ushered him down to the basement.

"I'm better now."

"Me too," he said, squeezing my hand as I pulled him down next to me on the couch. "But I wanna know how you're really doing. What's Drew been like about the whole thing?"

"You would know better than me. He hasn't spoken to me in

two weeks. He passes by me in the hallways like he doesn't even know me."

"He's been drinking a lot."

"And hooking up a lot from what I hear."

"Does that bother you?"

I thought about it for a minute. "Yes and no. In a way, I'm relieved. If he's with someone else then he can't lay that burden of sadness at my feet. But I think it will sting when he moves on, when I see him with his arms around someone else. I don't want him, though. Does that make sense?"

"Yeah, I guess."

"I was looking at the calendar today. It's so weird thinking that we're going to graduate in exactly three months."

"I can't wait" he said.

"I guess I'm looking forward to it."

"Did you make any decisions yet?"

"It's between Yale and UPenn. I'm leaning towards Yale."

I looked up at him, hoping he understood that I was trying to tell him I would be here, that I'd be around.

"New Haven, huh?"

"Forty-five minutes away."

"I think I could make that drive occasionally."

"Occasionally? You're a real prince," I said, scooting my butt a few feet away from him on the couch.

"Would you want me there?" he asked, effortlessly drawing me back and plopping me onto his lap.

I felt shy and exposed. "You know I would."

"How would I know that, Carolyn?" he asked, nuzzling my neck.

"You know I've wanted you since that first day at the lake...For way longer than that, really."

"I wanted you too. I thought about you pretty much every day. I had a vision of you in that blue checkered bikini. That's my favorite, by the way."

"Oh yeah?"

"*Oh* yeah," he murmured, nodding his head before he brought his lips up to mine and kissed me.

Never in my life was I kissed like this. He took my bottom lip just between his and then his tongue licked and pressed its way in to meet mine. Jeremy was a *good* kisser. Like, so good he could give doctoral level classes on the subject.

After what was probably only a few minutes but felt like a life-time—a life*line*—he pulled back and looked at me smiling, tender and gentle. "Now that right there? That was the best kiss of my life."

"Ditto," I breathed, drugged with longing for this boy.

That night—that *kiss*—was the beginning of one of the happiest times in my young life. But little did I know I was standing on a precipice.

I was about to descend into a nightmare.

<h1 style="text-align:center">Chapter Ten</h1>

CAROLYN

Happiness.

When everything is good. When someone you care about looks back at you with eyes that say: You're special to me, I want to be wherever you are, I want you.

He looked at me that way.

Jeremy: Come over?

Me: Sounds like a tempting offer

Jeremy: Let me sweeten the pot. I'll even cook for u

Me: Say wha?

Jeremy: student, artist, chef...I'm multi-faceted

Me: multi-talented

Jeremy: In ways you can't even imagine

Me: *sigh* maybe someday I'll get to do more than imagine

Jeremy: Do u like meat?

Me: Um...are we talking about dinner :/

Jeremy: Mind out of the gutter Harris

Me: The answer is YES

Jeremy: Down girl. See you in an hour?

Me: Yes

"Wow, it actually smells great in here. I'm impressed."

"Thanks, although that was a back-handed compliment."

"I didn't mean to doubt you, Jeremy, it's just that I don't know too many people our age who can cook. I can bake a mean brownie, but that's about the extent of my culinary prowess."

"I love when you talk those big, dirty words to me," he said as he tilted a spoon to my lips, urging me to taste.

I think I actually moaned when I tasted the wine reduction. It was better than anything my father had ever concocted, and I thought he was a seriously talented cook.

"This is *sooo* good. What are you making?"

"Nope," he said, placing the lid back onto the pan before I could sneak a look. "Five more minutes. Help me out and set the table."

"So this is like a fully separate apartment," I said as I opened drawers and cabinets, retrieving plates, glasses and utensils.

"Yeah, it is. I usually eat downstairs with my dad, though. The kitchen on the main floor is like three times the size of this box," he said, gesturing around the small but functional space.

"So you'll stay here after graduation?"

"Yeah, I have my privacy and everything here. I'm in no rush to get out and I need to sock away as much money as I can for the next two years. Going out on my own—that's my plan—means I have to be able to purchase equipment, trucks, all that stuff. I've been researching small business loans and how to establish credit and everything, but I want to have as much cash as possible on hand."

"Sounds like you've got everything all mapped out."

"Not really, but I know what direction I want to head in." I must have been staring absently in that moment because he tapped my nose and said, "Did you go somewhere just then?"

I smiled, shaking my head. "I was just thinking that you're pretty amazing."

"Yeah?" he asked, looking uncertain. "You think that what I'm going to do is good enough, even if I won't have a degree and all?"

"Of course! I admire people who own their own businesses. And I know you'll be successful, Jeremy."

"You think?"

"I know." I moved closer to him, positioning myself between him and the range top. I slid my arms up around his neck and kissed him once, softly. I wanted him to know, without any doubt, that I believed in him. "I know you *could* tackle college and get your degree, but if it truly isn't something you want to do, then you shouldn't. I just hope you're not choosing a path because you think you *can't* do it, you know?"

"I'm not. I mean, college classes would be a bitch and I know I'd struggle, but it's not that. It's just...I'm impatient. I feel older than most people my age. Hanging out at keg parties isn't appealing to me. I want to work, I want to earn a living, I want to...get started. Do you understand?"

He looked expectant. It was like he needed me to reassure him and alleviate the doubts that were plaguing him. I pulled him closer and whispered against his lips before I kissed him again, "I understand you. I do."

"Dammit woman, you're gonna make me burn the couscous!" he shouted, laughing as he gently pushed me aside and turned the burners off.

I touched my finger to my lips, tracing the swollen but satisfied flesh. *That* was a kiss. "I don't care if my couscous is burned, that was worth it."

"It was."

. . .

That weekend we were in our own little bubble. I was at his place again on Sunday, getting spanked in some football video game that I could hardly focus on.

"You're cheating," I whined when he scored yet another touchdown.

He paused the game and looked at me, eyes wide, mouth agape. "Thems fighting words. No one calls me a cheater and lives to tell about it."

"Oooh, I'm shaking with fear," I deadpanned.

"You should be." He took the controller from my hand and tossed it onto the floor with his. "Now you're gonna pay." He clasped both of my wrists in one of his hands and then slowly lifted them over my head. He shifted to sit beside me as he reclined me back into the couch cushions. "Now don't move," he commanded. "I'm going to let go of your wrists but do *not* move." When he looked down at me I felt content in a way that I never had before. "You're so beautiful, Carolyn." He began tracing a finger down my temple, to my chin and down my neck, stopping at the base. "I mean, you are so, so beautiful." His finger grazed my collarbone, slowly moving from one side to the other. My pulse rate sped up, my nipples were tight and the ache between my legs was closing in on unbearable. I think he could sense it, how much I wanted him to touch me. He continued his light touch, just one finger brushing down the valley between my breasts, down to the waistband on my jeans and back up again. He swallowed and then whispered, "We're gonna take our time, Carolyn."

"I trust you."

"I know you do."

He leaned down then and kissed me, pressing his broad, defined chest against mine. Later that night, I'd lie in bed reliving that kiss as I touched myself, imagining what it would be like to feel Jeremy in that way, inside of me. There was no fear, like there had been with *him*, and there was no reluctance like there was when Drew and I seemed to be heading in that direction. No, when I thought of Jeremy in that way, there was only a rush of want and need.

* * *

JEREMY

What I didn't tell Carolyn was that I wasn't willing to go any further down this road until she was mine. Really and truly mine. Until we were out in the open, there would be kisses—seriously body-rocking kisses—but nothing more. She was cute, though, begging me with her eyes and those sweet little sounds she made when I kissed her. I loved kissing her. I couldn't get enough and holding back was killing me, but I had an untapped reserve of self-control when it came to Carolyn.

It wasn't just the reassurance of being a full-on couple that I needed, I was also holding back because I wanted everything to be good for her, to be right. There was no getting around what happened to Carolyn that summer. For her, I wanted there to be a slow build-up to something great.

Looking at her, hands clasped above her head, hair fanned out around her, eyes clear and wanting me—I knew I'd never see a sight more beautiful than her. When she asked me later that afternoon if maybe I'd sketch her someday, I thought to myself that I'd already committed that earlier pose to memory, and as soon as I dropped her off that night I'd be transferring that memory to canvas.

Every day after school that week, she was at my place or I was in her room. I'd never been happier.

At school, though, I laid low. We laid low.

I'd sit in class daydreaming about the hours ahead. She made a cup of tea every day after school and I found that adorable. I pretty much thought everything she did, said or wore was freaking fantastic. I'd imagine her standing at the counter, as she did, dipping the teabag in and out of the cup slowly. I'd walk up behind her and place my hands on the counter, caging her in. I'd kiss her neck, exposed when she wore her hair in a ponytail. Her head would lean back against me and I'd trail my lips up and down her neck. She'd push her hips back into me, her breath quickening with mine. In reality I didn't go any further, but sitting in class my mind would take us all the way. When the bell rang, I'd have to take a moment to regain my sanity and some semblance of control over my lower body before I stood up.

On Thursday night I caved.

"All right, stop begging. I'll sketch you."

I laughed to myself, thinking this would probably be the hundredth time Carolyn was the subject of my art.

I dragged a counter stool to the middle of the room and turned on a lamp situated a few feet away. When she sat on the stool, I smiled. The lamp cast a warm glow on her skin. Perfect. Her hair was down, the loose waves reaching the middle of her back. She was wearing a black tank top and yoga pants.

"Now you're going to sit facing the window, but I want your shoulder tilted back towards me a bit. Like this," I said as I positioned her. "No whining, Carolyn. It can get tedious, sitting in one position."

She looked back to me with a sultry pout, batting her eyelashes. "No whining, Picasso. Got it."

Fuck, this girl is going to be the death of me, I thought as I went into my room to get my supplies. When I came out a minute later, Carolyn was perched on the stool facing away from me, wearing nothing but a pair of white cotton, low-riding hipsters. No, the white cotton thing didn't make them look innocent at all—they were tiny.

"What the hell, Carolyn?" I asked, dropping my shit on the couch as I grabbed an afghan to throw over her shoulders. "I didn't mean you had to strip!"

She waited a moment and then cleared her throat. "I know I'll never be fearless enough to bare it all like your models do, but I want you to draw me, Jeremy. I want you to *see* me."

"I don't know if I'm ready for this."

She looked to me, pleading, and the afghan slid off one shoulder as she turned, exposing her creamy skin. "Come on. Just pretend you're in class and I'm a model who came to pose. Pretend it's just another Tuesday."

"Yeah, that's not gonna work."

She turned her head defiantly and assumed the pose I'd dictated before. She let the afghan fall to the floor, exposing nearly all of her. My dick hardened immediately but I retrieved my gear from the couch, not even stopping to adjust myself or ease that ache in any way. I shook my head and then got to work setting up the easel and laying out my charcoals.

"What are you thinking about?" she asked when we were fifteen minutes in.

I shrugged. "I'm a guy. I was just thinking that your tits are pretty sweet." She blushed and looked down at herself. "Are you checking yourself out right now, Harris? I like it."

"I'm not checking myself out," she said, embarrassed.

"How are you doing? Still ok with this?"

"I'm good," she answered, nodding to reassure me. "This isn't as difficult as I thought it would be, you know?"

"Good."

"I actually feel kind of powerful right now. Like I'm wielding some sort of power over you."

"I am completely at your mercy right now."

"Ask me what I'm thinking about."

Deep breath. As I made sweeping strokes, I obeyed. "What are you thinking about?"

"I was thinking about you kissing me. Except this time you don't stop at my mouth. You kiss me everywhere."

"Well fuck, if you keep talking this drawing is gonna go to shit." I put the charcoal down and shook out my fingers. "You're making my hands shake with talk like that."

"Sorry," she said, giggling.

"One day I will do that, Carolyn."

"Promises, promises," she teased, but then we eased back into a comfortable silence as I worked.

About an hour in, I could see she was getting uncomfortable, shifting her weight from one hip to the other. I *really* didn't want to stop. I could tell this was some of my best work; it was more life-like and emotional than anything else I'd ever done. I'd just worked on the lips, and they looked to me as if Carolyn was mid-sentence, saying something evocative, maybe even something suggestive. She was my goddess, my muse.

But it was late.

"Hey, it's getting late."

"I can keep going," she reassured me.

"No, we're good. I have what I need."

I turned the canvas around when she craned her neck, trying to sneak a peek. "No. Can't see it until it's done. I'm serious."

"All right," she pouted as I grabbed the afghan, draping it back over her shoulders. Then I kissed the soft curve of her neck.

"Thank you," she whispered.

"I think that was a gift to me, angel."

Carolyn nudged one of my hands so that the afghan slid off one shoulder, then slowly led that hand to her breast. God, I had ached, physically ached to touch her this way. Holding back had been the right thing to do, but now? Now I just didn't seem to have it in me. She made a breathy sound that made my dick harden to steel as my fingers traced the curve of her breast. She twisted on the stool so that she was facing me and I was standing between her open thighs. We were lined up so that her body was pressed up against mine.

She whispered my name, a plea. "Please don't stop now, Jeremy."

I could barely get the words out when I said, "Hold onto me," as

I lifted her and carried her to the couch. She straddled my lap, her sweet, round breasts right at the level of my mouth. Oh, what I wanted to do to her in that moment. I wanted to lick, kiss and suck every inch of skin that covered her. I wanted to sink inside of her, make this girl mine.

She shifted a little, which made her tits bounce just slightly, and no sooner was the zipper of my jeans digging in. Carolyn gently pressed her mouth to mine and whispered between kisses, "Make me yours, Jeremy, please."

CAROLYN

"Rumor has it that you're single, Harris."

I was at my locker early Friday morning and he was too close, standing less than a foot away from me.

"Why would you care one way or the other, Chase?"

"Always wanted to get to know you better, I guess. I don't think anyone at Westerly *really* knows you, do they, Carolyn?"

I turned and faced off with him. "You might want to get to know me, but I have *no* desire to know you better. Go creep out some other lucky girl."

He ignored me and said, "I met a friend of yours last week." As he spoke, he did a slow perusal of my body, lingering on my chest for an extra beat. The way he looked at me made my skin crawl.

I turned my back on him to slam my locker closed. He moved closer and pressed his body up against mine as he whispered in my ear, "Haven't you heard, Harris? I'm a sought after lacrosse recruit. I was being wooed by Duke just this past weekend." The mention of *that* school had me frozen in place. "I liked it there," he cooed. "I had a great guy showing me around, Greg Henley. Turns out, he knows you. He had lots of really nice things to say about you, Carolyn."

"Get away from me, Chase."

He chuckled, obviously pleased with himself. "I'll see you at the party tonight, Harris," he said as he sauntered away.

I ran to the closest bathroom and up came everything I ate for breakfast. I sat through my morning classes like a zombie. I didn't go to the lunchroom, which probably pleased everyone. They didn't have to choose sides today. I'm sure my *friends* were relieved they could sit with Drew and the boys again.

My run-in with Chase made the decision to skip Samantha's party a no-brainer. She didn't want me there anyway. When I dropped a present off at her house that afternoon Samantha pouted, acting sad when I told her I was going to skip. Sporting a frown, she cocked her head to the side. "I'm bummed you won't be here, but I do think you're doing the right thing."

Samantha was *so* not bummed. She motioned zipping her lip to me when her mother said, "See you tonight, Carolyn." That would have been all sorts of awkward. Mrs. Cavanaugh was like a second mother to me and would have flipped if she knew Samantha was more than good with me missing her party.

I wasn't planning on sitting home alone by myself moping, though. I would be seeing Jeremy later that night.

I'd been floating on air since that night he sketched me. He didn't take things far, showing that same damned restraint I was coming to despise, but he did shower me with kisses, gentle touches and words that made me feel more cherished and loved than I ever had.

But now when I thought of Jeremy? Now I was scared.

I wanted to tell Jeremy. I wanted someone to help me, to protect me from this shit storm that I knew was brewing. I was fairly certain that Chase wouldn't be satisfied until he made me suffer. He was like that. He was cruel. I knew, though, that Jeremy couldn't protect me. Jeremy had gotten into a scuffle with one of his obnoxious teammates during a practice last year. I heard through the grapevine that Jeremy was informed, in no uncertain terms, that he would be "out on his ass" if there were any incidents even remotely resembling an assault. If Jeremy knew what Chase was saying to me, he would go after him. It's just how he was.

I wasn't about to risk Jeremy being thrown out of school a few months shy of graduation because of me.

I couldn't tell him the truth this time.

"I'm good," I lied when Jeremy asked how everything went between me and Samantha. "I dropped a present off for her earlier and she acted disappointed when I told her I wasn't coming to her party tonight."

"Maybe she is missing you."

I shook my head. "She's not. I'm pretty much on the outs with all of them. I'm not going to act all tough girl and say I don't care because I do care. It hurts."

"I never got it. She messes with you, cuts you down. It's fairly obvious that she's jealous of you."

I snorted. "No, I'm pretty sure she's one of the most confident girls on the planet."

"It's all an act. She's jealous, angel. Samantha cuts other people down to feel better about herself. She always did, even when we were kids."

"I remember once, back in fifth grade, she told me you liked that girl Mindy. I was so pissed. Even back then I didn't want to think about you with anyone else."

"Aw," he kissed my nose. "That's cute."

I shook my head, sad again. "I'm mad at myself for tolerating her put-downs for so long. And it's hard because I have so many good memories with Samantha. It hurts to believe that she doesn't want what's best for me, you know?"

"Not every friendship is meant to last a lifetime. Only the true ones are." He paused to wipe a tear from under my eye. "Now come here."

Jeremy eased me back onto the couch in my basement and kissed me as his body covered mine. His arms flexed with the effort it took to keep himself raised above me, but I didn't want any space. I ran my hands down his back and stopped at the lower curve, urging his hips closer. He pulled his face back a few inches and kept his eyes fixed on mine as he lowered his hips to my body. I couldn't help but raise my hips up to press against him. I think I actually moaned when I felt him, hard and rigid, the jeans we both wore doing nothing to lessen the feeling.

"Slow down."

"I'm trying," I said as I pulled his face down to kiss him, my body rising again to meet his. I wanted to lose myself in him. I wanted to touch him and I wanted him to touch me.

"I want you, Carolyn, so much that it's killing me to stop."

"Don't stop," I pleaded. I felt frustrated and foolish. Wasn't it the guy who usually pushed to go further and the girl who begged off?

"I've got to, angel."

He sat up then and took me with him so that I sat straddling him. I let out a breath and rested my forehead against his as he rubbed circles on my back. Those feelings of frustration ebbed, replaced by gratitude. Jeremy cared deeply for me. I knew that and was thankful for it.

I knew he was holding back for my sake but also for his own. Something he said a few nights ago came to mind—something about needing everyone to know. It was my idea to keep what we had private. I was afraid of the backlash, afraid of the judgement and afraid of hurting Drew. Jeremy wasn't forcing my hand at all, but by keeping us a secret, I now realized I was hurting him. And my horrible encounter with Chase had brought all those horrible memories from that summer to the surface again too, so I was a mess.

"I wish you could have been my first, Jeremy."

He kissed me softly. "I wish you were mine, too. You were the first girl for me, though. I think you've had a piece of my heart since I was twelve."

Even though I knew it wasn't a true declaration of love, his words made me feel safe and did make me feel loved. I thought of Jeremy as a boy and remembered the hours I spent daydreaming—a silly little girl hung up on a boy. I was still hung up on him. The thought made me smile.

"Well, I've got you beat then. I've pretty much been dreaming about our wedding since fifth grade...Ever since you came to my rescue that day."

"I wonder what ever happened to Trent."

"He's at Exeter or some other arrogant ass-in-training prep school. He left after eighth grade."

"Chase Sterling reminds me of Trent."

I stiffened at the sound of his name. "Yeah," I muttered. Jeremy didn't cue in to my unease.

"Fifth grade," he said, his lips curving up slightly. "I used to love listening to you read back then, Carolyn. You had the sweetest voice."

I smiled but my eyes were sad, imagining Jeremy sitting in class, too big for that desk, struggling. "I wish it hadn't been so hard for you. It kills me to think of what you went through. And all that time, I never knew that you'd lost your mother so young. I didn't know."

"Yeah, I think those early years would have gone a lot smoother for me if she was around."

"What was she like?"

"She was pretty and really kind," he said, smiling up at me. "You remind me of her, I guess because the clearest memory I have of my mother is her reading to me or teaching me."

"I saw the picture at your place, the one of you on her lap and your dad with his arms wrapped around her. They looked like they were so in love."

"I guess so, if my dad falling apart after she died was any indication of that. I think he found it really hard to go on without her. He does have a girlfriend now, though." He laughed. "It only took him little over a decade."

"Yeah?"

"That's part of the reason I moved to the bachelor pad upstairs. When she comes over...I mean she's really nice and all, but it just feels cramped."

"I thought you moved up there so you could bring your women home," I teased. After a moment I worked up the nerve and asked, "Have there been a lot? I mean, I won't judge. I really have no right to even ask you that."

"What kind of bullshit is that? Of course you have the right to ask me." He kissed my forehead and then leaned back, settling in. "There have been a few...Three in total. No one I'd call special. Most times I felt like I was either being used or using them. I'm not gonna lie, physically it was good for me...But there's an emptiness to that, you know?"

"Can I ask who your first was?"

"Taylor."

I burned with jealousy at the sound of her name, but then surprise took over. "Just last year? *She* was your first?"

He shrugged his shoulders. "Yeah, I'm not as worldly as you think I am."

"What was it like with her?"

He reached up with one hand, twisting his fingers gently through my hair, looking far off. "She was experienced and I wasn't. I mean it was good, but with Taylor...With every girl I've been with, really...They were all...It's hard to explain except to say that I missed out on that young lover experience." He smiled shyly. "You know what I mean? Two people who take it slow and kind of discover all of that good stuff together? I was never in love with Taylor, Willow, Beth—"

I cut him off. "Enough." I put a finger in each ear. "I don't want to know their names."

"It's always been you, Carolyn." He looked at me, uncertain. "I know it sounds pathetic, but I was fixated on you...All that time when you were with Drew. I almost can't believe that I have you now, that you're mine."

I regretted every minute I spent with Drew. "I wish I'd been yours all along." I kissed him and said, "I'm yours, Jeremy. I want everything with you."

I woke up that next morning, blissed out on thoughts of Jeremy, his kisses, and the sweet words he said to me. That contented feeling was short-lived though, as a paralyzing sense of fear crept over me.

Chase was at Samantha's party last night. Did he tell everyone my secret? I booted up my laptop and went onto Samantha's page. Of course she already had loads of pictures up. Samantha surrounded by a gaggle of well-wishers. She managed to have one snapped as she sat in Will's lap. That one made me laugh because Will was looking over his shoulder, clearly uncomfortable. She probably timed it, plopping into his lap the moment before Erica snapped the photo. There was another with Samantha on Chase's shoulders, the both of them laughing. The comments gave nothing away—the party was epic, love ya, happy birthday—nothing alluded to me. I let out a breath. When I went to Erica's page, my stomach dropped. Her page announced her new profile picture, one where she was sitting in Drew's lap, his arms wrapped around her waist, the two of them smiling at one another. Her relationship status read: So far, so good.

What. The. Fuck?

I picked up the phone and called Kerri. It was early, too early. Kerri sounded groggy and then annoyed. "What's so important that you needed to wake me up at eight in the morning on a Saturday?"

"I'm sorry, Kerri."

"Is this about Erica?"

"Yeah. Is she with him?"

She hesitated. "What did you see?"

"A post on her page. A picture of her and Drew looking cozy. I'm not jealous, Kerri, I just need to know."

"You're not?" Kerri asked, sounding as if she didn't truly believe me.

"No. I just feel betrayed. Samantha, Erica...Even you. I feel like you've all dropped me."

"I haven't!" she said defensively. "It's just hard, Carolyn. Will has been telling me how messed up Drew is over this whole thing. I just feel bad for him." She added quickly, "I'm still your friend."

"Will has been confiding in you? Since when?" I challenged.

That was my bad. I knew how she felt about Will and now her back was up.

"What, is that so unbelievable? Will Clarke couldn't possibly be interested in me, right?" She let out a huff. "You know what, Carolyn? I've been the *only* person defending you. What a joke."

"Kerri, wait. I'm sorry. I didn't mean that. I'm just...I feel like I'm all alone lately."

I sounded pathetic to my own ears.

"You're not alone. Yeah, Samantha and Erica are fair weathered friends, they always were, but you know I'll always be your friend, Carolyn."

"I know. I'm sorry I acted like a jerk."

"Me too."

"So how was the party, really?"

"Samantha was the belle of the ball. I think I posed for one picture with her and then she pretty much didn't even know I was there. For some reason she's all besties with Lara lately."

"Sharing blow job tips, maybe?" We both laughed. "So if Samantha didn't get her hooks into Will and Jeremy wasn't there, who was the lucky guy?"

"How did you know Jeremy wasn't there?"

"I saw him yesterday. He said he wasn't going." I left out the part about him being at my house, making out with me in my basement.

She gasped then, as if she'd just remembered something really important. "Holy crap! How's this for weird? Chase was asking about you. He wanted to know where you were and he wanted my advice on asking you to the prom."

My stomach sank. "I'd rather drink bleach."

"That's what I thought. What would even make him think about you that way? I'm not saying anything negative about you, Carolyn. I'm just saying that it's weird, right? He's Drew's teammate and he *knows* Drew is a hot mess right now. Why would he do that?"

Why would Chase do it? To inflict pain and suffering on someone—on me.

I wanted to change the subject, change it to anything other than Chase. "I really hate hearing that Drew isn't doing well. I care about him. I just don't want to be with him. I shouldn't be angry with Erica. If she makes him happy then that's what's important."

Kerri snorted. "Erica make Drew happy? Come. On. The only reason he's willing to let Erica grind in his lap in public is so that it will get back to you. Will told me he cries over you, Carolyn. Actual freaking tears! He feels like he lost the love of his life and he feels like a failure. He's drinking every night."

"It's so hard to believe that. When I see him in school he acts as if he doesn't even know me. He's so cold. I think he hates me."

"Hate and love...There's a fine line, right?"

"Should I talk to him?"

"I think I would if I were in your shoes."

On Monday morning I looked for Drew at his locker. No luck. I contemplated looking for him in the lunchroom but decided against it. I was still avoiding that scene. When I saw him leaning against his car after the last period bell, I decided to bite the bullet.

"Got a minute?"

He looked at me with cold indifference. "Got all day."

I shook my head. "Look, Drew, I just wanted to talk, to see how you're doing. You act like you don't know me anymore and that's ok...Whatever you need to do. We're not together but I still care about you. I always will."

His laugh was mocking and hateful. "Who are you kidding? You wouldn't care if I put a bullet through my head."

I fell back a step, stunned. "How could you say something like that?"

"Just calling it as I see it," he said, shrugging.

"I want only good things for you, Drew."

"Walk away, Carolyn," he said, making a condescending shooing motion with his hand. "I'm not interested in this bullshit sympathy routine."

I did walk away, and felt positively broken as I made my way back into school with my head down. My locker was right by the entrance and I needed to grab my physics notes. I would have gone without had I noticed who was waiting for me, but by then it was too late.

"What was that, Carolyn? Attempting a reconciliation?"

Erica's look was threatening. Samantha was standing behind her sporting a look that said: *What? I'm innocent here. I have no idea what's going on.*

I opened my locker, trying to look bored and unaffected when I shot back, "Rest easy, Erica. I was not looking to get back with *my* boyfriend, the person *I* dated for over a year. You know, the one *you* had no problem digging your claws into?"

"He came after me, sweetheart, not the other way around."

I slammed my locker shut and faced off with her. "So then be with him. I hope you make each other happy. Take that back...I hope you make *him* happy. I don't really give a shit about how you feel, Erica."

Samantha gasped. "Carolyn, is that really fair?"

"Excuse me?"

"I mean..." She looked back and forth between me and Erica.

I felt like saying: *Come on, honey, we all know whose side you're on.* This act, the faithful friend playing the role of mediator? It was a pathetic farce.

"I'm just saying, Erica didn't cause this, you did. You can't be mad at her for comforting Drew when he needed it."

I threw my head back, frustrated and just *so* done. "Why don't we just quit pretending we're friends?" I looked back to Samantha, stared at her, took her in for a moment before letting it all out. "You don't like me, admit it. And I don't like you. There, I said it."

Samantha affected her best hurt look as Erica's mouth dropped open. Erica looked like a stupid fish for a moment but recovered quickly.

"I told you, Samantha," she said as she put an arm around her shoulder, "it's all an act. Underneath it all, she's an icy, cold bitch."

I was shaking after the two of them walked away. I stood there for a while, waiting as the students cleared out and the hallways took on a deserted feel. It was official, I'd succeeded in completely alienating myself. Kerri wasn't even a sure thing. Once she got wind of this latest fiasco, she'd have to pick sides. Even though she said we'd be friends forever, I wasn't counting on it.

"What's up, baby?" He pressed his hips into my back suggestively. My skin went clammy and cold in an instant.

"Stay away from me, Chase."

"Stay away from my girl?" he teased.

"Are you delusional? I'll never be your girl."

I tried to get him to back off by throwing my shoulder into him, but he gripped my hips tight and leaned in to tug on my earlobe with his teeth. He whispered, "Hat Trick Henley. Remember him?"

I turned quickly and pushed him back with every ounce of strength I had. "Are you threatening me, Chase? I have to get with you or else you'll tell everyone about your sick friend? His hat trick? Three young girls he practically raped?"

He furrowed his brow and touched his index finger to his chin, lost in deep thought—a real fucking sadistic philosopher. "Three girls? Greg never mentioned that. He only spoke fondly of *you*, Harris. The hat trick was the three different ways he had you."

I was momentarily confused and then I froze. Chase reached down and thrust his hand up, hard and swift, cupping me roughly between my legs before releasing his hand.

"I have to say, Harris, at first I didn't think you had it in you. But I actually *can* picture you, bent over begging, taking it in that sweet ass. I've beaten off to that image every night this week."

I reached up to smack his face but he was faster and stronger. He grabbed my wrist, pressed his face in close and crushed his lips against mine. He pushed me back a few seconds later, so that my back hit the lockers. Then Chase turned and sauntered out the double doors, even having the nerve to whistle a tune—not a care in the world. I dragged the back of my hand across my mouth as I attempted to catch my breath.

When I looked up, I saw someone standing at the other end of the otherwise deserted hallway. Great. He was making his way towards me now. Double great. It was Will Clarke.

Could this day get any worse?

"What's up, Carolyn?" he asked cautiously.

I just shook my head and looked down. I couldn't face him. Chase had succeeded—I was now wracked with shame.

"Are you all right? I was far away, but from way back there it looked like you were kissing Chase Sterling." He cocked his head to the side, legitimately puzzled. "But I can't believe you'd do that. Is he bothering you?"

I snapped at Will, "I can handle it and I was *not* kissing him, ok? All I need is for Drew to hear that."

"I won't say anything to Drew. He's got enough shit to deal with as it is."

I looked up to the ceiling, shaking my head, fighting back tears. "It's all me, right? I'm the evil bitch who broke up with him."

He gently took me by the shoulders. "No one thinks that, Carolyn. I don't think that. I'm not gonna sugar coat it for you...I mean, he's been miserable since you broke up with him. But it's not just that...It's his father and all the pressure he's putting on Drew. It's too much."

"His dad should be happy." I was confused. "Drew got in."

Will shook his head. "Mr. Oliver's an asshole, but there's no telling Drew that. Drew got in but his dad hasn't stopped reminding him that he didn't get in on his own merit...That he didn't really earn it. Calls had to be made," he said in a ridiculously stern voice, mimicking Drew's father, "favors had to be called in."

"I feel terrible. He won't even talk to me."

"He can't right now. He's too hurt, too angry." Will tipped his head, gesturing in the direction Chase had gone. "If you need my help with anything, Carolyn, please ask. Just because you're not with Drew anymore doesn't mean that I'm not your friend."

I lowered my head and nodded. He was too good. Again I wanted to break down and spill everything. Scream to someone: *Please help me!* Instead I said, "I'm fine, Will, really."

I was so not fine.

"Hey," he greeted me shyly as I opened my door. Jeremy looked at me with a mixture of reverence, intimacy and still, some measure of uncertainty. I looked at him with longing.

When I was alone with Jeremy I could almost believe it would all be okay. That Chase and his threats didn't exist. I could forget for a while, imagine that it was just us and that everything would be fine.

I looked back to the kitchen where my mom was cooking and called out, "Mom, Jeremy's here. We're going to study."

I took his hand and led him upstairs to my room.

"So how was your Monday? I didn't see you all day."

My stomach quivered as my mind drifted back to school, feeling degraded and abused at the hands of Chase. Feeling powerless when he grabbed at my crotch and then laughed in my face. Feeling just like I did as a fourteen year old girl without a voice.

I wanted to tell Jeremy it was quite possibly one of the worst days of my life, but I didn't. I tucked it all away and willed myself to be in this moment with him, with this boy who made me feel so very safe and happy.

Pretending felt better than my reality.

"My Monday is getting better and better," I said as I pulled him down onto my bed with me.

"Hey, what's the rush?" he whispered, brushing my hair back from my face.

"I just missed you today."

"I missed you too."

He ran his hand across my jaw and then leaned in to kiss me. I melted into his kiss. He felt so good and he kissed me in a way that made my entire body spark with need. He laid his body over mine, and through his thin warm-up pants I could feel him growing long and hard. I rolled my hips, needing him closer, needing friction.

"Carolyn," Jeremy murmured, "you feel....Damn, you feel so good."

I licked and nipped his lower lip as I lifted my hips up again to grind against him, which elicited another rumbling groan from his chest. I was sliding my hand down between us then, desperate to touch him, when I realized we weren't alone.

"Hi, Jeremy! I didn't know you were coming for din—" Thomas

stopped chirping abruptly as he took in the scene. His eyes darted from me to Jeremy, back and forth. Jeremy jumped up off my bed and I sat up, cheeks flushed—busted. Thomas's faced morphed from horrified to confused to happy. "Is Jeremy your boyfriend?"

I looked over to Jeremy, who was now sitting upright on my bed, a pillow pressed over his lap. I suppressed a laugh. "Um, yeah, are you my boyfriend?"

He looked at me and then to Thomas, grinning. "Yep, I'm her boyfriend."

Chapter Twelve

JEREMY

Something was off. I parked my bike in my usual spot and cut the engine, but sat there for a minute feeling unsettled. And when I finally walked into school that Wednesday morning, the feeling intensified.

"What's up, stranger?"

I hugged Vanessa. "What's up with you?"

She clung to me an extra moment and I squeezed her back before looking down at her. She didn't look right.

"What's going on? Is that asshole bothering you again?"

She blew out a tired breath. "Same shit, different day." When I went to speak, she held up her hand to silence me. "I can't leave, so don't ask. Not that I don't appreciate the offer, Jeremy, I do."

"What happened?"

"I walked in from work last night and Bruce was shitfaced, nothing new. I went straight to my room and locked the door behind me." She looked up at me and said, "That creepy fuck was standing over my bed staring at me one night last week, so now I lock my door."

"And you won't leave, Vanessa?" I was pissed.

She looked up at the ceiling as she spoke, ignoring me. "They started arguing. I heard my mother comment on the fact that the cable bill was enormous because *someone* was ordering porn every day. Prince Charming retorts that if he could get his dick sucked more than once a month then maybe he wouldn't have to order the damn porn." She let out a laugh when she said, "Yes, I officially live in White Trash Nation." Her look turned serious again. "He slapped her, Jeremy. God, it was such a loud, cracking sound. I ran out there and my mother's holding her cheek, crying, and he's screaming, 'Look what you made me do, you stupid bitch!' I didn't yell, Jeremy. I didn't hit him, throw anything at him. I just stared at my mother, like, stupidly trying to convey some message to her without words. This is who you want to be with, Mom? This is who you *want*?"

"What did he do?"

"After a minute, he turned on me. 'Get back in your room,' he's screaming. I started laughing at him, the kind of laughing where you can barely catch your breath. I don't even know why. That pissed him off even more. 'What the fuck are you laughing at, Vanessa?' That made me laugh even harder, Jeremy. I don't know what came over me because usually when he says my name it makes my skin crawl. He raised his hand like he was gonna slap me but then he stopped for some reason. I don't know where it came from, but I just stopped laughing and said, 'That's right, motherfucker, you don't *touch* me. And if I find out you hit *her* again, I'm gonna make sure that *you* get beaten to within an inch of your life.' He stood there with his mouth hanging open for a minute. Then he just turned to my mother, kissed her, whispered something in her ear and they left together. He went from raging lunatic to loving boyfriend within a minute. And she fell for it. She falls for it *every* fucking time."

"Have you talked to your mother since then?"

"Nope. They slept in. I heard them stumble in together at around three this morning. Two drunken lovebirds, whispering 'I love you, baby' to one another as they crashed into every wall in the apartment on the way to their bedroom. Apparently, it's all good."

"And you feel some duty to stay there be—"

"Because if I wasn't there last night he would have done more than slap her once, Jeremy. That's why." She looked up to me pleading. "I love you for caring, but in this case you can't swoop in and make everything right, ok? Sometimes I just need you to listen."

I nodded my head as I ran my hand through her hair and then kissed her forehead. "All right, Vanessa. You know the offer always stands, though."

She had her hands on my chest, fisted in my shirt as she nodded against me. I heard her take in a deep breath then, trying to shake it all off. She stepped back and punched my arm. "You just want me there to cook and clean for your lazy ass."

"That wouldn't suck," I teased.

Frank and Vince approached then. After being interrogated about why I'd been missing in action lately, we agreed to meet at lunch.

I'd been making it to the cafeteria no more than once a week the past month. Carolyn was never there and I really didn't like spending time around Drew or anyone else in that crew lately. Watching Erica and Samantha comfort Drew was sickening. And even if Drew didn't know exactly what was going on between me and Carolyn, I felt his animosity. I'm not into kicking a guy when he's down, but if he asked, he was going to hear the truth.

I understood Carolyn's point, I did, but I was not keeping us a secret for much longer. She didn't want to rub Drew's nose in it, especially now, when he was walking around all dog-faced and hurt. I was tempted to tell Carolyn that his pain was bullshit—that he'd fucked around behind her back so he didn't deserve her concern. I held back, though. She had to want me for me. Didn't want to be some consolation prize when she found out what Drew had been up to.

Tonight I was alone. Carolyn said she couldn't get together because she had something to do with Thomas. We spent just about every other afternoon together these past few weeks, so I wouldn't have thought anything of it, except for her voice. There was something off.

I just could not shake the feeling that something was very wrong.

* * *

CAROLYN

"Hi, Carolyn."

There was no menacing edge to the voice but there was still no mistaking it was Chase.

I was sitting in my Calculus classroom preparing for a test next period. I had lunch this period, but no, I hadn't stepped foot into the cafeteria since my run in with Erica and Samantha on Monday. And no, Kerri had not reached out to me once since then.

When he approached, I'd been staring absently at the same section of my notes for probably ten or fifteen minutes. Lately, my ability to concentrate was lacking.

"What do you want, Chase?"

"I want to start over. I want to apologize for the way I acted last week."

"You've suddenly developed a conscience? That's rich."

He pulled a chair over and sat directly in front of me. "You may not be my biggest fan, but I really do like you as a person. I always have." Wow, he was laying it on thick, acting all sincere and concerned. "All that Greg Henley bullshit aside, I think you're a good girl. I'd never hold that against you."

A good girl? I cringed at those words and at hearing that bastard's name.

"Now that you're not with Drew, I really hope that you'll give me a chance. I think I went about everything all wrong, though, and I really do want to apologize."

"You think you went about it all wrong? You think?" I was shaking with rage and also a good measure of fear. Chase was intimidating, even when he was trying to act all sensitive male.

"I did, and I'll make it up to you. I want you to be my date for the prom, Carolyn."

Did this arrogant ass think he was bestowing some sort of gift upon me right now? I'm pretty certain my expression was alternating between bewildered and disgusted. His expression turned from expectant to offended as the seconds ticked by with no verbal response from me.

"Did you hear me? I just asked you to be my date for the senior prom."

I clasped my shaking hands together in my lap. I wanted to appear calm and self-assured even though I felt anything but.

"I'm not going to the prom with you, Chase."

"Let me guess, you're hoping that loser, Jeremy, is going to ask you?" He laughed cruelly in response to the way I flinched. "Yeah, I see the way you look at him. Guess you want a chance to ride him just like every other girl in this school." He leaned his face in close. "Is that it, Harris? Got some bad boy fantasies you want to play out?" When I didn't answer, he asked, "Or do you *actually* like him? Have you fallen for your special-ed charity case?" he mocked. A smile overtook his face. "I get it. You feel bad for the poor bastard. Can't read, can't write and you feel sympathetic towards a guy who you *know* is probably going to be fixing cars or flipping burgers, making minimum wage for the rest of his life." He took my chin in his hand then, forcing me to look at him. His voice took on its normal, hard edge. "But that's slumming, Harris.

You *don't* want to slum. And you don't want to be the back-up when he's already nailing that white trash slut on the side, do you?" Now he was back to his commiserating friend-voice. "Yeah, I hate to break it to you, but he's been fucking Vanessa steady since last year. Still is to this day." I shook my head and he said in response, "You hear a lot of guys' personal shit in the weight room, Harris."

I pushed my chair back and stood. He stood and took my shoulders firmly. "So no, Carolyn, you won't be wasting your time with Rivers. And you won't be crawling back to Drew, who also fucked around behind your back. You did know *that*, didn't you?"

"You're a liar."

He chuckled, as if he was explaining something to a simpleton. "Let me break it down for you, sweetness. Did you think he was cool with drawing blue balls all that time? No, babe. Feeling you up once a week didn't do it for Drew. He got his kicks here and there with Lara and," he dragged his words out for effect, "even hooked up with one of your besties, Erica."

"I already *know* he's with Erica now."

"Hate to be the one to clue you in, but he cheated on you all along. A certain rowdy party at Samantha's house last fall? I saw them, Drew looking all covert and shit, eyes darting every which way to see if anyone noticed as he led her into one of the upstairs bedrooms. Erica giggling as she trailed behind, that stupid slut."

I'm sure my face was a shade of ghostly white. Was it true? Drew was too honorable to cheat, wasn't he? And my so-called friends? Lying to me all along? A sick feeling of dread filled my belly when I thought back to how I'd sensed something had been up after that party. My thoughts darted to Jeremy then. What about him? Had Jeremy been with Vanessa? I mean, I'd suspected as much. I couldn't be upset over that, though, I reasoned. I had a boyfriend at the time. But he still obviously felt a connection to her now. What did it mean?

"You h-h-have to go," I stammered weakly as my classmates started to file into the classroom.

"You've got until tomorrow, Carolyn." He raised my chin roughly to his again. "I want an answer."

I sat back down and tried to compose myself as a few classmates eyed me curiously. I had to hold my shaking hands in my lap again until I managed to regain some control.

I handed in my test with half of it left blank. I texted Jeremy with some pretense about not seeing him today and then I walked out of school, skipping my last two periods. At the time, I would have rated that Wednesday the worst day ever.

Turns out, it wasn't even close.

Thursday before lunch I saw Samantha and Kerri waiting for me by my locker. I stopped a few feet away, paused, and then pushed forward, feeling so very drained. Kerri greeted me uncomfortably, "Hey," and in return, I managed only a feeble, "Hi." I was utterly at a loss for words. I felt weak in their presence and just so, so tired. I was awake most of last night, mulling over everything Chase had laid at my feet.

Kerri smiled at me sympathetically while Samantha averted her gaze, either uncomfortable or annoyed. Hard to tell.

Samantha spoke first. "Look, I don't know why I feel *any* loyalty towards you anymore, but I do." She cocked her head, smirking. "I know you think this thing you and Jeremy have going on is some big secret, but it's not."

Kerri reached out and took Samantha's forearm gently. "Carolyn, we've been friends for a long time and we don't want you making some big mistake. Not one of us," she said, gesturing between herself and Samantha, "wants to see you get hurt."

One of us. She was making it crystal clear that I was no longer a part of *us* where they were concerned. And I was okay with that now.

After all, if what Chase said was true, they were all in on Drew's deception.

"What's your point, Kerri?" I asked dryly.

Her hurt expression had no effect on me. I was pretty much done here. Samantha piped up. "*Our* point is that you need to take off your blinders where Jeremy's concerned. I'm sending you a picture. It was taken yesterday, by the way." She turned to Kerri now, who was looking at me sadly but with a faint trace of guilt in her expression. "Let's go, Kerri. This is total bullshit. I don't know why I'm even bothering."

They walked away, Samantha tapping into her phone. A moment later I heard the chirp of an incoming text. The picture had a message underneath it: *He's making a fool out of you.*

I studied the picture. It was taken very recently, as evidenced by the full sleeve of tattoos that now covered one of Vanessa's arms. She was leaning into Jeremy, her fists clutching the front of his shirt. I felt a surge of jealousy as I noted the mere centimeters that separated their bodies. His hands were cradling her face, fingers woven into her hair as he laid a kiss on her forehead. The pose wasn't carnal—I mean they weren't lip-locked or groping one another, but it was *intimate*, so intimate. It was exactly the way he held me, with what I thought was reverence, care and...love.

I made my way to an empty classroom to hide away. I stared at the picture, reassuring myself that it meant nothing. It could be easily explained. I shot Jeremy a quick text, knowing he was at lunch: *I need to talk to you.*

A moment later my phone chirped but it wasn't Jeremy.

Chase: I'd like an answer.
I ignored him
Chase: Now.
Me: I'm not going to the prom with you.
Chase: I'd reconsider if I were you.

Me: I've made up my mind.

Chase: Then get ready to suffer the consequences, bitch.

His last line hit me like an eighteen wheeler. Big, fat, ugly tears welled in my eyes before spilling over. My phone pinged again. It was Samantha. Another picture of Jeremy and Vanessa, this one shot from behind as they walked together, hand in hand, in what looked like the school parking lot. Again, Vanessa's newest batch of tattoos was visible, proving that this had been shot within the week. It didn't prove anything but it burned.

I took the phone and hurled it against the wall with force, watching as it connected and small pieces of plastic chipped off and scattered. I walked over and bent down to retrieve it, screen cracked beyond repair, hazy gray and white lines darting across its surface. I tossed it into my bag, and as I sat in the quiet of the empty classroom for those few remaining minutes, I was relieved to be out of everyone's reach for a while.

I sat through the next two periods in a daze. As I took my seat in AP European History, my last class of the day, I saw Jeremy peering in the door's window, looking as if he'd raced to try and catch me before the bell rang.

Too late, I thought bitterly, breaking our gaze and looking back down at my notebook.

We were sitting in groups of four, working on our last project of the year. I really hated group projects, as I always seemed to take on the bulk of the work. This one was no exception, as the two boys in the group were happy to let me and Tori basically complete the entire thing. I was glad to be working with Tori, though. She was smart and shouldered responsibilities with me. Happier still because even though I'd only considered her an acquaintance up until now, she was one of the few people in the "it" crowd who still spoke to me and treated me with some measure of civility. Those people were becoming more few and far between.

Twenty minutes into class, hushed gasps and low laughter seemed to overtake the room. At first I thought nothing of it, but then it became more widespread and louder. When the two boys in our group looked up at me in unison, wide-eyed and smirking, my heart sank into my shoes.

Chase.

Chase had threatened to ruin me and now he was making good on his promise.

Every eye in the room was on me. Tori looked down to her phone, which had pinged about twenty times within the last minute. A moment later she looked to me, horrified, and grabbed my hand. I felt stiff as a cold sweat swept over my body. "Grab your stuff," she whispered in an urgent tone. She murmured something to the teacher along the lines that I was sick. When the classroom door closed behind us and we were out in the empty hallway, she began chanting what sounded like a soothing mantra, "You're okay, Carolyn. I'm going to get you outta here. Everything's gonna be ok."

I followed along mute, nearly catatonic. I let her lead me out the door, across the parking lot and into her car. She even fastened my seatbelt for me. Then she drove. She drove past my house, past Main Street, and kept going until we were clearly out of town. She pulled off to the side of the road where there was an overlook. We sat in the parked car, both of us looking straight ahead for a few minutes.

"Let me see it," I finally said, devoid of emotion.

The message read:

Good girl or hot little piece of ass? You decide.

Attached was a picture of a naked girl bent over, being taken from behind. Her head had been photo-shopped, replaced with a picture of me, smiling happily. I opened the car door and vomited on the asphalt.

Tori gave me tissues and water.

"Let me see it again."

This time I saw there was also a link to a video. It looked as if it was being shot without Greg Henley's knowledge. As if someone—Chase—was holding the phone in his hand while aiming it at Greg, whose face would shift in and out of the frame. Didn't matter about the picture, really, because the audio was perfect. Greg's words were crystal clear.

Chase said, "I can't believe you were with that little goody-two-shoes, Carolyn Harris."

"Yeah, she was real sweet," Greg said, a sense of nostalgia dripping from his voice. "But not exactly innocent," he added, smirking.

"You were her camp counselor?"

"No, asshole, we were both counselors."

"Oh, right," Chase said. "So what's the Hat Trick Henley name mean, anyway."

"You know," Henley said, pausing to down a shot of some clear liquid. "The hat trick. I had her every which way."

Chase full-on guffawed. "Wait. So *you* are telling *me* that you nailed Carolyn Harris in the *ass*? Are you serious?"

Greg raised his hand as if he was being sworn in for President. "My hand to God."

"Damn, that's hot. I always suspected her A-student, pure as the driven snow-act was bullshit."

"She had a hot little body, even back then," Greg added.

At that point I had to let myself out of the car. I fell onto my knees and threw up again. Tori was right by my side, crying along with me.

"I don't want to tell you it's ok, Carolyn, because it's not. He's the lowest life form there is."

"It's not true, Tori. I didn't do *that*. It's not true."

"I know, honey."

"It doesn't matter if it's true or not, everyone will believe that it is. They'll get off on thinking that it's true."

"Fuck. Them. All. I mean it, Carolyn. Fuck anyone who is that cruel. I've got your back, do you hear me? People will have your back."

It was dark by the time Tori took me home. By then I'd watched the video, in its entirety, four more times. Each time I watched it, I imagined someone else seeing it. I imagined my parents finding out—their horror, their shame. I imagined Drew, disgusted and angry. It was safe to assume he would believe the worst about me. I imagined that Samantha and Erica would act stunned and sorrowful, but in truth they would be bursting with glee, just loving my fall from grace. Lastly, I imagined Jeremy seeing the video.

Jeremy.

Fear twisted its way through my body and took hold.

* * *

JEREMY

My eighth period Spanish class was rowdy to begin with—Senõra Nunez had zero classroom management skills—but today it was downright ridiculous. About halfway through class, the constant low murmur of chitchat and subtle laughter turned into full-on anarchy. Frequent calls of "oh shit" and "damn, baby" were the soundtrack to what felt like a movie rolling in slow motion. Everyone was either laughing or gasping in shocked amusement as they checked their own phones or held the screens out so others could view what was being shown.

My own phone was vibrating in my pocket. As I was reaching for it, Vanessa burst into the classroom, darted towards me, grabbed my hand and led me out into the hallway.

"What the fuck?" I forcefully shrugged her off.

"Don't do anything stupid, all right?"

"Vanessa, what are you talking about?"

"I sent you a picture this morning, a picture of your babe in a compromising position with that asshole, Chase Sterling."

"Yeah, I saw it. That was a shitty move."

"I don't think there's anything to that."

"I *know* there's not."

"I'm a bitch, Jeremy, I am. I wanted you to hate her. But damn, this is bad...This is fucked up."

I let out a frustrated breath. "I have *no* patience for you right now, Vanessa, so say whatever it is you want to say."

"Just don't do anything stupid. I know you care about her but she's not worth wrecking your life over."

With that, Vanessa cued up a video and I took the phone from her so that I could hear the grainy audio. About ten seconds in I knew exactly what I was listening to: Chase chatting up the guy who'd wrecked a part of Carolyn. Henley was just what I'd imagined: a pretentious little prick with a snooty-ass accent. What he said about her? The lies? Made me want to rip him limb from limb. I closed out the video only to see the foul picture and caption, Carolyn's sweet face a cruel joke.

Chase was going to die.

"Jeremy, wait," Vanessa pleaded.

"Take your phone," I said, shucking her off, "and get the fuck out of my way."

I ran back towards Carolyn's class again, Vanessa trailing behind me like an irritating pest. I peered through the window right as the last bell rang. No sign of her. I watched them file out, everyone buzzing, laughing, reveling in her agony. I wanted to choke each and every one of them as they walked out of the room and joined the cacophony of the crowded hallway.

No one noticed me, though. I had no connection to her as far as all of them were concerned. So they didn't censor their crude comments.

"Where's Carolyn Harris? Did she leave class early?"

He answered, laughing, "Back Door Harris? Yeah, she lef—"

He didn't get the last word out before having his head slammed into a locker. "What the fuck did you just call her?"

"Relax, Rivers. Jesus," he muttered, rubbing the back of his head.

I stormed out the doors, heading for my truck. Vanessa ran up and snatched my keys from my hand.

"You need to listen for a minute, Jeremy."

"Give me the fucking keys."

"Why? So you can drive to that asshole's house, beat him to death and then go to jail?" She stuffed the keys down her pants when I went to snatch them back. Vanessa grabbed my forearm and leveled me with her gaze. "Be. Smart. Rivers."

"He deserves what's coming to him."

"Yes, he does. But you need an insurance policy and I have it." Vanessa now had my attention. She gestured to the truck and said, "Get in."

$$Chapter\ Thirteen$$

CAROLYN

I was able to slink into my house that night without attracting much attention, feigning a headache, the need for a quick shower and bed.

Falling into a blissful sleep was not in the cards, though. My stomach was tight with agony as I lie in bed, the covers tucked up tight around my chin. When my mother entered my room, I draped the blanket to cover most of my head so that she couldn't make out the red splotches and swollen eyes that surely marked my face by this point. Her loving touch as she caressed my hair and then laid a kiss on the top of my head nearly broke me. How I wanted—no, *needed* her comfort right now. But no, Mommy could no longer step in and make it all better. I was alone in this.

All alone.

With my phone busted, Jeremy—one of the few people who would still *want* to communicate with me—couldn't reach me. He knew where I lived, though, right? *No, he won't abandon me,* I reassured myself. I believed that deep in my soul. Aside from my family, he was the one person in this world who would have my back.

Wouldn't he? But Samantha's comments, the pictures, that day back at the lake with Vanessa—doubt crept in and took hold.

When I was still lying awake, wide-eyed and fretting at four in the morning, I logged onto my page. My body tensed in fear when I saw the *hundreds* of new friend requests. That couldn't be good. The posted comments indicated that Chase's video was making the rounds. My peers at Darien, Weston, New Canaan and Wilton High Schools were now all in on the joke. Basically all of Fairfield County thought I was a slut.

So I had no intention of going to school that Friday—me, the girl with nearly perfect attendance. I couldn't do it. I couldn't face the biting laughter, the knowing leers, the gossip. I felt weak from lack of sleep, but weaker still from humiliation. It didn't matter that the worst part of Greg Henley's story was an abject lie. Perception was everything. Everyone would believe it, every word—the more sordid the details, the better.

"Tori? Come in, sweetheart. It's so nice to see you."

My mother's voice carried but I could barely make out Tori's words. "Let me see if she's ready," my mother went on. "She was really tuckered out last night. I think she slept twelve hours."

At the sound of the phone ringing, Tori called out, "You grab the phone. I'll go up and get her, Mrs. Harris."

"Hey," she whispered as she sat on my bed and nudged me.

I rolled over. The look on her face told me what I already knew: I was looking pretty wretched.

"I can't go in there, Tori. I'm taking the day."

"I get it…But seriously, Carolyn? Do you think it's going to be better on Monday? Maybe you should just face this head on. Show that asshole that you're not affected by his bullshit." She laughed as she said, "I wouldn't miss today for the world. I was up half the night thinking about the exact words I'll use when I curse Chase out."

The only reason I wanted to go to school was to see Jeremy. To make sure he was all right, that he didn't do something impulsive yesterday—something that would get him expelled. I also needed to know...was he still on my side?

"I don't know, Tori."

"I'll stick by you. Plenty of other people will too, you'll see."

I seriously doubted that last bit, but the need to see Jeremy was strong. So against my better judgement I dragged my ass into the shower.

Exiting the bathroom with wet hair pulled into a messy bun, dressed in gray sweats and a long-sleeved gray tee shirt, I was greeted by a wide-eyed Tori. "Oh, no, no, no," she declared, approaching my closet. "Today you need a power outfit. The way you're dressed now? You look like a puppy just begging to be kicked."

"I just want to be incognito, to blend into the background."

As she sifted through my clothes, pushing hangers along the metal rod noisily, she shook her head. "Nuh, uh. Today you want to wear an outfit that projects confidence. One that says: Don't fuck with me, bitches."

She pulled out my black skinny jeans, a snug, dark raspberry colored turtleneck, and my cropped black leather jacket. The tags were still on the jacket. It was edgy and hip, and although I loved it when I bought it, I never really felt like it was for me. Every time I tried it on with an outfit, it looked all wrong. Like I was a poseur, trying to be someone I wasn't. Carolyn Harris did not wear tight leather jackets. But apparently today, I did.

"Perfect," Tori crowed, laying the items out on the bed. She went back and rummaged through my shoes, pulling out a pair of black, low-heeled ankle booties that looked like cowboy boots.

"Love these. Love the pointy tip." She kicked her foot out like a ninja. "Perfect for damaging a certain particular guy's nut sack."

She wasn't done with me. I was usually a wash-and-go girl on school days, but today I went in with under eye concealer, foundation, blush, mascara and a liberal swipe of raspberry colored gloss on my lips. As I looked in the mirror, I had to admire, albeit indifferently, her skill as a make-over artist. I *almost* looked normal.

Twenty minutes later I reluctantly walked through the doors of Westerly High.

A janitor was furiously scrubbing my locker door as I approached. He was removing the T that completed the word SLUT, the remnants of each letter faded but not totally erased. Underneath, some pig had drawn a penis ensconced between two plump butt cheeks. The janitor hadn't gotten to that yet.

I stood frozen, not listening as Tori whispered empowerment sentiments in my ear. It was early but a few people were already milling about in the halls. Two boys who looked to be freshmen sniggered brazenly as they walked by. A girl I spoke with regularly in AP Calculus lowered her head as she went for her locker, actively avoiding contact with me.

I jumped when I felt a tap on my shoulder. I turned to see Taylor staring at me, expressionless. I assumed she was here to lay into me. To remind me that karma's a bitch. That when you slut shame other girls—as I had indirectly done by standing by passive as those in my group gossiped viciously about her—then you deserved what you got.

"Fuck them all."

"Excuse me?"

"Fuck them all, Carolyn. Hold your head up high and don't give any of those assholes the satisfaction. Own it."

I felt tears in my eyes then as Taylor did the most unexpected thing. She took my hand in hers and raised her chin up just a fraction, in a stance of defiance.

"Come on, let's go to homeroom."

Tori smiled at Taylor and then took her place on my other side. They walked me to class, buffering me from the stares and whispers as the hallways filled with the morning rush.

No sign of Chase.

No sign of Jeremy.

* * *

JEREMY

I winced when my sore knuckles hit the front door.

"Where's Carolyn?"

"Jeremy?"

Mrs. Harris stared at me wide-eyed, startled by my tone and by my appearance. I'd forgotten that my nose was busted and I was probably sporting a black eye. I'd forgotten that my knuckles were bloodied and swollen. And on this nasty, damp March morning, I was sporting only a threadbare t-shirt.

"What's happened to you?"

"I-I'll tell you later. I just need to talk to Carolyn." Fuck, I started to cry. "Where is she?"

It was too much: the shock, the sadness, the fucking grief, fear, confusion—all of it.

"She left already. Tori picked her up early this morning. Please, Jeremy," she pleaded. "Please tell me what's wrong."

I swallowed nervously, my throat feeling so dry and constricted that I barely got the words out. "Drew's dead." Mrs. Harris backed up a few steps, her gaze fixed on my bruised and swollen hands. "No! I mean, Drew, he...It was a gunshot. I don't know what happened." I slumped against the doorjamb as I added, "Will Clarke is dead too."

She gasped, one hand clutching her chest. Then, just like that, Mrs. Harris shifted gears. She moved at a frenzied, frantic pace. She instructed Thomas to finish breakfast and to be ready when the bus pulled up, grabbed her keys, slipped her feet into sneakers, pulled me towards their car and stuffed me into her passenger seat. "Oh my God," she repeated over and over. "Oh my God, my Carolyn."

Chapter Fourteen

CAROLYN

Slut. Bitch. Cunt. Whore.

I thought it couldn't get any worse, but those words? They were terms of endearment compared to what I was now being called.

Murderer.

They wanted me dead. Wanted someone to blame. Wanted someone to pay. Those two beautiful boys. Those two sons, brothers, friends, lovers.

Gone forever.

It was two weeks since my name was announced over the intercom, calling me out of homeroom, summoning me to the principal's office. Two weeks since Jeremy, bloodied and bruised, intercepted me on my way there, my mother in tears trailing behind him. Two weeks since I collapsed in the hallway, wailing in pain. Two weeks since I had to watch Tori's mouth go wide and hear her shrill scream as she was restrained by Mrs. Connolly upon hearing the news that her Will was also dead.

It was one week since I sat home, completely numb, on the day of both Drew's and Will's funeral. Their parents decided that since the two of them were inseparable in life, they would be together as everyone mourned their death.

I was not welcome there. His mother told me exactly that when I went to their home to express my condolences. She looked at me with disdain, with pure hatred. I stood on the stoop as Mrs. Oliver despondently stated, "You left him heartbroken. *You* killed my boy." Those were her parting words before shutting the door in my face.

It was one week since I'd broken down and told my parents everything. They were so confused. Didn't know why the menacing phone calls were coming in, the ones where men who sounded fullgrown said revolting and abhorrent things about their only daughter. They knew everything now.

It had been a few hours since I removed myself from every social media platform. I was told I'd become obsessed. Every day, twenty times a day, I checked. The dedications to Drew and Will on their pages were warm and heartbreaking. There were other comments—theories and assumptions as to what had unhinged Drew, what drove him to it, blind confusion and expressions of overwhelming grief.

I became equally as obsessed with checking the posts on my page. It was self-punishment, pure and simple. I deserved it all: the hatred, the blame, the cruel, brutal, sexually degrading comments. Thanks to Chase's video going viral, it wasn't just my classmates anymore—people of all ages from far and wide were now chiming in as well. The concensus? I was a cum-loving slut who begged for, and deserved, a good ass pounding. I deserved, according to my classmates and other well-wishers, to be bitch-slapped, gang-raped, punched in the face... murdered. I deserved the same fate as Drew and Will. After all, if it hadn't been for me, they would still be here.

You should just kill yourself, one "friend" posted on my page.

That comment got one hundred and twenty-five *likes* within an hour.

My page came down only after Mrs. Connolly paid me a house call. School was closed for juniors and seniors the entire week following their death, but I never returned. Hell, I could barely leave my bed.

The grief was paralyzing. I could scarcely muster up one-word responses to my parents' well-intentioned reassurances and questions. They fretted over me, pleading with me to drink sips of water and to eat a few meager bites at each meal. The food was brought to me. I only left my bed to use the bathroom and to drag my sorry ass into the shower each day to sob in private.

Mrs. Connolly entered my room that day and sat on the edge of my bed. "How are you, my darling?"

The words should have sounded overly familiar and awkward, but coming from her, there was nothing but comfort. There was something about her. Was it her words, her care, her concern, her connection to the place where I'd spent so much of my life with Drew, Will and Jeremy? Whatever it was, the floodgates were officially opened. I wept, struggling to get the words out for over an hour. She held me, comforted me, and gave me a few of the answers I so desperately needed.

"There was no mention of you in the note, Carolyn. It was very brief, a scribbled apology addressed to Will's sister, Anna. I didn't see the note, but the way the detective described it to me led me to believe that this was not something Drew had been planning or contemplating for long."

"How do you know?"

"Besides the note, there was just one quick text to Will. A goodbye of sorts. No true premeditation. I think he was intoxicated and sad in a way that would have been temporary, except that he didn't have to just *think* about killing himself, he also had the means to do it. Did you know there was a full arsenal of weapons in their home?"

"Yes. His father's line of work," I explained tearfully. "Drew trained with his father at the shooting range."

"A permanent solution to a temporary problem. That's what most suicides are. I don't believe Drew would have even followed through with it, if not for the fact that the gun went off in the struggle and Will was killed."

"Will," I said absently.

"Such a wonderful boy," she said, smiling. "Drew as well."

She moved closer to me, making sure she had my full attention. "This is an enormous tragedy, Carolyn, nothing less and nothing more. You are not at fault. I pray that you understand and believe that."

"It *is* my fault. I set it in motion. He knew that I didn't truly love him. I was a phony from the first day he asked me out. I led him to believe I wanted the same future. I strung him along. And I...I never told him everything. I was never honest with him."

"Seventeen, Carolyn. You. Are. Seventeen. It's not supposed to be all planned out already. You're supposed to experience joy, angst, happiness and uncertainty in your relationships. It's supposed to be great and it's supposed to be messy. You're supposed to fall in love, fall out of love and find your way. I know this may sound odd to you, but you're entitled to be the angry one here. In many ways, you've been wronged."

"I'm not dead. I'm not in the ground," I sobbed.

She pulled me close. "I know, but you've been robbed of something that I fear you'll never get back, dear. This can go one of two ways. You can believe the truth, that you are not to blame, or you can beat yourself up, day after day. You can let the hateful comments define you. You can punish yourself for something you had no hand in. I fear that's what you're doing."

"It feels good to make myself hurt, you know?"

I saw alarm flash briefly in her eyes before she regained her composure. "Grief is pain. In this situation, it's devastating. But I want you to let me help you. We need a plan of sorts."

"I'm not coming back to school," I said flatly, bracing myself, ready for her to argue with me.

"I think that's wise."

"What?" I choked out, surprised.

"There are seven weeks of school left. You've already secured acceptance into a number of universities. I think home schooling would be best at this point."

I dragged in a breath. "Do they hate me that much?"

"No," she assured me, shaking her head. "It's not that. I just imagine that sitting in class, concentrating, and yes, dealing with the select few who do not wish you well, would be difficult." She added, "It's also wholly unnecessary. What we need to focus on right now is you. I've been stalking social media and I want the two of us, right now, to take down your page. I have suggested to your parents that you don't expose yourself to the internet at all. It's not a discussion at this point, Carolyn, it's critical to your well-being."

I nodded and dragged my laptop from underneath my bed. I looked once, quickly, my eyes sweeping over the most recent nasty posts, and then went to my settings and removed my page. Mrs. Connolly then held out her hand, gesturing for me to hand over the computer. I did. In truth, I was relieved. I was weary from it. But although I liked the sound of what she was peddling with her affirmations and positive statements, I believed deep in my soul that I deserved every rotten thing that was being said and done to me. I believed that I was, in fact, to blame.

"Your home tutor is going to be coming here every morning from ten to one, paid for by the school district. I've spoken to her and instructed her that you should be doing college preparatory work. I've provided her with appropriate materials. This is pass-fail, Carolyn. No pressure. Do what you can. You *are* graduating and going on to great things. May not seem like that now, but I promise you, it will one day soon. I'm coming back to see you in two weeks. I reminded your mom that college responses are due by May first. No rush, but next time I come, let's talk about that."

She squeezed my hand and got up. Before leaving, she turned back and asked, "Have you spoken with Jeremy Rivers?"

I closed my eyes. "No."

Not since the day it all turned to nothing. The day he cradled me in the school hallway, rocking me as he cried with me and whispered that he loved me.

I was no longer worthy of that love.

I no longer wanted it.

I no longer wanted him.

And after Mrs. Connolly left? I made it a few hours cold turkey before smuggling my brother's old, outdated laptop into my room. I didn't reactivate my page. I didn't need to. My name was everywhere. I lapped it up—a glutton for my own demise.

* * *

JEREMY

Nothing.

Carolyn wouldn't respond to my calls or texts. She wouldn't see me when I came to her house. And her parents—her mother and father looked pale and shaken every time I stopped by. One of them would look through the peek hole in the door before cautiously opening it.

"Please," I practically begged Mrs. Harris one night. "I need to talk to her."

"Jeremy, I think talking to *you* would do her a world of good, but she doesn't want to see you. She won't see anyone."

"Do you tell her? Do you tell her every time I come by?"

186

"I do," she answered, eyes downcast.

I ran my hands through my hair in frustration. "Why?" I asked, knowing I sounded pathetic. "Why is she doing this?"

"It's been..." Mrs. Harris paused and let out a deep breath. I noticed her hands were shaking as she wrung them together. "It's been so difficult. Carolyn is being targeted. I can't even answer my telephone because these people say vile, terribly mean things about my daughter. Mr. Harris's tires were slashed the other night. The house has been egged twice." She was on the verge of tears. "I sent Thomas away to my sister's for two weeks. She lives close to Briarwood and being in this house...It's just not healthy for him to see this."

"She won't answer my calls or my texts."

"Her phone was broken the day before it happened and I haven't replaced it—I won't. I can't even imagine what people are texting her or saying in the voicemails."

"I want to help her."

She took my hand in hers. "I know you care deeply for her, Jeremy. Just give her some time."

I got back on my bike, dejected. I knew I could make it better. I knew if I just had the chance to hold her, comfort her, love her...then I could make it at least a little better.

That first day I went back to school, a full week after I was supposed to return, I almost got myself suspended. Some little prick, a sophomore who didn't know jack shit about this situation, was putting the finishing touches on some artwork on Carolyn's locker. After asking him what the fuck he was doing, I gave him an open-handed slap across the face to humiliate him in front of his adoring onlookers. I followed that up with a punch to his gut that left him reeling, doubled over on the floor and out of breath. I looked up to see that Carolyn's locker was covered in words and sick drawings that the janitor had done a half-assed job of removing.

Two security guards dragged me into the main office and Mrs.

Connolly intercepted on my behalf, once again. When the principal reminded me that assault resulted in expulsion, she went to bat for me, arguing that these were different circumstances and clearly my reaction was borne out of grief.

Did I grieve the loss of Drew and Will? Absolutely. That pre-dawn morning, when Frank told me the news he'd heard from his father, a town cop, I fell to my knees. I'd just gotten home, just exacted my revenge against Chase, and I collapsed from a combination of shock and fatigue.

Did I grieve them? Hell, yes. Did I grieve the loss of Carolyn? I did, with every aching cell in my body.

Just give her some time. I repeated Mrs. Harris's words in my head. I never imagined how long I would have to wait—do nothing but wait for Carolyn.

Chapter Fifteen

CAROLYN

Wash. Rinse. Repeat.

My days were as uneventful as a wash cycle.

The tutor came. I struggled to keep up, even though what she was dishing out was easy. Afterwards, I stayed downstairs and ate lunch with my mother. I knew how it pleased her, and after the shit storm my parents had endured these past few weeks, I felt as if I owed it to them. I heard the sharp thwack as the metal bat connected with the mailbox. Heard the eggs crack against the side of the house. Heard the slurred insults carrying through the night air as tires peeled down our street. For all that, I could manage a few minutes of empty conversation with her each afternoon.

After lunch, I'd nap for a few hours. I couldn't shake the fatigue. My body actually ached, sagging under the weight of this lingering grief and my own self-loathing.

Before dinner, I'd sit out back on the tire swing I hadn't used in years. Back and forth I'd go, thoughts drifting through my consciousness—painful thoughts and happy memories. Just no thoughts of the future. Whenever my mind drifted there, the landscape was bleak, empty.

Mrs. Connolly, however, thought of nothing *but* my future. She came back to my house once, twice and then a third time, pressing, in her kind and artful way, for me to make a decision. It was one week before schools required a commitment. Would it be Yale, Mrs. Connolly's suggestion, or UPenn, the school I was favoring simply because it was the farthest away from here?

I *needed* to get away from this place. In all this time, I'd ventured out of my home just once. By venturing out, I mean that I sat in the car with the windows rolled up and the doors locked as my mother went in to get groceries. I wasn't safe from the derisive looks even under those conditions. I imagined that everyone who walked down Main Street peered through the window, eyeing me with curiosity, some with scorn.

"Absolutely not," was my answer when my parents tentatively asked about attending graduation. They were relieved, I think. Prom? Graduation? No fucking way. I received my diploma, handed over by the mailman without pomp or circumstance. It saddened me some, but for the most part, I was numb.

As the spring gave way to summer, I barely took notice. I took no pleasure in the garden bursting with the flowers I'd picked out and helped to plant. I no longer cared if the birds came to feed, neglecting to fill the birdhouse with seed like I used to do each morning. The smell of steak on the grill used to make my mouth water but now it turned my stomach. Didn't dip my toes in our pool—not even once.

To placate my parents, I did cave and agree to leave the house on occasion. It was nearly always a disaster. I couldn't bear to face anyone. In my mind, the eyes of everyone were upon me. As we drove, I felt people turn in their seats to peer at me through car windows. I heard their laughter, even though we were separated by glass. When I dared to venture into a store, I would hear voices from aisles over, faceless people regaling their friends with tales about me —rumors and lies they portrayed as truths. I saw them and heard them—or at least I thought I did. There were lucid moments where I reasoned and suspected that I was most likely imagining it all, but there were other times when I was convinced that my paranoid thoughts were reality. It all seemed so real. It got to the point where I believed the mailman was leering at me knowingly when he dropped off packages. He too must have seen the video, the pictures, the posted comments—the summary of my sordid life in graphic detail.

I would no longer answer the door. There were entire days where I didn't even leave my bedroom.

In my room, I sat on my bed and stared at the walls, that is, when I wasn't trolling the internet obsessively. I'd taken to pulling out individual strands of my hair—for some reason it soothed me. And there were times I'd notice scabs on my forearms, unsure of how they got there, only to see the evidence of picked skin and blood underneath my own fingernails.

My increasingly odd and paranoid behavior worried my parents terribly, and fueled their belief, seconded by Mrs. Connolly, that I'd made a mistake in turning down Yale. I needed them close by, they would say. I needed home as a nearby refuge—just in case. They argued their point daily, gentle in their approach. I was convinced, though, that once I was away from the judgement of this town I would be better off. I would be free.

I refused to leave my bedroom when people came to see me. *There's a friend here to see you.* My parents were clueless—I had no friends. I couldn't trust that Tori, Mike Hanson or Taylor had come in the spirit of friendship. How could Tori feel anything but hatred for me? I'd taken away her love, her heart. And Mike. Gone were two boys who'd been like brothers to him since grade school. They were my friends once upon a time, but that was a lifetime ago. Before I'd driven Drew to kill himself. Before I had both boys' blood on my hands.

And Jeremy.

The first few weeks he came by every day like clockwork. I'd hear the doorbell at five, hear my mother talking with him, hear him kick the gravel as he made his way back down the driveway, and hear his bike sound an angry roar as he peeled away. As days turned to weeks and weeks turned to months, his visits tapered off.

I figured they would.

I winced in pain that day in late July as I sat on my bed, engrossed in my daily ritual of combing through various social media pages. On a whim, I looked up Vanessa. Pictures of her latest piercings and body art were posted. The girl seemed to have new ink every week and felt the need to advertise it to the world—still the same old angry narcissist. One post, dated a few weeks back caught my eye. MOVING DAY, the post read. Underneath the caption there was a picture of Jeremy carrying a very large, seemingly heavy box. He was smiling for the camera, pausing before stepping through his doorway. There were comments below from people I didn't know. *Jeremy, you better take care of our girl,* one post read. *Day-um, Vanessa, you are one lucky bitch,* read another.

I guess I wasn't entirely numb because this news brought me to tears. I sank back onto my bed and cried. Jeremy and Vanessa, living together, happily ever after—it was what I deserved.

He was better off without me.

And he knew it.

August dragged on. Thomas knocked on my bedroom door some days, other days we went the entire twenty-four hours without contact. I cringed inwardly when I noticed him staring at me. He now saw me as peculiar, an unknown and strange entity. He was better off spending his time elsewhere and my parents ensured that he was now at home as little as possible. Two weeks at sleep-away camp, a week on vacation in Maine with Zack's family, random activities to fill up other days. I barely saw him that summer.

A week before I was to leave for Penn, my mother chatted happily as we made our way to the mall to get all my necessities. Her tone and her attitude grated on me. She saw my willingness to accompany her to the mall as a major victory, and was now trying to make this outing into some mother-daughter bonding experience. A girls' day out. Like everything was normal. Like I was a normal girl shopping for her new bedspread, her room décor and toiletries. She fussed over which mini fridge to get while I looked around nervously, petrified of being spotted. No, I wasn't into it. I couldn't wait to escape back to the sanctuary of our car, our home, my room.

I cut the trip short with only half of the items on the list purchased. My mother acquiesced. She knew that venturing outside, leaving the house for any reason at all was a big deal for me. We should get while the going was good.

As we made our way past a cheap jewelry kiosk near the exit, I spotted her. Skinny, with hair dyed jet black, piercings that broadcast her tough, offish demeanor, and clothes that advertised too much of her young flesh. She looked very different from the sweet, fresh-faced blonde I remembered, but it was most definitely her. Will's little sister. Another person ruined, another life derailed by yours truly.

* * *

JEREMY

Work, sleep, eat, repeat.

I asked my boss for as many hours as possible. I had to keep working towards something, logging hours, ticking off tasks for my licensing requirements. I had to keep moving. Keep working. Stop thinking.

Stop.

Thinking.

Vanessa started crashing with me in July after mouthing off to her mother's boyfriend and then recoiling in shock when her mother backhanded her across the face. In that moment she knew that her mother would always choose her loser boyfriends over her. Why was she living there, miserable, when her mother chose him? I was glad she finally saw the light, but I knew I was shit for company these past few weeks. I tried for her sake, but living with me was no picnic.

I worked out like a madman, hitting the heavy bag my dad had set up in our shed. The punches helped to release some of the pain, not all. But falling onto my couch at the end of the day in a state of exhaustion was better than lying there thinking about everything I'd lost.

I heard no news of Carolyn. No one saw her. No one spoke with her. Whenever I'd run into Tori, talk would turn to Carolyn. Tori was hurting and looking for Carolyn to be her friend in the aftermath of what had happened. We both knew, though, that Carolyn wasn't callous or unfeeling. We both acknowledged sadly that there must be something very wrong there. That while we were grieving, she must have been damaged by this in a way we couldn't really comprehend.

Still, I scrounged like a starving dog for any scrap I could get. Her stubborn refusal to see me left me frustrated and angry. Did she imagine that she was the only one hurting? Did she even fucking care about me at all? I'd lost a friend in Will, a teammate in Drew—I'd lost *her*. It was a struggle each day to go on without her. Didn't she know she was breaking me?

"Jeremy," Vanessa chirped happily, "guess who I just saw?" When I didn't answer, still wrapped up in taking my aggression out on the heavy bag, she kept at it. "I'll give you a clue. He smiles kind of crooked now. I think the surgeon fucked up when he set his jaw."

I said nothing. I didn't give a shit about Chase Sterling. Just punched the bag harder, remembering the feeling of satisfaction from that night when my fists connected with his head, his jaw, his ribs.

I was grateful that Vanessa sent Frank out to follow me that night. He struggled to pull me off Chase when I wouldn't stop beating his limp, defenseless body. There was a chance I would have killed him if it wasn't for Frank. I owed him big. I owed Vanessa too, because without her, I would most certainly be rotting in jail right about now. She still had the spare thumb drive, in addition to having the video saved on her phone and hard drive. It was a crystal clear shot and audio of Chase purchasing a rather large quantity of coke and Special K from one of the tattoo artists in Vanessa's shop—a guy who doubled as a major supplier in the area. *His* face was not visible, you just saw Chase.

Before he lost consciousness that night, I dangled the threat before Chase. Let him listen to it, because his eyes had swelled shut by that point. Warned him that if he breathed a word about me to his daddy or to the cops, the video was ready to go, with copies addressed to the Westerly Police Department, the head lacrosse coach *and* the Dean of Students at Duke, The Westerly Tribune *and* his rich daddy.

Last I'd heard, Chase fabricated and spread a story that he was attacked by some gang thugs who were trying to rob and carjack him. According to Chase, the fact that his wallet and car were, in fact, still with him when he was found, was testament to how hard he'd fought them off. His jaw was wired for the better part of the summer. I considered myself a public servant in that regard, in that no one had to listen to Chase spew any of his nasty shit for nearly two months.

"Chase, dummy!" Vanessa crowed. "I saw Chase! He looked right at me and then the fucker nodded, like he was acknowledging defeat.

I am *so* glad that piece of shit knows that I was the one who fucked him over."

I stopped punching and set about unwrapping the tape from my hands. "Stay away from him, Vanessa, all right? He's not talking now but don't laud that shit over him. He'll look for a way to strike back. I want you safe."

She swallowed, humbled. "I'm sorry, baby, you're right. I'm glad I've got you looking out for me." I chuckled because articulating warmth and appreciation wasn't Vanessa's style. "I mean it. Even though I constantly give you shit, I appreciate everything you've done for me."

"You're the one who looks out for me, Vanessa."

She winked. "That's 'cause I love you."

"Love you back," I answered as she moved closer and wrapped herself around me. I hugged her back.

I knew to my father—hell, to anyone looking on from the outside—we seemed like a couple. That made us both laugh. Vanessa was my closest friend. Thankfully she hadn't pushed me to talk these past few weeks, but her presence, across from me as we ate dinner or sitting quietly on the couch watching a movie together at night, was a comfort to me. Even though I was torn up and brooding, I didn't want to be alone.

August dragged on. I hardly noticed as the days got a little shorter, ushering in fall. I still did my daily workouts, finishing off with sprints. Some days I'd find myself back at the lake, looking for that girl in the blue checkered bikini, missing her even more intensely when I stood at the shoreline than I normally did.

Today had been an especially shitty day. I'd run into town midday to grab some extra cable from the hardware store and came across Thomas, about to get his ass kicked by a group of slightly older boys.

"Whatcha got there, Legos, you pussy? You're in seventh grade and you still play with blocks?"

"Shut up," he answered back, attempting to get onto his bicycle even though one of them had a firm grip on his handlebars.

"Wait, Tommy, we just want to talk. What's the rush?" the ringleader taunted as he tightened his grip on the bike. Then he gestured to one of his little shit friends to grab Thomas's bag.

"There a problem here?" I asked, approaching and slapping Thomas on the back. "What's up, Thomas?" I greeted him with a smile before looking into the eyes of the tallest kid. I didn't exactly glare but I made my intentions clear: *Fuck with him and you'll be sorry.*

"Nope, no problem," the ringleader said, stepping back. "See you around, Tom," he said, smiling.

"Not if I see you first," I said, this time leveling him with a menacing stare.

Thomas jerked his bike around, his face an angry shade of red. "I can take care of myself, Jeremy."

"Um, oh-kay. They kind of had you outnumbered there, buddy."

"I'm not your fucking buddy, oh-kay," he mimicked my words, his face twisted.

I couldn't help but smile, listening to the unnatural way the curse word sounded on his lips. He jerked his bike around again quickly. I moved a step. I think the little twerp was trying to hit me in the shins.

"Thomas, what the hell? I was just trying to help you out. Would you like me to stand by and watch you get your ass kicked next time?"

"I don't need you. You're nothing," he hissed. His face fell then. "Why haven't you come for her? There's something...the matter with her." He was shaking now. He angrily wiped at his cheek as a tear slid down. He looked to me accusingly. "You were her boyfriend. Isn't a boyfriend supposed to take care of his girl?"

His words stung, hurt me deep in my soul. I put my hands on his shoulders gently, but with enough pressure so that he couldn't run off or attempt to ram the bike into me again.

"I did, Thomas. I did come. She wouldn't see me. Carolyn still won't talk to me. I'm sorry, buddy, I really am."

His shoulders slumped, the fight gone out of him. "I don't know what to do to make her like she used to be. She just stares out the window and looks sad all the time."

"I'll keep trying, Tom. I promise."

Driving home from work that night, I couldn't shake the guilt. Maybe I hadn't tried hard enough. I pulled down Carolyn's road just as I was about to pass it. Instead of knocking, which had gotten me nowhere in the past, I tossed a pebble at her window. Nothing. I tossed a bigger pebble, still nothing. I tossed another one, a little bit harder, which landed with a loud thwack and may or may not have made a small crack in the glass. She appeared, a pale and slight figure. When she looked down and saw me, she raised one palm to the window and pressed it flat against the pane. I raised my palm and mimicked her motion. *I want to touch you, to hold your hand*—that's the silent message I was sending her. What the hell, I went for it, mouthing the words: *I love you*. Damn, I saw immediately that it was too much. I'd fucked it up. She shook her head sadly as she lowered her hand. She moved back and closed the curtains.

Tori told me that Carolyn would be leaving for Pennsylvania next week. That, as they say, was that. I wanted answers but I wouldn't be getting them. I'd have to forget. I'd have to move on.

Sadness plagued me as I drove home along the darkened suburban streets. About a mile from my place, I made out a kid walking along the side of the road, glancing over her shoulder nervously as my headlights approached and my truck slowed next to her. As I got closer, I could see she wasn't dressed for this cool August night. Shit, she was barefoot.

"Are you all right?" I asked as I rolled down my window.

"I'm fine," she snapped nervously.

I got a closer look at her face when the wind whipped her long hair back. "Are you Will's little sister? Anna Clarke, right?"

Her head whipped back in my direction, her brow furrowed. "How do you know me?"

I'd come to a complete stop by then. I could tell this kid was cold, upset and scared. She was as edgy as a jackrabbit, ready to dart away.

"I'm Jeremy Rivers. I was a friend of Will's. We played football together. I met you once last year when I was at your house with Will."

"Oh," she said as she tucked her arms around her chest in an attempt to keep warm.

"Listen, let me give you a ride, ok? It's getting kinda cold out here and it's really not safe for a young girl to be walking along the side of the road alone in the dark."

"How do I know *you're* safe?" She asked, and with a snarky little attitude, I might add. This kid was a pistol.

"I guess you don't. But if you don't get in I'll be forced to call the cops and have them pick you up. I'm not leaving you out here alone. I owe at least that much to Will."

At the sound of her brother's name, she teared up, nodded, and let herself into the passenger side. Her feet were all dirty, with a few visible cuts. Her skin was covered in goosebumps. I cranked up the heat, even though it was the end of August.

"I'll take you home, Anna," I said as I started to pull away.

"No!" she wailed. Her tears were falling big and fast now. "Do *not* take me there. My parents are getting divorced. They're selling the house. That's what they told me today. It's like, just about the *only* thing they've said to me since Will died. All they do is drink. They don't give a shit about me. I'm telling you, they do *not* even realize I'm gone."

I remembered Will's parents—his mother, especially. She looked me over the first time I'd gone home with Will, taking in my clothes, my leather jacket, my longish hair. When she thought I was out of earshot, she asked Will about me and then made some stupid comment about not being the type that Will normally associated with. Her smile when she came back into the kitchen was tight and forced. *What a bitch*, I'd thought at the time. I disliked her—took her for the shallow, entitled woman that she was.

Yeah, I guess Anna didn't have to go *straight* home.

"Where to then?"

"I'm just telling it to you straight...What was your name again?"

"Jeremy," I said, trying not to laugh.

"Stop laughing, Jeremy. I am *not* going home tonight and if you call the cops, I'll run. Take me to a diner, to that movie theater on Oak Street...Take me anywhere that's open twenty–four hours. I don't really care."

I gripped the wheel hard. This was a dilemma. "I can't leave you at any of those places. Shit, don't you realize what could happen to a girl like you late at night?"

"I can take care of myself," she bit back.

"Yeah," I laughed, mocking her. "You've got great survival instincts. I see you left your shoes at home while planning to trek along the roadside tonight."

She looked down at her feet and then her bottom lip started to quiver in the cutest freaking way.

"I can't go home," she whispered.

"My place is a little cramped but you can take the couch. I'll share a room with Vanessa for tonight. Just for tonight," I warned. "Tomorrow you have to straighten things out with your parents."

The next few days went by in a blur. Anna became like our little mascot. That first night we cleaned and bandaged her feet, made her some soup and tucked her in, bundling her up on the couch. And then she just...stayed.

Every day when I got in from work, I'd tell her she had to go home, but I was outnumbered. Vanessa saw no reason for Anna to go back. "Hell," she'd whisper, reminding me, "it's not like they're even *looking* for her. No posters up in town, nothing on the news. They're not exactly doting parents."

Vanessa was well versed in being raised in a less than nurturing environment. She resisted every day when I argued that Anna staying with us was not a good idea. And I guess I really didn't want her to go either because every day, I'd relent.

We cooked for her at night like she was our kid. We dyed her hair to match Vanessa's. It suited her, I thought, and it let her escape for a little while, from her life and from all the shit she'd been enduring. And at Anna's badass insistence, Vanessa had happily pierced her ears in several spots, in addition to her upper lip and her eyebrow. *Holy shit*, I thought to myself one night, *maybe this wasn't such a good idea*. The kid looked like a mini Vanessa now. So different. Maybe we had no right. But damn, every night spent talking, laughing and occasionally crying with Anna made me feel a connection to Will. It gave me and Vanessa a way to remember him and to give something back to him by way of comforting his grieving little sister, who now seemed so lost without him.

When nearly a week had passed and Anna still refused to return home, I caved and called her father. I told him she was fine, that she'd crashed here with me and my friend, Vanessa, just so he didn't think I was some pervert. I told him where to come and get her. Well, the cops showed up instead and tried to haul me in for kidnapping. They only let me go when Anna screamed bloody murder, insisting that she'd run away. It helped that I also had Frank's father in my corner.

I never admitted to Anna that I'd given her up. I thought that would pile more heartbreak onto a kid who'd already had her fair share and then some. And when she left, I'll admit, it was a little heartbreaking for me.

Another person moving on.

Another reminder that Carolyn was gone.

Chapter Sixteen

THREE YEARS LATER...

CAROLYN

I stood at the starting line of the Rough Mudder, bouncing on my toes, adrenaline pumping throughout my entire being. I smiled with nervous excitement, flinching just slightly as the gunshot sounded the start of the race—momentarily rattled by the haunting sound but still able to focus. I dug down deep, scaling over walls, crawling commando-style across mud-filled pits, swinging over obstacles as my grip slid down the ropes—struggling but able to hang on.

Today was the best day I'd had in a very long time. There were breaks of sunshine along the way, but today? Today, for the first time in three years I felt like I was fully basking in the warmth and joy of the sun.

I laughed and smiled as I raced alongside my fellow competitors. And now that I was medication-free, like most people my age, I was able to enjoy a beer at the finish line with my friends.

Yes, I had friends. Not the kind of friendships I used to settle for. No, I now had true friends.

Sometimes I'd think about my past, regretting the time wasted, sorrowful over the person I'd become: a lowly sycophant aching for acceptance from hateful girls who weren't worth my time. When all the while, people like Tori and Taylor, genuine and loyal, were right in front of me.

But there are no do-overs, so I'd remind myself that where I stood today was what mattered. And today I was running a race, pushing myself to do something new and challenging with my closest friends by my side.

I just finished up my sophomore year at Fairfield, a local four-year university. Academically, it was a far cry from Yale or UPenn, but the work did challenge me. I should have been a junior but I was one full year behind. I lived at home, commuting each day. It just worked better for me.

That first semester I enrolled at Fairfield taking only nine credits, as opposed to fifteen. For someone who once easily shouldered five Advanced Placement courses at a time, I now struggled to concentrate. My anti-anxiety and anti-depressant medications hampered me in some ways, but I confess, there were days when those pills were the only thing that made getting out of bed in the morning possible.

I did what I could and was careful not to take on more than I could handle. That first year, after my release from the hospital, I took baby steps. I left the house for therapy appointments and to volunteer my tutoring services twice a week at Briarwood—that's all. My social anxiety wasn't as crippling as it had been the year before, but that didn't mean I was running around town or socializing. I generally avoided places where I expected my old classmates to congregate. Certain days were especially difficult. It pained me that just as I had on the day of their funerals, I remained cooped up indoors alone when a memorial service was held for Drew and Will on the one year anniversary of their deaths. Yes, days like those were rough.

I finally got my driver's license. Gradually, I also began to take on some responsibilities, such as going to the store and the dry cleaners. At first I would talk myself through these outings beforehand, trying to anticipate who I might see. I would role-play basic conversations in my head, giving myself a sort of script so that I didn't feel overwhelmed.

Sometimes I was embarrassed by how much effort it took for me to clear these low hurdles, to accomplish things that others did without a second thought. But I had to pat myself on the back every time I moved forward, because for so many months I had done nothing but stand still.

I slowly repaired my relationship with Thomas. Three years later we were nearly there. I think now he could understand what happened to me. When Thomas looked at me now, I think he saw the person that he knew and loved again.

He was so much older now, nearly fifteen. He still attended Briarwood, along with Zach and his other friends. Thomas had a girlfriend, too. A cutie by the name of Ingrid who played the cello like a sad angel. It was hard to reconcile the serious expression and the somber sound of her music with the lively, silly girl who emerged once she laid her instrument down. Ingrid and Thomas seemed to fit together like two pieces of a puzzle.

There were times I'd sneak a look at them, watching as Thomas pushed her on the tire swing in our backyard. I'd watch the two of them talking, hardly able to contain their smiles around one another. In those moments I felt as if I might burst with happiness for Thomas, because he deserved everything good and wonderful in life. But soon after I closed the curtains, a gnawing sense of loss and longing would plague me. I had no romantic life to speak of. No lips had touched my own since Jeremy.

It had been nearly three years since that summer night when I'd waved goodbye to Jeremy from my bedroom window. He was better off without me.

But not one day passed when I didn't think about him.

Jeremy had given up on me. I didn't blame him. I was an empty shell—nothing like the girl I once was. Nothing like the girl he'd fallen for.

For a very long time I felt as if I had nothing to offer.

"Holy crap, Carolyn, that guy who works in the coffee shop with Tori is totally checking you out right now."

Ava, a friend from school, was *always* trying to set me up.

"Robert? I don't think so, Ava. I see him all the time and we just talk...Like, no flirting whatsoever. Anyway, I'm covered in mud right now, so I'm pretty sure he is not checking me out."

"Maybe he's into getting down and dirty. Did you ever think of that?"

"Well then he's more your speed," I teased back.

"We *need* to hook you up, Carolyn. Maybe not with Robert, but there's got to be a guy you're into. *You* are a hottie and every hottie needs a man."

"Don't go all matchmaker on me, bitch, ok? The only thing I *need* right now is a job."

"Did I just hear someone say they need a job?" Robert asked as he approached us with fresh beers.

Ava chirped, "Hey, maybe you can work side by side with our girl, Carolyn. You can teach her everything there is to know about caramel soy latte frappe smoothies!"

"Uh, yeah," Robert said, looking at Ava liked the cracked individual that she was, "I don't know what that *is* exactly, but I am assistant manager there now, Carolyn. If you're interested, I'll definitely hire you."

"I appreciate the offer, but I need something in the evenings. I'm volunteering at Briarwood this summer as an assistant teacher."

"All right. I'll keep my ears open for you."

"Thanks."

Robert looked at Ava sort of like he wished she'd evaporate. When she stayed put, he looked back to me and asked, "Any chance I could take you out sometime?"

I'd become an expert in the art of the gentle let down. I didn't consider myself anything special in the looks department. I mean, I didn't have guys trailing behind me begging like Taylor seemed to have. But over the past few months, I guess the growing sense of self-confidence and well-being I was projecting was drawing the guys out of the woodwork.

I wasn't ready. Not even close.

"Thanks, Robert, but I'm not dating right now. I'm sorry."

"It's cool, Carolyn. I guess I'll see you at the shop?"

"Definitely. You know I can't get through my mornings without my java."

As soon as he was out of earshot, Ava threw her head back in exasperation. "What *was* that? I'm not *dating* right now?"

"I'm not," I answered, smiling.

That was another thing—I pretty much did what I wanted to do and said what was on my mind now. It felt...freaking great.

"You heard her, Ava. When the right guy asks her, she'll say yes," Tori chimed in as she wrapped her muddy arms around my muddy middle.

I peeled her arms from me, laughing. "I'd say yuck but I'm just as disgusting as you are."

"Who did you turn down, anyway?" she asked.

"Your boy, Robert."

"Oh yeah, he's sweet on you, Carolyn. He's nice enough but I'm with you on this, either the feeling is there or it's not."

"You two are out there." Ava threw her arms out to the side in frustration. "What ever happened to just giving someone a chance?"

"I've lived to regret that," Tori answered, rolling her eyes. "Anyone remember Darren?" We all laughed, thinking about Tori's high maintenance, metrosexual, overly man-scaped boyfriend who lasted all of three weeks. "Darren tweezed his eyebrows more than I did. His idea of fun was breaking out some tooth whitening strips. He was obsessed with watching pro soccer, not because he was into the sport, but so that he could copy their hairstyles."

"Anyone need to use the bathroom?" Ava asked. "I have to brave the portable potty."

"No," Tori and I said in unison, scrunching up our noses.

When Ava left, Tori asked, "You ok?"

"I'm good. No, I'm great, actually. Just not into Robert, even though he's a really nice guy and all. I'm just not ready for that."

"I get it."

"Have you seen him?" I asked cautiously.

"No," she answered, smiling. "But I love it when you break down and ask about him. I haven't seen him in a few months. The last time he came into the shop was around April. He told me he was taking on a big project in New Haven. He's working really long days and six-day work weeks."

"I saw him," I admitted in a barely audible whisper.

Tori's eyes went wide. "You did?"

I shook my head. "Not saw him like I was with him or talking to him or anything." I cringed when I admitted, "It was more like I *watched* him. He was walking into that gourmet food shop on Main and I just sat in my car and waited for him to come back out. Just to get a glimpse of him. Like a stalker," I added, laughing at myself.

"Oh, Carolyn, I wish I could tell him that. It would make his day."

"Yeah, but it would be *your* last day," I threatened. "Anyway, I think that ship has sailed. Not gonna play it off like I don't miss what I had with him, though, 'cause I do."

"I'd never know that, Carolyn." Tori took my hand and looked at me sadly. "You hardly bring his name up, like, ever."

I paused a moment to swallow back a tear and then shook my head and smiled to let Tori know I was all right, because I was. "I can't go back there. And I think I've built it up in my mind, making what we had more than it was. Anyway, it was a long time ago and he's moved on."

"You don't know that."

"Last I heard he was living with Vanessa."

Tori rolled her eyes. "She doesn't live there now...Hasn't for a *long* time."

"Doesn't matter anyway. I'm so much better now, I know that, but I'm still a lot for someone to take on, you know?"

"You're the best kind of wonderful to take on, Carolyn. I know that for a fact."

* * *

JEREMY

"I don't have time for a girlfriend right now."

"I don't recall saying you needed a girlfriend, I recall saying that you need to get laid," Frank pestered. He was annoying the crap out of me today. "Sadie has a friend. She's really nice and just your type... long brown hair, smoking body."

"How is that my type, asshole?"

Was he kidding me? Did he think I was looking to screw a Carolyn look-alike?

Frank ran his hands through his hair in frustration. His tone softened. "Look, I'm just saying that this isn't healthy. It's been a long time."

"Three years. I'm well aware."

"Exactly. I think you should let her go."

"I let her go three years ago."

"Great! So there's no reason for you *not* to come out with us this Saturday. You, me, Sadie and her friend."

"A double date? How adorable."

"Come on, Jeremy. I'm not asking you to marry her. Just have some fun. See how good it feels to have a girl in your life again."

"I'll think about it," I said. "Now will you please get outta here so I can finish up? I promised my dad I'd come by with dinner and I still have a shit-load to do."

Frank's words were ringing in my ears: *See how good it feels to have a girl in your life again.*

I did want a woman in my life. I wanted to feel again. I wanted to feel lips on mine, wanted to run my hands over soft curves, wanted to feel the sweet pleasure of sinking into the warmth of her. Problem was, I wanted one girl in particular and I couldn't have *her*.

Three years ago, the night she turned her back on me, a part of me died. I'll never understand it. I knew she was suffering, I did. But how could she just cut and run? One day we were falling in love and the next day we were over. I used to tell myself that she'd come around. I listened to everyone who told me to just give her time.

I finally gave up a year ago.

Sitting in the coffee shop with Tori during her break, I broke down and asked if Carolyn ever mentioned my name or asked about me. I felt like a needy, middle-school aged girl, but I had to know. Tori shook her head, her eyes sad. "No, she doesn't, but I also know she's not seeing anyone, Jeremy." Tori was trying to reassure me, but the knowledge that Carolyn was back in school, tutoring, socializing —carrying on without needing to know one iota of information about me? It was a slap in the face.

I buried myself in work. All that time I'd been missing her, waiting for her to come around, I worked. I set a goal for myself and did little else but work towards achieving it.

It paid off eventually. Denny, my first boss, was close to retirement. The day I passed my final licensing requirements, he offered me a fifty percent stake in his business. I jumped at the chance to buy into an established outfit. I was now officially a full partner in Tri-State Electrical.

Shit, I was so proud the day that our new invoices and business cards were delivered, listing Denny's name on one side and mine on the other, both with the word *proprietor* underneath. In that moment, though, I only wanted to call one person. I wanted Carolyn to know that I did it—that I was finally my version of a success.

When Tori shot all my hopes to hell that day in the coffee shop, I decided to literally wake up and smell the fucking coffee. I decided to move on.

Problem was that I couldn't.

Chapter Seventeen

CAROLYN

"That basket is for the golf getaway. The gift certificate for lessons, the weekend stay in Hilton Head, his and her golf gloves and the golf balls go in there."

"Aye, aye, captain," Ava teased as she set about arranging the basket. Having her help was great. She was one of those crafty girls who could stuff a basket and tie a ribbon in a way that made Martha Stewart look like a novice.

I looked around the first floor of my house with a satisfied, contented smile. This was the first year that I was fully back in planning mode for the annual Briarwood Gala. The gala was a huge deal every November, the school's biggest fundraiser, and my mother chaired the event. Along with the ten or so women that my mother recruited, I had Ava, Taylor and Tori helping. They fit right in.

I refreshed all the hors d'oeuvre trays and poured my friends another round of mimosas as they sat around my large kitchen island, where bits of tulle and ribbon were strewn all over. It was nothing crazy, but my mother liked to make these preparation days into somewhat of a social event to thank the women for donating their time.

"This is the basket I'm bidding on," Taylor said, as she looked over the service menu attached to the gift certificate donated by one of the most exclusive spas in Connecticut. "They fly mud in from the Aegean and slather you in it from head to toe."

"Didn't we do that last month?" Tori joked. "I don't recall my skin glowing after that mud run. I just remember finding bits of dried mud in all my private nooks and crannies for days afterward."

"I wish I was on basket duty with you girls." My back was to this woman's whiny voice. "You look like you're having so much more fun than the crew I'm with." I turned to see her tip her chin over her shoulder to where a group of my mother's friends were making table seating arrangements.

The group had changed. My mother still had her core crowd, but needed to recruit some new faces for the cause to replace people she was no longer on speaking terms with. Samantha's mother used to be her second in command and Erica's aunt was another old friend who worked tirelessly on this benefit. After my mother found out that my two *friends* were behind some of the most hateful garbage being hurled at me, though, she confronted them. I mean she *actually* went to Samantha's house and then Erica's house to give the girls *and* their parents a dressing down in person. Suffice to say, those women now volunteered for other worthy causes.

This woman was one of the newbies. She looked younger than the others and out of place. She was very attractive, sexy even, but it was like she was trying too hard. She was perfectly groomed, her make-up was flawless, and yet despite the fact that her clothes were obviously expensive, she looked cheap. With her plunging neckline and short skirt, she was showing too much skin for a casual Sunday morning among other ladies, and her wrists, fingers and neck were weighed down with a gaudy amount of gold.

"Do you have room for one more here?" she asked as she plopped herself onto a stool and took the mimosa I'd just poured for myself.

All righty then.

"Sure," I said, recovering. "You can be in charge of the Night on Broadway basket. Here are the show tickets, the gift certificate for dinner at Carmine's and the parking voucher."

"Great!" she chirped, dismissing me and turning back to my friends. "So girls, tell me about yourselves. I'm desperate. I've just spent the last hour listening to *those* ladies talk about hysterectomies and arthritis."

No one at our table laughed in response to her joke. And I certainly didn't take kindly to people insulting my mother's friends.

I dragged another stool over, now that she was sitting in *my* seat. "They might be a few years older than you, but you were paired up with a federal judge, someone who regularly competes in triathlons, and a fairly successful novelist. I seriously doubt they've been boring you with the details of their medical histories."

"I'm just joking, Carolyn," she said, rubbing my shoulder in an overly familiar manner. Jeez, I didn't even know this chick's name, but she soon remedied that. "I'm Beth, by the way."

All the girls introduced themselves. They were polite but on guard with this one. There was just something about her that rubbed me the wrong way. While Beth ingratiated herself with my friends, I went over to grab some more basket fillers.

"I see Beth Peterman has abandoned her post," my mother observed dryly.

"What's her story?"

"She's desperate for friends, I think. She married Bryce Peterman a few years ago. Wife number three. She's not from around here and I think she's had a hard time fitting in. She was very helpful last year, though, and I can use all the help I can get."

"What is she, like, thirty years younger than Mr. Peterman?"

"Maybe not quite thirty...More like twenty and change," my

mother answered, smiling. "Here, take these items for the Napa Getaway basket."

As I was making my way back over, I heard Beth rambling on about her high school days in Nevada. Apparently, she was the head cheerleader. Wow.

"Hate to interrupt this walk down memory lane," Taylor said, her smirk barely concealed, "but I have to run, Carolyn. I'm due at my mother's by two."

I hugged Taylor tight when I thanked her and walked her to the door. "I'm glad things are going well with your mom."

"Me too. You hit the jackpot with your parents, but my mom... Well, she's trying and I can't ask for more than that, right?"

I cringed listening to Beth's high-pitched giggling as I made my way back over. Ava was laughing along with Beth, while Tori sat there staring at the both of them with raised eyebrows. Guess I missed something good.

"Did you all go to Westerly High?"

"These two did," Ava said, gesturing to me and Tori. "I went to school in Darien."

"I have a friend around your age." She paused as she ran her index finger around the rim of her glass slowly. "Jeremy Rivers. He went to Westerly. Do you know him?"

Tori crossed her arms over her chest. "How do you know Jeremy?"

She shrugged her shoulders and smiled innocently. "He did some work on my house. We became, you know, friends."

It was clear what she was implying, but this lady wasn't completely stupid—she was too reliant on her sugar daddy's millions to spell it out completely.

"I'm good friends with Jeremy." Tori's tone was challenging and none too friendly. "I'll be sure to tell him I met you."

Beth was oblivious. "If you see him *please* tell him I was asking for him. He is *such* a great guy."

Oh. Come. On. Was she serious? It's not like she was ancient or anything, but still, someone her age should be saying: he's such a great *kid*.

My mind flashed back to a night years ago in my basement. Jeremy was telling me about his first. Taylor. *Taylor, Willow, Beth... they didn't mean anything.* Was she *that* Beth? Being in Taylor's presence never made me uncomfortable, but this chick? My skin was crawling. I was doing the math in my head. If she was the infamous Beth, then he was in high school at the time and she was...not.

"Were you *with* Jeremy?" I blurted out.

"Carolyn, let it go," Tori warned.

Beth's eyes went wide. Maybe I said that a little too loudly.

My mother approached then, sensing something was up. "Beth, I think these girls have the baskets under control. Maryanne and Madeline really need some help with the invitation list. Would you mind?" she asked, gesturing towards two women seated on the far side of the living room.

I shook my head as Beth slinked away. "She's repulsive and Jeremy is an ass."

"Easy. Don't assume what you don't know," Tori scolded me. "Jeremy is a good person. He doesn't go around banging married women."

"Beth kind of implies otherwise, no?"

Beth had a woman's body and I'm sure she was *very* experienced. It made me burn, the thought of Jeremy being with her. Me and Jeremy, when all was said and done, hadn't done much more than kiss. I was jealous, pure and simple.

Tori set about tying the bow atop her basket in earnest. Her lips were pursed in a thin line, but she broke her silence after a few moments. "Please know I'm saying this with love in my heart, but I will not listen to you talk shit about him. He was crazy about you and he was devastated after everything that happened. You weren't the only one grieving, you know? We all were." Meeting my eyes, she said, "He was in a lot of pain when he lost you. Do you realize that?"

I felt one hot tear slip down my cheek. I knew what Tori was really saying. For the longest time I only thought about my pain, my grief, my shame. I abandoned him and everyone else. I abandoned her when she needed me. I couldn't see it back then, but I could see it very clearly now.

Ava was sitting there stock still, taking it all in. She knew bits and pieces of our history, but not the whole story. She didn't know, for example, exactly how much Tori had lost when Will died. She didn't really know anything about Jeremy.

I took Tori's hand. "I'm sorry. I know I wasn't really a good friend to you, Tori. And I didn't mean what I said about Jeremy. He has every right and it's not my place to judge him."

"I get it," she said. Her eyes were still sad but one side of her mouth turned up in a teasing grin. "You're jealous. The fire still burns for the J-man."

I laughed her off, although deep inside I ached. The fire would always burn for him. And while I was better, so much better than I had been, I could not shake the feeling, deep-down, that I was damaged goods. Between what Henley had done to me, what Chase had put me through, and the regular, daily berating I took online for so long, I felt a deep, embedded sense of shame—of being dirty.

I could sit across from a therapist for the rest of my natural born life and that would never change.

* * *

JEREMY

"Well, look who it is," Tori called out as I entered the crowded coffee house. I scanned the seats, as I always did, simultaneously hoping and dreading that *she* would be here. It was amazing, I thought sometimes, how you could live in the same town as someone and never run into them. "I'm on break in five. Sit tight, Jeremy."

"What are you doing here? I haven't seen you in forever," Tori said as she plopped down into the seat across from me.

"You didn't make yourself a coffee?"

"I'm like the only barista on the planet who hates coffee."

"Barista, huh? Pretty fancy job title," I teased.

"That's assistant managing barista to you, ass wipe."

"Seriously? That's good, right?"

"More money, I guess...More hours, though. But I need it. I just wish I had more time in the day. Between work, classes and the boys, I feel like I'm running on a hamster wheel most days."

"Is everything all right?"

"Yeah," she waved me off, shaking her head. "Really, everything is good. The boys are doing great. I love my classes. I joined an adult volleyball league in Norwalk and I've been running again. Everything is good."

"Yeah?"

She nodded. "I did one of those mud warrior runs last month. You have to give that a try, it was awesome."

"I saw the picture you posted." I paused before adding, "She looks good."

Tori nodded. "Carolyn *is* good. I think she's finally made it to the other side, you know? I'm happy for her." When I didn't say anything in response, she switched subjects. "So what's new and exciting with you, Jeremy?"

"Working a ton, that's about it," I said, shrugging my shoulders. "Oh," I added with as much enthusiasm as I could muster, which was basically none, " and I've got a date tonight."

Tori's smile was crooked, hurt almost. What the hell?

"That's great, Jeremy. Who's the lucky girl?" she asked, trying to seem happy for me when it was clear that she wasn't.

"Uh, I don't even know her name. She's some friend of Frank's girl. I kind of got roped into this. I'm dreading tonight but I'm thinking maybe it's about time, right?" I couldn't ignore the change in her attitude any longer. "Is something wrong, Tori?"

"No." She smiled her warm, genuine smile. "I guess I'm just surprised because I've always held out hope. It's like, I'll never have a chance with Will again but I feel like you still have a chance with Carolyn."

I leaned over and kissed her cheek. I felt so goddamned bad whenever she brought up Will's name. "I don't believe that anymore. Three years is a long fucking time."

"Yep, it is a long time. It's just..."

Her eyes got that playful sparkle back.

"What?"

A laugh escaped before she turned away. "It's nothing."

"Holy shit, Tori. Start talking before I scream out loud that there's a cockroach in my coffee cup."

"You wouldn't!"

I nodded my head, rising slowly up out of my seat. "Oh yes I would."

"All right, Rivers, sit your ass back down." After I did, she grabbed a juice box from the case nearby and plopped back into her chair, undoing the wrapper from the straw, taking her sweet time. She was stalling and I wasn't having it. When I went stand again, she piped up. "Last weekend I was witness to Carolyn losing her shit when one of your old fuck buddies brought your name up. Carolyn was *beyond* jealous."

"One of my what?"

"Beth Peterman? Ring a bell? She's a little, um, mature, no? And a lot married?"

"Where did you see Beth?"

"So it's true!" she exclaimed, wide-eyed.

"It was a long time ago. I haven't seen Beth in a few years."

"Wow," she said, shaking her head, looking away from me.

"You still haven't answered the question, Tori. Where did you see her and how did my name even come up?"

Tori rolled her eyes. "*Mrs.* Peterman volunteers for the Briarwood Gala. She was at Carolyn's house last weekend. And *she* brought your name up. It was kinda creepy, Jeremy."

I shrugged. "I don't know what to say."

"She didn't come out and say it, but she implied you and her were more than friends. It was kinda gross. She *licked her lips* and then said you were a great guy. I thought Carolyn was gonna claw her eyes out."

There was a part of me that seriously doubted Carolyn was jealous, even though I hoped that she was. Kind of served her right. Did she expect me to be waiting on her for three years? Waiting for her to decide that I was worthy of her time? Carolyn thinking that I couldn't or wouldn't move on and be with someone else burned. It almost made me look forward to my date tonight.

Almost, but not quite.

We were meeting at Red's, a local bar and burger joint with pool tables and a relaxed vibe. I balked when Frank suggested venturing to Manhattan to check out some comedy club in the Village. I told him I didn't want to be trapped for six hours in case this was a bust.

I was there first and took one of the few available booths. The waitress came over and was making small talk with me when I saw Frank come in waving, with Sadie and her friend trailing behind. The waitress moved aside and gave them all a welcoming smile. I noticed that Sadie and her friend both immediately narrowed their eyes at her. So it was going to be like that, huh?

Sadie leaned over and kissed my cheek, whispering, "Kenzie," in my ear. *Thanks for the save*, I was thinking as I smiled back at her.

I stood up and introduced myself. "Hi, Kenzie, I'm Jeremy."

I offered her my hand, but Kenzie came right in for the hug and kiss on the cheek. "It's so great to finally meet you. Frank and Sadie are always talking you up to me."

She was pretty. She had long brown hair, blue eyes and a friendly smile. Not a lot of make-up, I liked that, but Kenzie dressed in a way that left nothing to the imagination. I had a full view of her breasts peeking out of her low-cut top every time she shifted her body towards me, which she did *every* time she asked a question or answered one of mine.

There was something the matter with me. Even after the second pitcher of beer was drained and the girls were laughing and flirty, I just could not muster up anything for this very attractive, very willing girl.

It all felt so contrived. Being set up, the forced getting-to-know-you questions, the coy, flirty glances, and now the whole *I'm a girly-girl who can't shoot pool so I need you to show me* act? At a certain point of the night I was close to rolling my eyes. Kenzie's ass was practically on display for me as she leaned over the table in her short skirt, giggling as she struggled with the pool cue. Begging for that movie scene bullshit where I bend over her, lining the cue stick up to the ball, pressing my dick into her backside in the process. Fuck that. I checked my watch when she looked over her shoulder a second time, beckoning me.

"Frank, I'm gonna head out. Can you drop her at home?"

He took a long pull off his beer. "Nope."

I took a deep breath. "You set this up. You're gonna act like a little bitch just because I don't want to, what, drop to one knee and propose to Sadie's friend?"

"No. It's just that you agreed to come. The girl was excited to meet you, got all dolled up and seems to really like you. If you're not planning on seeing her again, then I'd say you owe her the courtesy of telling her that yourself. That's all I'm saying."

He had a point.

"Kenzie, I've gotta work tomorrow. Can I take you home or

would you like to hang out and catch a ride home with Sadie and Frank?"

I looked back towards Frank as I asked her, and noticed he was now in a full lip lock with Sadie. I'm sure that was his way of flipping me off.

"I think I'll head home with you," Kenzie said, laughing nervously as she set eyes on the loving couple. "You work on Saturdays?"

"Most of the time, yeah."

"Sadie said you owned your own business. I guess you've got to be there if you're in charge, huh?"

"Yeah, but I don't really mind it. I like being busy," I said as I opened the door for her and we made our way through the parking lot.

"I'm about a half-hour drive from here. Is that all right?"

"It's no problem."

We made more small talk for the first five minutes and then the conversation lagged. She seemed uncomfortable with the silence, so she'd punctuate it with questions every few seconds.

"Where are you working tomorrow?"

"New Haven."

"Oh."

A minute later, she asked, "So do you have any brothers or sisters?"

"No, only child. What about you?"

"One sister."

I felt like a shit. I never should have agreed to go out with her. I had no interest, but still, she didn't deserve my indifference.

"Look, Kenzie, I shouldn't have wasted your time. I'm not really looking for a relationship right now. I'm tied up with work all the time and…" I was struggling to make sense of it but I couldn't.

Kenzie reached over and gently rubbed my hand that was rested on the gear shift. She swallowed nervously and said, "I know what you went through, Jeremy. Sadie told me everything. You lost some good friends and then you also lost a *girl* you were really serious about. I know how that feels."

She dropped her hand from mine and then her gaze shifted away, out the passenger side window. "My boyfriend, my high school sweetheart," she said, a smile of fond remembrance creeping up, "was everything to me. We started dating when I was sixteen. He was two years older. He enlisted as soon as he graduated from high school." She looked over at me, shaking her head, smiling wistfully. "I thought I'd die being separated from him, Jeremy." I took her hand then, wanting to comfort her, having some idea of where this story was going. "He wanted to go to college, but we didn't come from the kind of town where your parents make enough money to bounce you from high school right into the university of your dreams. Know what I mean? The plan was: Marines, marriage, college, kids...In that order."

I was pulling up to the address she plugged into the truck's GPS. The apartment complex looked fairly well kept, but it was in a somewhat gritty area on the outskirts of Bridgeport.

She turned to me as I brought the car to a stop. "He was deployed to Afghanistan. Didn't make it one month. Roadside bomb. He was twenty years old."

"Kenzie, that's awful. I really am sorry."

"When Sadie told me your story, I just felt like I was meant to cross paths with you."

"I don't know if you got the wrong impression, Kenzie, but the girl I was involved with...She's not dead. I did lose friends in a really tragic accident but I didn't lose her that way."

"I know that," she said, shaking her head apologetically. "And I don't know the whole story, but it made me feel like we have something in common anyway. To lose someone is devastating. Maybe losing someone the way you did is even worse. She's alive and she's gone, whereas my Michael...I know he's *really* gone."

I looked out my window then, still holding this girl's hand. *She's alive and she' gone. She's gone. She's gone.* The words were playing on repeat in my mind, tormenting me.

"I've been alone for a long time, Jeremy. I'm not looking for a serious commitment, but I think I am ready to *feel* something for another person again." She tugged on my hand gently, and when I turned back to her, she leaned over and placed one gentle kiss on my lips. "When you feel like you're ready, Sadie has my number. I'd really like it if you called me."

She slid across the seat again and went to open her door. I slid over some and grabbed for her hand.

"Wait." She turned back around and looked to me with hopeful expectation and desire in her eyes. "I don't know what I'm doing right now. I don' want to hurt you and I suspect that I'm going to be someone you regret."

Kenzie slowly turned her body and then moved across the seat and sat astride me, never taking her eyes off mine. "I'm a big girl, Jeremy. I won't break if you kiss me."

I didn't kiss her at first. I waited. There was a part of me screaming at myself to peel her off of me, put the car in drive and never look back. There was another part of me, though, the sad and fucking lonely guy, that melted at the feel of her nails scraping gently across the nape of my neck and heated at the feel of her soft core pressed against a part of me that was now thick and hard with lust.

She dipped her head forward and whispered, "Make me feel something," before she pressed her soft lips to mine. Her barely there skirt was already scrunched up over her hips, so when she pressed down onto me, there was just the satin of her underwear. She was grinding against the denim of my jeans. She wasn't shy, looking to take things slowly, or waiting on me to make the first move. She took one of my hands and placed it between us, urging me on. When my fingers made contact with the material, she moved her hips, inviting me to touch her. I nudged the material aside and felt her bare, smooth skin before sinking into her. "Oh, yeah," she said on a whimper, and then she claimed my lips feverishly, gripping the hair at the nape of my neck.

In and out, in and out—I closed my eyes and imagined, pretended. The feel of a woman, the smell. Warm breath on my neck, kisses and touches that started off soft but became feverish. It had been so long and in that moment it felt so damn good. This girl's cries sounded nothing like *hers*, but I was lost by then. With every *oh, yeah* and *fuck, baby* I was more driven to wring every bit of pleasure I could from this. And Kenzie was loud when she came. The stuff that came out of her mouth was filthy in a way that was hot, but for some reason I felt wrong and sickened by it at the same time. I worked to school my expression as she rode it out.

Kenzie opened her eyes slowly, smiling at me, now suddenly bashful. "Um, wow."

"Did I make you feel something?"

Her teeth dragged over her lower lip as she nodded. "That was...Wow."

She kissed me again as she reached down between us and went for my belt buckle. I reached down to stop her. "No, you don't have to do that. Tonight was about you."

"Fair is fair," she said, reaching down again to rub my dick through my jeans and then licking her lips. It was meant to be seductive but it left me feeling sorry for her.

"I don't want to take you in my truck. You deserve a hell of a lot better than that."

She smiled at me with awe and gratitude, as if I was some sort of prince. "I'd invite you up because I *really* want to continue this, but," she nodded her head towards the apartment building, embarrassed, "I still live with my parents."

"That's cool. I live in the upstairs apartment at my dad's place. Cheap rent, right?"

"Yeah." She traced her fingers along my jaw, gazing at me. "I really like you."

I placed my hand over hers, stopping her. "I have to take things slow and I can't make you any promises, Kenzie. To be honest, I think you should run like hell from me. I don't think I can be what you need."

"I'll take my chances," she said as she slid off my lap, slowly. "Give me your phone." She threw her long hair over one shoulder and snapped a selfie, her body at an angle that put her full breasts on prominent display. She entered her contact information and then handed the phone back over. "The ball is in your court, Jeremy. No pressure, but I hope you'll call me."

I sat and waited until I saw that she was safely inside the lobby before I drove off. I had to adjust myself several times on the drive home to alleviate that familiar, painful ache. The thought of Kenzie coming on my hand didn't have me worked up into this state. No, it was the memory of Carolyn, sitting in that same position all those years ago. Bared to me except for those little white panties, pleading with me to go further with her, to make her mine.

I wouldn't that night. I treated Carolyn like glass, like I had to be careful and go slow with her. If I *had* made her mine, would it all have turned out differently? Would she have trusted me? Let me know what Chase was doing to her? I bit back that old familiar anger, thinking about him threatening her, coercing her. Would she have let me in, let me take care of her? Would that act—connecting with her in that intimate way—would it have made her love for me strong enough?

Would it have made a damn difference?

I'll never know.

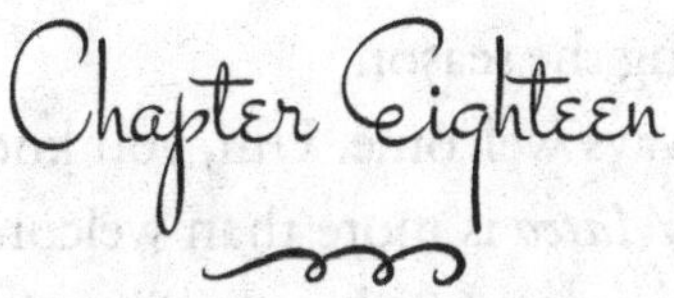

Chapter Eighteen

JEREMY

"What's up?" I answered happily, always glad to see Andie's name flash across my screen.

"You know, saving the world one learning disabled child at a time."

"I love that you're at Briarwood, Andie. How cool is that, teaching the next generation?"

"I hate to say I got lucky, because this position only opened up because Mr. Frazier had a stroke, but I do love this job. Like, I am *so* happy waking up every day. How many people can say they have a job like that?"

I smiled because her enthusiasm was infectious. Andie hadn't changed—she was still all that was happiness and light. "How's Mateo?"

"Awesome."

"Glad to hear it."

"Oh, he's angling for an invite up to Killington this winter. Just warning you."

I bought a place last winter, splitting the cost with my dad. It was nothing fancy, but it had a few extra guestrooms, a decent kitchen, a big ass fireplace and a location that couldn't be beat—ski-on, ski-off. We rented it out for the Thanksgiving, Christmas and February school breaks to offset the cost, but otherwise I tried not to miss too many weekends during the season.

"You two are always welcome. Um, you know what? On second thought," I teased, "*Mateo* is more than welcome but if *you* want to come up you have to promise that you'll at least attempt one run down the bunny hill."

"Gah! I was *not* made to ski. I'm a beach bum. You know this about me, Jeremy!"

"Then tell Mateo I'll see him soon."

"Make you a deal. I'll bring a giant pot of my killer vegetarian chili and some of my awesome space cakes...But I'm not skiing."

"It's a deal, but only if you stick some meat in that chili. Oh, and plain brownies for me, Andie. My space-caking days are officially over."

"You got it."

"I've actually got to head up there sometime in the next few weeks."

"Why so early?"

"Just to do some repairs and to tidy up. There's a nice sized hot tub on the deck but we couldn't use it last year. There are some wiring issues and the deck railing is kind of shot. I'm going to install some outdoor lighting too."

"Yeah, make sure you get that hot tub running since that's where I'll be spending most of my ski weekend."

"I haven't given up on you, Andie. I bet by the end of the winter me and Mateo will having you shredding up the slopes."

"Not happening. You need your very own little snow bunny to torture. And on that note...Anyone special in your life, Jeremy?"

"Not at the moment."

"No worries, handsome, she's out there. You just haven't met her yet."

No, I've met her.

Andie and I lost touch during those years I'd been at Westerly, connecting again after we met at an art show where Chuck Watters' work was being shown. She didn't know more than the most basic details of what I'd been through in recent years. She didn't know about Carolyn—the reason why I had no desire whatsoever to find myself a snow bunny of my very own.

"So," I said, changing the subject, "to what do I owe the pleasure?"

"Well, I kind of need a favor."

"Anything, Andie, you know that."

"I was hoping you'd say that. The Briarwood Gala is the first week of November. I'm the new kid here and I want to make a good impression on the board. In addition to the usual raffles and baskets, I suggested we have a silent auction art show. I'm asking students and former students to donate some of their work, with the proceeds going back to the school. Are you in?"

"Uh, I don't know if I have anything worthy of selling."

"Please, none of that self-deprecating bullshit, all right? Your work is insane, Jeremy. It will fetch some serious ducats."

"I don't know about that, but you're welcome to whatever you need. How many pieces and how big?"

"Two...Three if you're feeling generous. And any size is fine. Nothing is too small or too big."

"You got it. Any promising students?"

"Oh, you have *no* idea. There's this one boy, Travis. I feel like a complete fraud instructing him. He's totally more talented than I am. You'll see. His work will be displayed that night."

"I don't know if I'll be able to make it."

I knew Carolyn would most certainly be there, so I planned to steer clear. Then again, maybe I should go, see what happens. See how it is, now that she's *come out on the other side*, as Tori had put it.

"Well, I sure hope you can make it. But let's at least grab lunch the day you haul your stuff over here, all right?"

"It's a date."

That night I wandered around my place, flipping through canvases of various sizes, trying to find something that might fetch some money at auction. My best pieces had one thing in common: Carolyn was the subject.

* * *

CAROLYN

"Mom, I really need a job."

"I don't agree. You have your coursework to focus on. A job on top of school might be—"

"It won't be too much. I'd be working two shifts a week, just one night during the week and Saturday nights. I'll only take on more shifts during school breaks and holidays. Please don't fight me on this. I'm ready. I need to feel more independent."

"You've been doing so well." She stopped briefly to wipe her eyes. "I've been so happy watching you come back to us this year. I just don't want you to have any setbacks."

I hugged my mother close. Over the past three years, my parents had suffered as much, if not more than I had. Now that I was able to look back on everything, I can't imagine how hard it was for them to watch me change from a girl who seemed to have it all under control, to a scared and paranoid young woman who could not function without constant support. And my mother and father were nothing but supportive. How could I ever think they would have been angry at me or blamed me—that they wouldn't have backed me one hundred percent? No one had better parents than I did. Of that I was certain.

"You and Dad have been so good to me. I just need to start paying my own way. I know you had to eat the cost of that entire first semester of Penn and then...the hospital. I overheard you two talking one day. I feel so terrible that I've put you in debt."

"Do not *ever* mention that again, Carolyn. I mean it. We wouldn't have done anything differently. I'll never view anything that helped you as a financial burden. Do you understand?"

I nodded. "But I still want to take the job. I'm ready, Mom."

I don't know why I thought waitressing would be a mindless job, a breeze. Thursday and Saturday nights at La Viola were slammed every week. I trained during some afternoon lunches, which was a piece of cake—salads and mineral water for the after tennis, ladies who lunch crowd. At night, however, it was three course meals, opening wine bottles in the precise manner in which we were instructed to do so, and juggling up to nine tables at a time. It made the nights go quickly, though, and the tips were fantastic.

I was proud of myself after those first few weeks. Not only because I was able to handle the fast pace and the multi-tasking, but more so because I was able to handle the anxiety that sometimes still reared its ugly head when I was in a position to interact socially.

During my first week I waited on Mike Hanson's parents and my high school French teacher. With a few deep, calming breaths, I was able to do my job, smiling and keeping track of everything just fine. It was the little things, the small victories that I celebrated.

* * *

JEREMY

I didn't call Kenzie. I didn't see the point. She might say that she wasn't looking for any kind of commitment, but I believed that to be well-intentioned bullshit.

A week had passed since our date. Frank asked me about it once, told me that Kenzie really liked me, but then dropped it. I appreciated that. I knew that if a really good looking, seemingly kind and willing girl was doing nothing for me, then I just wasn't ready.

Sunday morning I woke up early and took a long run, as I did every week on my day off. I always stopped at the bake shop for a fresh crumb cake on my way back, and then have coffee with my grandfather as he polished off most of the sweets.

This year had been hard on him. He lost his way for a bit after my grandmother passed away, but he was keeping busy and putting one foot in front of the other. He spent his days tinkering, attempting to fix things around his house, even though his fingers weren't that nimble anymore. And he began sculpting again. Oddly enough, his arthritis gave an interesting quality to his work. The faces he sculpted had features that were a little distorted, but the work was really spectacular—it was emotional. He'd laugh me off when I complimented him, telling me that he wasn't blind yet so I should stop yanking his chain. I would work alongside him for an hour or so on Sunday mornings before heading out when he laid down for his mid-morning nap.

That Sunday I drove back into town again on my way home. I needed to grab some beer and chips to bring to Frank's place later that afternoon. Whenever the Jets played the Patriots we made a day of it. Sometimes we were lucky enough to snag tickets, but otherwise either me or Frank would invite everyone over. It was a mix of some old high school football buddies, work friends, and when Mike could make it, a few of his frat brothers tagged along too.

Mike originally planned to attend Stanford out west, but after everything happened, he decided on staying closer to home, accepting a seat at Yale instead. He told me once that he'd gone to see Carolyn, just to make sure she was all right and to let her know that she'd have him around at Yale if she ever needed anything, but like me, he was turned away.

I grabbed a baseball cap out of the glove compartment before I walked into the supermarket; I still hadn't showered since my morning run. I went straight for the beer section. I grabbed a case and then snatched a few bags of chips with my free hand. I was nearly at the end of the aisle when she turned into it from the opposite direction and we nearly collided. I dropped the chips and she scrambled to the floor at the same time I did, apologizing as she tried to pick them up for me.

"Leave it, Carolyn, I got it."

"I'm sorry…I'm such a spaz," she blurted out.

"How are you?"

"I'm good, and you?" Her tone was formal, like it was a rehearsed speech.

"I'm all right."

The air hung between us, not in an uncomfortable way, more like it was charged. After a moment of staring at each other, Carolyn broke the silence. "Um, looks like you're heading someplace fun today," she said, gesturing towards the beer.

"Frank's house…Just watching football. What are you up to?"

If she didn't have plans, I was going to do it, ask her to go somewhere with me right now. I envisioned the two of us sitting across from one another in a diner, telling each other everything, catching up on the last three years, giving each other explanations for what had gone wrong.

"Meeting my running group. I'm training for the Boston Marathon this spring."

"That's great, Carolyn. I'm impressed."

She turned away and lowered her head, like she was unsure of herself. Damn, she seemed so fragile. "Thanks. The running, it helps."

"Yeah, I know what you mean," I said, wanting to reassure her. "Running always clears my head and makes me feel good."

She nodded. "Anyway, I just ran in to grab some Gator—"

"Did you find them, Carolyn?" asked a guy around my height, slight build, dressed in running gear that I'd never be caught dead in. Skinny little bastard was wearing tights, a slim-cut top and a state of the art, giant ass training watch on his wrist. I mean, what self-respecting guy wears running tights? He looked me over from head to toe in return, certainly taking in my longish hair, my wrinkled, sweaty Tri-State Electrical t-shirt, my case of beer and my chips—which were *not* vegan, unsalted or gluten-free. This guy looked like he subsisted on tofu, chia seeds and almond milk.

"Um, Jeremy, this is Todd." Looking back to him, she said in explanation, "We went to high school together."

I winced. That hurt more than it should have. I nodded, probably tight-lipped and looking as pissed as I felt.

That's what we were, Carolyn, high school chums?

Fuck this, I'm outta here.

"It was good to see you, Carolyn. Take care of yourself."

I walked off, not bothering to say goodbye to Todd. That was for the best, as I had a strong urge to wrap my hands around his puny little neck and squeeze.

I needed to take my aggression out on the heavy bag for half an hour until the hurt and the anger bled out of me. After a long shower, I felt maybe not better, but resigned. Who knew if that guy Todd was her boyfriend even? I suspected he was, because she looked really uncomfortable when he came upon us. And if he wasn't, he wanted to be—that was clear. But even if he was nothing to her, it seemed like I fell into that category as well. *We went to high school together.* For some reason it also hurt that she looked great, beautiful —better than ever.

She looked happy—without me.

Frank was bringing the obnoxious to a whole new level. I was a die-hard Pats fan, while Frank's family, originally from Brooklyn, bled Jets green. As I walked up the steps to his second-floor apartment, I saw the Jets flag covering his window and the Gang Green sign on his door.

There were about ten of us here today, all seated around Frank's seventy-inch flat-screen. His place was basically a man cave, with the largest leather sectional couch I've ever seen, flanked by recliners on either side. There was ample room for ten large guys in his living room.

By half-time, the Pats had taken a comfortable thirteen-point lead and I was at least six beers in. I wanted to forget—to drink, to laugh and to move on.

At some point during the fourth quarter, Frank's door opened and in came Sadie, followed by a few of her friends. Cheers erupted when the guys saw they were carrying pizza boxes and more beer. Kenzie's eyes found mine and she smiled at me apprehensively. It's like she was silently asking: *Are you happy to see me or not?* I'm sure I gave her back a lazy-ass, borderline lewd smile, but she seemed pleased. She personally brought a slice over to me, and when she went to go back to the girls, I tugged her into my lap and whispered in her ear, "I'm glad you're here."

A few seconds later she whispered back, "Yeah, I get the idea that you're happy to see me," as she wiggled a little in my lap. Kenzie was wearing short shorts and a halter top, which wasn't out of place on this Indian summer kind of day. She was a petite little thing, probably no more than five-four, with Marilyn Monroe-like curves. She was hot. Me? I was horny, love-sick and angry.

"I'm heading out when the game's over."

"Do you wanna hang out?" she asked, hopeful.

"Yeah, I'd like that."

She took my keys, thankfully, and drove us back to my place.

My alarm went off at five–thirty, set for the time I usually took my short, pre-dawn run. That wouldn't be happening this morning. My mouth was dry, my head was a little fuzzy, and the smell of sex, I noticed, hung in the air.

Her soft, curvy ass nudged back against my morning wood. I'd nearly forgotten how nice it felt to have this. Kenzie was all soft skin, plump curves and willing. Taking the lead again, she reached down between us and eased me towards her entrance. Despite the mild hangover, I was into it, but I stopped.

"Wait, let me grab a condom."

She tugged on me again, gently. "We're good, Jeremy. We didn't use one last night. It felt awesome."

"Oh, shit," I murmured, rolling away from her onto my back.

She turned over, leaning up on one elbow, caressing my chest with her other hand. "I'm on the pill, baby, it's ok."

"I don't like taking chances."

"It was *your* idea last night. You said you needed to feel all of me...Nothing between us."

"Yeah, I'd say that was the ten or so beers talking. I shouldn't have done that. I'm sorry."

"It's all good, Jeremy, we're protected." She reached behind her where the condoms sat ignored from last night and ripped one off the strip. She straddled me, her tits swaying heavily with every slight move she made. "If it makes you feel better, let's cover you up," she said teasing, but there was a hint of hurt in her tone—like she clearly understood I'd be fucking miserable if she was ever to become pregnant.

She rolled the condom down, biting her lower lip as she watched the latex move down my length. Her voice was husky when she said, "I have to have you inside me again, baby. I need it."

As long as she needed *it* and not *me*, I was good to go. She rode me, arching her back, thrusting her tits out. She was uninhibited and looking to put on a show for me. She reached both hands up, lifted her long hair off her neck for a moment and then eased back, bracing her hands against my thighs. All the while she ground her hips in a circular motion as she bounced herself up and down along my shaft. She was losing control just like me, chanting my name, panting and moaning. When I was just there on the edge, Kenzie dipped her head down to kiss me and then whispered, "Tell me I'm beautiful, Jeremy."

Something about those words snapped me out of this mindless fucking. A memory. *Isn't that stupid, that I was so desperate to be told I was beautiful?* The memory of that painful secret Carolyn shared with me so long ago. Her shame at going along with that piece of shit, Greg Henley—an insecure girl so grateful to be told she was beautiful.

Whatever it was, Kenzie's demand deflated my boner like a pin to a blister. She was just about there, though, so I kept going, kept thrusting, and then—yes—I faked it. She didn't seem to notice that I rolled her off me immediately after letting out a series of lackluster grunts. She didn't notice that I peeled off an empty condom. She didn't acknowledge that I had not repeated those words back to her, as she'd asked me to.

Kenzie stretched like a contented cat and then rested her head on my chest, snuggling her body close to mine.

I had a strong urge to peel her off of me as I asked, "What time do you need to be at work?"

"Um, nine?"

"I'll drop you at home on my way up to New Haven. I'm gonna take a quick shower."

"Want company?"

I edged off the bed and grabbed a towel on my way to the bathroom. "No, I'm good."

I didn't want to hurt her, but the thought of letting her paw at me in the shower made my skin crawl and my heart ache.

What I did last night was just wrong. The fact that I'd indulged again this morning significantly upped my level of assholery.

Seeing Carolyn had totally screwed with my head. Wouldn't happen a second time. I wasn't going to lead Kenzie on anymore. I wouldn't hurt her. And I wasn't falling to pieces over Carolyn Harris ever again.

I contemplated calling Andie and asking her not to use the pieces I'd already dropped off at Briarwood for next Friday. It would look like a damn shrine to Carolyn if they displayed all three canvases together.

Fuck it.

Maybe it was for the best. Maybe it was time I got rid of everything that reeked of her.

Chapter Nineteen

CAROLYN

"No, it's not right. I think that piece would look better next to Travis's large canvas, right by the heart sculpture. Don't you?

I watched as this little sprite of a girl commanded three men.

"What about this one, Andie?"

"I want that right by Mitchell's series of watercolors."

One of the guys saw me standing there waiting and then gestured to Andie, the girl in charge.

"Hi," she said, smiling brightly. "Can I help you?"

I smiled back. It was kind of hard not to when you were in this girl's presence. She was energetic, full of life...exuberant.

"Hi, I'm Carolyn Harris. I'm just here to drop off the gift baskets for the raffle. Do you know where I'm supposed to put them?"

"You're Maureen Harris's daughter?" I nodded. "So then you're Tommy's sister...Love that kid. Do you want to see his contribution for the Gala auction?"

"He made something?" I asked, unable to hide the surprise in my voice. "I mean, I know he's creative but I just never thought he was into art."

"Oh, but he is. Feast your eyes on this," she said happily, as she gestured towards a large monarch butterfly made of papier-mâché.

I smiled, but before I knew it I was wiping away tears. Every year we would get one of those kits, the ones with live caterpillars. We'd check on them every day together after school, watching as they changed from caterpillar to chrysalis, and finally, to butterflies. We'd set them free then, watching as they landed tentatively on the purple butterfly bushes planted along the edge of our backyard before they went higher, moving further away.

In that moment, I realized that I'd let the ritual die three years ago. Was this Thomas's way of letting me know how much he missed *us*?

"I totally get it," Andie said, nodding. "My students' art can bring me to tears. Just knowing the feeling and the effort they put into making something so...so...beautiful."

"Yeah, this is really special to me. I'll definitely be bidding on this one."

"I'm so excited about this!" Andie sang happily, clapping her hands. "We have so many great pieces for the guests to bid on."

"The art auction was a great idea. It's definitely going to bring a lot more money in."

"Well it was *my* idea, so it better bring money in or I'll die of shame and embarrassment," she said, laughing. "Mateo, Daniel... Let's help Carolyn get the rest of the baskets from her car."

As we were walking in with the last load, Andie looked over to me with a puzzled expression. "I keep thinking we've met before. You look so familiar."

"I volunteered here over the summer. Maybe we ran into each other on campus?"

"No, I don't think so." She was still staring, trying to place me. "I just started teaching here in September. I mean, I *went* to Briarwood, but I've been away at college for the past four years."

I shrugged and she shook herself out of her dazed thoughts.

"Anyway, so I'll be seeing you on Friday, Carolyn?"

"I'll be here early setting up. I'm pretty much on duty the entire night."

"Me too. It'll be fun!"

"I'm so glad I met you, Andie."

* * *

JEREMY

There are many reasons why you shouldn't operate a hand-held phone while driving. The obvious reason would be to prevent a crash, grievous injuries and the like. Another reason? To prevent yourself from getting a fat ticket and a stern talking-to from the cops. But the most compelling reason I now had for never, *ever* doing it again? Calling someone without intending to do so.

I was trying to reach one of my electricians, Kevin, but was instead greeted by a giddy girl's voice chirping, "Jeremy! Hey, it's great to hear from you."

"Kenzie?"

"The one and only!"

"Um, hey, what's up? How's your week going?" I tried to be casual even though I was repeating: *fuck, fuck, fuck* in my head.

"Getting better and better," she practically sang.

"Listen, I—"

"Oh, I know why you're calling," she interrupted. "Sadie told me already. She set up plans for Saturday night—the four of us." I said nothing, stunned momentarily. Kenzie didn't seem to notice because she just kept on talking. "I forgot the name of the place. It's some

Italian restaurant that she said was awesome. Sadie said our reservation is for eight o'clock."

"Oh." That was the brilliant response I came up with.

"I think it's in Westerly. You don't need to drive all the way up here to get me. I can borrow my mother's car and park at your place."

She's a good person, I told myself. *You fucked her so the least you can do is take her out to dinner. After dinner, you can have a talk—tell her that it's not going to work out. Be kind and respectful to a girl who certainly deserves a lot better than you.*

"Did you hear me, Jeremy?"

Her question pulled me back from my rambling inner dialogue. "I'll come and pick you up, Kenzie."

"Are you sure?"

"Absolutely."

"Hey, dickhead, I said you could set up *one* date for me. I don't recall appointing you as my social calendar director."

"So good to hear from you, Rivers. For the record, Sadie set that up. I had nothing to do with it."

I let out a breath. "Seriously, Frank, please tell her to cut that shit out. Kenzie's a nice girl. I don't want to mess with her head."

"You're not interested? You seemed into her last weekend."

"I was drunk. I'm not proud of that. I'm a shit for leading her on like that, but all this double-dating crap is making it worse."

"You did fuck her, though, correct?"

"None of your business."

He laughed. "Kind of heard it through the grapevine already, but it's nice to know you're a gentleman."

"Great," I muttered.

"You *are* coming on Saturday though, right?" Frank asked cautiously. "I mean, she's *really* into you. Just give this a chance."

I was pressing my free hand into my forehead, trying to ward off the killer headache that was now inevitable.

"When I'm with her it doesn't feel right."

"You're just out of practice."

"I don't think so."

"Let's just go out as four friends, have some drinks, some laughs...See where it goes. I'm sorry, Jeremy, but I'm not gonna sit back and let you just exist—just keep up this miserable, lonely routine you've got going."

"I'm not miserable."

"But you're not happy. I want you to have what I have with Sadie, man. I'm *happy*."

I thought about Kenzie the rest of the week. Thought about her good looks, her smile, the way her body responded to mine. I thought about the pain she's endured in her young life. Tried to muster up some deeper sense of feeling for her.

I also thought about Carolyn a lot. I replayed the scene from the grocery store in my head. Before that asshole came strolling along, barging in on our reunion, I could swear she looked at me with some kind of—I don't know—longing. But then she introduced me as a classmate, nothing more. It was confusing as hell. And it was painful. Still painful after all this time.

I contemplated dropping into the coffee shop to drill Tori for information, but thought better of it. When Tori reached out to me Friday morning, dropping a text to ask if I was going to the Briarwood Gala, a simple *nope* was my reply. I felt hostile as I pounded those four letters out.

I wondered if Carolyn would see my work. If she would even recognize herself as my subject, my muse for every important piece I'd ever created.

I simultaneously prayed she would see them—feel my love for her through each stroke—and cringed thinking she may react by laughing at my immature need to hold onto her, when she'd probably moved on from me long ago.

* * *

CAROLYN

The gym had been transformed. Swaths of pale, glittery fabric hung from twinkling overhead light fixtures that cast a warm glow over the space. The tables were set with fine china, silver cutlery and crystal glassware that sparkled in the light.

I saw Beth Peterman setting spectacular fall-themed flower arrangements in the center of each table. I decided to extend an olive branch. This woman had done nothing to me, aside from making me seethe with jealousy. I can't say I was a fan, though, because if it was true, she hooked up with Jeremy while he was in high school and that was just flat-out wrong. But my new philosophy, in addition to speaking my mind and expressing myself honestly, also included things I was still working on: self-acceptance and letting go of the past. So I would let go of this hurt.

"My mother said you made these arrangements yourself. They're beautiful, Mrs. Peterman."

She turned, wide-eyed and wary when she saw it was me. "Thank you so much, Carolyn," she said, recovering. Smiling, she looked down and fussed with a few of the stems even though they looked perfect. "I love arranging flowers. I'm so glad I could do this for the Gala."

"Well, you're talented, and my mom said you've been a great help." That compliment rendered her childlike, beaming with delight and pride. I decided in that moment that I shouldn't judge her. Here she was, a fish out of water, married to a geezer who sought fit to marry a girl the same age as his daughter from his first marriage. Maybe Beth didn't have it as easy as I'd assumed.

I smiled and then told her I had to get back to work, gesturing towards the raffle table I was setting up. I was pleased. The baskets looked professionally done and the placards that Ava created on her laptop had great graphics and expressed the high quality of the merchandise within each one. *These should fetch some big bucks*, I thought to myself later as I took a step back and admired the finished display.

I waved to the other women when I was leaving, and then headed home, where Ava, Tori and Taylor were meeting me to get dressed for the night.

After I showered, I flopped back on my bed for a few minutes and admired my shiny, dark red mani-pedi. I didn't pamper myself much during the past three years, and it felt good. I looked over to the red dress hanging on my closet door. It was knee length, nothing too formal, but the satin fabric hugged my body. It looked a bit nineteen-twenties; sexy but elegant. I decided to get ready before they arrived. I dried and curled my hair into loose waves. I applied mascara, some blush and a tinted lip gloss that reddened my lips just slightly. I put on the satin bra and panties I'd purchased for tonight, slipped the dress over my head and then slid my feet into the black, strappy heels. I turned in the mirror, taking myself in from every angle. I looked good.

"You look good, girl!" Tori exclaimed as she entered my room, a garment bag draped over her arm. "Holy shit, Carolyn," she said, taking me in more thoroughly. "I'm serious, you look so beautiful."

"Thanks, Tori. Let's get you dressed."

"Hey," she said, cocking her head, "why do you look blue?"

"It's totally stupid."

"Tell me."

"I just...I'm hoping he'll be there tonight. And he won't be. I know he won't be. I'm just being an ass."

"No, you're not," she countered. "You still care about him. I get that."

"I acted so weird when I saw him in the supermarket last Sunday."

"How so?"

"I was totally awkward...Like I couldn't get a sentence out without sounding totally ridiculous."

"I'm sure he didn't think so. You're being overly critical of yourself."

"No, Tori, it didn't go well. He looked...I don't know, cold and offish by the time he walked away. You know, like...*See ya, have a nice life, Carolyn.* I felt like running after him and asking him for a do-over. I felt this need to talk to him, really talk."

"So then you'll do that. You'll talk to him. But," she added, shaking her head, "I'm pretty sure he won't be there tonight."

"You spoke to him?"

"Just texted. I asked if he was coming and he said no."

I nodded, resigned.

"He's off on Sundays, Carolyn. Comes in at eight-thirty nearly every Sunday morning, like clockwork. Grabs two coffees to go and a crumb cake." She smiled. "I think he times it so he gets there right as the crumb cakes come out of the oven."

"*Two* coffees?"

Tori rolled her eyes. "He goes to see his grandfather every Sunday morning." Rubbing her palms together and smiling, she said, "Anyway, I suggest you come in for coffee this Sunday morning."

"We'll see," I said, trying to sound undecided but unable to hide the grin that was spreading across my face.

After some last minute set-up, I stationed the girls at their respective posts. Tori and Ava would be walking about the room, selling raffle tickets, while Taylor, the most persuasive of our group, was manning the basket table, luring in prospective bidders with details about the decadent treats that awaited them if they were lucky enough to win.

I noticed that as the room started filling up, a great deal more men were stopping by the basket table, asking questions and dropping large amounts of raffle tickets into the bags. Taylor looked like she was having fun with it, breaking out her old wily charms. I smiled because this was play acting for Taylor now. She had grown up a great deal, committing herself to one person for the past year. Marcus was a slightly older guy who seemed to be head over heels for her.

"It's more crowded than usual, don't you think?"

"Definitely, Mom. I think tonight's going to top last year's total by a lot. Is there anything you need me to do?"

"Just keep selling. Everything else is under control."

All of us girls selling raffles had a silver balloon tied to a string around our wrists, so that we were easily recognized. I made my way about the room, generally only making it a few feet before being stopped by another patron. As the champagne flowed, the wallets opened.

Beth Peterman bought five hundred dollars-worth of tickets from me. I watched as she took them and approached the basket table, wondering which getaway she would bid on. I quickly caught on to her ulterior motive. She practically needed a crowbar to pry the very distinguished looking, but very *old* Mr. Peterman away from Taylor. Beth, I decided, probably lived under the constant worry of *when*, not if, Mr. Peterman was going to trade her in for a newer model.

"Now I know who you are!" I turned abruptly and was face to face with Andie, her expression pleased but a little stunned. She shook her head, bewildered. "You're true beauty."

"Uh...thanks for the compliment?"

Andie laughed. "You do look great tonight, Carolyn, but I'm referring to the painting. True Beauty? It was donated by a student... Well, a former student. It *has* to be you. Come see," she said as she took my wrist and led me into the adjoining space, which had been set up as a gallery.

Andie stopped in front of a large canvas, looking at me expectantly before she dropped my arm. I stood speechless, my mouth surely hanging open in shocked surprise.

It was me all right, perched on that stool in nothing but my tiny white skivvies. It was a modern piece. The female form was rendered in charcoal, but the borders were splashed in swaths of red with some yellow accents. It gave the impression of burning light surrounding the girl.

I swallowed back tears when I looked closely at the face. I was looking at him with an expression that conveyed my deep love and also my desire. My shoulder was arched back a little and one hand rested on my inner thigh. I remembered back to that night. I positioned myself so that he had no choice but to look at the curve of my breast as he worked. Jeremy wanted the session to be chaste, while I wanted to tempt him, break him down, get him into a state where he'd need me—have to have me.

"So you know Jeremy Rivers?" Andie asked softly, bringing me back.

"Yes," I whispered, nodding. "I knew him a long time ago."

"This piece is so hauntingly beautiful, so very evocative. It's spectacular, really. I almost feel bad that he parted with it. Someone is going to get a bargain tonight."

"Did he donate anything else," I asked, turning back to Andie.

"Um, yeah, two other pieces," she said, a sympathetic frown creasing her brow as she gestured across the room.

I felt like the wind was knocked out of me again as I took in *Blue Gingham*. It was me, standing at the water's edge. It was all charcoal, in black and white, but I smiled thinking about his obsession with that one particular bikini. I was dipping my toe into the lake tentatively, my arms out at my sides for balance, my face tilted down, peering into the water, possibly scoping it out for vipers? The detailing in the landscape was striking. It was if he'd given the reed grass movement; you could almost hear the whisper of a breeze passing through it. I smiled again as I took in the female form and noticed the slightly exaggerated size of my breasts. *Wishful thinking, Jeremy*.

A couple approached then and I went back to selling tickets as I moved about the gallery, looking for his third canvas. I made two loops and came up empty. I was just about to go find Andie when I came upon it. It was small in comparison, no more than two feet square, entitled *My Friend*. It was two kids—no, it was me and Jeremy at around age twelve. Our foreheads were almost touching and we were looking into each other's eyes, smiling in a way that was nearly imperceptible. My glasses were sliding down my nose. He was reaching a finger up, looking as if he was about to right them. There was such an intimacy in what passed between the two.

"His work takes my breath away, Carolyn. I hope someday he decides to pursue this. He's more talented than most people I know."

"He says the same thing about you, Andie."

She chuckled. "Yeah, well we have a long-standing mutual admiration society-thing going. But really, his style has changed. When I last saw his work, he was drawing portraits and figures, but they were bland. These are powerful and stripped down—raw in their intensity, you know?"

She was looking at me, gauging my reaction. I did my best to hold myself together. I simply nodded.

"Well, the auction ends in an hour. I have to work the room and get some of these people to part with their cash," she said, winking at me. "Oh, and by the way, two people have already bid on your butterfly but you can still snag that for a song. *True Beauty*, though, is commanding some nice bids. I don't know about you, but if *I* was the subject of that piece, I'd want to look at it hanging over *my* mantle when I turned old, wrinkly and gray. A nice reminder of what once was, you know?"

Before walking away, I looked at the bid sheet for *My Friend*. Three bids so far, with Beth Peterman topping the offerings at nine hundred. Making my way around the room, I noticed she also was among the several bidders for *Blue Gingham,* but not the top bidder. Under the guise of approaching patrons for raffle ticket sales, I stopped at each canvas. Funny, but her name wasn't on any other bid sheets. I stopped at Thomas's butterfly then, smiling as I put my name last on the list, outbidding the closest potential buyer by fifty dollars. Hopefully, no one else would want this and I could snag it for the eight-five dollars I'd bid. A few people were standing in front of *True Beauty* as I approached. An older couple stood close together, speaking in hushed tones that I strained to overhear.

"I really think we should snag this, dear. I mean, have you ever seen such a sensuous rendering?"

I blushed, knowing that it was my body they were looking at. But I realized in that moment that I didn't feel one ounce of shame. I looked at that girl and saw someone who *was* beautiful—someone who was in love. That *was* me and I had no sense of shame over the person I had been when I was with Jeremy.

"Someone's young lover," he replied, smiling wistfully.

"I'm upping the last bid," she whispered conspiratorially. "Jeez, this woman keeps outbidding me by a hundred dollars. Who is Beth Peterman?" she asked to no one in particular, annoyed.

"No idea, dearest."

After they walked away, I studied the bids. Yep, Beth had bid on this piece four times so far. My sympathy for her evaporated—was not liking her so much anymore. The highest bid was now two-thousand, eight hundred dollars.

For a brief, foolish moment, I contemplated writing in a bid of $2801. Fact was, I only had one third of that amount saved in tips from my job so far. It was out of my reach.

The thought also struck me that Jeremy had given them all away.

Maybe his willingness to part with his art, with these reminders of me, meant that he didn't want me.

"Hey, where you been?" Ava's bright smile drew me out of my funk.

"I was just working the gallery room. How did you do in sales?"

"I have no idea, but it has to be a lot. I kept going back to your mom with stacks of twenties and hundreds. These people don't mind dropping it, you know?"

"I think having beautiful girls selling the tickets doesn't hurt either," I teased.

"I was thinking the same thing," she said, giggling. "We all look smoking hot tonight. I mean, Taylor is workin' it. She has to have raked in a million dollars over there."

I looked over to see two tuxedo-clad, middle-aged men flirting shamelessly with Taylor as she laughed and batted her eyes while they dropped handfuls of tickets into various raffle bags. I shook my head, smiling. "She's too much."

There was a break in the dance music announcing that less than ten minutes remained before all silent art auction bids and raffle tickets sales were closed. I smiled at Ava. "Duty calls," I said, as I went back to working the perimeter of the room, selling more tickets.

A few minutes later, I noticed Beth come back into the main room, a scowl marring her face. Maybe that older couple had beaten her out. I really hoped they had. The idea of Beth owning that piece, owning something that was Jeremy's—something that was so intimately mine—burned. In comparison, the idea of those older art lovers owning the piece comforted me.

I stayed with my mother for the next twenty minutes. All of the volunteers were in a back room, recording the winners for the baskets and fifty-fifty drawings as names were picked out in a surprisingly formal and official manner. A different person was called up to pick a ticket from each raffle bag and the name was announced out loud for all to hear. My mother asked Ava to write the names of the winners on the large display board. Ava beamed, adding flourishes to the names as she wrote them. The girl had sick penmanship.

Beth was called up to pick the Spa Getaway basket winner. She hesitated before announcing my name. Her warm smile from before was gone. Yep, now her lip was curled into a barely concealed sneer. What the hell? And, hello, I didn't buy any raffle tickets.

"Yay!" my mother exclaimed. "Girls' getaway, Carolyn!"

I laughed, nodding, realizing my mother had purchased tickets in my name. She was awesome.

Dancing was still in full swing as desert was being served. After distributing the baskets, I wandered back into the gallery, my curiosity getting the best of me.

I purposely avoided Jeremy's pieces, first checking to see if I'd won Tom's butterfly.

"Winner, winner, chicken dinner," a voice called from behind me.

"Mateo, right?" I asked, and he nodded. "I'm so glad I won this. Would it be bad to lie to Thomas and tell him I plunked down a thousand, ending a fierce bidding war?"

"I'm sure he'll just be psyched you wanted it, no matter what you paid. Do you want me to box it up now? Most of the pieces are being delivered tomorrow but you could save me one trip," he said, cocking his head with a hopeful expression.

"Sure, I'll take it now."

"Great. I'll be back in five," he said, as he carefully lifted the piece from its display.

Bidders milled about, looking to see if they had won. *My Friend* had fetched twelve hundred. I didn't recognize the winner's name. Some large, modern abstract piece by a current student named Travis went for three thousand. He went by his first name only, so I'm guessing he was already a pretentious artist in the making. I was happily awestruck as I looked to the winning bids on each canvas. All went for substantial amounts. Andie must have been thrilled. I stopped at *Blue Gingham*. This name I recognized, as I saw the older woman's scrawl as she bid on *True Beauty*. She won over Beth's most recent bid of nineteen hundred. When I made my way over to *True Beauty*, now overcome with a burning curiosity, I saw that the wall space was blank.

A note was taped over the bid sheet that read: *The artist has requested this piece be removed from the auction. We are truly sorry for any inconvenience this last minute change has caused.*

I saw Andie standing off to the side, speaking with the older couple, smiling. When she saw me, she excused herself and made her way over. "Well this was a smashing success, don't you think?"

"You should be really proud, Andie. I can't believe how much money you raised with this."

"I know! I feel like giving myself a giant pat on the back!"

"Um, did Jeremy—"

"No," she answered, cutting me off. "All said, I think we raised close to thirty-thousand in the gallery alone. I held that piece back for you."

I took a deep, grateful breath but then I was apprehensive. "Andie, I can't just take it. That wouldn't be right."

She nodded, thinking. "You're right. I want twenty bucks for it. I won't take a penny less or a penny more." She looked at me point-edly. "I don't know the story behind that or the others, but I know that you are supposed to own *True Beauty*." She added, "You must be very special to Jeremy."

"I think I was at one time."

She smiled, her eyes sparkling with happiness and mischief. "Someone will be delivering it tomorrow," she said, looking over her shoulder as she walked away.

The next day I took a long run. My feet hit the pavement in a steady, rhythmic beat and my breath came in and whooshed out softly, adding another soothing sound. My breath and my steps were the only soundtrack I needed when I ran. I never ran with headphones, never needed the distraction of music. Running was my time for peaceful reflection. Over the course of the past three years, I believed that my return to running had done as much, if not more for me than my hours of therapy and the medication combined.

As I ran today, my thoughts were focused on the Gala—on Jeremy. Last night was so confusing. I was glad that I was now the owner of that painting, but I worried over what it all meant. Why did he donate those *particular* pieces? Was he trying to send me a message? I mean, he knew I'd be there. He knew I'd see them. If so, what message was he trying to send? Did he want me to know that he still felt something for me? That's what I hoped. The work, all three pieces, were so emotional and conveyed so much love. Was it possible that he still loved me? Or, I wondered sadly, was he trying to show me he could let go? That he was fine with the idea of a stranger owning pieces of us because I no longer meant anything to him.

As usual, I felt better after my run. I could face this, no matter what. I decided that tomorrow morning I *would* pay Tori a visit at the coffee shop at exactly eight-thirty. Tomorrow I wouldn't be startled by a surprise meeting or distracted by Todd's prying interest, as I had been last week. Tomorrow, I thought, psyching myself up, I would talk to Jeremy. For the first time in years, I would really *talk* to him. I felt determined and happy, looking forward to tomorrow.

Chapter Twenty

CAROLYN

I had a bounce in my step as I tied my apron around my waist.

Marco looked up as I came into the kitchen whistling. "What's got you so chipper?"

"Nothing," I said. "Just happy to be here."

"She's happy because she knows she's gonna make some *fat* tips tonight, Marco," Connie chimed in.

Connie trained me my first week. She was older than me, mid-thirties, I guessed. She was a little rough around the edges but sweet. Connie was a single mom with two kids, raising them without any help from their father. I guess that alone would toughen you up some. Although we couldn't have had less in common, she and I had forged a friendship. I'd even watched her kids a few times for her in a pinch, and in return she's cooked me some fabulous dinners. I enjoyed her company and her two boys were adorable. They were like young, rambunctious versions of Thomas.

"We *are* going to do well tonight," Nicholas, the other waiter added. "The reservation book is full."

After the three of us finished prepping salads, filling bowls with freshly grated parmigiana-reggiano cheese and setting up the coffee station, we sat for our pre-shift meal—my favorite part of the evening.

The chef poured us each a half glass of Chianti, which I now loved, and then plated a tasting menu with all of the night's specials. We studied the specials board as we tasted each offering, this way we were able to answer questions and recommend our favorites to customers. Tonight we feasted on duck breast with a balsamic cherry reduction, pear and pecorino-filled ravioli, roasted Maine diver scallops, and sautéed calf liver over polenta. Add sautéed calf livers to the list of things I was surprised to discover that I liked.

Nicholas's younger brother, Sal, who ran plates from the kitchen and bussed tables, joined us right before we sat down to eat.

"Nice of you to join us," Connie dripped sarcastically, her eyes fixed on the reservation book.

"Come on, Connie, after what we did together last night? I thought you'd be in a better mood," Sal teased.

"In your dreams, lover boy."

Sal set his sights on me then. "So, Carolyn, you gonna put Nick out of his misery and go out with him?"

"Seriously," Nicholas said, looking at me smiling, "you have my permission to slap him."

I laughed, now able to take the good natured teasing and quick banter that passed between the wait staff, surly cooks and the bartender.

Connie stabbed her fork in Sal's direction as she chewed on a piece of the ravioli, which was freaking fabulous in my opinion. That was definitely going to be a top recommendation for my customers tonight. "Hey, listen up, Sal. No goofing off tonight and no wasting time flirting with the female customers...or Carolyn," she added, winking at me. "We're going to be slammed, fully seated from...Let's see, five-thirty on. We're going to be running anywhere from six to ten checks at a time, *all night.*"

I asked, "Five-thirty?" Usually we weren't full until half-past six, nearly seven.

"Who the hell eats dinner at five thirty?" Nicholas asked.

"Grandma," answered Sal.

"Mr. and Mrs. Brandt, the Goldbergs, poor old Mr. Finch," I added.

"I think Mr. Finch is looking to make you his sugar baby, Carolyn."

"That wouldn't be half-bad, Sal. He's loaded," I joked.

"You've succeeded in grossing me out and that's not easy to do. Now I won't be able to get the picture of you making out with Mr. Finch out of my mind all night." We all laughed. "I'll be obsessed with the details," he went on. "Does he leave the dentures in or do you lovingly remove them for him, dropping them onto the night-stand before you ravage him?"

"Ugh, enough. Leave my Mr. Finch alone," I said, holding back giggles. I sobered then. "Really, though, he's such a lovely person. He's always telling me about Mrs. Finch. It's sad how much he misses her. My heart breaks watching him eat alone."

"You're such a softie, Carolyn," Connie said, smiling warmly at me as she stood up and started clearing our plates.

By seven o'clock the four of us were running on auto-pilot, a well-oiled machine. I served my early-bird regulars, like Mr. Finch, who always ate the same thing, week after week: hot antipasti, veal parmigiana with spaghetti, slice of cheesecake for desert. I didn't even give customers like him a menu; they appreciated the familiarity of La Viola, that we knew them like family. As usual, the later crowd brought both familiar and unfamiliar faces.

Nights like this, you didn't let your mind wander. You focused on details: drop salads on table twelve, a couple was just seated at three—get their drink order, the large group at five needs more bread. Keep working, keep moving.

When the hostess passed me and said, "I just seated you two new four-tops...tables eight and three," I took it in stride. I wrote down the dinner order from an older couple that was seated first and then made my way over to get drink orders and recite the specials.

I went to the first table, parents with their two teenage daughters, and then made my way towards the other table, two couples. The two girls were facing me, looking slightly annoyed as I approached.

"Hi, welcome to La Viola," I said, looking down to find the pen that had decided to go AWOL in the depths of my apron. "Can I get you something to drink while you look at the menu?"

"*That* would be nice," one girl said—a little sarcastically, I might add. What the hell? The hostess said they'd *just* been seated and you could see the place was jammed. I smiled and met her eyes. Kill them with kindness, the customer is always right—yeah, all that other crap. "I'll have a Cosmo," she said, dismissing me. *Of course you will, you sophisticated gal*, I mused.

I looked to the redhead next to her. "And what can I get you?" I asked, taking both girls in. They were attractive. Cosmo girl was especially pretty, but she kind of ruined the effect by wearing an obscenely low-cut top. Trying too hard.

Her friend was indecisive—tick-tock, tick-tock. I was looking behind her, checking my other tables and gesturing to Sal to clear my six-top, which looked ready to order desert.

"Um, I'm not sure," the girl said absently, nibbling on her lower lip between each word. "I'll give you my drink order when you come back."

Great, two trips to the bar.

"And what can I get you guys?" I asked. When I looked up from my pad, I saw two wide-eyed people who looked mighty uncomfortable. Make that three of us. "Frank, Jeremy...Um, hi."

"Hey, Carolyn," Frank spoke first. Shaking his head and

smiling kindly, he asked, "How have you been?" He glanced to Jeremy nervously when he added, "I didn't know you worked here."

From Jeremy's tight expression, it was obvious that he wouldn't have come within ten miles of this place had he known I was here.

"Yep," I answered. "I've been here for a few months." A brief, awkward silence ensued. "What can I get you guys to drink? And sorry for the wait," I said, looking to the very busty chick who was now eyeing me with curious suspicion. "It's really busy tonight."

"That's no problem," Jeremy said, recovering. "I'll have a Bud."

"Me too," Frank added. He looked to the girl across from him. I gathered that one was his. "Do you know what you want, Sadie?"

I'm thinking maybe my name registered with her, although I was certain I'd never met her. Her eyes were cold as she looked me over. "I'll have vodka with grapefruit juice."

Usually this is when I'd say, "I'll be right back with those," but I didn't have any intention of waiting on them. No way. I put in the bar order and then made a bee-line for the kitchen, where I was planning on asking Connie to cover them for me. She was in the middle of a full-on brawl with Marco, yelling that she did, in fact, alert him that the lady at table one had a shellfish allergy. I grabbed the baked clams my two-top was waiting for and approached Nicholas on my way out onto the floor.

"Nick, can you take the four-top on eight for me?"

"No can do. Just had a party of ten seated. Sorry."

I was desperate enough to ask Sal, our lowly runner, knowing full well that putting him on a table with two sets of boobs prominently displayed was a recipe for disaster. I didn't care. Just as I approached, though, a woman slid her chair out unexpectedly, knocking into Sal, causing him to drop a plate of mussels marinara. I turned at the sound of the plate crashing onto the marble floor.

I had no choice but to face Jeremy and his date.

Deep calming breath, Carolyn. In and out, in and out. Recite the

*specials, take their order, drop the check and you're done. You'll spend
no more than five actual minutes in their presence.*

I was back to giving myself pep talks.

"Here you are," I said as I served their drinks. I rambled off the
specials as quickly as I could. "Have you had a chance to look over
the menu or should I give you a few more minutes?"

Jeremy looked up and met my eyes briefly before looking back
down at his menu, studying like he was cramming for the bar exam.
"A few minutes, if that's ok."

"Yick! This is so *sour*!" Jeremy's babe made a puckered face.
"There's too much...something in this. It tastes nasty. Here," she
said, pouty faced, pushing the drink forward, "you taste it Jeremy."
She looked up to me, her tone short as she said, "I think you got the
order wrong."

Jeremy eyed her evenly. "I've never had one of those. I wouldn't
know if the bartender made it right or not, Kenzie."

*Kenzie...ugh. Hate that name. Actually, I like the name, I just
have a strong dislike for this bossy, bitchy, but...very pretty girl...Ugh!
Fuck me.* Realizing my mind was scrambling, I took another deep
breath and repeated my fight song: *Get yourself together, Carolyn. You
can do this.*

"Don't worry about it." Calm, cool as a cucumber Carolyn was
back. "That *is* a Cosmopolitan, though, so maybe I should just bring
you something else." I felt like dumping it over her head but I kept
my smile even and as sincere as humanly possible. Of course she took
her sweet time deciding. When I glanced up I saw my other table
looking at me expectantly. That other four-top had not even gotten
bread yet. I snagged Sal. "Get table three's appetizer order and bring
them bread right away."

"I guess I'll have a vodka cranberry," she murmured, pouting.

"Be right back." *Service with a smile, bitch.*

I took my other tables' orders, dropped a check and then came
back with Kenzie's drink. "Hope you like this one better," I said as I

placed it in front of her. Jeremy was still staring at the same section of the menu. Guess this was no picnic for him either.

She reached over, practically resting her D cups on the table, and stroked the top of Jeremy's hand, asking, "What looks good to you, Jeremy?" The gesture was familiar and intimate. I gathered that he knew what Kenzie looked like naked. But I also thought the gesture was somewhat forced—she wanted me to know Jeremy was hers. I'd brought out her territorial instincts.

He looked to me instead, moving his hand away from hers as he raised his menu, pointing to an item. "I'll have this one...The pacific grouper over—"

He stalled before attempting the next words: tagliatelli with porcini mushroom ragout.

I nodded, jumping in, noting his order. "I got it. You'll like that. The fish just came in this afternoon and the chef does a really great porcini mushroom sauce for the pasta."

His eyes met mine briefly. It wouldn't have been obvious to anyone else, but something passed between us: acknowledgement, a sense of gratitude, shared understanding—our shared past.Recognition that I knew he was struggling to read those words before anyone else noticed and that I'd covered for him.

I shifted my gaze to Frank before I allowed myself to get emotional.

"I'll have that ravioli special, Carolyn."

Frank's girl went with the chicken parm, no pasta, side of broccoli rabe. Great, moving right along. And then? We weren't. Kenzi scanned her menu indolently, taking her sweet time.

"Do you want me to give you another minute?" I asked.

"No," she said, dismissing me again. Cocking her head and fixing him with a look that said: *I need help from my man*, she asked, "Jeremy, would you get the shrimp scampi or the manicotti?"

"Depends on what you're in the mood for."

"I can't decide." Kenzie's pouty lips were back in place, her voice taking on that little-girl quality that some people find cute. I myself found it nauseating.

She studied the menu choices again. It was like watching a snail cross a wide stretch of deserted highway.

Jeremy stretched his collar away from his neck, his unease palpable. "The shrimp sounds good, Kenz," he offered, prompting her.

He didn't sound annoyed or impatient. The gentle tone Jeremy took with her led me to believe he had feelings for this girl—cue the knife twisting into my gut.

"All set?" I asked weakly.

"Yep," she said as she beamed her bright, white smile directly at Jeremy. "I'll go with the shrimp."

I left them and didn't approach the table again, save for one last time to ask them if they needed anything else before I dropped their check. I made sure that Sal delivered their entrees, asked if their food was ok and refreshed their drinks. I focused all the mental energy I could muster towards my other tables.

But I was dying inside, little by little with each minute that passed.

I stole looks at their table—at Jeremy and Kenzie in particular. She seemed very happy and totally into him. I couldn't read him, though. He didn't seem content and enamored like Frank did with his girl. But maybe he was just holding back, messed up and made uncomfortable by my presence—with the past rearing its ugly head.

Ambushing Jeremy at the coffee shop tomorrow morning? My quest for a reunion, or at the very least, closure? No, not happening. Mission aborted.

What I needed right now was a big piece of chocolate cake, a good cry and a hot shower—in that order.

The happy foursome didn't vacate the premises until quarter-past ten. Connie picked up the credit card receipt when I asked her to. I just couldn't go over there again—couldn't bear to do the awkward goodbye scene.

"Let me guess…An old boyfriend?"

"How did you know?"

"Because you're usually super organized and you fucked up two tickets tonight. Don't worry, Carolyn," she pressed on when I dropped my head into my hands. "I covered for you with Marco. But I *knew* something was up. You looked rattled. And that big, hot piece of man meat with the sexy, shaggy brown hair kept sneaking looks at you. The girl with him couldn't keep her dagger eyes off you either. And only a man who still holds a torch would leave a tip like this," she said, handing over the receipt.

The bill was for two hundred and thirty dollars. The tip was for one-twenty. Connie was smiling at me but that tip didn't please me —it made me feel like a loser. Jeremy wasn't pining for me. More like he wanted to be kind, to leave me some damn consolation prize to soften the blow.

I handed Sal sixty dollars as he was walking out the door.

"You already tipped me out, Carolyn."

"I know. This is extra. You helped me with that table so I'm splitting the tip with you."

"You sure? You don't have to do that."

"I insist."

"Ok, thanks." His face split into a wide grin. "Did you see the giant knockers on that brunette?"

"It's no wonder you don't have a girlfriend," Connie hissed as she smacked him on the side of his head.

It was nearly midnight.

Closing time.

Time to go home and lick my wounds.

* * *

JEREMY

I stood back, hidden in the darkness, debating whether or not I should approach. She was sitting in her mom's old model station wagon, parked behind the restaurant underneath a street light. Her forehead rested against the steering wheel.

I watched her.

After a few minutes, she raised her head. She looked drawn out, tired. I saw her wipe at her eyes and then turn the key in the ignition.

I watched Carolyn drive off.

Tonight was a disaster of epic proportions.

From the moment I picked up Kenzie, I was miserable. The effort she put into her hair and make-up, and the outfit—still border-line inappropriate but an obvious attempt on her part to look more upscale. It made me feel bad for her, guilty. It was obvious she believed this *thing* we had was moving in one direction, while I was certain it was going nowhere. Certain I had to end this tonight.

She was bubbly and chatty for the entire ride to the restaurant. I smiled, asked her questions, made conversation in return—tried not to be the heartless dick that I was.

When I opened her car door, she looked at me wide-eyed, as if no one had ever done that for her before, as if I was Prince fucking Charming. She flashed me a bright smile and said, "There are so many things I just love about you, Jeremy. You're so polite."

I couldn't wait for the night to be over. I just had this feeling, a sense of foreboding that sat like acid in the pit of my gut. I was afraid that with one or two drinks tonight, Kenzie would be professing her undying love for me.

And she thinks I'm polite? I wanted to remind her that after Sunday's fuck fest, I'd practically peeled her off me, couldn't look her in the eye, and pretty much left tire tracks as I sped away after drop-ping her off in front of her apartment. No, I was not polite and I was not good.

I was miserable.

When I was in her presence, I always had a simmering sense of irritation. I attributed it to the fact that our meetings were never initiated by me. But there was something else. Kenzie was pleasant enough and she'd shown me glimpses of her sweet side, but in the short time I'd known her, she flashed a little nasty as well. Tip-offs to what I assumed was a catty and possessive side. The *back off* look she shot to the waitress that first night at Red's, her constant need to grip my arm and hold my hand when we were together, and tonight, her impatience when our waitress didn't materialize within two minutes of our party being seated.

Our waitress.

I didn't have to look up to know it was her. That sweet lilt as she spoke her greeting? I'd know that voice anywhere. Her voice had been haunting my dreams for years.

Make me yours, Jeremy, please.

I raised my eyes slowly as I felt Frank nudge me under the table. Her hair was up in a ponytail, exposing her neck, giving me a full view of her face. Full pink lips, big brown eyes, creamy soft skin.

So beautiful.

I saw her expression change. She continued smiling but her brows puckered in a confused response to the subtle but snotty barb Kenzie lobbed. Carolyn stayed composed. I felt protective over Carolyn but also wanted to shield Kenzie. It was so fucking confusing. Kenzie's pettiness angered me but I was also embarrassed on her behalf. Carolyn's persistent kind smile and her refusal to stoop low left Kenzie looking the fool, and I felt bad for her. She was no match for Carolyn in any way.

When Carolyn finally looked my way, her shock was evident. It was clear she hadn't noticed me in the busy bustle of the restaurant before that very moment. Her eyes widened but I thought I saw one side of her mouth creep up. Could she possibly be happy to see me? If she was, the feeling was short-lived. She looked back and forth between me and Kenzie, and something that looked like painful recognition passed in her expression before she was back to business a moment later.

"Holy crap," Frank said, letting out a breath as soon as Kenzie and Sadie left the table to use the ladies' room.

We were already three rounds of drinks in. The girls were acting silly and were too loud. Kenzie was making a point of touching me at every given opportunity. I raised my head twice to see Carolyn's eyes fixed on that exact spot where Kenzie's hand rested over mine on the table, rubbing lazy circles into my skin. And when Frank, the idiot, mentioned how stoked he was for skiing this winter and the girls started making drunken plans for *the four of us* to spend weekends at my place in Killington, I could swear that Carolyn overheard.

I wanted to fucking scream.

I couldn't bear Carolyn's discomfort tonight—the awkward way she stumbled as she tried to recite the specials, the way her hand trembled just slightly as she wrote down our order. She was making mistakes, which was so unlike her. I watched, pained, as she set plates in front of customers who then informed her that they'd ordered something different.

I also couldn't stand the desperate way Kenzie was attempting to work her way in with me—the suggestive glances, the overly familiar touches. If I felt like things weren't quite right between us before, tonight just made it all the more obvious.

I felt nothing but disdain for her when she reprimanded Carolyn, and when she waffled over her dinner order, *needing* me to help her decide. Really? But my contempt for her was immediately replaced by guilt. The girl had lost the love of her life. She was looking for someone to care about her, looking for some kindness, some romance. Through my careless greed, my selfish need for the temporary comfort of a body next to mine—for a fuck—I'd led her to believe something about us that was not true.

"You know I had no idea she worked here, right?"

"I know, Frank. Just shut up about it, all right? I just wanna get through the night. No ordering fucking desert, either."

"Got it," he said, dejected.

"One more round?" Kenzie looked to Sadie, giggling as they sat back down.

"Yes, *if* we can get that waitress' attention," Sadie replied, heavy on the bitchy.

"Can I get you another round of drinks?" asked the kid who seemed to have taken over our table for Carolyn. The girls gave their orders and then he asked me and Frank if we wanted another round of beers. I noticed that as he spoke to us, his eyes stayed fixed on Kenzie's tits.

As he walked off, Sadie hissed, "What a little pervert."

"I know," Kenzie said indignantly. "He was totally rude."

"He's probably sixteen, seventeen tops," I said, dismissively, excusing his actions.

"Someone needs to teach him some manners," Kenzie huffed.

Did she think I was taking on that assignment? Defending her honor from a horny teenager whose only crime was ogling what she'd put out for public viewing? Not happening.

"If a boy sees those," I said, gesturing with my head towards her breasts, "he's going to look."

She took my statement as a compliment, not as a declaration of my indifference. When Sadie and Frank became involved in a side conversation, she looked down briefly towards her breasts, then raised her heated eyes to me and whispered, "These are only for you."

Fuck me.

Carolyn came over only once more, but it was enough to put the final nail in this coffin.

"I hope you enjoyed everything. Can I get you any coffee or desert, or would you like the check?"

I'm sure she was praying we'd ask for the check. She wanted us gone as much as I wanted to leave. This entire night was a fucking misery.

Frank said, "Everything was great. The check's fine, Carolyn, thanks."

I sat there silent, willing her to look at me. She didn't make eye contact as she placed the check on the table between me and Frank.

"I wanted a cannoli, Frank," Sadie whined.

Kenzie eyed me and then asked cautiously, "Who is that girl? How do you two know her?"

We answered simultaneously. Frank said, "We went to the same high school," while I said, "Carolyn was my girlfriend."

Kenzie's face paled, her expression morphing from hurt to anger. She crossed her arms underneath her chest. "Did you know she would be here?"

"No."

"That was a *long* time ago," Sadie reassured her.

"Was it, Jeremy? Is she long gone and forgotten?"

I just looked at her, attempting to come up with something to soothe her, to make her feel better. But the only thing that would make her feel better was a lie.

Kenzie excused herself, took her coat off the back of her chair and then left in a huff. I followed her out.

Kenzie had tears rolling down her cheeks when I caught up to her on the sidewalk outside. "Hey, I didn't know she was here. I'm so sorry, Kenzie. I feel terrible."

"You still care about her."

I looked up to the sky and blew out a tired breath. "Please get in, Kenzie," I said as I opened the passenger side door for her. "Let me take you home."

After fifteen minutes of uncomfortable silence, Kenzie turned to me and asked, "So she's the one? The one Sadie told me about? The one who totally screwed you over?"

Kenzie deserved a lot of things. She did *not* deserve my life story, though, and I was not listening to anyone talk shit about Carolyn. Not happening.

"That was a bad time. Carolyn didn't set out to hurt me or anyone else."

Her hands were in her lap, balled into fists. "I find it pretty hard to believe that you had no idea she worked there. This is a pretty small town."

"I *didn't* know. And remember, I didn't make these plans."

She nodded, and when she spoke her voice was bitter. "Come to think of it, Jeremy, you haven't made any plans with me. *Every* time... You make me feel like I'm being pushed on you and I should be happy to have any scrap of attention you throw my way. I'm nothing, right?" Her voiced went louder with each subsequent sentence. "Someone you fucked when you were drunk and horny, right? Fuck you, Jeremy! I deserve better than you!"

I let her rant because I deserved every word. "You do deserve better. And I never intended for us to be together in that way because I knew I wasn't ready. I told you that the very first night."

"But you *did* do it. And you wanted me. Not once, Jeremy, *three* times." She shook her head and added, "And that night...You told me you loved me."

Now it was my turn to put a quarter in the swear jar. "The *fuck* I did!"

She turned back to look at me. I could see the lie in her eyes.

"You did," she whispered before fresh tears slid down her cheeks.

"I was drunk that night, Kenzie, but I know for a fact that in my entire life, I've only said those words to one girl."

She let out a cheerless laugh as I pulled to a stop in front of her apartment. "You said it to *her*." Her voice was softer when she said, "That's a shame because she doesn't want you. That was as plain as day." After a moment she added, "I deserve better but so do you. Give us a chance. I know I could—"

"Shit," I said, slamming the steering wheel. "There's never going to be anything between us. I feel terrible because I've hurt you, but that's how it is. I'm sorry." I was desperate to end this conversation, to end this awful night. "Some guy is going to worship the ground you walk on. You deserve nothing less than that."

She nodded sadly, let herself out and made her way inside.

I drove south again, cursing myself as I passed my exit and drove right back—to her.

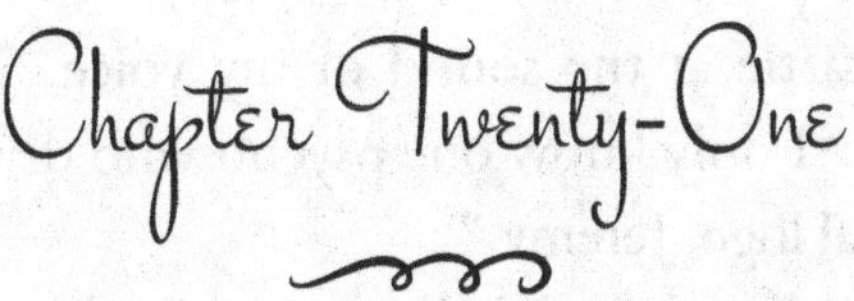# Chapter Twenty-One

JEREMY

When Carolyn drove off, I followed her home. It was midnight. Did she always get out of work so late? I worried about her driving home alone late at night—would always worry, would always care about her, no matter what. No matter if she didn't want me and it was *clear as day*. Kenzie's words hit me deep in my chest.

I slowed as she approached her street. Her brake lights and turn signal were on, but then she changed course and kept going straight. She drove. One mile turned to two, then three. Carolyn pulled into the field next to the lake. She pulled up as close as you could go, right to where the grass turned to sand.

I parked further back and got out of my truck slowly. I stood stock still for a moment, shoving my hands into my pockets. *Fuck it*, I thought as I stalked towards her car. Before I made it there, though, she got out.

She just stood next to her car, looking out over the lake. It was a calm night, fairly warm for mid-November. Moonlight danced over the surface of the water and lit Carolyn's features.

So much I wanted to say to her. So many things I needed to know, questions I needed answered. Instead I went with, "Are you fucking kidding me, Carolyn? Please tell me you don't usually come out here alone at night. I could have been some psycho following you."

She didn't startle at the sound of my voice. She kept her gaze fixed on the lake. "I only know one psycho who drives a truck with a Tri-State Electrical logo, Jeremy."

She looked back to me and then sank slowly into a sitting position. She patted the space next to her. An invitation—the first of its kind in three years.

"Where's your girlfriend?" she asked as I sat down.

On the way down, my arm brushed hers. And shit if my body didn't betray me, sending a jolt through my system at the mere proximity of her. It pissed me off.

"Not my girlfriend. It was just a date," I said defensively. "Frank and Sadie set us up."

"That was your first date?" Carolyn asked, smiling and cocking an eyebrow. Before I could answer, she called me on my bullshit. "She's, um, affectionate for a first date."

I shook my head. "Date three."

Her smile dimmed. "She's pretty."

I shrugged. It was quiet between us for a minute before I broke. "What am I supposed to say to you?"

She turned to me, her features weighed down with a heavy sadness. "I don't know, but I want you to talk to me, scream at me, lash out at me...Whatever you need to do." When I stayed silent, Carolyn let out a breath and said, "I know that I've been wanting for so long to tell you that I'm sorry." She paused and swallowed nervously before going on. "I had nothing, no feeling. I just...Things just got bad. But I'm sorry that I dropped you like that...Acted like I was the only one hurting."

"What happened, Carolyn?" Shaking my head, I added, "I've

been dying to know...For three fucking years I've been dying to know."

"I wish I had a good explanation, but the simple truth is that I lost my ability to cope for a long time—to see things clearly. After what Chase did? And then Drew and Will? I believed it was all on me. I started to believe every hateful thing people were saying about me. I became this fearful, paranoid girl. I didn't even recognize the person I'd become."

I took her hand. It was an instinct, something I needed to ground me. "I was so mad at you." I couldn't look at her again as I felt that old wound resurface. "You didn't trust me. I mean, why didn't you tell me what Chase was doing to you? All those weeks...And you would just pretend when we were together that everything was great?"

"It *was* great. I know how ridiculous it sounds now, but back then? It was like you and I were in this little bubble. It was my happiness. I could pretend he wasn't harassing me. That everyone, that my parents," she added, cringing, "wouldn't find out what I'd done. What I'd hidden from them."

"I would have gotten to him, Carolyn. He *never* would have sent that shit out if you would have just *trusted* me."

"I did trust you! But I knew if I told you, you'd go after him...You'd hurt him. After how hard you worked, knowing how much you struggled, I couldn't live with myself knowing I was the reason you were expelled."

I looked at her with disbelief, unable to hide my anger. "So I got my fucking diploma but I lost *everything*."

"I am sorry."

"I would have helped you. We could have helped each other. I felt like you never really...Like you weren't in as deep as I was."

"I know it sounds like a cop out, but I had no control at a certain point. I was vacant. You, my family...Everyone would be better off without me. I believed that." She looked to me again. "I know Tori never told you because, well, she's awesome like that," she swallowed, shoring herself up, "but I had a breakdown. I spent nearly two months in a hospital after I put my fists through my dorm window freshman year."

I lowered my head. It was that same feeling: the desire to wrap her up in my arms while simultaneously wanting to shake her and scream. Frustration and pain. Why did she go through it all alone when she could have had me by her side?

"I didn't know."

"No one did," she said with a faint smile. "I was at Silver Springs, psychiatric facility for the rich and famous. Didn't matter if you were schizophrenic, suicidal or completely psychotic—your diagnosis was exhaustion. No trail. Nothing that could affect your next movie deal or your daddy's political aspirations, know what I mean?"

"Were you? Suicidal, I mean?"

"I don't think I intended to die when I lost it that night. I did want all the pain to stop, though. But no, I don't think so. Right after it all happened, after Drew...It's like I wanted to inflict as much pain on myself as I possibly could. Reading what our classmates— what *friends* were saying about me? Then the vile things the internet creeps were writing? I needed to see it every day like I needed air to breathe. I fed off it. I was obsessed. I wanted to be punished. But then it all became too much. I could feel it—my sanity slipping away. I knew...It's like I was standing outside of myself watching, knowing I was going crazy."

"Cut yourself some slack, Carolyn. That was a bad time."

"But it scares me that I sunk that low." She looked away as she said, "Sometimes I think about my college roommate. She wasn't exactly kind to me, but I do feel sort of sympathetic towards her now. Aubrey found me that night. Apparently, there was blood everywhere and I was totally out of it, screaming at the top of my lungs." She stopped for a moment, taking in a few shaky breaths before continuing. "I'm better now, really, but I'm also terrified that it could happen again, you know?"

I nodded, feeling so low, so sad for her.

"What changed? How did you get better?"

"Silver Springs does have some of the best doctors and therapists money can buy, so that set me on the right path, I guess. I found out later that my parents went heavy into debt keeping me there. Two months at a place like that sets you back a *lot*. But it did put me on the road back. Therapy, lots of therapy. And I was on medication for more than a year." She looked up to me, uncertain. "I still feel ashamed about that."

"You shouldn't," I said, squeezing her hand.

Her expression was grateful. "I still see a therapist, but now it's just once or twice a month, when I feel like I need it. Running really helps me. I also eat a certain way—very little sugar, lots of veggies. Having my family close and letting friends back in, though, that's helped me the most."

"So you're still in school?"

She laughed ruefully. "Yeah, and at the rate I'm going, my undergraduate will take six or seven years."

"So what?"

"I know. It's just that I used to have it all mapped out. Four years at an ivy league, then onto a top-rated graduate program, doctorate in neuropsychology, then off to change the world. Everything carefully planned—my upward trajectory according to my rigid little timetable."

"And now?"

"That plan isn't completely off the table, it's just that I've been forced to become more flexible on how long it takes me to get there. Right now I'm studying early childhood education, specializing in reading disabilities. Someday down the road I may be on the research side, but for now, I think I'm happiest working directly with kids like Thomas."

"And like me," I said, nudging her shoulder. "Those kids will be really lucky to have you as a teacher."

"I hope so." She wiped at her eyes and then smiled brightly. "So, I've kept tabs on you," she said, in an attempt to take the focus off of her. "You did it, huh? You own your own business?"

I shrugged my shoulders. "Co-own, but yeah."

She elbowed me, teasing. "Don't be modest. That's a huge big deal, Jeremy."

"It's a lot of work but I like it." I paused. "No, I *love* being my own boss," I admitted, smiling.

"I knew you could do it. I'm surprised it happened so fast for you, though. It's impressive."

"Thanks."

"Do you still make time to sketch?"

"Yeah. It does something for me...Helps me work through issues I might be having with work or just other shit that's driving me crazy." After a pause, I said, "I'm assuming you were at the Gala."

She nodded, looking ahead, and then her fingers went straight to a strand of hair that had escaped from her ponytail. That old nervous habit.

"Can I ask you something, Jeremy?"

"Anything."

"Did you want me to see them, or was it more that you were cleaning house? Wanting to get rid of every reminder of me?"

I looked up at the sky, unsure of how I should answer. "For the past three years...It's like every time I go somewhere, anyplace where I think you might be, I'm hoping I'll see you and also praying that I won't. I can't explain it. It's like I'm still fucking desperate for you, but I hate myself for feeling that way." I took her hand when I noticed she was looking away, trying to hide the fact that she was crying. I went on, softly. "I wanted you to see them, especially *that* one of you. It's like I wanted you to know I still care about you, but I wanted to hurt you at the same time."

"I get it, I think."

"I don't know if you do, Carolyn. I don't even know if *I* get it. But I know that this past year, hearing Tori talk about spending time with you again, seeing Taylor's posts with pictures of you all laughing, knowing that you're doing all these great things again—it fucking hurts. You look so good, so happy. How could you let *them* back in? Why not me?"

She didn't answer right away and I felt tired all of a sudden, so fucking tired. I dropped her hand from mine and was a second from getting up and leaving when she said, "How could I think after everything that's happened, that you'd want anything to do with me? And I worry, too...Maybe I'm not good for you, Jeremy."

"What the hell is that supposed to mean? Is that some kind of let me down easy bullshit? You're not good enough for *me* but you're good enough for that uppity asshole, Todd?"

She looked at me like I had two heads. "What are you even talking about? I'm not *with* Todd, he's just a friend of mine." Her expression changed from surprised to pissed off. "And who are you to talk, mister I love big tits?"

I looked at her, wide-eyed, laughing. "Come again?"

"Your *date*, Kenzi." She looked irritated and...jealous? Good. "And just for the record," she went on, "I may have hurt you that summer, but you did move on pretty quickly."

"Three and a half years is pretty quickly? How do you figure?"

She looked away, shaking her head. "Please, you moved on right after."

"I'm still not following."

"They warned me, they'd been sending me pictures even before everything went down with Drew. I didn't believe them. I mean, I knew that Samantha, Erica and Kerri were *not* my friends. I thought there had to be some logical explanation. I knew you and Vanessa were close, but shit, Jeremy, it hurt. And when I saw that just a few months later she moved in with you?" Carolyn shook her head. "And you know what's crazy? I remember feeling crushed, but I was also kind of relieved for your sake. I was damaged goods, you know? I didn't want you to be burdened with me."

I wanted to kiss her senseless and push her into the lake at the same time. "Vanessa's gay. Gay since the day she was born. You do know that, right? She owns a tattoo shop in New Jersey with her girlfriend."

She looked at me with a blank expression. "I didn't know." Carolyn suddenly looked very worn down.

"I was the only person who knew and I didn't tell anyone," I said, softening. "No way you could have known," I muttered.

"You don't know how much time I've wasted, wishing I could go back, to do things over. There's so much I regret. But there aren't any do-overs."

After a minute, I asked, "Are you happy, Carolyn? I mean, you look great. From the outside, if I didn't know your past, I'd think you were just your average college girl."

She mulled that question over for a moment. "I am happy...Or grateful might be a better way to put it. I'm overwhelmed with gratitude to have my family back, to have *real* friends, and to feel like now I can handle whatever comes my way. I don't take little things for granted anymore. So I guess I'm good, better than I have been in such a long time." After a beat, she asked, "Are you?" Before I could answer, she added, "Does she make you happy, Jeremy? I...I really couldn't tell by watching you two together. I mean, I hope she does."

"Do you? Do you hope she makes me happy?"

Carolyn shrugged. "I've only ever wanted good things for you. Even after everything, I'm sure you know that."

"I have a good life. I'm proud of who I am. Kenzie doesn't factor into all that, though."

* * *

CAROLYN

Did I hope Kenzie made him happy? Jeremy asked me that and I responded with some bullshit about only wanting what's best for him. Hell. No. I hoped she made him miserable. I hoped she snored, was a kleptomaniac, acted like a raging bitch at regular intervals—anything that would drive him away.

Drive him straight to me.

Kenzie doesn't factor into all that. That declaration gave me some hope, but he didn't really come out and say she meant nothing to him. If my intuition was even remotely accurate, they had slept together. The pain of that realization burned straight to my soul. But did I expect that Jeremy had been alone this entire time? Pining away for me? A foolish girl could hope, I guess.

"That was a lie."

"Come again?" he asked.

"I don't hope that she makes you happy. Truth is, I kind of hate her and I don't even know her." I looked up at him cautiously. "It was hard to see you with another girl." After another pause, I shook my head and said, "That was a lie too. It was more than hard to see you with her, it was...heartbreaking. I know I have no right to say that to you, but there it is."

Jeremy's features hardened as he ran his hands through his hair in frustration. "After I saw you last weekend in that store...The way that guy acted towards you? Todd? He was possessive. I was so sure you were together. I drank myself into a puddle that day. I barely knew Kenzie before that night and then I went—"

"And you slept with her," I interjected, quietly. "That was pretty obvious. Just in the way she touched you. I knew."

"But do you understand that for *three years* before that night, *last fucking week*, that there was no one? Not one girl...Not so much as one kiss?"

The tears came slowly, enough so that I could bat them away one by one. The frustration and sadness over missed opportunities, over failed communication.

"No, I never imagined that you were alone." I added, "I'm sorry you were alone because of me."

"Stop doing that," he said, angrily. "Stop putting the fucking weight of the world onto your shoulders, ok? Maybe I didn't want there to be anyone. That was *my* choice."

I nodded, unconvinced.

My phone chirped, interrupting the moment. "That's my dad texting, making sure I'm all right. Shit, it's almost two. I never let him know I'd be late."

I texted back quickly that I was fine, that I was talking to Jeremy and that I'd be home soon.

"We should head home."

"Yeah," I reluctantly agreed, hoping the disappointment in my voice wasn't too obvious.

He stood up and reached down to pull me up. I smiled weakly. "I'm glad you followed me tonight."

"Me too," he said, chuckling.

I got in my car, started it up and then lowered the window. Jeremy hadn't moved and the silence was suddenly heavy and awkward.

"I'd say I'll see you around, Carolyn, but we've managed to live in the same town and not run into one another for a long ass time."

"That's what you used to say to me." Pain seared my chest at the memory. "Every time we'd part ways at the lake. 'See you around, Carolyn'."

"That was so long ago," he said absently, looking off at a point in the distance.

"I don't know what to say. This feels strange, but good."

He nodded and then looked to me with uncertainty. "I'd like to see you...To talk to you again. Maybe have coffee with me sometime?"

"I'd really like that."

"Then that's what we'll do," he said, resigned. He didn't exactly seem happy about it, though, which made my heart sink. "Good night, Carolyn," he said as he turned and made his way back to his truck.

* * *

JEREMY

I caught a look at myself in the rearview mirror when I got back into my truck. I was grimacing.

As we were leaving, it took everything in me not to grab her by the waist and press into her as I took her right against the side of her car.

All night, every time she walked past our table or I caught sight of her across the room, I thought about kissing her. Thought about those afternoons spent in her room, in her basement or at my place. We'd only just started to know each other in that way, and since then, I always had this sense of feeling robbed when I thought back to that time. For the past three years I had to survive on daydreams about what touching and making love to Carolyn *would* have been like, instead of getting to replay images of the real thing. And seeing her tonight, being close to her again, actually hearing her story and knowing she regretted the loss of us—it left me wanting her with a renewed sense of desperation.

I still loved her. That had never changed.

Would tomorrow be too early to get that coffee together? *Slow down, Jeremy,* I told myself in warning. *Be careful.* Yeah, tomorrow was too soon. I wanted to jump right in but I needed to test the waters first.

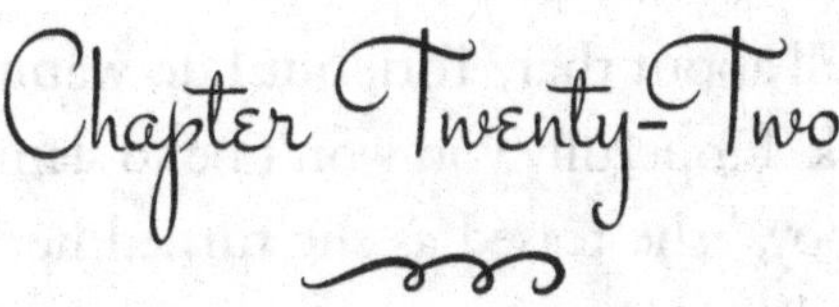

Chapter Twenty-Two

JEREMY

"Good morning, sunshine," I said as I finally reached the front of the line. "It's more packed than usual today."

"And the new hire called in sick," a harried-looking Tori replied as she worked the register. "I put a crumb cake aside for you. I'm nearly sold out already."

"On behalf of Grandpa, thanks."

Tori kept looking past me, towards the door. "You expecting someone? You're kind of hurting my feelings," I said, laughing.

"Nope," she said, snapping her attention back to me. "Why don't you hang out for a few minutes?"

I looked at the ten or so people in line behind me. "Doesn't look like you'll be getting a break anytime soon."

"Ugh," she muttered, frustrated. "I just thought we could catch up. I feel like I haven't hung out with you in, like, forever."

She looked at the door again. What was up with her?

"Sure everything is all right, Tori?"

She nodded, looking back to me. "I'm good." As she handed me my cake box and my two coffees, she asked, "How did things go with that blind date? You never came back to fill me in."

I wasn't getting into it, especially when the testy lady behind me huffed to anyone who was listening, "They should have more people working on a Sunday morning."

"Nothing to tell about that, Tori, but I do wanna talk. I'll pop in sometime this week. Hopefully you won't be so slammed."

"Later, lover boy," she teased as she turned her attention to the cranky lady next in line.

"That was so fucking awkward," Frank huffed as he plopped down onto my sofa.

"I can't believe you actually had a Carolyn Harris sighting," Vinny said. "I haven't left this town for the past three years and I have not seen the girl once."

A bunch of guys were over watching the Patriots' game. When my dad left after the first quarter, the events of last night were rehashed in agonizing detail. Frank piled on the drama thick.

"Brutal, just brutal. Jeremy thinks *he* had it bad," he lamented, gesturing to me. "Meanwhile I'm the one who had to listen to Sadie bitch and moan for the entire ride home and then I went through it again after she spent an hour on the phone that night with Kenzie."

"I kinda feel bad for that girl but I feel worse for Carolyn," Mike Hanson said. "I wouldn't want to be waiting on an ex and his new girl."

"Kenzie's not my girl," I shot back defensively.

Mike was there with two of his frat brothers, guys I'd come to call friends of my own. Never thought much of frat boys before, but Mike's friends had changed my opinion of that entire scene. They were good people. "How is she?" Mike asked, looking almost hurt on her behalf, concern in his eyes. I understood. The mere mention of

Carolyn's name was a direct link to Will and Drew. I knew Mike would never truly get over their loss.

"She *looks* good," Frank said, his expression uneasy.

I spoke quietly, directly to Mike. "I think she's doing a lot better. I talked to her last night. I didn't realize how bad things had gotten for her."

"I heard rumors but I never knew anything for sure. The last time I saw Erica, like a year ago, she told me Carolyn was in a *nuthouse*. Said she'd *wigged out* and *gone postal* at Penn." He shook his head and grimaced. "Yeah, the bitch used those exact words."

I wouldn't confirm or deny. Not my story to share.

"I know things were rough but she's doing well now. She looks incredible. She seems happy." I added, "She's running the Boston Marathon this spring. She organized some group that's raising money for the victims of that terrorist bombing."

"That's awesome."

Yeah, it is. I was proud of Carolyn.

I caught wind of Frank's side conversation. "Kenzie's gorgeous," he said to Vinny. "Totally nuts about that moron, too," he said, nodding his head back in my direction. "But you know Jeremy. Now that he got a taste of Carolyn again, it's all about her."

That's right. It just might kill me this time, but it's all about her.

"So when am I going to get an invite to Killington?" Mike asked, acting miffed. "I'm jealous. Vinny said the location is sick. And I'll have you know, I'm an après-ski legend at The Lookout."

"Since when do you need an invite? Mi casa es tu casa, asshole. Depending on the forecast, I'll be up there every weekend after Thanksgiving."

"Finals those first two weeks of December," he said, shaking his head. "After that, I'm in. Just say the word. I'm basically free from Christmas until January twentieth."

"Must be nice, college boy," Frank chimed in from across the room. "Some of us have to work. But I'm counting on some week-ends, Rivers. Just ordered my new Burton."

"The only weeks we're renting out this year are Christmas and February break. And the family that's renting for Christmas is taking it early. I'm thinking a New Year's bash may be in order."

"Did you have any luck with the hot tub?" Vinny asked, looking hopeful.

"That was a bitch but well worth it. It took me and my dad a full weekend to get it up and running. I cannot wait to soak my sore ass in that after a day on the slopes."

"Kristi can come with?" Mike asked.

"Absolutely. There are five bedrooms all together and stragglers can crash on the couches. There's room for everyone."

Five rooms.

I knew who I wanted to be sharing a room with.

* * *

CAROLYN

"So?"

"So it was good, I guess," I answered noncommittally. I couldn't help the smile that stretched across my face, though.

"Holy crap! You better give me some details right now, Harris. I'm dying here."

"It was good because we talked about a lot of things, Tori. It felt so good to talk to him. But," I said, shaking my head, "I'm not getting all swoony over this. Jeremy's hard to read. Like, he didn't pledge his undying love to me or even ask me out for that matter. He *did* say he wanted to meet for coffee. I think he said he wanted to get together to talk some more. I'm fuzzy on the details." I looked up at her, embarrassed.

"I was so freaking wired up, Tori. I wanted to crawl into his lap the entire time and just telepathically will him to kiss me." I couldn't help but laugh. "I'm a mess!"

Tori looked up over the edge of her wineglass cautiously. "He came in to see me yesterday, Carolyn."

"You're holding out on me? I feel so betrayed!"

She laughed when I flung a piece of popcorn at her face and then deftly caught the next two pieces I tossed right in her mouth. "I wasn't holding out," she said while chewing. "It's just weird being friends with you both. Like, he says stuff to me and I kind of think he wants me to pass it along, but I'm not sure if I should, you know?"

"You don't have to. Just...be my friend. Tell me if I'm pining away for the idea of something that's never going to happen. He has every reason to move on, to walk away. But the way he was the other night? It was confusing. I felt like he wanted more, but then I also felt like maybe I was reading too far into things. Maybe he just wants to be friends. I'm afraid to hope."

"He wasn't exactly divulging his deepest, darkest secrets. And I think he's also confused...Unsure of where you stand. I can say with certainty that he has no feelings *whatsoever* for that girl he was with at La Viola. And by the way, you poor baby, that must have been awful for you."

"You have no idea."

"Well, she's history."

"You're sure?"

"I'm pretty certain, Carolyn. He barely mentioned her."

I wasn't totally convinced but felt a little relieved. "She was really pretty and so curvy. She looked like a pin-up girl. I hate feeling so jealous."

"She's pretty?" Tori asked, laughing. "Have you gotten a good look at yourself lately?" I shook my head, brushing her off. I still found it hard to take a compliment. "Let me quote your boy, Robert, shall I?" Tori teased. "I think his exact words were something along the lines of, 'She's the total package—sweet and also drop dead gorgeous'."

"Well," I said, deflecting, "he obviously hasn't seen Kenzi."

Now it was my turn to be pelted with popcorn.

More than a full week passed since that Saturday night at the lake. It's not like I was expecting to grab that coffee with Jeremy the next day or anything, but as time went on, my hopes fell.

Tori said he seemed confused. I got it, really, I did. Taking me on, especially after I laid out everything I'd been through the past few years, was a risk. The prospect of having me in your life would be daunting.

So I waited—and my heart sank just a little bit more with every passing day.

I ran every morning, read ahead on my class assignments, helped my mother with the Thanksgiving preparations—anything to keep myself busy. I tried to resign myself to the idea that Jeremy and I would be nothing more than casual acquaintances.

And then on that following Tuesday, an unknown number flashed on my screen.

Hallelujah.

"Hello."

"Hi, uh, Carolyn?"

"Jeremy?"

"Yeah, it's me. I got your number from Tori. I hope you don't mind."

My pulse spiked and I was filled with this almost giddy-like excitement. I took a deep calming breath, silently chastising myself. Coming off as overly eager when I wasn't sure where he stood was foolish. For all I knew, Jeremy was calling to tell me that on second thought, rekindling even a friendship with me wasn't a good idea.

"No, it's fine. Of course I don't mind."

"So...I was hoping we could get together for that coffee if you're not too busy."

"Is tomorrow good for you?" The words were out of my mouth before I could stop myself. So much for not looking too eager. "I mean, it's just that I don't have classes tomorrow since it's the day before Thanksgiving. But you're probably busy so just forget—"

"No, tomorrow's good," Jeremy cut in, interrupting my rambling nonsense. "You want to meet at one o'clock at Le Évier? Instead of coffee, we can grab some lunch. I've been hooked on their chicken soup ever since you brought it to me that time I was sick."

"Yeah," I answered, smiling as a tear simultaneously slid down my cheek. "I'm hooked on that soup too. That sounds good."

"Great. I'll see you there."

I was always punctual but today I was downright itchy. I'd been sitting in my car outside Le Évier since quarter to one. I forced myself to wait until just a few minutes before one and then took a seat in a cozy booth close to the window.

I've always loved this place. It's just a little café that serves breakfast and lunch, then caters to the dinnertime take-out needs of their upscale clientele. My parents were an anomaly in these parts—either Mom or Dad cooked dinner nearly every night. But they loved this place too, and I'd been enjoying Sunday morning croissants that were light as air and buttery good since I was a toddler.

I looked around—no sign of him yet. When the waitress came over, I was tempted to order myself a big, giant glass of Cabernet to calm my nerves, but I opted for an iced tea.

Wine was something I enjoyed in moderation. I loved having a glass with my girlfriends or with my parents after we cooked a great meal together, but I had a strict policy of avoiding anything akin to self-medicating. If I was anxious, I'd just have to work through it.

I sat there, talking myself back into a calm state, reassuring myself that no matter what happened, Jeremy was a kind and good person. Nothing could happen that would make me regret meeting up with him today.

Maybe I spoke to myself too soon.

She turned from the counter holding take-out bags in both hands. Deeply tanned, with hair five shades blonder than I remember, Samantha stopped dead in her tracks when she locked eyes with me. I contemplated turning away but I didn't. She stood transfixed as well.

What to say? What to say? I didn't really want to know what she'd been up to these past few years so I wasn't asking, and really, I didn't want to know how she was in general, so the generic "How are you?" wasn't happening either. I just went with, "Samantha," paired with what I hoped was a comfortable, confident looking smile.

"Carolyn? I can't believe it's you! How *are* you?" she gushed as she approached the table.

You're still as fake as ever, I mused. I should say: *You know me, I'm still the same slutty bitch I was back in high school. That's how you referred to me in those friendly posts, correct?*

I shrugged with a smile as I answered, "I'm doing well." I was going for the not rude, yet not friendly vibe.

As she began lowering herself into the booth across from me, she used a super-duper upbeat voice as she said, "I'd love to catch up with you!"

I held my hand up and shook my head just slightly to let her know that was not happening. "I'm meeting someone."

"Oh," she said, eyes wide, dejected and surprised. I'm sure being rebuffed was a very rare occurrence in her life.

With that, who comes striding in but Mr. Gorgeous himself—all six-foot-three of him. Hair adorably tousled, dressed in a snug long-sleeved thermal shirt, jeans and work boots. I smiled at Jeremy, nearly forgetting that Samantha was still standing there, now with her mouth hanging wide open.

He slid into the booth across from me and automatically took my hand across the table, giving me a reassuring squeeze. "Sorry I'm late," he said, ignoring Samantha entirely.

"Jeremy, it's me, Samantha! Oh my God, it's been *sooo* long!"

And what Jeremy did next? Let's just say I wanted to marry him and have his babies right there on the spot.

Jeremy looked up at her, cocked his head and repeated her name absently, as if it barely registered with him at all. Then he smiled politely and looked back to me. "Well, Samantha, I've got to be back at my job site in an hour, so Carolyn and I had better get started on lunch." He pretty much dismissed her when he added, "Good seeing you."

I didn't look at Samantha, but the weak way in which she replied, "Um, yeah, it was great seeing both of you, too," pretty much told me that Jeremy's words and lack of interest had worked better than any smack down I could have delivered.

I couldn't help but chuckle as she walked away. "You're my hero, you know that?"

He looked down at his menu, shaking his head while failing miserably at reining in his smile. "I cannot stand that girl."

"That's the first time I've seen her."

"Yeah, since high school?" he asked, looking up, surprised.

I nodded. "I think it was you who once told me that some friendships aren't meant to last forever." Shaking my head, I added, "My friendship with Samantha should have ended in seventh grade. And our mothers are no longer on speaking terms either. My mom made it her mission to confront everyone who wronged me back then," I added, rolling my eyes.

"Good for her. I always liked your mom and dad. How's Thomas doing? Andie told me he's quite the artist."

"Yeah, he was never into art before. I think his newfound interest is because Andie is so adorable. He has a girlfriend but I think he also has a crush on your friend. I mean," I added, laughing, "I even kind of have a girl crush on her. She's one of the nicest, most genuine people I think I've ever met."

"Girl crush? Should I be worried?"

The waitress came over then, interrupting our nice easy conversation. I realized in that moment that I felt completely and totally at ease.

Jeremy ordered us both chicken soup and then I convinced him to trust me when I ordered a grilled cheese sandwich for us to split. At Le Évier, grilled cheese wasn't your typical white bread fare, greasy with butter and sticky yellow American slices. No, it was an experience.

"Damn," he whispered reverently as he savored the lightly toasted French bread slathered with herbed butter, oozing creamy Gruyère. "This could be my new addiction."

"*You* could scarf one of these down every day and you'd still look like that." I blushed, catching myself as I gestured to him.

"I'm sure you could, too. How many miles are you logging each week?"

"It depends. I do a six-mile loop most days. Sundays I do my longer run, usually ten to twelve."

"That's when you run with Todd?" Jeremy raised his eyebrows, smiling as he said his name.

"Yes. That's when I run with my *entire* group," I teased back.

"Ummm," he moaned as he took another bite. Lordy, he made my insides quiver when he made those sounds. "There's a place up in Killington that makes great fondue and all sorts of good cheesy sandwiches, but I think this one has them beat."

"My family always skied at Bromley when I was younger. I haven't been there in years."

"Did you like skiing?"

"I used to love it and I was pretty decent. I'm out of practice now, though."

He was staring into his empty soup bowl then, deep in thought.

After a minute he looked up and asked, "Would you...I mean if there was like, a group of people going and it was like, Andie and Tori... Would you want to come up and ski with us...Stay at my house?"

His foot started tapping, which forced his knee to bump the tabletop. He was still too big for his own good, and I realized suddenly, he was nervous. Was he worried that I wouldn't take him up on the invitation, or did he regret it now that the words were already out of his mouth? Was he thinking that getting close to me again may not be a good idea? The second possibility pained me. I stalled. "I didn't know you had a place up there."

"Just got it last year. Me and my dad own it. It's not exactly a palace now, but our aim is to fix it up, little by little."

"That's great."

He cleared his throat. "So Andie and her boyfriend Mateo are coming up the weekend after next. I could invite Tori up too, and Taylor. You interested?"

I looked down at the table. "Are you sure?"

He took my hand. "Are you asking me if I want you there? With me?"

I was certain he was going to tell me that I was being silly—that we were just friends. *Way to go, Carolyn*. I'd just made myself look presumptuous and foolish.

"Hey," he said, and then waited until I looked up. "I want you there. I...I want to get to know you again. But I'll never push you. I'm taking my cues from you. I mean," he smiled and started laughing, "for all I know you want nothing to do with me."

Screw looking too eager. I couldn't help the smile that spread wide across my face. "I'd really like to go skiing with you next weekend, Jeremy."

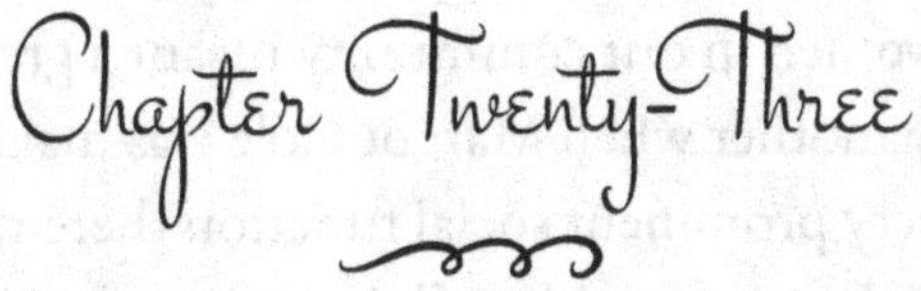

Chapter Twenty-Three

CAROLYN

This was the slowest night I'd ever worked at La Viola and I was grateful for it. My mind was elsewhere and my heart had been doing happy backflips since my lunch date with Jeremy on Wednesday.

Thanksgiving Day I woke up to a text from Jeremy. It was just an emoji of a turkey but it may as well have been a declaration of his love and devotion. I sent him back a picture of me and my dad at the starting line of the Turkey Trot run and then he texted: *show off* :)

The next day I braved the Black Friday crowds at the mall and got myself some new skiwear. I didn't want to look like I was trying too hard, but hell, I was. I needed to look good—so good that Jeremy would never ever even think about Big Boobs again.

So as I worked the few tables that came in on that Saturday after Thanksgiving, my head was pretty much in the clouds.

"Carolyn, dear," a familiar voice called to me from over by the ladies' room.

"Mrs. Cole! How are you?"

Margot Cole was another person who came out of the woodwork after the tragedy. One of several people who showed me that true kindness and selflessness did exist in this world.

When I was at my very lowest, she made a point of regularly coming over and visiting with my mother. Being that my family had become the town pariahs, friendship from one of the most powerful and influential women in our community meant a great deal. No one dared dismiss my mother when Margot Cole was making it a point to include her in every prominent social function there was.

For the past three years, Mrs. Cole had made it her mission to also help me out in whatever way she could. The fact that Will Clarke was her beloved nephew made the kindness she directed towards me and my family something that I would never, ever forget.

"I'm well," she replied, taking me in from head to toe. "But *you*, my lovely, look positively radiant."

I giggled. "Thank you."

"So is everyone treating you well here?"

"Yes, and I love working here. Thank you again for putting in a good word for me."

"Pshaw, they're lucky to have you. And giving an overly qualified, stunningly beautiful girl a job is the least they could do for one of their best customers."

I took in her effusive compliments with raised eyebrows and a smile. "Who are you here with, Dylan?"

"No, in fact, I'm here with my niece, Anna."

"Will's little sister," I said, my voice trailing off. I collected myself again. "How is she doing?"

"Pop over and ask her yourself," she said, smiling over her shoulder with a reassuring nod and a wink.

Not only did I approach Anna, but I went ahead and asked if she would meet me for coffee the next morning. And I'm so very glad that I did.

In her own way, Anna was more enlightened than most people twice her age. Listening to her talk about the past few years—everything she'd gone through and how she felt now that she'd had time to process everything—well, she inspired me. More importantly, she lifted a burden off of me when she forgave me and reassured me that I was, in no way, to blame.

After all this time, had I entertained the idea that it wasn't my fault? Of course I did. But there was always a lingering sadness, a niggling doubt. If only I had reached out to Drew again. Those awful, prophetic words he'd said in the parking lot still haunted me. If only I had reached out to his parents or to someone in school who could have helped him.

If only.

Anna got up to leave, hugging me tight before she turned to go. I flopped back down into the plush chair in the corner of the coffee house and let out a deep breath as a few tears escaped.

"You okay?" Tori asked, looking deflated.

"Yeah. What about you? Seeing her has to be rough."

Tori settled into the chair opposite me. "Not in the way you probably think."

"How so?"

"Seeing her makes me feel invisible. Like, Anna doesn't really even know who I am. She'll never know who Will was to me or who I was to him. And then I question if I really meant anything to him at all, you know?"

Shaking my head and holding her hand, I tried to reassure her. "Everyone knew he was crazy about you, Tori." I smiled then. "Lordy, I had to listen to Samantha whine about it incessantly. It burned so bad...The fact that Will was into you and wouldn't give her the time of day."

"As far as most people are concerned, though, he and I were no more than friends. And that was on me. After he died, I resented everyone and everything—just the cards I'd been dealt. I was furious with my father for just sitting back and allowing me to take on all that responsibility, mad at my brothers for needing me so much... Hell, I was mad at my poor mom for dying." She looked away for a moment, collecting herself. "If I had a normal life, like every other girl he knew, things might have been different."

"I always felt bad that you had to take care of your brothers, but I also admired you for it. I'm sure Will did too."

She smiled. "He did. And he'd always try and help me out. He was there whenever I needed him. But I blame myself sometimes, like, was I there for him?"

"What do you mean?"

She looked out the window. It had started to rain, hard. "I can still barely think back to that day without wanting to cry and punch a wall," she said, shaking her head. "He betrayed me in the worst way and I wanted to hate him, but I couldn't...I blamed myself for it."

"Kerri?"

"Yeah. I mean, if I had ever *allowed* myself to go to a party, then it might never have happened. It wasn't exactly an ideal situation for him to be with me, someone who barely ever socialized.

"Will came over right after he dropped her off that morning. He was so sick that he threw up in my backyard. Then I remember him crying. It scared me to death. The only man I'd ever witnessed crying was my father, so I thought something tragic had happened. But I guess it had, you know?"

I squeezed her hand. "I can't imagine how that felt, Tori. But I was still friends with Kerri at that point and I can tell you, she had no idea what had happened. It was like they were drugged or something."

"Or just really drunk," she added, looking doubtful and disgusted. "I'd just lost my virginity to Will the month before so I took it pretty hard."

"Really?" I blurted out.

She nodded with raised eyebrows. "See, you never would have guessed that. No one knew. It was Will's first time too."

"Wow," I added absently, lost in thought.

"So after he came clean, groveled and whatever, I took the high road and all that, but it just gutted me. And I *did* hate her. I never thought she'd orchestrated it or anything, but I just hated the idea that Kerri had gotten a part of him. And how she looked at him after the fact, all smitten and infatuated? And Will," she shook her head, fighting back tears, "with his inability to be mean to anyone, it's like he still needed to reassure her and make sure she was all right. I hated that he was concerned about her, you know? I was so damn jealous that sometimes I couldn't see straight. I could still scream just thinking about it."

"God, who could blame you?"

"But I was mad at myself—mad at my circumstances. Sometimes I still just want a do-over. I want to go back and have the chance to really be his girlfriend."

The rain had tapered off and a few more customers had now joined the line. Tori wiped her eyes with the corner of her apron and then forced a smile. "Seeing Anna just dredged that all up."

I was going to mention Jeremy's invitation to the ski house but figured that could wait. I squeezed her hand as she stood. "Thanks for sharing all that with me, Tori."

"Love you, Carolyn."

"Love you, too."

It was another one of those moments when you realize that everyone has their own issues to deal with, their own long-buried stories. Everyone, not just me, had reasons to wish for a do-over.

Chapter Twenty-Four

JEREMY

Things weren't going exactly as planned. For the past few nights I'd been staying overnight in New Haven, close to this disastrous job site. I got a late-night call from the local fire department on Thanksgiving, alerting me that a small fire had been put out. The police had a suspect in custody, a squatter with a history of arson. The fire was contained, but a whole lot of damage had been done. My crew had to come in to re-do already completed work. This was setting us back big time, and being that I had other jobs lined up, I needed to be as close to on-schedule as possible.

Owning your own business had its perks...and its drawbacks.

Even with all this going on, Carolyn and our upcoming ski weekend was still front and center in my mind. We texted back and forth a few times, one-liners, nothing big, but she let me know that Taylor and Tori were in. That was good because in all this mess, I'd forgotten to invite them. I did ask Andie and Mateo, and let out a relieved breath when they said yes. Andie and her kookiness would reduce the chance of any awkward silences, and she was guaranteed for a constant stream of laughter. Frank had angled for an invite, but I put him off. I liked Sadie, she made Frank happy, but I wasn't taking any chances. I needed to get myself on solid ground with Carolyn before I had her around anyone who was linked to Kenzie.

Everyone was coming up Friday night except for Carolyn. She swapped Saturday for Friday night at La Viola. She said she'd leave early enough so that she could hit the slopes with us on Saturday morning.

I left New Haven early on Friday, before lunch, so that I'd have some time to set up. They were all working Friday so I wasn't expecting them until late, but when the clock read seven, then eight and then nine o'clock, I turned on the radio to listen to the news. The snow had been falling all day, but it didn't seem like anything too out of the ordinary. A little to the south, though, a band of heavy snow had passed through, dumping over two feet and closing some stretches of highway. I called Tori and it went straight to voicemail—same with Andie. It was midnight before I received texts from them both, letting me know they'd turned back.

I cracked a beer in front of the fireplace, disappointed, and resigned myself to a weekend of skiing solo.

I was up at six, planning to hit the slopes early. I liked being one of the first out there to take advantage of the powdery snow and empty trails. There was a quiet heaven in that solitude. I could eat later in the morning, when all the sleepyheads finally dragged themselves out of bed and crowded the chairlift lines.

When I was dressed and ready, though, I encountered a minor obstacle. Couldn't open my front door. I wiped the frost from the window only to see what looked like a four-foot drift wedged up against it. From the sliding glass doors on the back deck I looked out onto a winter wonderland. It was serene and quiet. The snow was coming down heavy now, but without the biting wind that I could hear howling during the night.

I trudged across the deck, around to the front of the house and surveyed my truck, as well as the road that led from my house to the main street. *No, I'm not going anywhere just yet.*

I busied myself shoveling the deck and clearing out the front steps and porch. Damn, the snow was heavy. It took me a full hour just to clear that small area. I was about to head back inside and peel off my soaking wet clothes when I heard a distant voice call my name like a question. I turned and saw a girl half-way down my long drive-way, her lower half enveloped by a snow drift.

It was Carolyn.

Holy shit, it was her.

I started running towards her but I wasn't really running. It was more like taking slow, awkward steps through what felt like a stone wall. When I got closer, I could see that she had all but stopped trying to walk, a large aluminum tray resting next to her on the snow, which was up to her thighs.

"How the hell did you get here?"

"It was fine when I left at four in the morning." She looked past me. "Oh my God, what's with the long-ass driveway, J. R. Ewing?"

"Who?"

"That's right, I forgot you don't do television re-runs or classic eighties movies."

"I think your brain is frostbitten," I said when I was finally next to her, grabbing her backpack. "How bad was the ride?"

"Actually, not that bad on the highways, they were plowed. But once I got to the base of the mountain, I chickened out after I my car swerved once or twice."

"Jesus, you should have called me."

"I did try. No reception. Anyway, I hitched a ride with a couple driving a gigantic SUV. But even that was nail-biting, coming up the mountain with all those turns. The guy took one look at your driveway and asked, 'You good from here?'"

The wind was picking up again. You could barely make out ten feet in front of you. We trudged through the snow slowly, Carolyn carrying the large tray while I had her huge knapsack. We laughed at our awkward steps and how long it was taking us to make it such a short distance. But it *was* taking long. When we got to my porch, Carolyn all but collapsed on the stairs, shivering.

"I didn't realize you had jeans on. Shit, Carolyn, let's get you inside and out of those. I threw her bags inside, abandoned the tray on the porch, and then I reached down and carried her inside and sat her in front of the fire. She shimmied out of her jacket and peeled off her thin gloves to reveal stiff, pink fingers. She couldn't undo the button on her jeans because her hands were trembling so bad. I looked to her for consent and then did my best to peel the wet denim down her legs without looking directly at her. Holy awkwardness. My hands were shaking by the time I grabbed an afghan off the couch and wrapped her up in it.

"Sit tight. I'm gonna make you some tea."

"I'm f-f-fine, Jeremy."

"Sure you are," I called back over my shoulder, smiling. Couldn't help it. I *liked* taking care of her.

The radio was still on in the kitchen. "Looks like another two feet or so will be dumped on us before this is all said and done. Sorry, folks," the weatherman joked, "I hate getting it wrong as much as you hate me when I get it wrong. Smuggler's Notch and Stowe have lots of freshly dumped powder. Trails are open. Killington and Bromley, though, total white-out. No lifts running at this time."

Handing her the steaming mug, I couldn't help but think to myself that she was beautiful. I took in the wet strands clinging to her face, cheeks pink from the frosty snow pelting her, and her purple-painted toes peeking out from beneath the blanket.

"I'm afraid to ask, but where is everyone?" She looked around, uneasy.

"They all turned back last night...Bad driving conditions. You're stuck with me."

"I suppose I am," she said, cracking a shy smile. Her eyes

widened. "I'd better call my parents. My father's probably watching the weather channel, thinking I'm in a ditch somewhere." She threw her head back. "Oh, crap! I left my phone on the charger in my car. It's probably a little block of ice by now."

I tossed her my phone and then gathered up her jacket, gloves and jeans. "I'm gonna throw these in the dryer, all right?"

She smiled and nodded at me as she waited for her call to connect. As I made my way downstairs to the laundry room, panic gripped me. The feeling was fleeting, though, and soon replaced by anticipation. We were stuck here together, me and Carolyn. Snowed in, just the two of us.

This could be interesting.

"Hey, you should still be by the fire. What are you doing?"

Carolyn was crouched by the open front door, reaching over and sliding in the giant tray we'd left on the porch.

"I'm not letting some hungry raccoons get at this. I spent most of yesterday morning slaving over a hot stove."

She lifted the tray off the floor once she got it inside. When she stood, the afghan slid off one shoulder.

"Whoops! Grab this for me Jeremy," she said, gesturing to the tray. She readjusted the small blanket, pulling it higher, so now it revealed every inch of her long legs, the skin still pink from the cold. She looked up at me and I realized I was standing there holding the tray while, like an asshole, ogling her legs. She cleared her throat. "You wanna stick that in the fridge? Um...I'm going to hop in the shower quick and then change into some dry clothes, okay?"

"Yeah," I said, recovering. "Take the first room off the hallway. It has a bathroom. I'll run you a bath if you want."

I'll run you a bath? Holy shit, you sound like a damn pervert.

"Um...I'm good with a shower. But thanks," she added awkwardly.

Carolyn wet. Carolyn naked and wet. This was going to be torture. *No, asshole, it's going to be good. You're going to make this a* good *weekend for her. Get your shit together and stop acting like a horny teenager.*

"Wow, this is huge, Jeremy. I hope you're not giving up your room for me," she called out from the bedroom.

"Nah, no assigned rooms," I answered as I came in with her bags. "You like it, though? I did decorate it myself."

"It's very you. It's got the whole brawny, masculine, log cabin vibe going on. It's homey. I love it," she replied, smiling.

"Whatcha got in here? This knapsack is heavy."

"Well, us girls planned out a dinner. I was bringing the main dish and the wine, so those are the wine bottles that are so heavy. But we'll be doing without desert—that was Taylor's contribution—and without Tori's amazing salad and...Oh, crud, she was bringing the pasta. Hope you don't like spaghetti with your meatballs."

"I've got spaghetti, Harris. Are you forgetting that I keep a well-stocked kitchen? And did I just hear you say that *you* cooked meatballs? Since when do you cook?"

"Since I spent two years practically housebound." She laughed and then looked up to me, cocking her head apologetically. "I spent a lot of time learning to bake with my mom and cooking with my dad...It was easier for me to talk and connect through cooking." Upbeat again, she added, "My meatballs rock, by the way. There's freshly ground veal in them, pecorino cheese, and I make my own breadcrumbs. Then there's my secret ingredient."

"Secret ingredient? What's that?"

"Nope. I'll take it to the grave, Rivers."

"You think I won't be able to taste it? I'm like a meatball aficionado."

"We'll see," she teased as she pranced her fine self into the bathroom, shutting the door in my face with a smile.

"*What* are you doing?"

Damn, caught red handed. "Nuttin'," I attempted to mumble around the full meatball in my mouth.

"Well?"

I shook my head as I chewed. "I don't know. The first one I was thinking that you mixed pork, veal and beef, but that's no secret. Then I was thinking red pepper flakes or sardine paste? Cause it's got a nice tang to it. Then—"

Eyes wide, she pretended she was angry but I saw the smile hidden beneath. "How many have you eaten?"

"I don't know...four?"

"They're cold, Jeremy!"

Damn, she was cute with that scrunched up face, acting like she was mad at me when we both knew she wasn't.

"That's the test of a good meatball. They have to taste good cold. These," I said, tipping a fifth meatball into my mouth, "are awesome."

"Thanks," she said, blushing with pride. "But put them away. Who knows, we might be snowed in for a week and that's all we'll have to live on."

"I wouldn't mind that at all."

Did I say that out loud? Fact was, I would give my right arm to be cooped up with her for the next, well, forever.

She smiled back at me shyly. "So, the slopes are really closed?"

"Probably just for today. Tomorrow we'll be able to get out there."

"I have to warn you, I haven't skied in four years."

"Have you ever snowboarded?"

"No. Tommy loves it but I nearly got killed by an out of control boarder careening down the mountain when I was in eighth grade. I basically looked down my nose at it ever since then. Anyway, it looks like it's so much harder than skiing."

"Not harder, just different. Come on, try something new. I'll teach you."

"All right. You asked for it."

Yes I did.

I took her in as she stood not two feet in front of me. Her hair was damp, drying in waves, cheeks flushed, lips sweet and full. She was dressed in a pair of leggings and a tank top, a men's flannel shirt over it with sleeves rolled up. Her feet were bare. Carolyn never needed anything fancy or expensive to make her desirable and today was no exception. She looked hot as hell.

She fingered the collar of the shirt. "Sorry. Do you mind?"

Shit, got caught staring again. "Sorry."

"No," she said, confused. "Do you mind that I grabbed this out of the closet?"

"That's mine?" Heat crept up my neck and colored my cheeks. My shirt, on her, touching her skin. Yes, something was clearly wrong with me. I turned away as I reassured her, "No, help yourself to anything you want."

"Ok, thanks."

She went back into the room and came out balancing three wine bottles in her arms. "A housewarming present," she said as she lined them up on the counter and then went back in for something else. She then set each bottle into an opening on a rustic wine rack. It looked like it was carved out of a tree trunk.

"It kind of matches the décor, right?"

"It's perfect." *Everything you do is perfect.* "You didn't have to get me a gift."

"I wanted to."

"Jeez, you're like Mary Poppins. What else you got tucked into that bag?"

She waggled her eyebrows. "You'll have to wait and see, now won't cha?"

* * *

CAROLYN

This day, this so called boring day, stuck inside while the snow continued to fall—it was ranking right up there with my all-time best ever days.

Jeremy and I spent the morning and afternoon installing window blinds in the spare guest bedrooms, and then made those beds up with the sheet sets and comforters that were still sitting in shopping bags in the storage room.

He'd try to get me to stop every twenty minutes or so, saying he didn't want me doing work, but I was enjoying myself. Being in close proximity to Jeremy was making my body hum, and if I got to ogle that strip of skin on his torso every time his shirt rode up? Well, that was just a bonus.

When I broke out the wood polish and started dusting the furniture in those rooms, Jeremy grabbed me around the waist and made a game out of wrestling the can and the rag out of my hands.

"No. You're off duty, Harris. Who knew you were such a clean freak?"

The feeling of his hands wrapped around my waist? It felt so good that it almost brought me to tears.

I missed touching. I missed having a boy touch me, kiss me. And Jeremy was no longer that boy. He was even bigger and more manly than I'd thought of him back then. His unshaven face, his broad shoulders and the square, defined set of his jaw? He was a man. The man I wanted touching me.

I could swear that as he set me back down on the ground, he leaned in for just a second and breathed in the scent of my skin. Maybe I was imagining it. I hoped not.

He broke the moment, stepping back and smiling as he held my shoulders. "I owe you lunch. Prop your feet up in front of the fire and I'll whip us up something."

I took in my surroundings as I settled into the corner of the soft leather couch. The large picture windows overlooked an endless forest of fir trees, the branches laden with new fallen snow.

"It's really beautiful here, Jeremy."

He walked in with two steaming bowls of something that smelled really good. "I know. It's peaceful, right?"

I think I actually moaned when I got a taste of his broccoli cheddar soup. "You made this?"

He nodded smugly as he slurped a big spoonful. "Glad you like it."

We sat together in companionable silence for the next few minutes, enjoying our soup. He sat on the opposite end of the couch, facing me. Our toes grazed one another's once, twice, and then Jeremy took his two giant feet and plopped them entirely over mine.

"Hey!" I said, acting affronted, when in reality I loved the feeling of his feet on mine, of any physical contact from him I could get.

"Hey, yourself," he countered, smiling.

I was taken back to an afternoon so long ago, when I sat like this with him, spilling my painful secrets. So relieved to be able to say it all out loud, knowing that with him I would be all right. Jeremy was so good to me that day. He made me feel protected and safe.

"Hey, where'd you go?"

I shrugged, trying to recapture my smile. "I was remembering what it was like, sitting like this and studying at your place." Then I went for broke. "I was thinking about that day I told you every-thing...about Henley." He nodded, frowning. "You were really good to me."

"I wanted to find him and kill him...After it all happened."

"Henley?"

"Yeah."

"What happened with Chase?"

"He got what he deserved."

"I figured that was you...The carjacking."

Jeremy nodded solemnly, scooping the last spoonful of soup into his mouth. "I haven't seen him since that night. Taylor told me he wound up going to some school on the west coast."

"I heard that too. Guys like Chase always seem to land on their feet, though, you know? I predict he'll be a senator—"

"Or one of those preachers who collects bazillions from his flock, preaching piety while he's knee deep in dirt."

My voice broke when I said, "That's another one of those things I'd like to do over. That first day he threatened me, I should've just called his bluff, told him to tell everyone for all I cared." I had to look away as the memories flooded back. "I also wish I would have told my parents what happened that summer at camp. Reported Henley. I still feel guilty about that. He went back to camp that next year...Did one more summer. Did he find some other girl and ruin her innocence?"

"I'd bet money on it, Carolyn. But that's not your fault and you know it."

I shrugged. "I just wonder how different life would have been had I spoken up. What was I thinking? How could I have not trusted my parents? They would have been in my corner. I let myself suffer all that time. I let what he did...change me."

He picked my feet up and put them on his lap, squeezing and rubbing them gently like he did that day.

"No do-overs, right?" I said, trying to smile. "I know it's not healthy to keep looking back."

"There's a whole lot I regret, too. I knew something was off with you that last week...Especially those few days leading right up to it. I never pressed you about it. If I had, maybe you would have told me what was going on."

"Do you ever think about why Drew did it?"

"Back then I wondered all the fucking time."

"I worry that Chase's post sent him over the edge. Maybe he believed it all, and he was upset that I'd lied to him and was disgusted that...that he'd dated someone like me."

"No way. It wasn't like that. Drew loved you, Carolyn. I think he was just hurting...He was hurting for you just like I was. Bottom line is that he was sad, drunk and had ten different guns in his house to choose from...Not a good combination."

"It'll be four years this March."

"Yeah." After a moment he said, "I've been to the memorial service every year. It's the same people, although the crowd last year was a little light in comparison to years past."

"I still wouldn't be welcome there. I do my own sort of memorial a few days after the date. It feels kind of crappy, though, visiting their graves like a thief in the night, still praying that no one spots me out there."

"No one with half a brain ever blamed you, and I'll be honest, I still feel so angry—with you and with everyone else—thinking about you going through all that shit alone." Jeremy's hands were balled into fists now, his irritation palpable. "If there's one thing that I could go back and fix, it would be that instead of standing outside your house every day like a pathetic chump, I would have pushed past your parents and *made* you talk to me."

I leaned over and took one of his hands. "I wish I would have opened the door one of those nights. You were like clockwork...Five o'clock on the dot. I needed you. I wish I would have let you in. I'm sorry."

* * *

JEREMY

"I understand now, I really do, Carolyn. And what's done is done. We can only make sure we don't repeat the same mistakes, right?"

She reached for a strand of hair, twisting it around her finger. "Right."

We needed a break from the heavy. "You hungry?"

"Nope."

"Thirsty?"

"Nope."

"Tired."

She laughed. "Nope."

"All right, what do people do when they're snowed in, stranded and adrift from civilization?"

"We're not exactly roughing it, chief. We've got heat, hot water, cable—"

"Wanna watch a movie?"

She shrugged. "Not really. Got any games?"

"I actually do." I opened the cabinet underneath the television console. "Let's see. We've got Monopoly, chess, Yahtzee and Scrabble." I looked back to her smirking. "My dad and I play Scrabble all the time. Two dyslexics squaring off...It's pretty comical."

"I didn't know your dad has a reading disability. I mean, it makes sense. It often runs in families."

"Yeah. He didn't get himself help until after he saw how much the teachers at Briarwood helped me. It was kinda weird seeing my dad with his tutor, but I was so proud of him."

Carolyn swallowed, emotion taking over her features. "I think that's great. It takes a lot of courage to get help when you're an adult." She shook it off then and leveled me with a challenge. "I'm kind of a Scrabble ninja. Think you can take me?"

I can take you in so many ways, missy.

Being this close to Carolyn after wanting her for so long was screwing with my head, my body...with everything. I schooled my expression before turning back to her. "Game on, sweetheart."

I poured us a small glass of wine and joined her in front of the fire where she was setting up the game. "Maybe we'll have dinner at around seven?"

"Sounds good." Her eyes widened then. "I almost forgot!" She jumped up and made her way back into the bedroom, returning with two loaves of semolina bread tucked under her arm.

She stopped on her way to the kitchen at the sound of my voice. "Don't even tell me you just pulled those out of your bag, too."

She was practically doubled over laughing. "I know, I'm like a freaking magician! You'll be glad I hauled these along, though. La Viola gets their bread from some bakery in the Bronx that's been around for nearly a century. It's *so* good." She paused then, her smile falling. "Oh, but you tried it the other night, right?"

"No, I didn't. That grouper looked great, too, but I didn't have much of an appetite."

"Gotcha." She nodded in understanding and then continued on into the kitchen. Walking back out, she teased, "You didn't peak in the bag when you picked your letters, did you?"

"C'mon, I don't get any accommodations on account of my disability?"

"Screw that, Rivers."

We each picked one letter. I drew an E, she drew the Z.

"You get to go first. That's a slight advantage."

"Not when you're pretty much stuck with all vowels." I grumbled as I put down EAT as my first word. "Holy shit, I'm gonna get creamed. What is that, six points?"

"Yep. Thank goodness you snagged the double word score."

She hesitated a minute and then looked up at me with a guilty expression.

"What is it?"

"I'm not trying to be obnoxious, really," she said, breaking into laughter as she took all of her seven letters and laid them down, piggy backing off the letter T in EAT to spell out QUIXOTIC.

"Holy shit! Did you just get a double word score, too? That's just not right."

She could barely get the words out she was laughing so hard. "No! Just a double letter on the Q and...the O and the I. Total score," she emulated a drumroll, "eighty-eight points." She cringed as she announced it.

"No feeling bad for the reading disabled kid allowed," I joked. "Shit. I'm gonna go down like the Titanic. I forgot you get that fifty point bonus for using all seven letters."

I built off of her Q and laid down the word QUONDAM. "Thirty-eight points." I looked at her, smug. "I'll catch up."

"What the hell is *that*? Is that even a real word?"

"Do I smell a challenge, Harris?"

She backed down. "No. I'd lose. You always had a great vocabulary. So what does it mean?"

"From long ago...Like a former time."

"Hmph." She nodded as she went about rearranging her letters.

"Crazy, right? I could tell you what any word means but for the longest time, I couldn't recognize the word, read it."

"Is it better? I mean the other night at the restaurant..."

I smiled, warming to the memory of how she looked at me tenderly when she made that save. "Yeah, I almost tanked on one of those foodie words, thanks. I think that was nerves more than anything."

She put down MOOL. "Now I'm just trying to stump you," she teased.

"Nice try. Soil right, but like specifically the dirt on a grave."

She let out a frustrated, "ugh," as she reached back into the bag for more letters.

"I like that word. I like quixotic the best, though."

"Oh yeah, smarty pants?"

"Yeah, it's a word that fits you."

She looked up at me, her brow furrowed. "Am I idealistic to the point of being ridiculous?"

"No, I think of it as being a dreamer, seeing what's best in a situation maybe even when there's not so much that's good to begin with."

She studied me as she took a sip of her wine. "Maybe that's how I *used* to be."

"You always saw the best in me, even when I was an angry little punk."

"You were never a punk. Even when we were kids I saw you as this strong, silent type...But I always thought you were sweet."

"That day I pushed you, you thought I was sweet?"

"The next morning you proved to me that you were." After a pause, she said, "You know I still have that peace offering?"

"What?"

Nodding, embarrassed, she chuckled. "I mean, I ate the candy bar that night, but I saved the note. I held onto that note crying every night after you left school."

"No way."

"I did. I'd conjured up all these terrible scenarios. Where did they take you? Were you in some sort of juvenile detention hell hole? I felt terrible. You were falsely accused and I never stood up for you."

"See? Always putting the weight of the world on your shoulders. Anyway, it didn't feel like it then, but that was the best thing that could have happened to me."

"I know."

"I did miss you, though."

"Me, really?"

I nodded. "I was totally hung up on you when I was twelve."

She lowered her head to hide the blush creeping across her cheeks. She met my eyes again when she said, "I loved that piece you did...*My Friend*. That was me and you, right?"

"More like how I imagined it was between us back then. Even though I hardly ever spoke to you, I did always feel like you were my friend. But you were good to everyone. I think every boy in that class was crushing on you."

"Right," she said with a smirk. "Anyway, I couldn't afford *My*

Friend or any of your other pieces at the Gala. You drew the big bucks. There were bidding wars happening."

"So Andie tells me. She's already conned me into donating a few pieces for next year."

"Did she tell you about *True Beauty*?"

I flinched. "Did you freak when you saw it?"

Carolyn smiled as she reached over and grabbed my hand. "For a minute I freaked. I mean, it took me back, you know? But it was more like I was in awe. I love it, Jeremy."

"It was hard to part with that one."

It *was* hard. I wrapped the canvas up and put it in the truck, only to take it out and haul it back upstairs, repeating the process two more times before deciding to take it to Andie.

"Well, that one caused the biggest stir. There were a few patrons who kept trying to outbid one another. It got a little heated. And then Andie took it down, telling everyone that the artist requested its removal from the auction."

"Why'd she do that?" *And why hadn't she told me?*

We'd pretty much abandoned the Scrabble game by then. Carolyn was raking her hands over the board and scooping the tiles back into the bag.

She took a moment before answering, "Because she wanted me to have it."

Relief washed over me. Andie was a genius. "You should have it. It always should have been yours."

"It's still wrapped up. I think I'll wait until I have my own place to hang it." Her shy smile was drawing me in, making me think about kissing her. "It's art, and my parents don't have hang-ups about that sort of thing, but I don't know if my mom or dad could handle seeing me that way. I mean, the look on my face...It's pretty obvious what's on my mind, you know?"

I did know what was on her mind that night and the memory made my dick painfully hard. I was wearing sweats. I thought I was smooth when I casually reached up to grab a throw pillow to place over my lap, but she looked right at my crotch and then smiled wide as she rose up and stretched.

"I'll get started on dinner, ok?"

"Um, yeah. I'm gonna grab a quick shower, all right?"

She made her way to the kitchen but then peeked her head back in and teased, "You do that."

I was busted and therefore decided to take full advantage by rubbing one out in the shower.

"Hey, you didn't tell me we were getting all fancy for dinner." Carolyn looked down at her get-up and then gestured to the loose bun atop her cute little head. "I feel like a shlub."

I looked down at my outfit. I had on new jeans and a button down with the sleeves rolled up. I guess I had put a little extra effort in, but I mean, I was barefoot. "A shlub? You've finally stumped me in the vocab department. Whatever shlub means, I think you look great."

"I might have made that word up. And I'm not changing," she added defiantly. "I packed a lot of crap in my bags. With my ski clothes, the wine, the bread, the olive oil...I didn't have any extra room for formal dinner wear."

I shook my head in disbelief. "You packed olive oil?"

"When I told Marco, the cook, I was stealing some bread, he insisted I take some of his favorite olive oil for dipping."

"Nice."

I leaned over her shoulder as she stirred the pot of meatballs and breathed in. "That smells so good." I was referring to Carolyn, really. Her skin smelled clean and sweet. She didn't smell like vanilla or roses or honey—she smelled like Carolyn, and if you could bottle that scent you'd be a millionaire ten times over.

She bumped her butt backwards. Her hands were full, so that

was her way of getting me to back off, but her ass pushing into me had the opposite effect. I was as hard as steel again, my skin felt heated, and it took everything in me not to lean in again and drag her hips back into mine. *Back off*, I scolded myself, and then willed myself to turn away.

I busied myself slicing the bread and then setting the table for two. "Carolyn, can I pour you another glass of wine?"

"Yeah, I just downed a big glass of water so I'm good to go. I like that Chianti, don't you?"

"I'm usually a beer guy, but yeah, that was really good."

I handed her the glass. "Cheers. I'm glad you're here."

She clinked her glass with mine. "Me too, Jeremy." Her eyes held mine for a moment before she smiled shyly and then went back to stirring the pot.

* * *

CAROLYN

I was burning up. Standing over the stove, wearing his flannel shirt, the proximity of his body—it was all working together to make me hot, flustered and itching with a need to strip myself out of these clothes. While he was busy setting the table, I unbuttoned his shirt and tossed it. I was in leggings and just a tank—one that hugged me tight and left a strip of exposed skin at my midriff.

I could feel it when he turned back around. I knew he'd stopped in his tracks and I could feel his eyes trained on me. It's what I was aiming for but his reaction made me nervous. I didn't feel particularly schooled in the art of seduction, and with Jeremy I really didn't know where I stood. I mean, the two of us being here alone was a fluke, and while he seemed happy about this unexpected turn of events, I just couldn't be sure. And the thought of being rejected by him—no, I just couldn't let my mind go there.

To busy my shaking hands, I reached up to let my hair down and then fixed it into another topknot to trap the strands that had come loose. My throat felt tight. I cleared it before saying, "Do you have a strainer? I think the pasta's done."

"Um, what?"

"The pasta. I think it's done."

"Oh, got it."

We stood side by side at the counter. Jeremy dumped the contents of the pot into the colander and then heaped a giant mound of pasta onto each of our plates. I topped each with meatballs and sauce.

"Hey, I'm not a lumberjack."

He bumped my hip. "All of you runners carb load, right?"

"That's enough pasta for three of me."

"Nah, you need to fatten up," he teased as he pinched my butt.

I think I yelped and jumped about a foot from shock. "Hey, mister grabby hands."

Jeremy just smiled his sly smile, cut me a glance and then turned as he took both plates to the table. I relaxed a bit as I thought, *Maybe he is into me.*

You couldn't get a more romantic setting: the rustic log cabin, the fireplace, the warm lighting, the wine. I was already feeling the wine. When he went to refill our glasses, I stopped him.

"That's enough for me."

He rose from the table and headed back into the kitchen. "I'll get you some water."

"Thanks," I said as he placed my glass in front of me. "I'm careful with alcohol. I drink but I try and keep it to two."

His brow furrowed. "Did you have a problem with it?"

"No. It's just...I guess it's a need to be in control? Those months after, um, everything, I hated the way the medication made me feel all fuzzy and dull."

"I can understand that."

He popped another meatball in his mouth and went on to groan in pleasure.

"Whoa, doggie. It sounds like you're having a religious experience."

"What's the secret?" he asked mid-chew, the food still in his mouth.

God, he made me happy. I was transfixed for a moment, watching his strong jaw work, staring at the drop of sauce that sat on his full lower lip. He was a work of art. Strong—so much bigger and more defined than he was. He was making my head swim more than the wine.

"Carolyn?"

"Hmm?"

"The secret ingredient. What is it? C'mon, give it up."

"Oh, well you were half-right. There *are* crushed red pepper flakes, but I also dice some prosciutto into the mixture."

He nodded, seemingly impressed, and then speared another with his fork. "I don't want you to go getting a big head or anything, but these are the best I've ever tasted."

"That's high praise coming from a cook of your caliber."

"Next time I'll cook for you. I've got some new tricks up my sleeve."

"I'd like that."

"Yeah, me too," he said absently.

Jeremy's eyes were fixed on my chest. I could feel my skin heat under his stare. I reached for my water and downed half the glass. He didn't seem to notice that I was positively wound up. While I was forcing myself to nibble on my food, he cleaned his plate and then went in for seconds.

We talked about everything and nothing, and I found myself relaxing again. There were times when being with him was so effortless. As I twirled my last remaining forkful of pasta and popped it into my mouth, I was overwhelmed by the realization that if nothing else, Jeremy was a friend of mine and I believed he always would be.

He stood up and started clearing the table. "That was delicious, Carolyn. Thanks." When I went to follow, he turned. "Nope. You park yourself in front of the fire. You cooked, I clean."

"Aye, aye, captain," I said, saluting him as I made my way to the couch and flopped down. I felt warm, sated and loose from the wine. I watched him as he made his way from the table to the sink and back again. He was talking to me about snowboarding the entire time but I barely registered what he was saying.

He popped back out of the kitchen, eyes wide, the small bakery box in his hand. "What's in here?"

"I lied. We do have desert. Marco's famous cannolis."

"Oh, woman," he murmured, closing his eyes. "You know the way to my heart."

My eyes popped open in surprise. He didn't look away or look to take the words back. He kept his eyes locked on mine as the air between us crackled louder than the logs in the fire.

This was really happening.

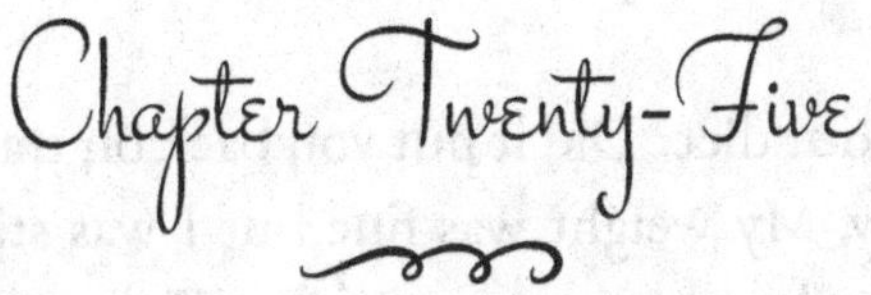

Chapter Twenty-Five

CAROLYN

Jeremy flopped down opposite me, his back against the other arm of the couch. "You wanna watch that movie now?" he asked, handing me a cannoli. "The kettle's on. I'll make us some tea in a minute."

"Ummm," I murmured, smiling as I bit into it. "I have to watch it with these. If I could, I'd have one after every meal."

"Why do you watch your weight, Carolyn? You're in great shape."

I shrugged. "I don't really. I just like to eat healthy. My doctor actually told me I had to start eating more healthy fats, but I don't think this counts." I smiled, holding up the cannoli. Absently, I added, "The running was interfering with my cycle." He cocked his head to the side. *Shit...Way to go, Carolyn.* "Sorry, that was a little TMI."

"What cycle?"

Oh lordy. I felt myself turning a deep shade of scarlet.

"It happens to a lot of female runners. My, um, time of the

month? I was skipping a lot. Please," I pleaded, "let's change the topic before I die of embarrassment."

He nudged my foot with his. "Don't be weird. It's just your body." Jeremy left the room and came back a minute later with two mugs. As he handed me my tea, he asked, "So, did it work?"

"What?"

"Changing your diet? Did it put you back on track?"

"Not entirely. My weight was fine but I was still skipping a lot. The doctor prescribed birth control pills. They regulate my cycle. I really didn't want to take anything and fought my mother and doctor on it for a while. After weaning myself off the other meds, even though it's an entirely different scenario, I just...you know."

He nodded. "So you're on them now?"

"Yeah, I gave in. It's actually really bad for you if your cycle stops. It can weaken your bones. So now, um, it's all good."

I wanted to crawl under a rock in that moment. I started fiddling with the remote but couldn't turn the thing on.

"Here, I got it." He took it and started scrolling through the channels. He looked over to me, ignoring the cable guide on the screen. "If it makes you feel any better, my menstrual cycle is kind of messed up too."

I hurled a throw pillow at him, laughing. "You idiot! And why is it that boys can't pronounce that word?"

"I said it just fine," he protested.

"No, you annunciated each syllable. Men-stru-al."

Eyes innocent, he asked, "How are you supposed to say it?"

"Nope, I'm not telling you." Reaching over, I grabbed the remote from his hand. "Gimme that."

As our hands touched, there was a clicking sound and then we were shrouded in darkness. The only source of light was the dim output from the dwindling fire.

"If you messed up my remote, woman, you're gonna pay."

"Wow, Mr. Electrician, haven't you noticed that *everything* is off?"

"Shit." He jumped off the couch. "Let me find the flashlight."

He was back a minute later, handing me a flashlight and then making his way to the door where he pulled on his boots, gloves and jacket. He switched on his halogen, which lit up everything, and winked at me before leaving. "Be right back."

I walked into the kitchen, balancing the mugs in one hand and the flashlight in the other. I looked for candles but couldn't find any.

About fifteen minutes later Jeremy came back in, kicking the snow off his boots on the doorjamb before coming all the way inside. As he stripped out of his jacket, gloves and hat, he told me, "Nothing's wrong *here*, but the power is definitely out. None of the houses around here look to have power either. I hope a transformer didn't blow or something."

"Well, at least we've got the fireplace."

"We're going to need it. It's gotta be around ten below out there now and the gas furnace doesn't run without power." He looked to me sheepishly. "I've been meaning to bring up a back-up generator but I haven't gotten around to it."

"I'm going to report you to the union."

"I know, I'm a disgrace to my profession."

"Yes, you are. And now, since you've put us in mortal danger and we might not make it through the night and all, I propose that we eat the two remaining cannolis. It would be a shame if we froze to death and the raccoons got to enjoy them."

"I'm in agreement with that proposal. More tea?"

"A little more wine for me. Just a little. Red wine tastes really good with cannolis."

I grabbed the cannolis off the counter and Jeremy poured us some wine. He placed the glasses on the coffee table.

"Be right back. I'm gonna change."

My breaths came in shallow while he was gone. I sipped my wine nervously. Not a day had gone by when I hadn't thought of Jeremy, thought of what I'd missed out on. I wanted so much from tonight, so much from him. And when he came out, the shirt and jeans replaced by a snug tee and sweats that hung low on his hips, my mouth watered for the taste of his kiss, for the taste of his skin.

* * *

JEREMY

She was so damn sweet, looking up at me all wide-eyed, lips parted, taking in a shaky breath that I wanted to steal right back from her.

That little bit of skin peeking out from beneath her tank top held my attention and then my eyes moved up. In my fantasy, she'd part her lips and wet them as she slowly pulled the top down just enough so that her plump, round—

"If you don't grab that cannoli soon, I'm gonna eat your's too."

"What?"

"I said I'm about to eat your cannoli."

I snatched it out of her hand and wolfed it down in two bites.

"Don't think so," I mumbled with my mouth full.

"Pig," she teased, laughing.

I plopped down right next to her so that our hips were touching. I wanted her on my lap, wanted her soft pressed up against my hard. But I was a patient man and every single step was going to be on Carolyn's terms.

We sat in comfortable silence for a few minutes, sipping the last of our wine, mesmerized by the flickering flames. She broke the silence, blurting out, "Why did you hold back that night? The night I posed for you?" She looked down to her lap then, embarrassed. Shaking her head, she added, "Don't answer that."

I adjusted the boner that was now becoming painful. "I was afraid you'd regret it."

"Why would you think that?"

"I don't know, really. I was just afraid of hurting you. I didn't want you to see me like you saw him, Henley…Taking something you weren't ready to give."

"You're nothing like him. I wouldn't have regretted it."

"I'm the one who was left with regret. You know how many times I thought about that night and imagined the alternate ending?"

"I was so mad at you, Jeremy. I *was* ready and I was mad that you wouldn't. But then that next day, I remember feeling so…cherished. You said the sweetest things to me that night. You made me feel like I was special."

"You were…You are." I shifted her so that she was sitting across me, straddling my lap, moving slowly to make sure she was on board with this. "Can I kiss you?"

* * *

CAROLYN

It was all I could do not to press down right onto him. But I wanted to. I wanted him pressed right up against me, in me. I wanted his lips and his hands everywhere. I wanted him to fill my mouth, my sex. I wanted him to devour me.

Can I kiss you, he asks me? I'm sure I nodded repeatedly in my lust-induced haze.

He kissed the corner of my mouth, teasing, licking—his lips as full and soft as I remembered. The sweet taste of the cannoli cream mixed with the wine leaving the best taste on my lips. I needed more.

As his tongue swept into my mouth, I reached back and undid the clasp on my bra with one hand. Then both of my hands, seemingly with a will of their own, went to pull my top down to expose myself to him. My breasts felt heavy, achy with a need to be touched, kissed, sucked. His hands moved to my shoulders and he moved me back just slightly as he broke the kiss. He stared at my breasts, swallowing and then licking his lips. Then he looked up to me. I knew what he was doing. He was looking for consent every step of the way. Protecting me. Making sure I was all right. Always taking care of me.

I didn't take my eyes off his as I pushed my arms out of the straps and pushed the tank down around my waist as my discarded bra fell to the floor. Wanting him to know I was offering myself to him.

Jeremy's mouth kissed mine again and then he lowered his head as his hands gently pressed my breasts together. His greedy mouth went from one nipple to the other, licking, nipping, sucking. My hands threaded through his hair, using the hold for leverage to push my body down. I couldn't help moving, rocking against him for the friction I craved, that I needed. I could feel him large, thick, so hard, but the thin fabric was still too much between us. I think I moaned when his hand made contact, slipping between my belly and the waistband of my leggings, moving down and finally hitting me where I was begging him to. My lips locked onto Jeremy's as my body responded of its own accord, rocking against his hand as he cupped me and then against him when he pushed inside. *Fuck me, fuck me, fuck me*, I begged in silence.

"Tell me what you want, Carolyn," he whispered, urging me when I didn't answer him right away. "*Tell* me."

Breathy and desperate, I sighed as I said the words, "I need...I need—"

"I need *you*, Carolyn. I need to be inside of you. That's what *I* want. What do *you* want, baby, because once we do this," he paused, "there's no going back. I'm all in. Are you?"

"I want you. I want everything with you," I breathed as I pushed his hand against me, greedy for my release.

"Show me," he rasped as he worked me until my sex clenched, my muscles tightening with my orgasm. "You're so damn beautiful," he murmured into my hair.

I slumped against him for a moment and breathed him in, my

lips still hungry to kiss him, my tits still heavy in his hands. Wanting more, I stood and slowly hooked my fingers into the waistband, taking my leggings and panties down as I tugged. I swallowed as I stood bared to him, tentative but unashamed.

He stood as he took me in from head to toe with a look of pure reverence. He moved closer and then two large, callused hands caressed my hips, slid over my ass and down the backs of my thighs before he grasped me there and lifted me up, wrapping my legs around his waist.

"I'm taking you to my bed. Is that all right?"

"Yes," I answered, lowering my lips to his then and kissing him with everything I had.

We entered his darkened room. Before going to the bed, Jeremy wrapped one arm around my back to secure me, using his free hand to whip open the curtains. The moon reflected off the snow, casting a faint glow throughout the room.

He laid me in the center of the bed. "I want to see you."

He undressed, never taking his eyes off my body. I fisted my hands in the sheets to keep from touching myself. The sight of him standing there, his hard cock upright against his belly, left me as achy as I was before. When he took one hand and began to stroke himself, I gave in and let one hand roam over my breasts and down between my legs. I was wet.

"Fuck," he blew out on a breath. Climbing over me, he reached with one hand for the nightstand drawer and then tossed a foil packet onto the bed next to us. He lowered himself, taking each of my hands in one of his as he gently pinned them above our heads. "Is this okay?"

"Yes," I answered, nodding my head, my chest heaving. "Yes."

He kissed my lips, kissed along my jaw, kissed down my neck and along my collarbone. He kissed down along one side of my ribcage, my body writhing with need when his warm breath whispered over my breasts. He skimmed kisses across my belly and then looked up to me, waiting for consent that I gave him with my eager, lust-filled eyes before plunging his tongue between my legs.

Never felt *that* before.

Oh.

Dear.

Now I knew what all the fuss was about.

Kisses and nips along my inner thighs then. And kisses back up over my belly, my breasts, my neck and my mouth. The idea that I was tasting myself on his lips made me hotter, more wetness pooling between my legs. Again...*fuck me, fuck me, fuck me*, I begged silently.

"Are you ready, Carolyn?" he asked me.

"Yes."

"You sure you want this?" he repeated, his jaw clenched with the effort of holding back.

"Please," I begged, my body rising up to meet his.

He kissed me once more, so tenderly, before he kneeled to put the condom on.

"I'm on the pill, Jeremy."

He continued rolling it down over himself. "I know," he said, his face pained, "but I need to protect you."

If what he said had registered at that moment, it might have ruined it for me. But I was blissful and oblivious and just wanting him so very badly.

* * *

JEREMY

Yes...yes...yes.

The best homecoming I will ever have in this lifetime.

She flinched when I entered her the first time, and I stilled, never wanting to be a man who hurt her.

"No," she urged me, gently digging her heels into my ass. "It's good, Jeremy."

"So good, Carolyn, so good." The words came out on a breath. A prayer, a chant—words that were so simple, when really, I was overcome with the feeling of being inside of this woman. Being so close to *her*. Nothing could ever be as good as this. *I love you, I love, I love you*, I wanted to shout out every time I pushed inside of her. But I didn't.

I moved into her, moved with her, as I sucked, licked and kissed any inch I could claim with my mouth.

Heaven.

"Why did you say you had to protect me?"

"Hmm?" I hummed into her hair, lazy and sated and just so, so *good* after the best sex of my life. This girl. So beautiful. Her sexy little whimpers, the way she moved her body, the way she said my name. Me—like I was someone special and beloved.

"I mean, I get it. I'm all for being extra careful," she said as she drew lazy circles onto my back, dragging her nails lightly across my skin. Just that, her touch—everything she did felt so fucking good. "It's not like I want to be a mom right now or anything," she went on.

Shit. I did not want to have this conversation. No, I wanted just me and Carolyn in this room—nothing ugly, nothing stupid that I'd done. But she had to know. So I raised my head and met her eyes, suddenly feeling desperate. "Hear me out, ok?"

"All right," she answered, her voice now hesitant and wary.

"I was drunk and I had sex without protection. Recently."

"Oh."

"I've never done that before."

"With Kenzie," she said, her voice flat.

I rolled over onto my back and looked up at the ceiling, clasping her hand in mine. "I don't want to bring all that into this room with us. I'm telling you, it meant nothing and I know that makes me sound like a shit. I *was* a shit to her." A moment passed. "Say something, Carolyn," I pleaded.

"I feel...such hateful jealousy towards her. I hate that there was someone else. And I know that's ridiculous for me of all people to say."

I rolled towards her and leaned in over her body. "I told you this already, but for the longest time there was no one and I...I never saw her as special to me in any way. There never has been anyone else. There's no one but you."

"Are you certain? It's completely over between you and Kenzie?" There was no anger or accusation in her voice when she quietly pressed, "Just tell me."

"One hundred percent over."

"Okay," she whispered. And to show me it really was okay, Carolyn laced her fingers with mine, lifted my hand up and kissed it tenderly.

"I meant what I said. I'm all in."

"I know. No turning back. I am too," she said as she rolled up and over, straddling me and draping her body over mine.

She felt so unbelievably good. I felt as if my heart would burst. I ran my hands down over her back, her ass and back up again, cradling her close to me. "No one else. I'm yours, Carolyn. Always was, always will be."

She raised her head and looked down upon me, shaking her head. "I never once stopped loving you. Never."

"Are you happy now? Right now, Carolyn, are you happy?"

She punctuated each whispered word with kisses to my chest, neck, jaw and finally, my lips. "So...so...happy...happy...happy."

Chapter Twenty-Six

CAROLYN

Jeremy walked in with two steaming mugs.

"Rise and shine, sweetness. The power's back on, snow's stopped falling and the trails are open. Don't think I'm gonna let you off the hook or anything."

I wasn't asleep, just pretending to be. I'd been listening to him putter around as I lie in bed, praying with everything I had that there would be no morning-after awkwardness between us. I pulled the covers down slowly over my face to see him standing at the foot of the bed, his smile stretching from ear to ear, infectious.

"Good morning," I murmured, unable to contain my own smile.

I yawned then and stretched my arms overhead, not realizing that the sheet was no longer covering me.

"Don't move," he commanded, setting the mugs down on top of the nightstand. The smile now gone, he shook his head. "Do you know how beautiful you are?" he asked as his hands moved slowly to trace the sides of my breasts. Then he cupped them, one in each hand, gently running his thumbs over my sensitive skin.

I wanted him again. I shifted my thighs, rubbing them against one another, seeking some friction, some relief.

"Good morning," I murmured again.

"Love these," he murmured as he lowered his lips to my breasts.

"You're a boob man, huh?"

I said it in a lighthearted way, but the comment only came to mind because, deep down, I was still jealous of that chick.

"I'm a boob man for Carolyn Harris's boobs." In between the kisses and licks he laid on one and then the other, he reached down and gripped my ass. "I'm an ass man for Carolyn's ass." He moved down the bed then and lifted one of my legs, tracing his fingers down to my foot. "I've even got a foot fetish for Carolyn Harris's feet," he said before popping my big toe into his mouth and sucking. I groaned. "But this," he said, moving back up, "this is my heaven." And he went right there, tongue delving in, lips kissing and sucking on my most sensitive places.

I fisted the sheets. Didn't know what to do with the sensation. He pressed my hips into the mattress to still me as he worked me over, relentless. I wanted to grab the back of his head and press his face in even closer but I wasn't sure if that was wrong. I rocked my hips instead, and once I started I couldn't stop. My hands moved up to grasp my own hair at the roots. I felt, I felt...I felt too much. He hummed against me, "Let go, baby," as he snaked two fingers inside of me. In between nips and kisses he whispered, "I can feel you, Carolyn. You feel that? So fucking good."

I could feel it. I could feel my insides pulsing against his fingers, every nerve ending humming, tingling. As I came back down, my fingers twisted in his hair and he looked up to me with a satisfied, cocky smirk.

"You're pretty good at that, huh?" I teased lazily.

"You seem to think so."

I nodded, feeling so close to him in that moment that a sensation of warmth blanketed my chest, spreading all over my body. I rose to my knees, completely exposing my nudity to him. "Now you. Let's trade places."

"You don't have to, Carolyn." But he did ease back down onto the bed, so I'm guessing, yeah, he wanted this.

"Yes, I do." I looked down at him as I sat up on my knees, settling between his thighs on the bed. "I want to," I said as I lowered his sweats. The waistband caught, and when I tugged, he literally sprang free. Long and hard, silken skin covering his shaft. I lowered my head to him and moved my hair over one shoulder so that I could concentrate on the task at hand. I didn't feel that confident, but really, how hard could this be? From the little I knew about sex, I knew that just looking at a guy could get him excited.

Just me kissing the tip had Jeremy moaning, "Holy fuck." So I went with it, licking and sucking, but never taking him too deep. I could feel his eyes on me, and after less than two minutes he took my shoulders and gently guided me back up.

"No good?"

He shook his head. "So good, but I want in."

I moved up more and straddled him, lowering myself to grind back and forth along his cock. It felt so good.

He took hold of my hips, moving me back and forth, his head thrust back. I wanted so much for him to just glide into me, to fuck me skin on skin. I moved up so the head of his cock lined up with my opening. He held me tight then, stilling my movement. "Grab one. That drawer," he said, tipping his chin towards the nightstand.

He was right—I knew that. I ripped a condom off the strip and once I had it out, I fumbled trying to roll it down over him. His hands covered mine, trembling too as he helped me to finish the job.

"Inside of you, Carolyn. I always want to be inside of you."

I raised myself up a bit and held him, guiding him into me. I felt powerful in this position and sexy. I liked the feel of my breasts bouncing gently as I moved up and down, taking him in over and over again. I loved hearing him moan, his head thrown back in ecstasy, knowing *I* was doing this. *I* was making it good for him.

And watching him come down from it—his heavy breaths slowing, his lips curving into a smile, shaking his head just slightly as he said, "You're killing me, baby." He pulled me down to him, hugging my chest close to his, part of him still inside of me. "I love you."

"This is real then? You and me?"

I couldn't look at him. All of a sudden I was nervous, afraid this would all change once we were back in Westerly.

Jeremy lifted my chin so we were face to face. "Hey, listen carefully. I'll tell you how I want this to go, ok?" I nodded, needing to hear the words. "I want to be your boyfriend." He smiled for a moment but then the lighthearted air was gone and he was serious again. "I want you to be my girl. Every day, Carolyn, I want to call you whenever something funny happens, or something crappy happens, or when I'm thinking about you and just want to tell you. I want you to sneak over to my place after your Saturday night shift and climb into bed with me so I can wrap my arms around you. I want you to come with me when I hang out with my Grandpa and I want to sit with your family and have dinner on Sunday nights like I used to."

"I want all of that, too. I want you, Jeremy."

"You've got me."

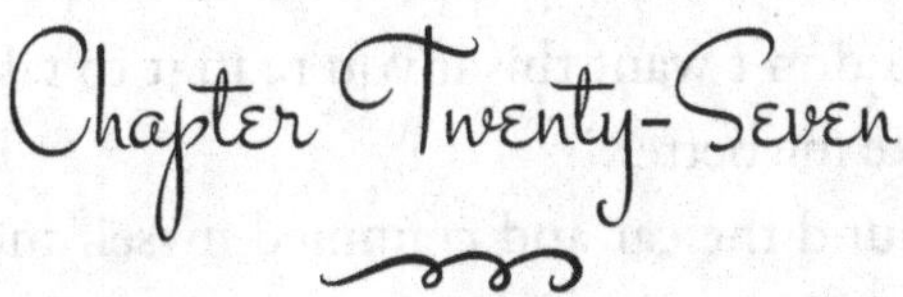

Chapter Twenty-Seven

JEREMY

"You got this? You sure?"

Carolyn rolled her eyes. "I've been driving around for the past two years without your help. Yes, I've got this."

It took us over half an hour to clear the snow from her car and to clear the ice from her windshield. Now she was sitting in the driver's seat, rubbing her hands together, looking impatient.

"I mean the roads look decent, but I'm sure there are still some slick spots. Is your phone fully charged?" She ignored me, busying herself by adjusting her mirrors. "I'll be right behind you."

She shot me a look. "You're following me home? Uh, no. It's Monday, you have to be at work."

"I told them I'll be on site late today."

"So you're going to follow me all the way home and then turn around and drive back up to New Haven? Why?"

"I just want to make sure you get back safe."

Carolyn's teasing smile turned into a frown. "You can't do this."

"What?"

"You can't follow me, protect me…Make me feel like I can't do things without your help."

I took in her words and her expression. "That's not what I meant."

"Maybe it is." Carolyn gripped the steering wheel, looking straight ahead. "I don't want this if you're in it to take care of me, or fix me, or to make me better."

I walked around the car and crammed myself into the passenger seat of her new, ridiculously small Mini Cooper. "I'm not looking to be your babysitter. I get it. But I want to take care of you, to protect you. I'd want to do that even if the past had never happened."

"But I *need* to feel like I'm capable, Jeremy. Do you understand? Even if I fall, it's better that I fall and pick myself back up. If you treat me like I'm incompetent or vulnerable, I'll lose faith in myself."

"I get it."

"Good," she said, cracking a smile. "Now get out of my car and go to work."

"I am following you until New Haven, though. Your car's been buried for the past two days. Just call me when you get home, all right?"

"I will."

"And we're still on for dinner tomorrow night?"

She leaned over to kiss me—a hot, smoking kiss that lasted so long and got me so worked up that I wanted to recline the seats and stay in her cramped little car forever. She broke the kiss. "We're on for dinner tomorrow night. I just got you back so you're not getting rid of me anytime soon."

And so it went. Carolyn and I slipped into a routine. We saw each other most nights. But when work was crazy or when Carolyn was bogged down with schoolwork, we spoke to one other on the phone at least a couple of times each day. She still waitressed on Saturday nights but would occasionally come up to ski when she could switch a shift with someone else. I got in the habit of leaving the mountain after taking a few runs early on Sunday mornings because I officially had my seat back at the Harris family table on Sunday nights. I'm not going to say that was the highpoint of my week—no, the times when I was able to hold Carolyn naked in my arms and sink inside of her topped anything—but Sunday dinners were a close second.

I was happy, truly happy for the first time in a really long time. And I was comfortable. I wasn't expecting the axe to fall anymore. I wasn't waiting for it all to come crashing down.

I wasn't expecting it to end.

* * *

CAROLYN

"Hey, I just sat three guys at table twelve. The big, burly one wants your cannoli, sweetness...Insisted on sitting in your section," Sal said, waggling his eyebrows.

"Why is everything you say laced with innuendo?"

Sal was promoted to host-runner-busboy on Saturday nights. At least that's what he told everyone when the hostess up and quit last weekend.

"Go get that big sausage, Carolyn. You know you want it."

"Nick, I don't know how much longer I can take him." I could barely stifle my giggle, though. Sal was gross and immature, but he made laugh and he made the night fly by.

"See, you're laughing. Don't encourage him!"

My smile got even bigger when I came out of the kitchen to see my man sitting with his father and an older gentleman whom I assumed was his grandfather. "Hi! This is a nice surprise."

When Jeremy caught sight of me, he stood up and his smile stretched across his face to match my own. The way he looked at me

made me feel like I was someone amazing and extraordinary and...
loved. He made me feel loved.

All three of the Rivers men were standing now. "It's nice to see
you, Mr. Rivers."

"You've gotta start calling me Mike, please."

"All right, Mike," I answered, but I could feel the blush creeping
across my face as I said it. Jeremy's dad was also a big, imposing guy. I
felt like Mr. Rivers fit him better.

"And Carolyn, this is my grandfather, James Walker."

"Hello, dear. You can call me Jimmy."

Jimmy was tall but slight. You could tell he'd once had the same
lumberjack build that Jeremy and his dad shared, but time had
thinned his frame and stooped his posture some. He had piercing blue
eyes that stood out from the wrinkles that framed them. The creases
that framed his eyes and mouth looked like the result of many years
spent smiling. I liked him instantly. The man just radiated happiness.

"I have a feeling this is going to be the best dinner I've had all
month," Jimmy announced as he took in a deep whiff. "Nothing
better than the smell of garlic and olive oil, am I right?"

"Spoken like a true Englishman," Mike commented dryly.

"You're English?"

Jeremy shrugged. "I think we're mutts...A little bit of everything,
right?" he asked, looking towards his father.

Jimmy interjected, "Speak for yourself. I'm one hundred percent
Englishman. Your grandmother was part French, part Dutch, and
your dad's family was—"

"Spanish and Irish," Mike said wistfully.

I think I was a little bit loco in love, because any little thing I
learned about Jeremy made me fall head over heels that much more.
"That explains the tan and the skilled French accent."

"Oh, he's been pulling out the mon chérie on you, has he?" his
grandfather teased.

"Oui, oui."

"Ok, ok, can we hear the specials?" Jeremy begged me, cheeks flaming red.

After I told them about the specials, with emphasis on the excellent pork braciole I'd had the pleasure of sampling earlier, I turned to Jeremy. "What are you doing here, anyway? Wasn't this the big guys-only ski weekend?"

He looked uncomfortable when he answered, "Yeah, it didn't turn out as planned. I came back early." He held his menu up in front of him before whispering, "Can you stay with me tonight?"

"Yeah." I was probably nodding like a goof but I didn't care. *Jeremy wants me.* I couldn't imagine that the excitement over being with him would ever fade. "I'll work it out."

My parents, thank goodness, were not sticklers like that. I still lived at home, although Ava and I had been talking more seriously about splitting a place off campus for next year. My parents were fine with me staying overnight at Jeremy's occasionally, as long as I let them know ahead of time.

They were fine with it because it was Jeremy.

***

JEREMY

"Well, she's a keeper," my grandfather announced as Carolyn took our menus and went to her next table. I saw Carolyn's mouth turn up in a smile as she wrote down her other table's order. My grandfather was slightly hard of hearing and tended to speak at megaphone decibel level. The entire restaurant now knew that Grandpa approved of Carolyn.

I was glad I'd made the decision to bail today and come see her. I spent a lot of time with her family, so it made me feel good to have her spend some time with mine. And it was clear to see that my father and grandfather were enamored with her, just like I was.

I would have taken off even without the promise of being able to have Carolyn tonight, though. This weekend was supposed to be me, Frank, Vinny, Mike and Mike's older brother at the house. The plan was to ski Saturday, watch football Sunday, head home Monday. Good friends, beers and laughs.

We'd just gotten back from the mountain. I was bringing firewood in from the back deck when I heard the laughter. Female laughter. Frank looked back towards me with a guilt-ridden expression and eyes that pleaded: *I didn't know,* as he grabbed Sadie's bag. *I'm gonna kill him.* Of course Sadie was accompanied by four friends, Kenzie among them. How fucking convenient—five guys, five girls. Vinny looked ecstatic while I'm sure I was turning an angry shade of purple.

"This is a nice surprise." Frank looked nervously between Sadie and me. "I'm just gonna throw the girls' bags into my room for now."

I set about starting the fire, so irate that I didn't trust myself to speak. The other guys went over to help with their bags. They were all relaxed, making small talk with the girls—no big deal. I, on the other hand, felt ambushed, pissed off and disappointed. My closest friend and his girl were not looking out for my best interests.

I walked by Frank when he tried to pull me aside. He wanted to spin some bullshit story about having no idea that Sadie was planning to come up and I wasn't having it. As I passed, I heard him say, "Now that they're here, let's just have fun. No reason to make it awkward, right?"

No reason at all, asshole. Sure, Carolyn would be totally cool with me spending the night partying with Kenzie. Just like I'd want her hanging out at a ski house and drinking with Todd or whatever that fucktard's name was. *Deep breath, Rivers.*

Mike came into the kitchen, eyeing me warily. "You good?"

"I'm sorry to bail on you guys, but I'm outta here."

"I get it. Kristi would be none too happy about this either. I'd grab a ride home with you but my brother is pretty excited about the change in plans. Hey, the guys will be outnumbered so maybe he can have two."

"I'm out."

He came in for a one-armed hug. "Let's go out to dinner before I head back up to school next week. I'd really like to catch up with Carolyn and I want her and Kristi to get to know one another."

"Sounds good."

Kenzie stood in the corridor as I walked by and made my way into my bedroom. She had tears in her eyes. Maybe it makes me a cold-hearted bastard, but I didn't give two fucks that she was upset.

"Can we talk for a second?" I ignored her. "I told Sadie this wasn't a good idea and now I can see that it *really* was *not* a good idea."

"It wasn't. I don't like being blindsided."

"Jeremy, we can just hang out as friends."

"We're not friends, Kenzie."

She took a defiant stance, hand on her hip, chin raised. The crocodile tears were gone all of a sudden. "What, is your girlfriend the jealous, insecure type? Can't handle you being around me?"

"So you know? You know that I'm with her now and you decided to come here anyway?"

Kenzie closed my door behind her and advanced on me. She stopped abruptly and lowered her head before raising it again to reveal a sad, concerned expression. This girl was gunning for an Oscar. "Sadie has told me nothing good about her. From what I've heard, you're falling right back in with some girl who's clearly trouble. She thought nothing of crushing her last boyfriend, then dumped you without—"

"Stop!"

She kept coming. She was less than a foot away from me when

she put her hands on my chest and whispered, pleading, "Didn't her last boyfriend kill himself? This girl has mental problems, Jeremy. Can't you see that?"

I gripped her wrists harder than I intended to and shoved her away from me. "Shut your fucking mouth!"

I wasn't explaining shit to Kenzie or to anyone else. And Sadie spreading lies and bullshit? Can't say I was done with Frank, but I'd never see Sadie in the same light again. The people who mattered to me knew Carolyn. They knew she was good and that she was good for me.

As I was stuffing gear into my bag at a furious pace, Kenzie made one last ditch effort. "I care about you. I just want you to consider the idea of us. No complicated past, no drama. I *really* care about you, Jeremy."

I slung my bag over my shoulder. "But I *don't* care about you, Kenzie. I *never* will. Find someone who does care because this bullshit you're spinning is wasted on me."

I pushed past her and quietly made my way to my car. Frank just watched as I passed by. He knew better. He knew I was about one stupid comment away from knocking his teeth loose.

* * *

CAROLYN

The door was open when I got to Jeremy's after midnight. He was asleep on the couch. He looked delicious, with his hair mussed and his bare torso on display, but he also looked like a little boy with his eyes closed and his lips parted, one hand tucked underneath his cheek.

I put my bag in the corner and made my way to the bathroom as quietly as possible. I needed a shower. I always smelled like garlic bread after a shift at La Viola, so of course Jeremy would tell me that he craved garlic bread, that he lived to eat garlic bread. I giggled as I thought back to him chasing me around his apartment the last time I came over after work.

Ooh that feels good. The hot water soothed my tired muscles as I worked Jeremy's manly smelling shampoo into my hair.

"You do know that you're every boy's fantasy right now, don't you?" I turned to see him looking at me through the shower glass door, reaching down to push his sweats off. "Dripping wet, soap suds sliding down those beautiful tits, that round ass just begging to be touched."

I felt so turned on when I was around him. "So come on in here and touch me."

"Touch yourself. I want to watch you."

He opened the shower door half-way. Heat pulsing through me and so drugged with desire, I could barely keep my eyes open as I did what he commanded. I made a conscious decision to let go and then barely recognized the moan that escaped my lips a few moments later.

"Tell me."

"I'm close, close...feels so good it almost hurts."

"Fuck," he let out on a strangled breath.

He stepped in and directed the spray away from me when he caught me moving to kneel down before him. "Are you sure?" I nodded before licking my lips and taking him in as far as I could. "Oh fuck," he groaned.

Who was I? Before this boy, the thought of sex scared me. There was nothing good associated with it in my past. But my life with Jeremy was entirely different. I could be all of those things that scared me before. With Jeremy I could say anything, do anything. There was no fear of judgement. In his eyes I'd never be weird or deviant or laughable. He loved me and it gave me a sense of freedom that I've never known.

I moaned as I rocked my hips against my hand and the vibration set him off. He said my name like a pained whisper as he jerked his hips and came in my mouth. I swallowed him down and then raised my face to the stream of water as he pulled out.

"Come here," he said, gripping me by my elbows and raising me up. He crushed his lips to mine as he ran his hands over my ass. "That was the hottest thing ever."

"Oh, I'm hot, am I?"

"You're hot and you're mine."

And what he did next really did feel so good that it was painful. I was tingling and aching—on the verge of exploding. I wanted him to stop and just fuck me, but my body was moving, pushing back against him, taking everything he'd give me. "More," I heard myself begging. "Please."

"Please, what? What do you want me to do?"

"I want you inside of me."

And then I could feel him, thick, pulsing, hard—so deep inside me. "Don't stop."

He pumped into me over and over again, tugging me hard against his body. I would think back to that moment later on, analyzing it, and it's then that I understood why the French call it *la petite mort*—the little death. Quivering, temporarily detached from rational thought, it was as if I'd drifted outside of my body—living somewhere between this earth and what I imagined heaven to be like.

We were both speechless for a moment, catching our breath, our bodies still joined together.

His soft laughter and the feeling of him slipping out of me brought me down to earth. "Something funny?"

"I was just thinking that I wanna get down on my knees and worship you," he said as he turned me back around to face him. "Do you realize what this is like for me? I never thought of myself as unhappy, but this kind of happiness? It just never occurred to me that I could be this happy. I look forward to talking to you on the phone every day because I love hearing what you have to say...about anything. I think about you whenever we're apart. When we're together I want to hold onto you, kiss you as much as possible. And this," he said, gesturing between us, "I've never experienced this before. Do you know what you look like when we're together?" I looked away, suddenly shy. "No, really, do you realize how incredible you are?" He turned me again as he took some more shampoo and began to lather my hair. "Carolyn, your mouth parts in this incredibly sexy way. Your head tilts to the side, exposing this part of you," he whispered as he leaned down to kiss my neck. "And the look in your eyes...You look at me like no one else has ever made you feel this way before. It makes me feel like a king."

"I've never felt this way. Only with you."

He rinsed my hair and then let his hands roam lovingly over my breasts and my belly, pulling me in close to him. "I've never felt this way either. It's only you."

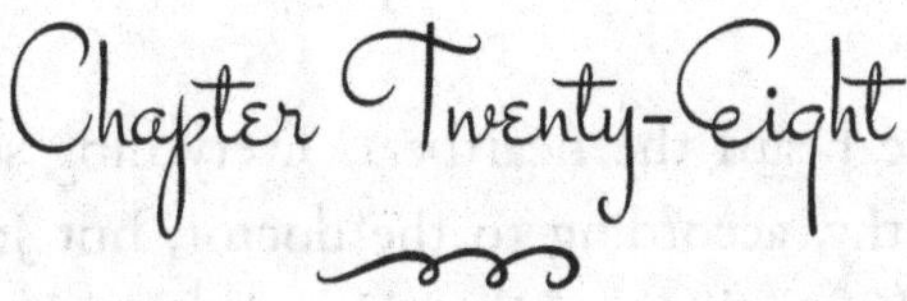

Chapter Twenty-Eight

CAROLYN

Look at him. I know he hates wearing a suit but he looks so damn fine.

I love him just as much when he's in his grease splattered t-shirt, jeans and work boots, but the way he looks tonight? I'm ready to haul him home and role play some alpha male billionaire tames his smart-mouthed secretary fantasy.

I spy two middle-aged women standing a few feet away from Jeremy. They're whispering, stealing looks at him and then giggling like two teenagers crushing on the hot guy. *No, no, no, ladies...He's mine.*

He is mine—heart and soul and body.

And I am Jeremy's in every way.

A part of him grows inside of me now. Everyone describes pregnancy as a miracle, but since finding out that we're expecting, I occasionally have to stop and catch my breath. I'm awestruck. It's amazing to think that we made this. Jeremy making love to me created life that grows inside of me.

It's been our secret this past week. I'm only seven weeks along. We decided to wait a few more weeks to tell our family, and then we'll let the rest of the world in on our big news when we're three months along.

Yesterday we heard the heartbeat. Everything sounded perfect, strong and healthy, according to the doctor, but Jeremy and I are being careful. We've held our friends' hands after they've shared their happy news only to suffer a crushing loss a few weeks later. We know it's not uncommon with the first pregnancy, so for now we're keeping this between us two. But it's impossible to keep from dreaming about this little person, and it's nearly impossible to contain this overwhelming desire I have to dance, and to scream to everyone within earshot that I'm so damn happy!

Telling Frank and Sadie will be hard. They've had two miscarriages back to back. My heart breaks for them, even though every loss makes Sadie all that more difficult to be around. I'm guessing that when she hears our news, the few times a year we see them will dwindle down to nothing.

I hurt for Jeremy because this once-close friendship has been fading away slowly but surely ever since I came back into the picture. Jeremy doesn't see things that way, though. Life is short in his opinion. Too short to spend time with people who don't have your best interests at heart. I can't say that I miss dodging Sadie's snarky comments or the way she'd regularly bring up Kenzie's name in conversation. Not that she's done that recently, though. Sadie and Kenzie had a major falling out a year ago over something ridiculous. I guess when you put two catty kittens in a cage together it won't be long before they try to claw one another's eyes out.

We have a full life now filled with friends who are true. Tori, Andie, Matteo, Taylor, Mike, Vinny and Ava are all regulars at our house on Saturday nights. And whenever Vanessa and her partner

Marie are able to get away from their business, they have their own personal guestroom in our home. Yes, Vanessa is someone I have come to understand and to love like a sister. Chuck Watters is also a regular guest, and others who have shared in our past, like Anna Clarke and her Declan.

Having Anna in our life doesn't bring me pain or grief. No, Anna brings me solace as few other people can. What we all went through, separately but connected, is a tie that will bind us forever.

More than eight years have passed since that fateful night. It took me two years to climb out from the darkest depths of despair, and another year to feel like I was truly healing and on the road back.

The past few years haven't been without setbacks or self-doubt, but I can say now that fear has no place in my life. I'm confident that I can handle whatever comes my way, just like the Carolyn Harris I was at fourteen: the karaoke loving captain of the Science Olympiad team, the steadfast friend, the girl who dreamed big...the Girl Most Likely to Succeed.

* * *

JEREMY

I finger my collar, trying to create some space as it presses tight against my neck. *It's only for a few hours. For her I can suffer.*

I hate wearing a suit. This number is of the custom-fit, high-end variety and it still makes me feel stiff and trapped. Any day of the week you'll find me in jeans, boots and a thermal shirt. My "topcoat" is a flannel button down. My most important business meetings warrant no more than khakis and a polo shirt. Carolyn bought me this suit for tonight though, so I wasn't about to complain. Especially after she told me I looked "delicious" and she was looking forward to "unwrapping" her prize later on tonight.

And she looks incredible, so I needed to step up my game anyway.

I smile as I watch her work the room in her strapless sequined dress. She's wearing heels that are sky high, so I can easily make her out amid the crush of bodies surrounding her. She's selling, and these rich old geezers are eager to buy whatever my beautiful girl is peddling. Her hair is up, revealing the soft curve of her neck and the promise of beautiful breasts hidden beneath the taut fabric of her dress. The longer I watch, the more I'm dying, desperate to just pull her into a closet and claim her.

My desire for her will never let up. I want her right now just as much as I did years ago.

"Looks like tonight is going to be another smashing success! Thanks again, Jeremy." I turn to look at my old friend and smile. "Can you stop admiring your woman for a few minutes so I can pimp you out in the gallery?"

"Sure, Andie, anything for the cause."

Andie taps an older woman on her shoulder and then gestures to me. "This is the artist."

"Oh my word," she says, clutching her chest. "You're gorgeous, young man!"

The woman in front of me has to be pushing seventy-five. After that awkward greeting, we have a long conversation about color and perspective—she's a fellow artist and a collector of Chuck Watters' work. She's interested in a piece I donated for tonight's fundraiser called *My Life*. Carolyn is the subject—no surprise. She posed for this one just last week.

Every piece I create is special to me, but the ones of Carolyn are especially hard to part with. Tonight was no exception. As I stood looking at Carolyn on canvas, discussing details of the work with this woman, I had the strong, familiar urge to lift it off the wall, pack it up and take it back home.

Carolyn would laugh at me, reminding me that our new home had limited storage space, persuading me with the argument that

Briarwood needed the funds more than we needed yet another picture of her.

She didn't understand. Every piece triggered a memory for me—a look, something she said, her touch.

The woman was now long gone, off to look at other works, but I was still standing in front of my Carolyn. Andie broke the spell. "I'm telling you, Jeremy, every year it's the same. Don't these bidding wars tell you anything? You should be doing this. All. The. Time."

"Uh, no. I'm not the starving artist type."

"Yeah, you're the stinking rich general contractor type. Sellout," she teased, poking me in my ribs.

I just shrug. Since my partner retired last year, Tri State Electrical is all mine and we're doing well—very well. It's a good feeling. No, it's a *great* feeling knowing that all that hard work—the twelve-hour work days, the six-day work weeks—that it's all paying off.

There are times when the realization that I now have serious money will hit. And it's not really the money, but the luxury of security. That I could afford the kindly home health aides who attended to my grandfather every day last year before he passed, that I can relieve my father of any and all financial concerns, that I'm secure in the knowledge that I can provide well for my family—where I come from, that's luxury.

Most recently, it was the day I surprised Carolyn with a plot of land, a beautiful two-acre piece of property in Darien, and asked her if she'd like to help me design a house on it. As she paced the lot, yammering on about which side the kitchen should face and what angles would offer the best views, she stopped in her tracks and looked at me. "Who are we designing a house for?"

I just smiled wide as she ran towards me and tackled me to the ground. "For us? For you and me? Are you asking me to move in with you?"

"If you'd let me up, I'd kneel like I'm supposed to, Carolyn. I'm asking you to marry me."

I never got up. She never let me, and I figured that lying in the grass with this beautiful girl's body covering mine was a better way to do it anyway.

"Excuse me, Mr. Rivers. My name is Madeline and this is my husband, Arnold."

"Hello."

"I have to tell you, I'm a great admirer of your work."

"We both are," her husband says. "My bride, though," he gestures to his elderly wife, "I think she enjoys getting into catfights with the other bidders over your work every year. It's like an Olympic sport to her."

She playfully hits his chest as she looks back to me. "It's partly true. I find myself scheming to keep everyone away from your pieces so that I can snag them for myself. And it never works! I've only managed to get my hands on one, *Blue Gingham*. And I want to tell you, it gives me such joy. I find myself looking at it almost every day."

"Wow, thank you. I appreciate that. And I remember that piece. It was hard to part with it."

"But this one," she reflects as she studies *My Life*, "this one speaks to me in a different way. I may be imagining it but I'd guess there's a strong connection between you and the subject. I don't know if it would be possible to evoke this level of feeling if there wasn't."

Her eyes light up as realization sets in. "But the subject is the same! She's the same one, the girl from that oversized piece." She hits *my* chest then, and with some force I might add. "Do you know how crestfallen I was that night?" Her husband is shaking his head, exasperated but amused. "I plotted, calculated my bids, only to be outbid repeatedly. And then when I was giddy with the certainty that I was going to win? That I was going to beat out the insipid little tart who'd been outfoxing me at every turn?" She sighs dramatically. "I turned only to see them removing the piece from the wall. *True*

Beauty…I still remember the name. Oh, I was heartbroken. I wanted it so badly."

I can't help but smile. "It hangs in my house. In my bedroom, in fact."

"As it should," she says, resigned. "Please tell me you won't be pulling this one," she pleads as she gestures towards this image of Carolyn. In this piece she's looking at me with affection, her two hands resting lovingly across her flat belly—already devoted to the little person growing inside of her.

Just one week before, Carolyn stood in front of the bathroom sink, her lips rounded in a surprised O, the stick with the pink plus sign in her hand. I fell to my knees before her and rested my head against my child. I'd never felt a rush of pure love so intense in my life. A week later now and I still struggle to put my feelings into words. The picture tells the story best. That image of Carolyn and our baby is *My Life* in every sense.

"This one's for you," I say as I reach up to remove it from the display. "But just so you know, it's not one of a kind."

"Let me guess, you have one just like it at home?"

I gesture towards a volunteer and tell him to pack it up as I make a note of the highest bid on the sheet so I can cover the cost. "Yeah, this one is special to me."

She takes my hand. Her skin is papery thin, just as my grand-mother's once was, and her eyes hold me with their intensity. "I'm guessing they're all very special to you, so I thank you. We'll treasure this."

As they walk off hand in hand, my woman comes and wraps her arm around my waist. "I was going to interrupt but that looked intense. I remember them. That was the older couple I was telling you about. She was the one going toe to toe with Beth Peterman over your paintings, especially the one of me practically bare-assed. It got pretty heated. I was rooting so hard for them."

"You were?"

"Of course! I couldn't afford it myself and that just about killed me. I just remember feeling desperate that night. We weren't together anymore but I...I wanted something of ours. Maybe it was more that I wanted some piece of you. But they were all so far out of my price range. I was watching the two of them walk around the gallery that night. It was obvious they were together for a long time but were still so in love. Anyway, if I couldn't have it, I wanted them to have it. To keep us safe, you know?"

"I get it. And I'd be a little creeped out by Beth having a naked picture of you on her wall. Or worse, that Mr. Peterman would be ogling your fine ass on a daily basis."

"You noticed that she's not here, right?" When I shake my head and shrug, Carolyn teases, "Sure you didn't. Anyway, the gossip gals in my mother's group said she's gone and Mr. Peterman has found himself a new young honey. I feel bad for her. I hope Beth picks more wisely next time."

"Are you done selling? Maybe you shouldn't be on your feet so much."

Another eye roll. I get one every time I say or do something that Carolyn views as overprotective. "I'm fine. This little fella is like the size of a kidney bean right now."

"Little fella? Do you know something I don't?"

"Nope...And we're not finding out, ok? I want to be surprised. I'll be shocked if it's a girl, though. I just keep imagining a little boy who looks just like you."

Just like me.

Since we moved into our house, Carolyn has been going back and forth to her parents' place to clear out odds and ends. A few days ago she came home with some photos and a small box of keepsakes. I came across her laughing on our couch, flipping through a notebook. She made a half-hearted effort to hide it when I came into the room so I had to wrestle it from her, copping a feel in the process.

"Do *not* read that!" she shrieked. But she was laughing so hard that I knew whatever this was, it wasn't something seriously private.

My eyes went wide looking at the bubbly script that was clearly the work of a child. "Mrs. Carolyn Rivers?"

"No!" she cried as she tried to grab the notebook that I was now holding up and out of her reach.

"Who's Rory Rivers and Jared Rivers?"

She was laughing so hard she had tears streaming down her cheeks. "Our children," she blurted out, covering her face in embarrassment.

"You named our kids? In sixth grade?"

"Fifth grade."

I couldn't contain my smile or my pride. So she really *was* into me way back then.

I read over the names again: Mr. and Mrs. Jeremy Rivers. That's who we were. And we were going to be naming our baby soon. "I'm not a fan of Rory... Sounds like something you'd name a big Irish Setter. Jared isn't half bad, though. Jared Rivers."

"It's after Jared Leto."

"That actor guy? Are you serious? Not happening. Now I don't feel so great about you crushing on me back then."

"Why not?"

"I was in the same category as *him*?"

She hit me with a knowing smile. "Oh, he was a hottie, and still is. You know, the sensitive, brooding type."

"Whatever...Jared's off the table."

Carolyn was looking down at a small battered piece of notepaper in her hands. She wasn't laughing anymore. She turned the paper over to me. "Remember this?"

The paper had a cluster of tiny bluebirds in the upper left hand corner. It was the notepaper my grandmother kept in their kitchen.

The handwriting was mine. I felt my features harden as I took in the barely legible scrawl. At the same time I felt Carolyn's arm snake around my waist.

"You can't imagine what that note meant to me at the time."

It was simple. It just read: I'm sorry, with only my first name written underneath.

I swallowed and nodded, feeling sadness and empathy for that boy. "I remember that I wanted to write more. I wanted to tell you that I'd never do that again and that I felt really badly about what I'd done. But I knew how babyish my writing looked, and I knew that if I wrote more, I'd definitely misspell something and look even more stu—"

"Don't say that word—ever." Carolyn cut me off and then rested her head on my chest, wrapping her arms around me again, covering me in her warmth. "I remember feeling special that day. Even though everything crashed and burned for you that morning, I remember feeling something deep in my heart. I just wanted to believe that you saw me as someone special. That note was everything...I knew you cared about me, Jeremy."

After a quiet minute, I mustered up the courage to ask the question that had been bothering me since long before Carolyn told me we were expecting. "Are you worried at all?"

"About what?"

"That our baby will be like me in that way."

Carolyn turned and sat on my lap straddling me, running her fingers through my hair. "I'm kind of betting on it."

Tears burned my eyes as I fought to hold them in. "Really? How can you say that?"

"Jeremy," she whispered in a way meant to soothe me. "We both carry a strong genetic predisposition. You, your dad, my brother...My mom thinks my grandfather's brother may have struggled with it too." She leaned in to kiss my forehead and then each cheek before she went on. "But I look at it another way. I mean, who on earth could raise a child with a learning disability better than you and me? I teach reading disabled children, for heaven's sake. And you? You're a role model. Your life is a testament to the idea that with hard work you can achieve anything if you set your mind to it." She lifted my chin so that she had my full attention before she announced with conviction, "We've got this."

Carolyn always had faith in me, even when I had no faith in myself. I had to trust in us. I had to trust that we would be in this together, that we'd have each other to lean on—forever.

That next day, inspired by Carolyn, I popped into a jewelry store near my current job site in Greenwich. It was an upscale place but not too formal or stuffy. Turns out the place was perfect. The shop-keeper knew exactly what I wanted, even though I was struggling to describe my vision in words.

I held the silver chain in my hands a few weeks later, thinking of the day I would place the necklace around my wife's neck. It would be the day we brought our first child into this world.

The chain held three round, hammered silver pendants. Each one was engraved with the words I've used to describe this perfect woman, my Carolyn, over the years:

My Friend
My True Beauty
My Life

* * *

A Note From Lily

Thank you for reading *Let Me Fall*. Jeremy emerged out of left field while I was writing Anna and Declan's story, *Let Me Heal Your Heart*. Although Jeremy's role was small, it was clear to me from very early on that he had his own story, one that just had to be told. Jeremy and Carolyn touched me deeply, and I hope their story touched you, too.

Ready for more? The final book in the Let Me series is the conclusion to Dylan Cole's story: *When I Let You Go*.

Twelve years ago I ruined my life.
Lost the one girl I've ever truly loved and I've been living a lie ever since. I go home to my wife...most nights. But I'm just going through the motions, living the life I was born into, married to a girl predestined for me. It's not my wife's fault, but sometimes I can barely stand the sight of her.

Do I sound like a heartless bastard?
That's exactly what I am. Go ahead and hate me if you want, but you couldn't possibly hate me more than I already hate myself.

My name is Dylan Cole.
It's a name synonymous with power. I am rich beyond measure, domineering, and ruthless when it comes to getting what I want. But I cannot have her.
This is what happened...When I Let You Go

Dylan Cole's story is a seriously steamy, forbidden age gap romance intended for the 18 and older crowd due to mature content.

Visit the website to learn more:
LilyFoster.com